PRAISE FOR
THE FINAL DETAIL

"In a genre crowded with accidental detectives who seem invented only to lure cat-loving vegetarians and other special-interest readers, Myron Bolitar stands out. The Edgar Award–winning author gives his characters memorable personalities . . . they are never plain-vanilla."
—*USA Today*

"*The Final Detail* captures the author's trademark humor, but don't let Coben's wry observations fool you. They gift wrap keen insights into our society, particularly America's obsession with sports figures."
—*The Washington Post Book World*

"Coben has melded sly humor, sophisticated plotting, and solid storytelling with bizarre yet believable characters. Coben has sculpted Myron into one of the most likable guys. . . . [*The Final Detail*] secures even further Coben's place as a writer of substantial mysteries."
—*Chicago Tribune*

"An amusing whodunit with an endearing sports agent . . . a hilarious tour of over-the-top New York."
—*Los Angeles Times*

"This is a terrific entry in a terrific series."
—*Kansas City Star*

"A crackerjack mystery."   —*Kirkus Reviews*

"The strongest entry yet in a series that deftly balances realism with excitement."   —*Publishers Weekly*

Please turn the page for more extraordinary acclaim. . . .

BOOKS BY HARLAN COBEN

Harlan Coben

A MYRON BOLITAR

NOVEL

THE
FINAL
DETAIL

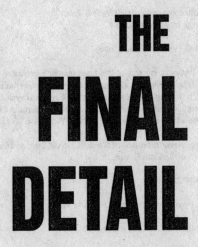

Dell

Published by
Dell Publishing
a division of
Random House, Inc.

Cover photo copyright © 2000 by Will Ryan
Cover design by John D. Sparks

Copyright © 1999 by Harlan Coben

ISBN: 0-440-22545-0

Reprinted by arrangement with Delacorte Press

Printed in the United States of America

Published simultaneously in Canada

February 2000

20 19 18 17 16 15 14

OPM

For Aunt Evelyn in Revere,
with lots and lots of love

And in memory of Larry Gerson
1962–1998
Close your eyes and you can still see the smile

Myron lay sprawled next to a knee-knockingly gorgeous brunette clad only in a Class-B-felony bikini, a tropical drink sans umbrella in one hand, the aqua clear Caribbean water lapping at his feet, the sand a dazzling white powder, the sky a pure blue that could only be God's blank canvas, the sun as soothing and rich as a Swedish masseur with a snifter of cognac, and he was intensely miserable.

The two of them had been on this island paradise for, he guessed, three weeks. Myron had not bothered counting the days. Neither, he imagined, had Terese. The island seemed as remote as Gilligan's—no phone, some lights, no motorcar, plenty of luxury, not much like Robinson Crusoe, and well, not as primitive as can be either. Myron shook his head. You can take the boy out of the television, but you can't take the television out of the boy.

At the horizon's midway point, slicing toward them and ripping a seam of white in the aqua-blue fabric, came the yacht. Myron saw it, and his stomach clenched.

He did not know where they were exactly, though the island did indeed have a name: St. Bacchanals. Yes, for real. It was a small patch of planet, owned by one of those mega-cruise lines that used one side of the island for passengers to swim and barbecue and enjoy a day on their "own personal island paradise." Personal. Just them and the other twenty-five hundred *turistas* squeezed onto a short stretch of beach. Yep, personal, bacchanallike.

This side of the island, however, was quite different. There was only this one home, owned by the cruise line's CEO, a hybrid between a thatched hut and a plantation manor. The only person within a mile was a servant. Total island population: maybe thirty, all of whom worked as caretakers hired by the cruise line.

The yacht shut off its engine and drifted closer.

Terese Collins lowered her Bolle sunglasses and frowned. In three weeks no vessel except the mammoth cruise liners—they had subtle names like the *Sensation* or the *Ecstasy* or the *G Spot*—had ambled past their stretch of sand.

"Did you tell anybody where we were?" she asked.

"No."

"Maybe it's John."

John was the aforementioned CEO of said cruise line, a friend of Terese's.

"I don't think so," Myron said.

Myron had first met Terese Collins, well, a little more than three weeks ago. Terese was "on leave" from her high-profile job as prime-time anchorwoman for CNN. They both had been bullied into going to some charity function by well-meaning friends and had been immediately drawn to each other as though their mutual misery and pain were magnetic. It started as little more than a dare: Drop everything and flee. Just disappear with someone you found attractive and barely knew. Neither backed down, and twelve hours later they were in St. Maarten. Twenty-four hours after that they were here.

For Myron, a man who had slept with a total of four women in his entire life, who had never really experienced one-night stands even in the days when they were fashionable or ostensibly disease-free, who had never had sex purely for the physical sensation and without the anchors of love or commitment, the decision to flee felt surprisingly right.

He had told no one where he was going or for how long —mostly because he didn't have a clue himself. He'd called Mom and Dad and told them not to worry, a move tantamount to telling them to grow gills and breathe underwater. He'd sent Esperanza a fax and gave her power of attorney over MB SportsReps, the sports agency they now partnered. He had not even called Win.

Terese was watching him. "You know who it is."

Myron said nothing. His heartbeat sped up.

The yacht came closer. A cabin door in the front opened, and as Myron feared, Win stepped out on deck. Panic squeezed the air out of him. Win was not one for casual drop-bys. If he was here, it meant something was very wrong.

Myron stood. He was still too far to yell, so he settled for a wave. Win gave a small nod.

"Wait a second," Terese said. "Isn't that the guy whose family owns Lock-Horne Securities?"

"Yes."

"I interviewed him once. When the market plunged. He has some long, pompous name."

"Windsor Horne Lockwood the third," Myron said.

"Right. Weird guy."

She should only know.

"Good-looking as all hell," Terese continued, "in that old-money, country-club, born-with-a-silver-golf-club-in-his-hands kinda way."

As though on cue, Win put a hand through the blond locks and smiled.

"You two have something in common," Myron said.

"What's that?"

"You both think he's good-looking as all hell."

Terese studied Myron's face. "You're going back." There was a hint of apprehension in her voice.

Myron nodded. "Win wouldn't have come otherwise."

She took his hand. It was the first tender moment between them in the three weeks since the charity ball. That might sound strange—lovers alone on an island, the sex constant, who had never shared a gentle kiss or a light stroke or soft words—but their relationship had been about forgetting and surviving: two desperate souls standing in the rubble with no interest in trying to rebuild a damn thing.

Terese had spent most days taking long walks by herself; he'd spent them sitting on the beach and exercising and sometimes reading. They met up for food, sleep, and sex. Other than that, they left each other alone to—if not heal—at least stave off the blood flow. He could see that she too had been shattered, that some recent tragedy had struck her deep and hard and to the bone. But he never asked her what had happened. And she never asked him either.

An unspoken rule of their little folly.

The yacht stopped and dropped anchor. Win stepped down onto a motorized dinghy. Myron waited. He shifted his feet, bracing himself. When the dinghy was close enough to the shore, Win snapped off the motor.

"My parents?" Myron called out.

Win shook his head. "They're fine."

"Esperanza?"

Slight hesitation. "She needs your help."

Win stepped gingerly into the water, almost as though he expected it to hold his weight. He was dressed in a white button-down oxford and Lilly Pulitzer shorts with colors loud enough to repel sharks. The Yacht Yuppie. His build was on the slight side, but his forearms looked like steel snakes coiling beneath the skin.

Terese stood as Win approached. Win admired the view without ogling. He was one of the few men Myron knew who could get away with that. Breeding. He took Terese's hand and smiled. They exchanged pleasantries. Fake smiles and pointless bandies followed. Myron stood frozen, not listening. Terese excused herself and headed to the house.

Win carefully watched her saunter away. Then he said, "Quality derrière."

"Would you be referring to me?" Myron asked.

Win kept his eyes keenly focused on the, er, target. "On television she's always sitting behind that anchor desk," he noted. "One would never guess that she had such a high-quality derrière." He shook his head. "It's a shame really."

"Right," Myron said. "Maybe she should stand a couple times during each broadcast. Twirl around a few times, bend over, something like that."

"There you go." Win risked a quick glance at Myron. "Take any action snapshots, perhaps a videotape?"

"No, that would be you," Myron said, "or maybe an extra-perverse rock star."

"Shame."

"Yeah, shame, I got that." Quality derrière? "So what's wrong with Esperanza?"

Terese finally disappeared through the front door. Win sighed softly and turned toward Myron. "The yacht will take half an hour to refuel. We'll leave then. Mind if I sit?''

''What happened, Win?''

He did not answer, choosing instead to sit on a chaise longue and ease back. He put his hands behind his head and crossed his ankles. ''I'll say this for you. When you decide to wig out, you do it in style.''

''I didn't wig out. I just needed a break.''

''Uh-hmm.'' Win looked off, and a realization smacked Myron in the head: He had hurt Win's feelings. Strange but probably true. Win might be a blue-blooded, aristocratic sociopath, but hey, he was still human, sort of. The two men had been inseparable since college, yet Myron had run off without even calling. In many ways Win had no one else.

''I meant to call you,'' Myron said weakly.

Win kept still.

''But I knew if there was a problem, you'd be able to find me.'' That was true. Win could find a Hoffa needle in a Judge Crater haystack.

Win waved a hand. ''Whatever.''

''So what's wrong with Esperanza?''

''Clu Haid.''

Myron's first client, a right-handed relief pitcher in the twilight of his career. ''What about him?''

''He's dead,'' Win said.

Myron felt his legs buckle a bit. He let himself land on the chaise.

''Shot three times in his own abode.''

Myron lowered his head. ''I thought he'd straightened himself out.''

Win said nothing.

''So what does Esperanza have to do with this?''

Win looked at his watch. "Right about now," he said, "she is in all likelihood being arrested for his murder."

"What?"

Win said nothing again. He hated to repeat himself.

"They think Esperanza killed him?"

"Good to see your vacation hasn't dulled your sharp powers of deduction." Win tilted his face toward the sun.

"What sort of evidence do they have?"

"The murder weapon, for one. Bloodstains. Fibers. Do you have any sunblock?"

"But how . . . ?" Myron studied his friend's face. As usual, it gave away nothing. "Did she do it?"

"I have no idea."

"Did you ask her?"

"Esperanza does not wish to speak with me."

"What?"

"She does not wish to speak with you either."

"I don't understand," Myron said. "Esperanza wouldn't kill anyone."

"You're quite sure about that, are you?"

Myron swallowed. He had thought that his recent experience would help him understand Win better. Win had killed too. Often, in fact. Now that Myron had done likewise, he thought that there would be a fresh bond. But there wasn't. Just the opposite, in fact. Their shared experienced was opening a whole new chasm.

Win checked his watch. "Why don't you go get packed?"

"There's nothing I need to bring."

Win motioned to the house. Terese stood there, watching them silently. "Then say good-bye to La Derrière and let's be on our way."

Terese had put on a robe. She leaned against the doorway and waited.

Myron was not sure what to say. He settled for "Thank you."

She nodded.

"Do you want to come along?" he asked.

"No."

"You can't stay here forever."

"Why not?"

Myron thought about it for a moment. "You know anything about boxing?"

Terese sniffed the air. "Do I detect the distinct odor of an upcoming sports metaphor?"

"I'm afraid so," he said.

"Ugh. Go on."

"This whole thing is sort of like a boxing match," Myron began. "We've been ducking and diving and weaving and trying to keep away from our opponent. But we can only do that for so long. Eventually we have to throw a punch."

She made a face. "Christ, that was lame."

"Spur of the moment."

"And inaccurate," she added. "Try this. We've tasted our opponent's power. It dropped us to the canvas. Somehow we managed to get back to our feet. But our legs are still rubbery, and our eyes are still hazed over. Another big blow and the fight will be over. Better to keep dancing. Better to avoid getting hit and hope to go the distance."

Hard to argue.

They fell into silence.

Myron said, "If you come up to New York, give me a call and—"

"Right."

Silence.

"We know what would happen," Terese said. "We'd meet up for drinks, maybe hop back in the sack, but it won't be the same. We'll both be uncomfortable as all hell. We'll pretend that we'll get together again, and we won't even exchange Christmas cards. We're not lovers, Myron. We're not even friends. I don't know what the hell we are, but I'm grateful."

A bird cawed. The small waves hummed their soft song. Win stood by the shore, his arms crossed, his body frighteningly patient.

"Have a good life, Myron."

"You too," he replied.

He and Win took the dinghy to the yacht. A crew member offered Myron his hand. Myron grabbed it and hoisted himself on board. The yacht took off. Myron stood on the deck and watched the shore grow smaller. He was leaning on a teakwood rail. Teakwood. Everything on this vessel was dark and rich and teak.

"Here," Win said.

Myron turned. Win tossed him a Yoo-Hoo, Myron's

favorite drink, kind of a cross between a soda pop and chocolate milk. Myron smiled. "I haven't had one of these in three weeks."

"The withdrawal pains," Win said. "They must have been agony."

"No TV and no Yoo-Hoo. It's a wonder I survived."

"Yes, you practically lived like a monk," Win said. Then, looking back at the island, he added, "Well, like a monk who gets laid a lot."

They were both stalling.

"How long until we get back?" Myron asked.

"Eight hours on the boat," Win said. "A chartered jet is waiting at St. Bart's. The flight should take about four hours."

Myron nodded. He shook the can and popped it. He took a deep swig and turned back toward the water.

"I'm sorry," he said.

Win ignored the statement. Or maybe it was enough for him. The yacht picked up speed. Myron closed his eyes and let the water and gentle spray caress his face. He thought a moment about Clu Haid. Clu hadn't trusted agents—"a small step below pedophile" was how he put it—so he asked Myron to negotiate his contract, even though Myron was merely a first-year student at Harvard Law. Myron did it. He liked it. And MB SportsReps soon followed.

Clu was a lovable screwup. He unapologetically pursued wine, women, and song—not to mention any high he could get his hands/nose/veins on. Clu never met a party he didn't like. He was a redheaded big guy with a teddy bear gut, handsome in a boyish way, an almost old-fashioned cad, and immensely charming. Everyone loved Clu. Even Bonnie, his long-suffering wife. Their marriage was a boomerang. She'd throw him out, he'd spin in the air for a while, and then she'd catch him on the return.

Clu had seemed to be slowing down a bit. After all the times Myron had gotten him out of trouble—drug suspensions, drunk driving charges, whatever—Clu had gone puffy, reached the end of his charm reign. The Yankees had traded for him, putting him on strict probation, giving him one last chance at redemption. Clu had stayed in rehab for the first time. He'd been attending the AA meetings. His fastball was back up in the nineties.

Win interrupted his thoughts. "Do you want to hear what happened?"

"I'm not sure," Myron said.

"Oh?"

"I screwed up last time. You warned me, but I didn't listen. A lot of people died because of me." Myron felt the tears come to his eyes. He pushed them back down. "You have no idea how bad it ended."

"Myron?"

He turned to his friend. Their eyes met.

"Get over yourself," Win said.

Myron made a noise—one part sob, two parts chuckle. "I hate when you coddle me."

"Perhaps you would prefer it if I served up some useless platitudes," Win said. He swirled his liquor and tasted a bit. "Please select one of the following and then we'll move on: Life is hard; life is cruel; life is random; sometimes good people are forced to do bad things; sometimes innocent people die; yes, Myron, you screwed up, but you'll do better this time; no, Myron, you didn't screw up, it wasn't your fault; everyone has a breaking point and now you know yours. Can I stop now?"

"Please."

"Then let us begin with Clu Haid."

Myron nodded, took another swig of Yoo-Hoo, emptied the can.

"Everything seemed to be going swimmingly for our old college chum," Win said. "He was pitching well. Domestic bliss seemed to reign. He was passing his drug tests. He was making curfew with hours to spare. That all changed two weeks ago when a surprise drug test produced a positive result."

"For what?"

"Heroin."

Myron shook his head.

"Clu kept his mouth shut to the media," Win said, "but privately he claimed the test was fixed. That someone had tampered with his food or some such nonsense."

"How do you know that?"

"Esperanza told me."

"He went to Esperanza?"

"Yes, Myron. When Clu failed the test, he naturally looked to his agent for help."

Silence.

"Oh," Myron said.

"I don't want go into the fiasco that is MB SportsReps right now. Suffice to say that Esperanza and Big Cyndi did the best they could. But it's your agency. Clients hired you. Many have been more than unhappy by your sudden disappearance."

Myron shrugged. He would probably care one day. "So Clu failed the test."

"And he was immediately suspended. The media moved in for the kill. He lost all his endorsement deals. Bonnie threw him out. The Yankees disowned him. With nowhere else to turn, Clu repeatedly visited your office.

Esperanza told him that you were unavailable. His temper rose with each visit.''

Myron closed his eyes.

''Four days ago Clu confronted Esperanza outside the office. At the Kinney parking lot, to be more exact. They had words. Harsh and rather loud words. According to witnesses, Clu punched her in the mouth.''

''What?''

''I saw Esperanza the next day. Her jaw was swollen. She could barely talk, though she still managed to tell me to mind my own business. My understanding is more damage would have been inflicted had Mario and several other parking attendants not pulled them apart. Supposedly Esperanza made threats of the I'll-get-you-for-this-you-limp-dick-son-of-a-bitch variety as they were being held back.''

Myron shook his head. This made no sense.

''The next afternoon Clu was found dead in the apartment he rented in Fort Lee,'' Win continued. ''The police learned about the earlier altercation. They were then issued a slew of search warrants and found the murder weapon, a nine millimeter, in your office.''

''My office?''

''MB's office, yes.''

Myron shook his head again. ''It had to be a plant.''

''Yes, perhaps. There were also fibers that matched the carpeting in Clu's apartment.''

''The fibers are meaningless. Clu was in the office. He probably dragged them there.''

''Yes, perhaps,'' Win said again. ''But the specks of blood in the trunk of the company car might be harder to explain.''

Myron almost fell over. ''Blood in the Taurus?''

''Yes.''

"And the police confirmed the blood as Clu's?"

"Same blood type. The DNA test will take several weeks."

Myron could not believe what he was hearing. "Had Esperanza been using the car?"

"That very day. According to the E-Z Pass records, the car crossed the Washington Bridge back into New York within an hour of the murder. And as I said, he was killed in Fort Lee. The apartment is maybe two miles from the bridge."

"This is crazy."

Win said nothing.

"What's her motive?" Myron asked.

"The police don't have a solid one yet. But several are being offered."

"Such as?"

"Esperanza was a new partner at MB SportsReps. She'd been left in charge. The company's inaugural client was about to walk out the door."

Myron frowned. "Pretty flimsy motive."

"He had also recently assaulted her. Perhaps Clu blamed her for all the bad things that were happening to him. Perhaps she wanted vengeance. Who knows?"

"You said something before about her not talking to you."

"Yes."

"So you asked Esperanza about the charges?"

"Yes."

"And?"

"And she told me that she had the matter under control," Win said. "And she told me not to contact you. That she did not wish to speak with you."

Myron looked puzzled. "Why not?"

"I haven't a clue."

He pictured Esperanza, the Hispanic beauty he had met in the days when she wrestled professionally under the moniker Little Pocahontas. A lifetime ago. She had been with MB SportsReps since its inception—first as a secretary and now that she'd graduated law school, as a full-fledged partner.

"But I'm her best friend," Myron said.

"As I am well aware."

"So why would she say something like that?"

Win guessed the question was rhetorical. He kept silent.

The island was out of sight now. In every direction there was nothing but the churning warm blue of the Atlantic.

"If I hadn't run away," Myron began.

"Myron?"

"What?"

"You're whining again. I cannot handle whining."

Myron nodded and leaned against the teakwood.

"Any thoughts?" Win asked.

"She'll talk to me," Myron said. "Count on it."

"I just tried to call her."

"And?"

"No answer."

"Did you try Big Cyndi?"

"She now rooms with Esperanza."

No surprise. "What's today?" Myron asked.

"Tuesday."

"Big Cyndi still bounces at Leather-N-Lust. She might be there."

"During the day?"

Myron shrugged. "Sexual deviancy has no off hours."

"Thank God," Win said.

They fell into silence, the ship gently rocking them.

Win squinted into the sun. "Beautiful, no?"

Myron nodded.

"Must be sick of it after all this time."

"Very," Myron said.

"Come below deck. I think you'll be pleased."

CHAPTER 3

Win had stocked the yacht with videos. They watched episodes of the old *Batman* show (the one with Julie Newmar as Cat Woman and Lesley Gore as Pussycat— double meow!), the *Odd Couple* (Oscar and Felix on *Password*), a *Twilight Zone* ("To Serve Man"), and for something more current, *Seinfeld* (Jerry and Elaine visit Jerry's parents in Florida). Forget pot roast. This was comfort food. But on the off chance that it wasn't substantial enough, there were also Doritos and Cheez Doodles and more Yoo-Hoos and even rewarmed pizza from Calabria's Pizzeria on Livingston Avenue.

Win. He might be a sociopath, but what a guy.

The effect of all this was beyond therapeutic, the time spent at sea and later in the air an emotional pressure chamber of sorts, a chance for Myron's soul to adjust to the bends, to the sudden reemergence into the real world.

The two friends barely spoke, except to sigh over Julie Newmar as Cat Woman (whenever she came on the screen in her tight black cat suit, Win said, "Puuuurrrrfect"). They'd both been five or six years old when the show first aired, but something about Julie Newmar as Cat Woman completely blew away any Freudian notions of latency. Why, neither man could say. Her villainy perhaps. Or something more primal. Esperanza would no doubt have an interesting opinion. He tried not to think about her—useless and draining when he couldn't do anything about it—but the last time he had done something like this was in Philadelphia with both Win and Esperanza. He missed her. Watching the videos was not the same without her running commentary.

The boat docked and they headed for the private jet.

"We'll save her," Win said. "We are, after all, the good guys."

"Questionable."

"Have confidence, my friend."

"No, I mean us being the good guys."

"You should know better."

"Not anymore I don't," Myron said.

Win made his jutting jaw face, the one that had come over on the *Mayflower*. "This moral crisis of yours," he said. "It's *très* unbecoming."

A breathy blond bombshell like something out of an old burlesque skit greeted them in the cabin of the Lock-Horne company jet. She fetched them drinks between giggles and wiggles. Win smiled at her. She smiled back.

"Funny thing," Myron said.

"What's that?"

"You always hire curvaceous stewardesses."

Win frowned. "Please," he said. "She prefers to be called a flight attendant."

"Pardon my oafish insensitivity."

"Try a little harder to be tolerant," Win said. Then: "Guess what her name is."

"Tawny?"

"Close. Candi. With an *i*. And she doesn't dot it. She draws a heart over it."

Win could be a bigger pig, but it was hard to imagine how.

Myron sat back. The pilot came over the loudspeaker. He addressed them by name, and then they took off. Private jet. Yacht. Sometimes it was nice having wealthy friends.

When they reached cruising altitude, Win opened what looked like a cigar box and pulled out a telephone. "Call your parents," he said.

Myron stayed still for a moment. A fresh wave of guilt rolled over him, coloring his cheeks. He nodded, took the phone, dialed. He gripped the phone a bit too tightly. His mother answered.

Myron said, "Mom—"

Mom started bawling. She managed to yell for Dad. Dad picked up the downstairs extension.

"Dad—"

And then he started bawling too. Stereo bawling. Myron held the phone away from his ear for a moment.

"I was in the Caribbean," he said, "not Beirut."

An explosion of laughter from both. Then more crying. Myron looked at Win. Win sat impassively. Myron rolled his eyes, but of course he was also pleased. Complain all you want, but who didn't want to be loved like this?

His parents settled into a meaningless chatter—meaningless on purpose, Myron supposed. While they could undoubtedly be pests, Mom and Dad had a wonderful ability to know when to back off. He managed to explain where he'd been. They listened in silence. Then his mother asked, "So where are you calling us from?"

"Win's airplane."

Stereo gasps now. "What?"

"Win's company has a private jet. I just told you he picked me—"

"And you're calling on his phone?"

"Yes."

"Do you have any idea how much that costs?"

"Mom . . ."

But the meaningless chatter died down in a hurry then. When Myron hung up seconds later, he sat back. The guilt came again, bathing him in something ice cold. His parents were not young anymore. He hadn't thought about that before he ran. He hadn't thought about a lot of things.

"I shouldn't have done that to them," Myron said. "Or you."

Win shifted in his seat—major body language for him. Candi wiggled back into view. She lowered a screen and hit a switch. A Woody Allen film came on. *Love and Death*. Ambrosia of the mind. They watched without speaking. When it was over, Candi asked Myron if he wanted to take a shower before they landed.

"Excuse me?" Myron said.

Candi giggled, called him a "Big Silly," and wiggled away.

"A shower?"

"There's one in the back," Win said. "I also took the liberty of bringing you a change of clothes."

"You are a friend."

"I am indeed, Big Silly."

Myron showered and dressed, and then everyone buckled their seat belts for approach. The plane descended without delay, the landing so smooth it could have been choreographed by the Temptations. A stretch limousine was waiting for them on the dark tarmac. When they got off the plane, the air felt strange and unfamiliar, as though he'd been visiting another planet rather than another country. It was also raining hard. They ran down the steps and into the already-open limo doors.

They shook off the wet. "I assume that you'll be staying with me," Win said.

Myron had been living in a loft down on Spring Street with Jessica. But that was before. "If it's okay."

"It's okay."

"I could move back in with my folks—"

"I said, it's okay."

"I'll find my own place."

"No rush," Win said.

The limousine started up. Win steepled his fingers. He always did that. It looked good on him. Still holding the steeple, he bounced his forefingers against his lips. "I'm not the best one to discuss these matters with," he said, "but if you want to talk about Jessica or Brenda or whatever . . ." He released the steeple, made a waving motion with his right hand. Win was trying. Matters of the heart were not his forte. His feelings on romantic entanglement could objectively be labeled "appalling."

"Don't worry about it," Myron said.

"Fine then."

"Thanks, though."

Quick nod.

After more than a decade struggling with Jessica—years of being in love with the same woman, having one major breakup, finding each other again, taking tentative steps, growing, finally moving in together again—it was over.

"I miss Jessica," Myron said.

"I thought we weren't going to talk about it."

"Sorry."

Win shifted in his seat again. "No, go on." Like he'd rather have an anal probe.

"It's just that . . . I guess part of me will always be enmeshed in Jessica."

Win nodded. "Like something in a machinery mishap."

Myron smiled. "Yeah. Like that."

"Then slice off the limb and leave it behind."

Myron looked at his friend.

Win shrugged. "I've been watching *Sally Jessy* on the side."

"It shows," Myron said.

"The episode entitled 'Mommy Took Away My Nipple Ring,' " Win said. "I'm not afraid to say it made me cry."

"Good to see you getting in touch with your sensitive side." As if Win had one. "So what next?"

Win checked his watch. "I have a contact at the Bergen County house of detention. He should be in by now." He hit the speakerphone and pressed in some numbers. They listened to the phone ring. After two rings a voice said, "Schwartz."

"Brian, this is Win Lockwood."

The usual reverent hush when you first hear that name. Then: "Hey, Win."

"I need a favor."

"Shoot."

"Esperanza Diaz. Is she there?"

Brief pause. "You didn't hear it from me," Schwartz said.

"Hear what?"

"Good, okay, long as we understand each other," he said. "Yeah, she's here. They dragged her through here in cuffs a coupla hours ago. Very hush-hush."

"Why hush-hush?"

"Don't know."

"When is she being arraigned?"

"Tomorrow morning, I guess."

Win looked at Myron. Myron nodded. Esperanza would be held overnight. This was not a good thing.

"Why did they arrest her so late?"

"Don't know."

"And you saw them drag her in cuffs?"

"Yep."

"Didn't they let her surrender on her own?"

"Nope."

Again the two friends looked at each other. The late arrest. The handcuffs. The overnight. Someone in the DA's office was pissed off and trying to make a point. Very not a good thing.

"What else can you tell me?" Win asked.

"Not much. Like I said, they're being quiet on this one. The DA hasn't even released it to the media yet. But he will. Probably before the eleven o'clock news. Quick statement, no time for questions, that kind of thing. Hell, I wouldn't know about it if I wasn't a big fan."

"A big fan?"

"Of professional wrestling. See, I recognized her from her old wrestling days. Did you know Esperanza Diaz used to be Little Pocahontas, the Indian Princess?"

Win glanced at Myron. "Yes, Brian, I know."

"Really?" Brian was big-time excited now. "Little Pocahontas was my absolute fave, bar none. An awesome wrestler. Top drawer. I mean, she used to enter the ring in this skimpy suede bikini, right, and then she'd start grappling with other chicks, bigger chicks really, writhing around on the floor and stuff—swear to God, she was so hot my fingernails would melt."

"Thank you for the visual," Win said. "Anything else, Brian?"

"No."

"Do you know who her attorney of record is?"

"No." Then: "Oh, one other thing. She's got someone, well, sort of with her."

"Sort of with her, Brian?"

"Outside. On the front steps of the courthouse."

"I'm not sure I'm following you," Win said.

"Out in the rain. Just sitting there. If I didn't know better, I'd swear it was Little Pocahontas's old tag team partner, Big Chief Mama. Did you know Big Chief Mama and Little Pocahontas were Intercontinental tag team champions three years running?"

Win sighed. "You don't say."

"Whatever Intercontinental means. I mean, what is that, Intercontinental? And I'm not talking about recently. Five, eight years ago, at least. But, man, they were awesome. Great wrestlers. Today, well, the league has no class anymore."

"Grappling bikini-clad women," Win said. "They just don't make them like they used to."

"Right, exactly. Too many fake, inflated breasts nowadays, at least that's how I see it. One of them is going to land on her stomach and bam, her boob is going to blow out like a worn tire. So I don't follow it much anymore. Oh, maybe if I'm flipping the channels and something catches my eye, I might watch a little—"

"You were talking about a woman out in the rain?"

"Right, Win, right, sorry. Anyway, she's out there, whoever she is. Just sitting there. The cops went by before and asked her what she was doing. She said she was going to wait for her friend."

"So she's there right now?"

"Yep."

"What does she look like, Brian?"

"Like the Incredible Hulk. Only scarier. And maybe greener."

Win and Myron exchanged glances. No doubt. Big Chief Mama aka Big Cyndi.

"Anything else, Brian?"

"No, not really." Then: "So you know Esperanza Diaz?"

"Yes."

"Personally?"

"Yes."

Silent awe. "Jesus, you lead some life, Win."

"Oh, indeed."

"Think you can get me her autograph?"

"I'll do my best, Brian."

"A picture autograph maybe? Of Little Pocahontas in costume? I'm a really big fan."

"So I gather, Brian. Good-bye."

Win hung up and sat back. He looked over at Myron. Myron nodded. Win picked up the intercom and gave the driver directions to the courthouse.

CHAPTER 4

By the time they arrived at the courthouse in Hackensack, it was nearly 10:00 P.M. Big Cyndi sat in the rain, shoulders hunched; at least Myron thought it was Big Cyndi. From a distance, it looked like someone had parked a Volkswagen Bug on the courthouse steps.

Myron stepped out of the car and approached. "Big Cyndi?"

The dark heap let loose a low growl, a lioness warning off an inferior animal who'd wandered astray.

"It's Myron," he said.

The growl deepened. The rain had plastered Big Cyndi's hair spikes to her scalp, as if she were sporting an uneven Caesar coif. Today's color was hard to decipher— Big Cyndi liked diversity in her follicular tint—but it didn't look like any hue found in the state of nature. Big Cyndi sometimes liked to combine dyes randomly and see what happened. She also insisted on being called Big Cyndi. Not Cyndi. Big Cyndi. She had even had her name legally changed. Official documents read: Cyndi, Big.

"You can't stay here all night," Myron tried.

She finally spoke. "Go home."

"What happened?"

"You ran away." Big Cyndi's voice was childlike, lost.

"Yes."

"You left us alone."

"I'm sorry about that. But I'm back now."

He risked another step. If only he had something to placate her with. Like a half gallon of Häagen-Dazs. Or a sacrificial goat.

Big Cyndi started to cry. Myron approached slowly, semileading with his right hand in case she wanted to sniff it. But the growls were all gone now, replaced by sobs. Myron put his palm on a shoulder that felt like a bowling ball.

"What happened?" he asked again.

She sniffled. Loudly. The sound almost dented the limo's fender. "I can't tell you."

"Why can't you?"

"She said not to."

"Esperanza?"

Big Cyndi nodded.

"She's going to need help," Myron said.

"She doesn't want your help."

The words stung. The rain continued to fall. Myron sat on the step next to her. "Is she angry about my leaving?"

"I can't tell you, Mr. Bolitar. I'm sorry."

"Why not?"

"She told me not to."

"Esperanza can't bear the brunt of this on her own," Myron said. "She's going to need a lawyer."

"She has one."

"Who?"

"Hester Crimstein."

Big Cyndi gasped as though she realized she'd said too

much, but Myron wondered if the slip had been intentional.

"How did she get Hester Crimstein?" Myron asked.

"I can't say any more, Mr. Bolitar. Please don't be mad at me."

"I'm not mad, Big Cyndi. I'm just concerned."

Big Cyndi smiled at him then. The sight made Myron bite back a scream. "It's nice to have you back," she said.

"Thank you."

She put her head on his shoulder. The weight made him teeter, but he remained relatively upright. "You know how I feel about Esperanza," Myron said.

"Yes," Big Cyndi said. "You love her. And she loves you."

"So let me help."

Big Cyndi lifted her head off his shoulder. Blood circulated again. "I think you should leave now."

Myron stood. "Come on. We'll give you a ride home."

"No, I'm staying."

"It's raining and it's late. Someone might try to attack you. It's not safe out here."

"I can take care of myself," Big Cyndi said.

He had meant that it wasn't safe for the attackers, but he let it pass. "You can't stay out here all night."

"I'm not leaving Esperanza alone."

"But she won't even know you're here."

Big Cyndi wiped the rain from her face with a hand the size of a truck tire. "She knows."

Myron looked back at the car. Win was leaning against the door now, arms crossed, umbrella resting on his shoulder. Very Gene Kelly. He nodded at Myron.

"You're sure?" Myron asked.

"Yes, Mr. Bolitar. Oh, and I'll be late for work tomorrow. I hope you understand."

Myron nodded. They stared at each other, the rain cascading down their faces. A howl of laughter made both of them turn to the right and look at the fortresslike structure that contained the holding cells. Esperanza, the person closest to them both, was incarcerated in there. Myron stepped toward the limousine. Then he turned back around.

"Esperanza wouldn't kill anyone," he said.

He waited for Big Cyndi to agree or at least nod her head. But she didn't. She hunched the shoulders back up and disappeared within herself.

Myron slid back into the car. Win followed, handing Myron a towel. The driver started up.

"Hester Crimstein is her attorney," Myron said.

"Ms. Court TV?"

"The same."

"Ah," Win said. "And what's the name of her show again?"

"Crimstein on Crime," Myron said.

Win frowned. "Cute."

"She had a book with the same title." Myron shook his head. "This is weird. Hester Crimstein doesn't take many cases anymore. So how did Esperanza land her?"

Win tapped his chin with his forefinger. "I'm not positive," he said, "but I believe Esperanza had a fling with her a couple of months back."

"You're kidding."

"Well, yes, I am such a mirthful fellow. And wasn't that just the funniest line?"

Wiseass. But it made sense. Esperanza was as perfect a bisexual as you could find—perfect because everyone, no matter what his or her sex or preference, found her immensely attractive. If you're going to go all ways, might as well have universal appeal, right?

Myron mulled this over a few moments. "Do you know where Hester Crimstein lives?" he asked.

"Two buildings up from me on Central Park West."

"So let's pay her a visit."

Win frowned. "Why?"

"Maybe she can fill us in."

"She won't talk to us."

"Maybe she will."

"What makes you say that?"

"For one thing," Myron said, "I'm feeling particularly charming."

"By God." Win leaned forward. "Driver, step on the gas."

CHAPTER 5

Win lived at the Dakota, one of Manhattan's swankiest buildings. Hester Crimstein lived two blocks north at the San Remo, an equally swanky building. Occupants included Diane Keaton and Dustin Hoffman, but the San Remo was perhaps best known as the building that had rejected Madonna's application for residence.

There were two entranceways, both with doormen dressed like Brezhnev strolling Red Square. Brezhnev One announced in a clipped tone that Ms. Crimstein was "not present." He actually used the word *present* too; people don't often do that in real life. He smiled for Win and looked down his nose at Myron. This was no easy task—Myron was at least six inches taller—and required Brezhnev to tilt his head way back so that his nostrils looked like the westbound entrance to the Lincoln Tunnel. Why, Myron wondered, do servants of the rich and famous act snootier than their masters? Was it simple resentment? Was it because they were looked down upon all day and thus needed on occasion to be the one doing the looking down? Or—more simply—were people attracted to such jobs insecure asswipes?

Life's little mysteries.

"Are you expecting Ms. Crimstein back tonight?" Win asked.

Brezhnev opened his mouth, stopped, cast a wary eye as if he feared Myron might defecate on the Persian rug. Win read his face and led him to the side, away from the lowly member of the unwashed.

"She should be back soon, Mr. Lockwood." Ah, so Brezhnev had recognized Win. No wonder. "Ms. Crimstein's aerobics class concludes at eleven."

Exercising at eleven o'clock at night. Welcome to the nineties, where leisure time is sucked away like something undergoing liposuction.

There were no waiting or sitting areas at the San Remo —most of your finer buildings did not encourage even approved guests to loiter—so they moved outside to the street. Central Park was across the roadway. Myron could see, well, trees and a stone wall, and that was about it. Lots of taxis sped north. Win's stretch limousine had been dismissed—they both figured they could walk the two blocks to Win's place—but there were four other stretch limousines sitting in a no parking zone. A fifth pulled up. A silver stretch Mercedes. Brezhnev rushed to the car door like he really had to pee and there was a bathroom inside.

An old man, bald except for a white crown of hair, stumbled out, his mouth twisted poststroke. A woman resembling a prune followed. Both were expensively dressed and maybe a hundred years old. Something about them troubled Myron. They looked wizened, yes. Old, certainly. But there was more to it, Myron sensed. People talk about sweet little old people, but these two were so blatantly the opposite, their eyes beady, their movements shifty and angry and fearful. Life had sapped them, sucked out all the goodness and hope of youth, leaving them with a vitality based on something ugly and hateful. Bitterness was the only thing left. Whether the bitterness was directed at God or at their fellowman, Myron could not say.

Win nudged him. He looked to his right and saw a figure he recognized from TV as Hester Crimstein coming toward them. She was on the husky side, at least by today's warped Kate Mossian standards, and her face was fleshy and cherubic. She wore Reebok white sneakers, white socks, green stretch pants that would probably make Kate snicker, a sweatshirt, a knit hat with frosted blond hair sticking out the back. The old man stopped when he saw the attorney, grabbed the prune lady's hand, hurried inside.

"Bitch!" the old man managed through the good side of his face.

"Up yours too, Lou," Hester called out after him.

The old man stopped, looked like he wanted to say something more, limped off.

Myron and Win exchanged a glance and approached.

"Old adversary," she said in way of explanation. "You ever hear the old adage that only the good die young?"

"Uh, sure."

Hester Crimstein gestured with both hands at the old couple like Carol Merrill showing off a brand-new car. "There's your proof. Couple years back I helped his children sue the son of a bitch. You never saw anything like it." She tilted her head. "Ever notice how some people are like jackals?"

"Pardon?"

"They eat their young. That's Lou. And don't even get me started on that shriveled-up witch he lives with. Five-dollar whore who hit the jackpot. Hard to believe looking at her now."

"I see," Myron said, though he didn't. He tried to push ahead. "Ms. Crimstein, my name is—"

"Myron Bolitar," she interrupted. "By the way, that's a horrid name. Myron. What were your parents thinking?"

A very good question. "If you know who I am, then you know why I'm here."

"Yes and no," Hester said.

"Yes and no?"

"Well, I know who you are because I'm a sports nut. I used to watch you play. That NCAA championship game against Indiana was a frigging classic. I know the Celtics drafted you in the first round, what, eleven, twelve years ago?"

"Something like that."

"But frankly—and I mean no offense here—I'm not sure you had the speed to be a great pro, Myron. The shot, sure. You could always shoot. You could be physical. But what are you, six-five?"

"About that."

"You would have had a tough time in the NBA. One woman's opinion. But of course the fates took care of that by blowing out your knee. Only an alternate universe knows the truth." She smiled. "Nice chatting with you." She looked over at Win. "You too, gabby boy. Good night."

"Wait a second," Myron said. "I'm here about Esperanza Diaz."

She faked a gasp of surprise. "Really? And here I thought you just wanted to reminisce about your athletic career."

He looked at Win. "The charm," Win whispered.

Myron turned back toward Hester. "Esperanza is my friend," he said.

"So?"

"So I want to help."

"Great. I'll start sending you the bills. This case is going to cost a bundle. I'm very expensive, you know. You can't believe the upkeep of this building. And now the doormen want new uniforms. Something in mauve, I think."

"That's not what I meant."

"Oh?"

"I'd like to know what's going on with the case."

She scrunched up her face. "Where have you been the last few weeks?"

"Away."

"Where away?"

"The Caribbean."

She nodded. "Nice tan."

"Thanks."

"But you could have gotten it at a tanning booth. You look like the kind of guy who hangs out at tanning booths."

Myron looked at Win again. "The charm, Luke," Win whispered, doing his best Alec Guinness as Obi-Wan Kenobi. "Remember the charm."

"Ms. Crimstein—"

"Anyone who can verify your whereabouts in the Caribbean, Myron?"

"Pardon me?"

"Hearing problems? I asked if anyone can verify your whereabouts at the time of the alleged murder."

Alleged murder. The guy is shot three times in his home, but the murder is only "alleged." Lawyers. "Why do you want to know that?"

Hester Crimstein shrugged. "The alleged murder weapon was allegedly found at the offices of one MB SportsReps. That's your company, is it not?"

"It is."

"And you use the company car where the alleged blood and alleged fibers were allegedly found."

Win said, "The key word here is *alleged.*"

Hester Crimstein looked at Win. "It speaks."

Win smiled.

Myron said, "You think I'm a suspect?"

"Sure, why not? It's called reasonable doubt, sweet buns. I'm a defense attorney. We're big on reasonable doubt."

"Much as I'd like to help, there was a witness to my whereabouts."

"Who?"

"Don't worry about it."

Another shrug. "You're the one who said you wanted to help. Good night." She looked at Win. "By the way, you're the perfect man—good-looking and nearly mute."

"Careful," Win said to her.

"Why?"

Win pointed at Myron with his thumb. "Any minute now he's going to turn on the charm and reduce your willpower to rubble."

She looked at Myron and burst out laughing.

Myron tried again. "So what happened?" he asked.

"Excuse me?"

"I'm her friend."

"Yeah, I think you already said that."

"I'm her best friend. I care about her."

"Fine. Tomorrow I'll pass her a note during study hall, find out if she likes you too. Then you can meet at Pop's and share a soda."

"That's not what I—" Myron stopped, gave her the slow, slightly put-out-but-here-to-help smile. Smile 18: the Michael Landon model, except he couldn't crinkle the eyebrow. "I'd just like to know what happened. You can appreciate that."

Her face softened, and she nodded. "You went to law school, right?"

"Yes."

"At Harvard no less."

"Yes."

"So maybe you were absent the day they went over a little something we call attorney-client privilege. I can recommend some wonderful books on the subject, if you'd like. Or maybe you can watch any episode of *Law & Order*. They usually talk about it right before the old DA grouses to Sam Waterston that he's got no case and should cut a deal."

So much for charm. "You're just covering your ass," Myron said.

She looked behind her and down. Then she frowned. "No easy task, I assure you."

"I thought you were supposed to be a hotshot attorney."

She sighed, crossed her arms. "Okay, Myron, let's hear it. Why am I covering my ass? Why am I not the hotshot attorney you thought I was?"

"Because they didn't let Esperanza surrender. Because they dragged her in in cuffs. Because they're holding her overnight instead of getting her through the system in the same day. Why?"

She dropped her hands to her sides. "Good question, Myron. Why do you think?"

"Because someone there doesn't like her high-profile attorney. Someone in the DA's office probably has a hard-on for you and is taking it out on your client."

She nodded. "Good possibility. But I have another one."

"What?"

"Maybe they don't like her employer."

"Me?"

She started for the door. "Do us all a favor, Myron. Stay out of this. Just keep away. And maybe get yourself a lawyer."

Hester Crimstein spun around and disappeared inside then. Myron turned toward Win. Win was bent at the waist, squinting at Myron's crotch. "What the hell are you doing?"

Still squinting. "I wanted to see if she left you with even a sliver of a testicle."

"Very funny. What do you think she meant about them not liking her employer?"

"Not a clue," Win said. Then: "You mustn't blame yourself."

"What?"

"For your charm's seemingly lackluster performance. You forgot a crucial component in all this."

"That being?"

"Ms. Crimstein had an affair with Esperanza."

Myron saw where he was going with this. "Of course. She must be a lesbian."

"Precisely. It's the only rational explanation for her ability to resist you."

"That, or a really bizarre paranormal event."

Win nodded. They started walking down Central Park West.

"This is also further proof of a very frightening adage," Win said.

"What's that?"

"Most women you encounter are lesbians."

Myron nodded. "Almost every one."

CHAPTER 6

They walked the two blocks to Win's place, watched a little television, went to bed. Myron lay in the dark exhausted, but sleep remained elusive. He thought about Jessica. Then he tried to think about Brenda, but the automatic defense mechanism deflected that one. Still too raw. And he thought about Terese. She was alone on that island tonight for the first time. During the day the island's solitude was peaceful and quiet and welcome; at night the solitude felt more like dark isolation, the island's black walls closing in, silent and cloying as a buried coffin. He and Terese had always slept wrapped in each other's arms. Now he pictured her lying in that deep blackness alone. And he worried about her.

He woke up the next morning at seven. Win was already gone, but he'd scribbled a note that he'd meet up with Myron at the courthouse at nine. Myron grabbed a bowl of Cap'n Crunch, discerned with a digging left hand that Win had already extracted the free toy inside, showered, dressed, checked his watch. Eight o'clock. Plenty of time to reach the courthouse in time.

He took the elevator down and crossed the famed Da-

kota courtyard. He had just reached the corner of Seventy-
second Street and Central Park West when he spotted the
three familiar figures. Myron felt his pulse quicken. FJ,
short for Frank Junior, was bookended by two huge guys.
The two huge guys looked like lab experiments gone very
wrong, as if someone had potently mixed genetic glandu-
lar excess with anabolic steroids. They wore tank tops and
those drawstring weightlifting pants that looked suspi-
ciously like ugly pajama bottoms.

Young FJ silently smiled at Myron with thin lips. He
sported a purple-blue suit so shiny it looked like someone
had sprayed it with a sealant. FJ didn't move, didn't say
anything, just smiled at Myron with unblinking eyes and
those thin lips.

Today's word, boys and girls, is *reptilian.*

FJ finally took a step forward. "Heard you were back
in town, Myron."

Myron bit back a rejoinder—it wasn't a very cutting
one, something about the nice welcoming party—and kept
his mouth shut.

"Remember our last conversation?" FJ continued.

"Vaguely."

"I mentioned something about killing you, right?"

"It might have come up," Myron said. "I don't remember. So many tough guys, so many threats."

The Bookends tried to scowl, but even their faces were
overmuscled, and the movement took too much effort.
They settled back into the steady frowns and lowered the
eyebrows a bit.

"Actually, I was going to carry through with it," FJ
continued. "About a month ago. I followed you out to
some graveyard in New Jersey. I even sneaked up behind
you with my gun out. Funny thing, no?"

Myron nodded. "Like Henny Youngman wrote it."

FJ tilted his head. "Don't you want to know why I didn't kill you?"

"Because of Win."

The sound of his name was like a cold glass of water in the faces of both Bookends. The two giants actually stepped back but recovered quickly with a few flexes. FJ remained unruffled. "Win doesn't scare me," he said.

"Even the dumbest animal," Myron said, "has an innate survival mechanism."

FJ's eyes met Myron's. Myron tried to maintain contact, but it was hard. There was nothing behind FJ's eyes but rot and decay; it was like staring into the broken windows of an abandoned building. "Sticks and stones, Myron. Sticks and stones. I didn't kill you because, well, you already looked so miserable. It was as though—how to put this?—as though killing you would have been an act of mercy. Like I said before, funny, right?"

"You should consider stand-up," Myron agreed.

FJ chuckled and waved a well-manicured hand at nothing in particular. "Anyway, bygones. My father and uncle like you, and yes, we see no reason to antagonize Win unnecessarily. They don't want you dead, so neither do I."

His father and uncle were Frank and Herman Ache, two of New York's legendary leading leg breakers. The elder Aches had grown up on the streets, slaughtered more people than the next guy, moved up the ladder. Herman, the older brother and big cheese, was in his sixties now and liked to pretend he wasn't scum by surrounding himself with the finer things in life: restricted clubs that didn't want him, nouveau-riche art exhibits, well-coiffed charities, midtown French maître d's who treated anyone who tipped with less than a Jackson like something they couldn't scrape off the soles of their shoes. In other words, a higher-income scum. Herman's younger brother, Frank, the psycho who had produced the equally psycho offspring who now stood in front of Myron, remained what he had always been: an ugly hatchet man who considered K mart velour sweatsuits haute couture. Frank had calmed down over the last few years, but it never quite worked for him. Life, it seemed, had little meaning for Frank Senior without someone to torture or maim.

"What do you want, FJ?"

"I have a business proposition for you."

"Gee, I just know this is really going to interest me."

"I want to buy you out."

The Aches ran TruPro, a rather large sports representation firm. TruPro had always been devoid of any semblance of scruples, recruiting young athletes with as much moral restraint as a politician planning a fund-raiser. But then their owner stacked up debts. Bad debts. The debts that attract the wrong kind of fungus. The appropriately named Ache brothers, the fungi in question, moved in and, like the parasitic entities they were, ate away all signs of life and were now gnawing on the carcass.

Still, being a sports agent was a legit way of making a living, sort of, and Frank Senior, wanting for his son what all fathers wanted, handed young FJ the reins straight out of business school. In theory FJ was supposed to run TruPro as legitimately as possible. His father had killed and maimed so that his son wouldn't have to—yep, the classic American dream with, granted, a rather deranged twist. But FJ seemed incapable of freeing himself from the old familial shackles. *Why* was a question that fascinated Myron. Was FJ's evil genetic, passed down from his father like a prominent nose, or was he, like so many other children, simply trying to gain his father's acceptance by proving the acorn could be as ferociously psychotic as the oak?

Nature or nurture. The argument rages on.

"MB SportsReps is not for sale," Myron said.

"I think you're being foolish."

Myron nodded. "I'll file that under 'One Day I Might Even Care.' "

The Bookends sort of grumbled, took a step forward, and cracked their necks in unison. Myron pointed to one, then the other. "Who does your choreography?"

They wanted to be insulted—you could just tell—except neither one of them knew what the word *choreography* meant.

FJ asked, "Do you know how many clients MB Sports-Reps lost in the last few weeks?"

"A lot?"

"I'd say a quarter of your list. A couple of them went with us."

Myron whistled, feigned nonchalant, but he was not happy to hear this. "I'll get them back."

"You think so?" FJ again smiled the reptilian smile; Myron almost expected a forked tongue to dart out between his lips. "Do you know how many more are going to leave when they hear about Esperanza's arrest?"

"A lot?"

"You'll be lucky to have one left."

"Hey, then I'll be like Jerry Maguire. Did you see that movie? Show me the money? I love black people?" Myron gave FJ his best Tom Cruise earnest. "You. Complete. Me."

FJ remained cool. "I'm willing to be generous, Myron."

"I'm sure you are, FJ, but the answer is still no."

"I don't care how clean your rep used to be. Nobody can survive the sort of money scandal you're about to go through."

It wasn't a money scandal, but Myron was not in the mood to issue corrections. "Are we finished, FJ?"

"Sure." FJ gave him one last scaly smile. The smile seemed to jump off his face, crawl toward Myron, and then slither its way up his back. "But why don't we get together and have lunch?"

"Any time," Myron said. "You have a cellular?"

"Of course."

"Call my partner right away and set it up."

"Isn't she in jail?"

Myron snapped his fingers. "Drat."

FJ found that amusing. "I mentioned that some of your old clients are now using my services."

"So you did."

"If you contact any of them"—he paused, thought it over—"I'd feel obliged to retaliate. Do I make myself clear?"

FJ was maybe twenty-five years old, less than a year out of Harvard Business School. He had gone undergrad to Princeton. Smart kid. Or powerful father. Either way, rumor had it that when a Princeton professor was about to accuse FJ of plagiarism, the professor disappeared and only his tongue was found—on the pillow of another professor who had considered leveling the same charges.

"Crystal, FJ."

"Great, Myron. Then we'll talk again."

If Myron still had his tongue.

The three men slid into their car and drove off without another word. Myron slowed his heart rate and checked his watch. Court time.

CHAPTER 7

The courtroom in Hackensack looked very much like the ones you see on television. Shows like *The Practice* and *Law & Order* and even *Judge Judy* capture the physical appearance pretty well. They can't of course capture the essence emanating from the little things: the faint, underlying stench of fear-induced sweat, the overuse of disinfectant, the slightly sticky feel to all the benches and tables and handrails—what Myron liked to call the ooze factors.

Myron had his checkbook ready so bail could be posted immediately. He and Win had gone over it last night and figured the judge would come in around fifty to seventy-five grand. Esperanza had no record and a steady job. Those factors would play in her favor. If the money was higher, no problem. Myron's pockets might be only semideep, but Win's net worth was on par with the GNP of a small European country.

There were droves of reporters parked outside, tons of vans with wrapped cables and satellite dishes, and of course phallic antennas, stretching toward the heavens as though in search of the elusive god of higher ratings. Court TV was there. News 2 New York. ABC News.

CNN. Eyewitness News. Every city in every region of the country had an Eyewitness News. Why? What was so appealing about that name? There were also the new sleazoid TV shows, like *Hard Copy, Access Hollywood, Current Affair,* though the distinction between them and the local news was becoming murky to the point of nonexistent. Hey, at least *Hard Copy* and the like were somewhat honest about the fact that they served no redeeming social value. And they didn't subject you to weathermen.

A couple of reporters recognized Myron and called out. Myron put on his game face—serious, unyielding, concerned, confident—and no-commented his way through them. When he entered the courtroom, he spotted Big Cyndi first—no surprise since she stuck out like Louis Farrakhan at B'nai B'rith. She was jammed into the aisle of a row empty except for Win. Not unusual. If you wanted to save seats, send Big Cyndi; people did not relish excusing themselves to squeeze past her. Most opted to stand. Or go home even.

Myron slid into Big Cyndi's row, actually high-stepping over two knees that looked like batting helmets, and sat between his friends.

Big Cyndi had not changed from last night or even washed up. The steady rain had rinsed out some of the hair dye; purple and yellow streaks had dried on the front and back of her neck. Her makeup, always applied in amounts thick enough to make a plaster bust, had also suffered under the rain's onslaught, her face now resembling multicolored menorah candles left too long in the sun.

In some major cities, murder arraignments were commonplace and handled in factory-line fashion. Not so here in Hackensack. This was big time—a murder case involving a celebrity. There would be no rush.

The bailiff started calling cases.

"I had a visitor this morning," Myron whispered to Win.

"Oh?"

"FJ and two goons."

"Ah," Win said. "Was the cover boy for *Modern Mobster* voicing his usual medley of colorful threats?"

"Yes."

Win almost smiled. "We should kill him."

"No."

"You're just putting off the inevitable."

"He's Frank Ache's son, Win. You just don't kill Frank Ache's son."

"I see. Then you'd rather kill somebody from a better family?"

Win logic. It made sense in the scariest way possible. "Let's just see how it plays out, okay?"

"Don't put off until tomorrow what must be exterminated today."

Myron nodded. "You should write one of those life-instruction books."

They fell into silence. Cases went by—a breaking and entering, a couple of assaults, too many car thefts. Every suspect looked young, guilty, and angry. Always scowling. Tough guys. Myron tried not to make a face, tried to remember innocent until proven guilty, tried to remember that Esperanza too was a suspect. But it didn't help much.

Finally Myron saw Hester Crimstein sweep into the courtroom, decked out in her best professional civvies: a sleek beige suit, cream blouse, and a tad overcoiffed, over-frosted hair. She took her spot at the defense table, and the room fell silent. Two guards led Esperanza through an open door. Myron saw her, and something akin to a mule kicked him in the chest.

Esperanza was dressed in a court-issued fluorescent orange jumpsuit. Forget gray or stripes—if a prisoner wanted to escape, he was going to stick out like a neon light in a monastery. Her hands were cuffed in front of her. Myron knew that Esperanza was petite—maybe five-two, a hundred pounds—but he had never seen her look so small. She kept her head high, defiant. Classic Esperanza. If she was afraid, she wasn't showing it.

Hester Crimstein put a comforting hand on her client's shoulder. Esperanza nodded at her. Myron tried desperately to catch her eye. It took a couple of moments, but eventually Esperanza turned his way, looking straight at him with a slight, resigned, I'm-okay smile. It made Myron feel better.

The bailiff called out, "The People versus Esperanza Diaz."

"What's the charge?" the judge asked.

The assistant district attorney, a fresh-faced kid who barely looked old enough to sport a pubic hair, stood by a pedestal. "Murder in the second degree, Your Honor."

"How do you plead?"

Esperanza's voice was strong. "Not guilty."

"Bail?"

The fresh-faced kid said, "Your Honor, the People request that Ms. Diaz be remanded without bail."

Hester Crimstein shouted, "What?" as if she had just heard the most irrational and dangerous words any human being had ever uttered under any circumstance.

Fresh Face was unfazed. "Miss Diaz is accused of killing a man by shooting him three times. We have strong evidence—"

"They have nothing, Your Honor. Circumstantial nothings."

"Miss Diaz has no family and no real roots in the

community," Fresh Face continued. "We believe that she presents a substantial flight risk."

"That's nonsense, Your Honor. Miss Diaz is a partner in a major sports representation firm in Manhattan. She is a law school graduate who is currently studying for the bar. She has many friends and roots in the community. And she has no record whatsoever."

"But, Your Honor, she has no family—"

"So what?" Crimstein interrupted. "Her mother and father are dead. Is that now a reason to punish a woman? Dead parents? This is outrageous, Your Honor."

The judge, a woman in her early fifties, sat back. "Your request to deny bail does seem extreme," she said to Fresh Face.

"Your Honor, we believe that Miss Diaz has an unusual amount of resources at her disposal and very good reasons to flee the jurisdiction."

Crimstein kept up with the apoplectic. "What are you talking about?"

"The murder victim, Mr. Haid, has recently withdrawn cash funds in excess of two hundred thousand dollars. That money is missing from his apartment. It's logical to assume that the money was taken during the commission of the murder—"

"What logic?" Crimstein shouted. "Your Honor, this is nonsense."

"Counsel for the defense mentioned that Miss Diaz has friends in the community," Fresh Face continued. "Some of them are here, including her employer, Myron Bolitar." He pointed to Myron. All eyes turned. Myron stayed very still. "Our investigation shows that Mr. Bolitar has been missing for at least a week, perhaps in the Caribbean, even in the Cayman Islands."

"So what?" Crimstein shouted. "Arrest him if that's a crime."

But Fresh Face was not done. "And next to him is Miss Diaz's friend Windsor Lockwood of Lock-Horne Securities." When all eyes turned to Win, he nodded and gave a small regal wave. "Mr. Lockwood was the victim's financial adviser and held the account where the two hundred thousand dollars was withdrawn."

"So arrest him too," Crimstein ranted. "Your Honor, this has nothing to do with my client, except maybe to prove her innocence. Miss Diaz is a hardworking Hispanic woman who struggled her way through law school at night. She has no record and should be freed immediately. Short of that, she has a right to reasonable bail."

"Your Honor, there's just too much cash floating around," Fresh Face said. "The missing two hundred thousand dollars. Miss Diaz's possible connection with both Mr. Bolitar and, of course, Mr. Lockwood, who comes from one of the wealthiest families in the region—"

"Wait a second, Your Honor. First, the district attorney suggests that Miss Diaz has stolen and hidden away this alleged missing money and will use it to run. Then he suggests that she'll ask Mr. Lockwood, who is no more than a business associate, for the funds. Which is it? And while the district attorney's office is busy trying to manufacture some kind of money conspiracy, why would one of the already wealthiest men in the country deem it appropriate to conspire with a poor Hispanic woman to steal? The whole idea is ludicrous. The prosecution has no case, so they've come up with this money nonsense that sounds as plausible as an Elvis sighting—"

"Enough," the judge said. She leaned back and strummed her fingers on the big desk. She stared at Win for a second, then back at the defense table. "The missing money troubles me," she said.

"Your Honor, I assure you that my client knows nothing about any money."

"I'd be surprised if your position were different, Ms. Crimstein. But the facts presented by the district attorney are sufficiently troublesome. Bail denied."

Crimstein's eyes widened. "Your Honor, this is an outrage—"

"No need to shout, Counselor. I hear you just fine."

"I strenuously object—"

"Save it for the cameras, Ms. Crimstein." The judge hit the gavel. "Next case?"

Suppressed mumbles broke forth. Big Cyndi started wailing like a widow in a war newsreel. Hester Crimstein put her mouth to Esperanza's ear and whispered something. Esperanza nodded, but it didn't look like she was listening. The guards led Esperanza toward a door. Myron tried to catch her eyes again, but she didn't—or maybe wouldn't—face him.

Hester Crimstein turned and shot Myron a glare so nasty it almost made him duck. She approached him and fought to keep her face neutral. "Room seven," she said to Myron, not looking at him, barely moving her lips. "Down the hallway and to the left. Five minutes. Don't say anything to anyone."

Myron did not bother with a nod.

Crimstein hurried out, already starting with the no comments before she hit the door. Win sighed, took a piece of paper and a pen from his jacket pocket, began to scribble something down.

"What are you doing?" Myron asked.

"You'll see."

It did not take long. Two plainclothes cops accompanied by the stench of cheap cologne made their approach. Homicide division, no doubt. Before they could even introduce themselves, Win said, "Are we under arrest?"

The cops looked confused. Then one said, "No."

Win smiled and handed him the piece of paper.

"What the hell is this?"

"Our attorney's phone number," Win said. He rose and ushered Myron toward the door. "Have a special day."

They arrived in the defendant's conference room before the anointed five minutes. The room was empty.

"Clu withdrew cash?" Myron said.

"Yes," Win said.

"You knew about it?"

"Of course."

"How much?"

"The district attorney said two hundred thousand dollars. I have no reason to quibble with that estimate."

"And you just let him?"

"Pardon?"

"You just let Clu withdraw two hundred grand?"

"It's his money."

"But that much cash?"

"It was none of my business," Win said.

"You know Clu, Win. It could have been for drugs or gambling or—"

"Probably was," Win agreed. "But I am his financial adviser. I instruct him on investment strategies. Period. I am not his conscience or his mommy or his baby-sitter— or even his agent."

Ouch. But no time for that now. Once again Myron suppressed the guilt and mulled over the possibilities. "Clu okayed us receiving his financial statements, right?"

Win nodded. MB SportsReps insisted that all clients use Win's services and meet with him in person at least quarterly to go over their accounts. This was for their sake more than Myron's. Too many athletes get taken advantage of because of ignorance. But most of Myron's clients had copies of their statements sent to Myron so that he too could help keep track of the ins and outs, set up some automatic bill paying, that kind of thing.

"So a withdrawal that big would have come up on our screen," Myron said.

"Yes."

"Esperanza would have known about it."

"Yes again."

Myron frowned. "So that gives the DA another motive for the murder. She knew about the cash."

"Indeed."

Myron looked at Win. "So what did Clu do with the money?"

Win shrugged.

"Maybe Bonnie knows?"

"Doubtful," Win said. "They've separated."

"Big deal. They're always fighting, but she always takes him back."

"Perhaps. But this time she made the separation legal."

That surprised Myron. Bonnie had never gone that far before. Their turmoil cycle had always been consistent: Clu does something stupid, a big fight ensues, Bonnie throws him out for a couple of nights, maybe a week, Clu begs forgiveness, Bonnie takes him back, Clu behaves for a little while, Clu does something stupid, the cycle starts anew. "She got a lawyer and filed papers?"

"According to Clu."

"He told you that?"

"Yes, Myron. That's what 'According to Clu' means."

"When did he tell you all this?"

"Last week. When he took out the cash. He said that she had already begun divorce proceedings."

"How did he feel about it?"

"Badly. He craved yet another reconciliation."

"Did he say anything else when he withdrew the cash?"

"Nothing."

"And you have no idea—"

"None."

The conference room door flew open. Hester Crimstein came in, red-faced and fuming. "You dumb bastards. I told you to stay away."

"Don't put this on us," Myron said. "This is your screwup."

"What?"

"Getting her bail should have been a slam dunk."

"If you weren't in the courtroom, it would have been. You played right into the DA's hands. He wants to show the judge that the defendant has the resources to run away, and boom, he points to a famous ex-jock and one of the country's richest playboys sitting right in the front row."

She started stomping about as though the industrial gray carpet contained small brushfires. "This judge is a liberal schmuck," she said. "That's why I started with all that hardworking Hispanic crap. She hates rich people, probably because she is one. Having the *Preppy Handbook* here"—she gestured with her head at Win—"sit in the front row was like waving a Confederate flag at a black judge."

"You should drop the case," Myron said.

Her head jerked toward him. "Are you out of your mind?"

"Your fame is playing against you. The judge may not like rich people, but she doesn't much like celebrities either. You're the wrong attorney for this case."

"Bullshit. I've had three cases before this judge. I'm three and oh."

"Maybe she doesn't like that either."

Crimstein seemed to lose a little steam. She moved back and collapsed into a chair. "Bail denied," she said more to herself than anyone else. "I can't believe they even had the nerve to ask for no bail." She sat a bit straighter. "All right, here's how we play it. I'm going to press for answers. In the meantime you guys say nothing. No talking to the cops, the DA, the press. Nobody. Not until we figure out what exactly they think the three of you did."

"The three of us?"

"Weren't you listening, Myron? They think it's a money scheme."

"Involving the three of us?"

"Yes."

"But how?"

"I don't know. They mentioned your going to the Caribbean, maybe the Cayman Islands. We all know what that means."

"Depositing cash in offshore accounts," Myron said. "But I left the country three weeks ago—before the money was even withdrawn. And I never went anywhere near the Caymans."

"They're probably still grasping at straws," Crimstein said. "But they're going to go after you in a big way. I hope your books are in order because I guarantee you they'll have them subpoenaed within the hour."

Money scandal, Myron thought. Hadn't FJ mentioned something about that?

Crimstein turned her attention to Win. "Is that stuff about a big cash withdrawal true?"

"Yes."

"Can they prove Esperanza knew about it?"

"Probably."

"Damn." She thought about this a moment.

Win moved into a corner. He took out his cell phone, dialed, started talking.

Myron said, "Make me co-counsel."

Crimstein looked up. "Excuse me?"

"As you pointed out last night, I'm a bar-appointed attorney. Make me her attorney, and anything she tells me falls under attorney-client."

She shook her head. "One, that'll never fly. The judge will see it for what it is, a loophole to make sure you can't testify. Two, it's moronic. Not only will it reek of a desperate defensive move, but it'll look like we're shutting you up because we have something to hide. Three, you may still be charged in all this."

"How? I already told you. I was in the Caribbean."

"Right. Where nobody but Preppy Boy could find you. How convenient."

"You think—"

"I don't think anything, Myron. I'm telling you what the DA *might* be thinking. For now we're just guessing. Go back to your office. Call your accountant. Make sure your books are in order."

"They're in order," Myron said. "I've never stolen a dime."

She turned to Win. "How about you?"

Win hung up the phone. "What about me?"

"They'll subpoena your books too."

Win arched the eyebrow. "They'll try."

"Are they clean?"

"You could eat off them," Win said.

"Fine, whatever. I'll let your lawyers handle it. I got enough to worry about."

Silence.

"So how do we get her out?" Myron asked.

"We don't get her out. I get her out. You stay away."

"I don't take orders from you."

"No? How about from Esperanza?"

"What about Esperanza?"

"This is her request as well as mine. Stay away from her."

"I don't believe she'd say that."

"Believe it."

"If she wants me out," Myron said, "she'll have to tell me to my face."

"Fine," Crimstein said with a heavy sigh. "Let's go take care of that now."

"What?"

"You want her to tell you herself? Give me five minutes."

Win said, "I have to get back to the office."

Myron was surprised. "You don't want to hear what Esperanza has to say?"

"No time."

His tone slammed the door on further discussion. Win reached for the knob.

"If you need my special talents," he said, "I'll have the cellular."

He hurried out as Hester Crimstein entered. She watched him disappear down the corridor. "Where's he going?"

"His office."

"Why's he in such a rush all of a sudden?"

"I didn't ask."

Hester Crimstein raised an eyebrow. "Hmm."

"Hmm what?"

"Win was the one in charge of the account with the missing money."

"So?"

"So maybe he had a reason to silence Clu Haid."

"That's ridiculous."

"Are you saying he's incapable of murder?"

Myron did not reply.

"If even half the stories I've heard about Windsor Lockwood are true—"

"You know better than to listen to rumors."

She looked at him. "So if I subpoena you to testify and if I ask if you've ever witnessed Windsor Horne Lockwood the Third kill someone, what would you say?"

"No."

"Uh-huh. Guess you also missed the class on perjury."

Myron did not bother with a comeback. "When can I see Esperanza?"

"Come on. She's waiting for you."

Esperanza sat at a long table. She still wore the orange prison suit, her now-uncuffed hands folded in front of her, her expression serene as a church statue's. Hester signaled to the trooper, and they both left the room.

When the door closed, Esperanza smiled at him. "Welcome back," she said.

"Thanks," Myron replied.

Her eyes took him in. "If your tan was any darker, you could pass for my brother."

"Thanks."

"Still got the smooth tongue with the ladies, eh?"

"Thanks."

She almost smiled. Even under these conditions, Esperanza still looked radiant. Her supple skin and ink black hair shimmered against the fluorescent orange backdrop. Her eyes still brought forth thoughts of Mediterranean moons and white peasant blouses.

"Are you feeling better now?" she asked him.

"Yes."

"Where were you anyway?"

"A private island in the Caribbean."

"For three weeks?"

"Yes."

"By yourself?"

"No."

When he didn't elaborate, Esperanza simply said, "Details."

"I ran off with a beautiful anchorwoman I barely knew."

Esperanza smiled. "Did she—how to put this delicately?—did she boff your brains out?"

"As it were."

"Glad to hear it. If any guy needed to have his brain boffed out—"

"Right, I'm the guy. Voted Most Boff Needy by the senior class."

She liked that one. She leaned back and crossed her legs cocktail-lounge casual. Odd in these surroundings, to put it mildly. "You didn't tell anybody where you were?"

"That's right."

"Yet Win still found you in a matter of hours," she said.

It surprised neither of them. They sat in silence for a moment or two. Then Myron asked, "You okay?"

"Fine."

"Do you need anything?"

"No."

Myron was not sure how to continue, what subject to broach or how to broach it. Once again Esperanza took the ball and started dribbling.

"So are you and Jessica through?" she asked.

"Yes." It was the first time he had said it out loud. It felt weird.

That made her smile, big time. "Ah, the silver lining,"

she said triumphantly. "So it's really over? Queen Bitch is gone for good?"

"Don't call her that."

"Is she gone for good?"

"I think so."

"Say yes, Myron. It'll make you feel better."

But he couldn't. "I'm not here to talk about me."

Esperanza crossed her arms, said nothing.

"We'll get you out of this," he said. "I promise."

She nodded, still playing casual; if she were a smoker, she'd be blowing rings. "You better get back to the office. We've already lost too many clients."

"I don't care about that."

"I do." Her voice had an edge now. "I'm a partner now."

"I know that."

"So I own part of MB SportsReps. If you want to self-destruct, fine. But don't drag my lusted-after ass down with you, okay?"

"I didn't mean it like that. I just meant we've got bigger worries right now."

"No."

"What?"

"*We* don't have bigger worries. I want you to stay out of this."

"I don't understand."

"I have one of the top criminal defense attorneys in the country working on my case. Let her handle it."

Myron tried to let her words settle in, but they were like unruly children after a sugar fix. He leaned forward a bit. "What's going on here?"

"I can't talk about it."

"What?"

"Hester told me I shouldn't talk about the case with anyone, even you. Our conversations are not protected."

"You think I'd tell?"

"You can be forced to testify."

"So I'd lie."

"You won't have to."

Myron opened his mouth, closed it, tried again. "Win and I can help here. We're good at this."

"No offense, Myron, but Win is psycho. I love him, but his kind of help I don't need. And you"—Esperanza stopped, looked up, unfolded her arms, lowered her gaze back to his—"you're damaged goods. I don't blame you for running away. It was probably the right thing to do. But let's not pretend you're back to normal."

"Not normal," he agreed. "But I'm ready for this."

She shook her head. "Concentrate on MB. It's going to take all your efforts to keep her afloat."

"You're not going to tell me what happened?"

"No."

"That doesn't make any sense."

"I just spelled out the reasons—"

"You're really afraid I'd testify against you?"

"I didn't say that."

"So what is it? If you think I'm not up for this, okay, maybe I buy it. But that wouldn't stop you from talking to me. In fact, you'd probably tell me just to keep me from poking around. So what's going on here?"

Her face slid closed. "Go to the office, Myron. You want to help? Save our business."

"Did you kill him?"

He regretted it the moment the words came out of his mouth. She looked at him as if he'd just reached across the table and slapped her face.

"I don't care if you did," he pressed on. "I'll stand by you no matter what. I want you to know that."

Esperanza regained her composure. She slid her chair back and stood. For a few moments she stared at him, studying his face as though searching for something that was normally there. Then she turned away, called for the guard, and left the room.

CHAPTER 9

Big Cyndi was already manning the reception desk when Myron reached the offices of MB SportsReps. They had a prime location, right smack on Park Avenue in midtown. The Lock-Horne high-rise had been owned by Win's family since Great-Great-Et-Cetera Grandpa Horne (or was it Lockwood?) had torn down a tepee and started building it. Myron rented space at a premium discount from Win. In return Win handled all the finances for Myron's clients. This deal was a bargain for Myron. Between the *primo* address and the ability to guarantee his clients the financial services of the near-legendary Windsor Horne Lockwood III, MB SportsReps had an air of legitimacy few small firms could boast.

MB SportsReps was on the twelfth floor. An elevator opened directly into their reception room. *Muy* classy. The phones were beeping. Big Cyndi put people on hold and looked up at him. She looked even more ridiculous than usual. No easy task. In the first place, the furniture was too small for her, the desk legs actually teetering on her knees like something a father might experience when visiting his child's elementary school. In the second place, she still had not washed up or changed from last night. Normally Myron, the image-conscious entrepreneur, would comment on this, but now did not seem an appropriate (or safe) time.

"The press is pulling out all the tricks to get up here, Mr. Bolitar." Big Cyndi always called him Mr. Bolitar. She liked formalities. "Two of them even pretended to be prospective clients coming out of Division One schools."

Myron was hardly surprised. "I told the guard downstairs to be extra wary."

"A lot of clients are calling too. They're concerned."

"Patch them through. Get rid of everybody else."

"Yes, Mr. Bolitar." Like she wanted to salute. Big Cyndi handed him a pile of blue slips. "These are this morning's calls from clients."

He started thumbing through the stack.

"For your information," Big Cyndi continued, "we told everyone you were just gone for a day or two at first. Then a week or two. Then we started faking emergencies for you: family illnesses, helping a sick client, that sort of thing. But some clients got tired of the excuses."

He nodded. "You have a list of who left us?"

It was already in her hand. She handed it to him, and he started toward his office.

"Mr. Bolitar?"

He turned. "Yes?"

"Will Esperanza be okay?"

Again the tiny, distant voice belied her bulk, as though the looming form in front of him had swallowed a small child and the small child were now calling for help. "Yes, Big Cyndi. She'll be fine."

"You'll help her, won't you? Even though she doesn't want you to?"

Myron gave her a half nod. That didn't seem to satisfy her. So he said, "Yes."

"Good, Mr. Bolitar. That's the right thing to do."

He had nothing to add to that so he entered his inner office. Myron had not been to MB in six weeks. Strange. He had worked so hard and so long to build up MB SportsReps—M for Myron, B for Bolitar, snappy name, no?—and he had just abandoned her. Just like that. Abandoned his business. And his clients. And Esperanza.

The renovations had been completed—they'd sliced a bit of space out of the conference room and reception area so that Esperanza could have an office of her own—but the new room remained unfurnished. So Esperanza had been using his office. He sat at his desk and immediately the phone started ringing. He ignored it for a few seconds, his eyes latched on the client wall, the one with action photos of all the athletes MB represented. He zeroed in on Clu Haid's image. Clu was on the pitcher's mound, leaning forward, about to go into a stretch, his cheek bulging with tobacco chaw, his eyes squinting at a sign he would undoubtedly shake off.

"What did you do this time, Clu?" he said out loud.

The photo didn't reply, which was probably a good thing. But Myron continued to stare. He had pulled Clu out of so many jams over the years that he had to wonder: If he had not run off to the Caribbean, would he have been able to pull Clu out of this one too?

Useless introspection—one of Myron's many talents.

Big Cyndi buzzed him. "Mr. Bolitar?"

"Yes."

"I know you told me to only patch through clients, but Sophie Mayor is on the line."

Sophie Mayor was the new owner of the Yankees.

"Put her through." He heard a click and said hello.

"Myron, my God. What the hell is going on here?" Sophie Mayor wasn't big on chitchat.

"I'm still trying to sort it out myself."

"They think your secretary killed Clu."

"Esperanza is my partner," he corrected, though he was not sure why. "And she didn't kill anyone."

"I'm sitting here with Jared." Jared was her son and the "co-general manager" of the Yankees—*co meaning shares the title with someone who knows what he's doing because he got the job through nepotism. Jared meaning born after 1973.* "We need to tell the press something."

"I'm not sure how I can help, Ms. Mayor."

"You told me Clu was past all this, Myron."

He said nothing.

"The drugs, the drinking, the partying, the trouble," Sophie Mayor continued. "You said it was in the past."

He was about to defend himself but thought better of it. "I think it's better if we talk about all this in person," Myron said.

"Jared and I are on the road with the team. We're in Cleveland right now. We're flying home tonight."

"How about tomorrow morning then?"

"We'll be at the stadium," she said. "Eleven o'clock."

"I'll be there."

He hung up the phone. Big Cyndi immediately put through a client call.

"Myron here."

"Where the hell have you been?"

It was Marty Towey, a defensive tackle for the Vikings. Myron took a deep breath and let loose his semiprepared oration: he was back, things were great, don't worry, the financials are terrific, got the new contract right here, busy securing new endorsements, blah, blah, soothe, soothe.

Marty was a tough sell. "Dammit, Myron, I chose MB because I didn't want underlings handling me. I wanted to deal with the big boss. You know what I'm saying?"

"Sure, Marty."

"Esperanza's nice and all. But she ain't you. I hired you. Do you understand?"

"I'm back now, Marty. Everything is going to be fine, I promise. Look, you guys are in town in a couple of weeks, right?"

"We play the Jets in two weeks."

"Great. So I'll meet you at the game and we'll go out to dinner afterward."

When Myron hung up, it dawned on him that he'd been so uninvolved in his clients' affairs that he didn't even know if Marty was playing at an All-Pro level or nearly waived. Christ, he had a lot of catching up to do.

The calls went on in a similar vein for the next two hours. Most clients were assuaged. Some sat on the fence. No additional ones left him. He had not fixed anything, but he had managed to lessen the blood flow to a serious trickle.

Big Cyndi knocked and opened the office door. "Trouble, Mr. Bolitar."

An awful, though not unfamiliar, stench started emanating from the doorway.

"What the hell . . . ?" Myron began.

"Out of the way, hot stuff." The gruff voice came from behind Big Cyndi. Myron tried to see who it was, but Big Cyndi blocked his line of vision like a solar eclipse. Eventually she yielded, and the same two plainclothes officers from the courthouse hurried past her. The big one was fiftyish, bleary-eyed, world-weary and had the kind of face that looked unshaven even after a shave. He wore a trench coat with sleeves that barely reached his elbows and shoes that had more scuff marks than a Gaylord Perry baseball. The smaller guy was younger and really, well, ugly. His face reminded Myron of a magnified photo of head lice. He wore a light gray suit with vest—the Sears Casual Law Enforcer—and one of those *Looney Tunes* ties that screamed 1992.

The awful smell started permeating the walls.

"A warrant," the big guy groused. He wasn't chewing on a cigar, but he should have been. "And before you tell me we're out of our jurisdiction, we're still working with Michael Chapman, Manhattan North. Call him, you got a problem. Now get out of the chair, asshole, so we can search this place."

Myron crinkled his nose. "Jesus, which one of you is wearing the cologne?"

Head Lice gave a quick look toward his partner. The look said, Hey, I'll take a bullet for this guy, but I'm not taking the fall for that smell. Understandable.

"Listen up, dip shit," the big one said. "My name is Detective Winters—"

"Really? Your mother named you Detective?"

Barely a sigh. "—and this is Detective Martinez. Move out here now, dim wad."

The smell was getting to him. "Yo, Winters, you got to stop borrowing cologne from male flight attendants."

"Keep at it, funnyman."

"Seriously, does the label include the words *glaze liberally*?"

"You're a real comedian, Bolitar. So many bad asses are funny it's a pity they don't televise Sing Sing."

"I thought you already searched the place."

"We did. Now we're back for the financials."

Myron pointed to Head Lice. "Can't he do it alone?"

"What?"

"I'll never get the smell out of here."

Winters took out a pair of latex gloves, this so as not to mess up possible fingerprints. He snapped them on in dramatic fashion, including finger wiggling, and grinned.

Myron winked. "You want me to bend down and grab my ankles?"

"No."

"Dang, and me needing a date." Want to needle a cop? Use gay humor. Myron had yet to meet one who wasn't a complete homophobe.

Winters said, "We're going to trash this place, funnyman."

"Doubtful," Myron countered.

"Oh?"

Myron stood, reached into the file cabinet behind him.

"Hey, you can't touch anything in here."

Myron ignored him, pulled out a small videocamera. "Just keeping a record of your doings, officer. In today's climate of false police corruption charges, we wouldn't want any misunderstandings"—Myron snapped on the camera and aimed the lens at the big guy—"would we?"

"No," the big guy said, staring straight into the lens. "We wouldn't want any misunderstandings."

Myron kept his eye in the viewer. "The camera captures the real you, Detective. I bet if we played it back, we'd still smell your cologne."

Head Lice hid a smile.

"Please get out of our way, Mr. Bolitar," Winters said.

"Sure thing. Cooperation is my middle name."

They began the search, which basically consisted of packing every document they could lay their hands on in crates and carrying them out. The gloved hands touched everything, and it felt to Myron like they were touching him. He tried to look innocent—whatever that looked like

—but he couldn't help being nervous. Guilt was a funny thing. He knew that there was nothing amiss in any of the files, but he still felt oddly defensive.

Myron gave the video camera to Big Cyndi and started making calls to clients who had left MB. Most didn't pick up. The few who did tried to defect. Myron played it soft, figuring that any overaggression would backfire. He merely told them that he was back and would like very much to speak with them at their earliest convenience. A lot of hemming and hawing from those who actually spoke to him. Not unexpected. If he were to regain their confidence, it would take time.

The cops finished up and left without so much as a good-bye. Manners. Big Cyndi and Myron watched the elevators close.

"This is going to be very difficult," Myron said.

"What?"

"Working without any files."

Big Cyndi opened her purse and showed him computer disks. "Everything is on these."

"Everything?"

"Yes."

"You backed up everything on these?"

"Yes."

"Letters and correspondences, okay, but I need the contracts—"

"Everything," she said. "I bought a scanner and ran every paper in the office through it. There's a backup set in a safety-deposit box at Citibank. I update the disks every week. In case of fire or other emergency."

When she smiled this time, Myron's cringe was barely perceptible.

"Big Cyndi, you are a surprising woman."

It was hard to tell under the melted Masque de Crayola, but it almost looked like she was blushing.

The intercom buzzed. Big Cyndi picked up the phone. "Yes?" Pause. Then her voice grew grave. "Yes, send her up." She replaced the receiver.

"Who is it?"

"Bonnie Haid is here to see you."

Big Cyndi showed the Widow Haid into his office. Myron stood behind his desk, not sure what to do. He waited for her to make the first move, but she didn't. Bonnie Haid had let her hair grow out, and for a moment he was back at Duke. Clu and Bonnie were sitting on the couch in the basement of the frat house, another major kegger behind them, his arm draped over her shoulder, she wearing a gray sweatshirt, her legs tucked under her.

He swallowed and moved toward her. She took a step back and closed her eyes. She put a hand up to stop him as though she could not bear the pain of his intimacy. Myron stayed where he was.

"I'm sorry," he said.

"Thank you."

They both stood there, two dancers waiting for the music to begin.

"Can I sit down?" Bonnie asked.

"Of course."

She sat. Myron hesitated and then chose to go back around his desk.

"When did you get back?" she asked.

"Last night," he said. "I didn't know about Clu before then. I'm sorry I wasn't here for you."

Bonnie cocked her head. "Why?"

"Pardon?"

"Why are you sorry you weren't here? What could you have done?"

Myron shrugged. "Help maybe."

"Help how?"

He shrugged again, spread his arms. "I don't know what to say, Bonnie. I'm flailing here."

She looked at him a moment, challenging, then dropped her eyes. "I'm just lashing out at whoever's in front of me," she said. "Don't pay any attention."

"I don't mind; lash away."

Bonnie almost managed a smile. "You're a good guy, Myron. You always were. Even at Duke there was something about you that was—I don't know—noble, I guess."

"Noble?"

"Sounds silly, doesn't it?"

"Very," he said. "How are the boys?"

She shrugged. "Timmy is only eighteen months old so he doesn't have a clue. Charlie is four so he's just pretty confused right now. My parents are taking care of them."

"I don't want to keep sounding like a bad cliché," Myron said, "but if there's anything at all I can do . . ."

"One thing."

"Name it."

"Tell me about the arrest."

Myron cleared his throat. "What about it?"

"I've met Esperanza a few times over the years. I guess I find it hard to believe she'd kill Clu."

"She didn't do it."

Bonnie squinted a bit. "What makes you so sure?"

"I know Esperanza."

"That's it?"

He nodded. "For now."

"Have you spoken to her?"

"Yes."

"And?"

"I can't talk about specifics"—mostly because he didn't know any; Myron was almost grateful that Esperanza had not told him anything—"but she didn't do it."

"What about all the evidence the police found?"

"I can't answer that yet, Bonnie. But Esperanza is innocent. We'll find the real killer."

"You sound so sure."

"I am."

They fell into silence. Myron waited, mapping out an approach. There were questions that needed to be asked, but this woman had just lost her husband. One had to tread gently lest one trip an emotional land mine.

"I'm going to look into the murder," Myron said.

She looked confused. "What do you mean, look into?"

"Investigate."

"But you're a sports agent."

"I have some background in this."

She studied his face. "Win too?"

"Yes."

She nodded as if something suddenly made sense. "Win always scared the crap out of me."

"That's only because you're sane."

"And now you're going to try to figure out who killed Clu?"

"Yes."

"I see," she said. She shifted in her chair. "Tell me something, Myron."

"Anything."

"What's your priority here: finding the murderer or getting Esperanza off?"

"One and the same."

"And if they're not? If you learn Esperanza killed him?"

Time to lie. "Then she'll be punished."

Bonnie started smiling as though she could see the truth. "Good luck," she said.

Myron put an ankle up on a knee. *Gentle now,* he thought. "Can I ask you something?"

She shrugged. "Sure."

Gently, gently. "I don't mean any disrespect, Bonnie. I'm not asking this to be nosy—"

"Subtlety is not your strong suit, Myron. Just ask your question."

"Were you and Clu having problems?"

A sad grin. "Weren't we always?"

"I hear this was something more serious."

Bonnie folded her arms below her chest. "My, my. Back less than a day and already you've learned so much. You work fast, Myron."

"Clu mentioned it to Win."

"So what do you want to know?"

"Were you suing him for divorce?"

"Yes." No hesitation.

"Can you tell me what happened?"

In the distance the fax machine started its primordial screech. The phone continued beeping. Myron had no fear that they'd be interrupted. Big Cyndi had worked for years as a bouncer at an S&M bar; when the situation called for it, she could be as nasty as a rabid rhino with a bad case of piles. Er, even when the situation didn't call for it.

"Why do you want to know?" Bonnie asked.

"Because Esperanza didn't kill him."

"That's becoming something of a mantra for you, Myron. Say it often enough and you start to believe it, right?"

"I believe it."

"So?"

"So if she didn't kill him, someone else did."

Bonnie looked up. "If she didn't kill him, someone else did," she repeated. Pause. "You weren't just bragging before. You really do have a background in this."

"I'm just trying to find out who killed him."

"By asking about our marriage?"

"By asking about anything turbulent in his life."

"Turbulent?" She let out a stab of a laugh. "This is Clu we're talking about here, Myron. Everything was turbulent. The hard thing to find would be patches of calm."

"How long were you two together?" Myron asked.

"You know the answer to that."

He did. Junior year at Duke. Bonnie had come bopping down to the frat house basement dressed in a monogram sweater and pearls and, yep, ponytail. Myron and Clu had been working the keg. Myron liked working the keg because it kept him so busy he didn't drink as much. Don't get the wrong idea here. Myron drank. It was pretty much a college requirement in those days. But he wasn't a very good drinker. He always seemed to miss that cusp of fun, that floaty buzz between sobriety and vomiting. It was almost nonexistent for him. Something in his ancestry, he assumed. It had actually helped him in recent months. Before running away with Terese, Myron had tried the old-fashioned approach of drowning one's sorrows. But, put bluntly, he usually threw up before reaching oblivion.

Nice way to prevent alcohol abuse.

Anyway, Clu and Bonnie's meeting was pretty simple. Bonnie walked in. Clu looked up from the keg and it was as if Captain Marvel had zapped him with a thunderbolt. "Wow," Clu muttered, the beer overflowing onto a floor so coated with beer that rodents often got stuck on it and died. Then Clu leaped over the bar, staggered toward Bonnie, dropped to one knee, and proposed. Three years later they tied the knot for real.

"So after all these years what happened?"

Bonnie looked down. "It had nothing to do with his murder," she said.

"That's probably true, but I need to get the full picture of his life, travel down any possible avenue—"

"Bullshit, Myron. I said it had nothing to do with the murder, okay? Leave it at that."

He licked his lips, folded his hands, put them on the desktop. "In the past you've thrown him out because of another woman."

"Not woman. Women. Plural."

"Is that what happened again this time?"

"He swore off women. He promised me that there'd be no more."

"And he broke that promise?"

Bonnie didn't answer.

"What was her name?"

Her voice was soft. "I never knew."

"But there was someone else?"

Again she didn't answer. No need. Myron tried to put on his attorney skin for a moment. Clu's having an affair was a very good thing for Esperanza's defense. The more motives you can find, the more reasonable doubt you can create. Did the girlfriend kill him because he still wanted to be with his wife? Did Bonnie do it out of jealousy? And then there was the missing money. Wouldn't the girlfriend and/or Bonnie have known about it? Couldn't that be an added motive for murder? Yep, Hester Crimstein would like this. Throw enough possibilities into a trial, muddy the waters enough, and an acquittal is almost inevitable. It was a simple equation: Confusion equals reasonable doubt equals a not-guilty verdict.

"He's had affairs before, Bonnie. What was different this time?"

"Give it a rest, Myron, okay? Clu isn't even in the ground yet."

He pulled back. "I'm sorry."

She looked away. Her chest rose and fell, her voice fighting to stay steady. "I know you're just trying to help," she said. "But the divorce stuff . . . it hurts too much right now."

"I understand."

"If you have other questions . . ."

"I heard Clu failed a drug test." So much for backing off.

"I only know what I read in the papers."

"Clu told Win it was a fix."

"What?"

"Clu claimed he was clean. What do you think?"

"I think Clu was a marvelous screwup. We both know that."

"So he was taking again?"

"I don't know." She swallowed and locked eyes with him. "I hadn't seen him in weeks."

"And before that?"

"He seemed clean, actually. But he was always good at hiding it. Remember that intervention we tried three years ago?"

Myron nodded.

"We all cried. We all begged him to stop. And finally Clu broke down too. He sobbed like a baby, said he was ready turn his life around. Two days later he paid off a guard and sneaked out of rehab."

"So you think he was just masking the symptoms?"

"He could have been. He was good at that." She hesitated. "But I don't think so."

"Why not?"

"I don't know. Wishful thinking, I guess, but I really

thought he was clean this time. In the past you could almost see he was going through the motions. He was playing a part for me or the kids. But this time he seemed more determined. Like he knew this trade was his last chance to start fresh. He worked at it like I've never seen him work at anything. I thought he was beating it too. But something must have pushed him back off. . . ."

Bonnie's voice tailed off, and now her eyes filled. She was wondering, no doubt, if she had been that push, if Clu had indeed been clean and if she had thrown him out of their house and plunged him back into the world of his addictions. Myron almost told her not to blame herself, but good sense kept the grating cliché at bay.

"Clu always needed someone or something," she went on. "He was the most dependent person I ever knew."

Myron nodded, encouraging her.

"At first I found that attractive, that he needed me so much. But it got weary." Bonnie looked at him. "How many times did someone pull his ass out of the fire?"

"Too many," Myron admitted.

"I wonder, Myron." She sat up a bit, more clear-eyed now. "I wonder if we all did him a disservice. Maybe if we weren't always there to save him, he would have had to change. Maybe if I had dumped him years ago, he would have straightened himself out and survived all this."

Myron said nothing, not bothering to point out the inherent contradiction in her statement: She finally did dump him and he ended up dead.

"Did you know about the two hundred thousand dollars?" Myron asked.

"I heard about it from the police."

"Do you have any idea where it might be?"

"No."

"Or why he might have needed it?"

"No." Her voice was far away now, her gaze drifting over his shoulder.

"Do you think it was for drugs?"

"The papers said he tested positive for heroin," she said.

"That's my understanding."

"That would be a new one for Clu. I know it's an expensive addiction, but two hundred thousand seems extreme."

Myron agreed. "Was he in any trouble?"

She looked at him.

"I mean, besides the usual. Loan sharks or gambling or something like that?"

"It's possible, I guess."

"But you don't know."

Bonnie shook her head, still looking off at nothing. "You know what I was thinking about?"

"What?"

"Clu's first year as a pro. Class A with the New England Bisons. Right after he asked you to negotiate his contract. Do you remember that?"

Myron nodded.

"And again, I wonder."

"Wonder what?"

"That was the first time we all banded together to save his ass."

The late-night phone call. Myron swimming out of sleep and clutching the receiver. Clu crying, almost incoherent. He had been driving with Bonnie and his old Duke roommate, Billy Lee Palms, the Bisons' catcher. Drunk driving, to be more precise. He had smashed the car into a pole. Billy Lee's injuries were minor, but Bonnie had been rushed to the hospital. Clu, not a scratch on him, of course, had been arrested. Myron had hurried out to western Massachusetts, plenty of cash in hand.

"I remember," Myron said.

"You'd just signed Clu to that big chocolate milk endorsement. Drunk driving was bad enough, but with an injury to boot, well, it would have destroyed him. But we took care of him. The right people were bought off. Billy Lee and I made a statement about some pickup truck cutting us off. We saved him. And now I wonder if we did the right thing. Maybe if Clu had paid a price right then and there, maybe if he'd gone to jail instead of skating by . . ."

"He wouldn't have gone to jail, Bonnie. A suspended license maybe. Some community service."

"Whatever. Life is about ripples, Myron. There are some philosophers who think that everything we do changes the world forever. Even simple acts. Like if you left your house five minutes later, if you took a different route to work—it changes everything for the rest of your life. I don't necessarily buy that, but when it comes to the big things, yeah, sure, I think the ripples last. Or maybe it started before that. When he was a child. The first time he learned that because he could throw a white sphere with amazing velocity, people treated him special. Maybe we just continued the conditioning that day. Or brought it up to an adult level. Clu learned that someone would always save him. And we did. We got him off that night, and then there were the assault charges and the lewd behavior and the failed drug tests and whatever else."

"And you think his murder was the inevitable result?"

"Don't you?"

"No," Myron said. "I think the person who shot him three times is responsible. Period."

"Life is rarely that simple, Myron."

"But murder usually is. In the end someone shot him. That's how he died. He didn't die because we helped him through some self-destructive excesses. Someone murdered him. And that person—not you or me or those who cared about him—is to blame."

She thought about it. "Maybe you're right." But she didn't look convinced.

"Do you know why Clu would strike Esperanza?"

She shook her head. "The police asked me that too. I don't know. Maybe he was high."

"Did he get violent when he got high?"

"No. But it sounds like he was under a lot of pressure. Maybe he was just frustrated that she wouldn't tell him where you were."

Another wave of guilt. He waited for it to recede.

"Who else would he have gone to, Bonnie?"

"What do you mean?"

"You said he was needy. I wasn't around. You weren't talking to him. So where would Clu go next?"

She thought about it. "I'm not sure."

"Any friends, teammates?"

"I don't think so."

"How about Billy Lee Palms?"

She shrugged an I-don't-know.

Myron tossed out a few more questions, but nothing of consequence was batted back to him. After a while Bonnie feigned a check at the time. "I have to get back to the kids," she said.

He nodded, rose from his chair. This time she did not stop him. He hugged her and she hugged him back, gripping him fiercely.

"Do me one favor," she said.

"Name it."

"Clear your friend," she said. "I understand why you

need to do that. And I wouldn't want her to go to jail for something she didn't do. But then let it be.''

Myron pulled back a bit. ''I don't understand.''

''Like I said before, you're a noble guy.''

He thought about the Slaughter family and how it all ended; something inside him was crushed anew. ''College was a long time ago,'' he said softly.

''You haven't changed.''

''You'd be surprised.''

''You still need justice and neat endings and to do the right thing.''

He said nothing.

''Clu can't give you that,'' Bonnie said. ''He wasn't a noble man.''

''He didn't deserve to be murdered.''

She put a hand on his arm. ''Save your friend, Myron. Then let Clu go.''

CHAPTER 10

Myron took the elevator up two floors to the nerve center of Lock-Horne Securities and Investments. Exhausted white men—there were women and minorities too, more and more each year, but the overall numbers were still woefully inadequate—darted about, particles under blaring heat, gray phones tethered to their ears like life-sustaining umbilical cords. The noise level and the open space reminded Myron of a Vegas casino, though the toupees were better. People cried out in joy and agony. Money was won and lost. Dice were rolled and wheels were spun and cards were dealt. The men constantly glanced up at an electronic ticker, awe in their faces, ardently watching the stock prices like gamblers waiting for the wheel to settle on a number or ancient Israelites peering up at Moses and his new stone tablets.

These were the trenches of finance, armed soldiers crowded together, each trying to survive in a world where earning low six figures meant cowardice and probably death. Computer terminals twinkled through an onslaught of yellow Post-It notes. The warriors drank coffee and buried framed family photos under a volcanic outpouring of stock analyses and financial statements and corporate reviews. They wore white button-down shirts and Windsor-knotted ties, their suit jackets neatly arrayed on the backs of chairs as though the chairs were a tad chilly or preparing for lunch at Le Cirque.

Win did not sit out here, of course. The generals in this war—the rainmakers, big producers, heavy hitters, what have you—were tented on the perimeter, their offices running along the windows, cutting off from the foot soldiers any hint of blue sky or fresh air or any element endemic to human beings.

Myron headed up a carpeted incline and toward the left corner suite. Win was usually alone in his office. Not today. Myron stuck his head in the door, and a bunch of suitheads swiveled toward him. Lots of suits. Myron couldn't say how many. Might have been six, maybe eight. They were a lumpy blur of gray and blue with streaks of tie-and-hankie red, like the aftermath of a Civil War reenactment. The older ones, distinguished whitehaired guys with manicures and cuff links, sat in the burgundy leather chairs closest to Win's desk and nodded a lot. The younger ones were squeezed onto the couches against the wall, heads down, scratching notes on legal pads as though Win were divulging the secret of eternal life. Every once in a while the younger men would peer up at the older men, glimpsing their glorious future, which would basically consist of a more comfortable chair and less note taking.

The legal pads gave it away. These were attorneys. The older men probably over four hundred bucks an hour, the younger ones two-fifty. Myron didn't bother with the math, mostly because it would take too much effort to count how many suits were in the room. Didn't matter. Lock-Horne Securities could afford it. Redistributing wealth—that is, the act of moving money around without creation or production or making anything new—was incredibly profitable.

Myron Bolitar, Marxist Sports Agent.

Win clapped his hands and the men were dismissed. They rose as slowly as possible—attorneys billed by the minute, sort of like 900 sex lines minus the guaranteed, er, payoff—and filed out the office door. The older men departed first, the younger men trailing not unlike Japanese brides.

Myron stepped inside. "What's going on?"

Win signaled for Myron to sit. Then he leaned back and did the steeple thing with his hands. "This situation," he said, "has me troubled."

"You mean Clu's cash withdrawal?"

"In part, yes," Win said. He bounced the fingertips before resting the indexes on his lower lip. "I become very unhappy when I hear the words *subpoena* and *Lock-Horne* in the same sentence."

"So? You have nothing to hide."

Win smiled thinly. "Your point being?"

"Let them look at your records. You're a lot of things, Win. Honest being chief among them."

Win shook his head. "You are so naive."

"What?"

"My family runs a financial securities firm."

"So?"

"So even the whiff of innuendo can destroy said firm."

"I think you're overreacting," Myron said.

Win arched an eyebrow, put a hand to his ear. "Pardon *moi*?"

"Come on, Win. There's always some Wall Street scandal or other going on. People barely notice anymore."

"Those are insider trading scandals mostly."

"So?"

Win paused, looked at him. "Are you being purposely obtuse?"

"No."

"Insider trading is a completely different animal."

"How so?"

"Do you really need me to explain this to you?"

"Guess so."

"Fine then. Stripping it bare, insider trading is cheating or stealing. My clients do not care if I cheat or steal—as long it is done for their benefit. In fact, if a certain illegal act were to increase their portfolios, most clients would probably encourage it. But if their financial adviser is playing games with their personal accounts—or equally awful, if his banking institution is merely involved in something that will give the government the right to subpoena records—clients become understandably nervous."

Myron nodded. "I can see where there might be a problem."

Win strummed the top of his desk with his fingers. For him, this was major agitation. Hard to believe, but for the first time Win actually appeared a touch unnerved. "I have three law firms and two publicity firms working on the matter," he continued.

"Working on it how?"

"The usual," Win said. "Calling in political favors, preparing a lawsuit against the Bergen County DA's office for libel and slander, planting positive spins in the media, seeing what judges will be running for reelection."

"In other words," Myron said, "who can you pay off."

Win shrugged. "You say tomato, I say tomahto."

"The files haven't been subpoenaed yet?"

"No. I plan on quashing the possibility before any judge even thinks of issuing them."

"So maybe we should take the offensive."

Win resteepled. His big mahogany desk was polished to the point where his reflection was near-mirror clear, like something out of an old dish detergent commercial where a housewife gets waaaaay too excited about seeing herself in a dinner plate. "I'm listening."

He recounted his conversation with Bonnie Haid. The red phone on Win's credenza—his Batphone, so enamored with the old Adam West vehicle that he actually kept it under what looked like a glass cake cover—interrupted him several times. Win had to take the calls. They were mostly from attorneys. Myron could hear the lawyerly panic travel through the earpiece and all the way across the desk. Understandable. Windsor Horne Lockwood III was not the kind of guy you wanted to disappoint.

Win remained calm. His end of the conversation could basically be broken down into two words: *How*. And *much*.

When Myron finished, Win said, "Let's make a list." He didn't reach for a pen. Neither did Myron. "One, we need Clu's phone records."

"He was staying at an apartment in Fort Lee," Myron said.

"The murder scene."

"Right. Clu and Bonnie rented the apartment when he first got traded in May." To the Yankees. A huge deal that gave Clu, an aging veteran, one last chance to squander. "They moved into the house in Tenafly in July, but the apartment's lease ran for another six months. So when Bonnie threw him out, that's where he ended up."

"You have the address?" Win asked.

"Yep."

"Fine then."

"Send the records down to Big Cyndi. I'll have her check through it."

Getting a phone record was frighteningly easy. Don't believe it? Open your local yellow pages. Choose a private investigator at random. Offer to pay him or her two grand for anyone's monthly phone bill. Some will simply say yes, but most will try to up you to three thousand, half the fee going to whatever phone company minion they bribe.

Myron said, "We also need to check out Clu's credit cards, his checkbook, ATM, whatever, see what he's been up to lately."

Win nodded. In Clu's case, this would be doubly easy. His entire financial portfolio was held by Lock-Horne Securities. Win had set up a separate management account for Clu so that he could manage his finances easier. It included a Visa debit card, electronic payments of monthly bills, and a checkbook.

"We also need to find this mystery girlfriend," Myron said.

"Shouldn't be too difficult," Win said.

"No."

"And as you suggested earlier, our old fraternity brother Billy Lee Palms might know something."

"We can track him down," Myron said.

Win raised a finger. "One thing."

"I'm listening."

"You will have to do the majority of the legwork on your own."

"Why's that?"

"I have a business to run."

"So do I," Myron said.

"You lose your business, you hurt two people."

"Three," Myron corrected. "You forgot Big Cyndi."

"No. I am speaking of Big Cyndi and Esperanza. I left you out for all the obvious reasons. Again if you require the prerequisite cliché, please choose one of the following: You made your bed, now lie in it—"

"I get the point," Myron interrupted. "But I still have a business to protect. For their sakes, if not my own."

"No question." Win motioned toward the trenches. "But at the risk of sounding melodramatic, I am responsible for those people out there. For their jobs and financial security. They have families and mortgages and tuition payments." He pierced Myron with the ice blues. "That's not something I take lightly."

"I know."

Win leaned back. "I'll stay involved, of course. And again if my particular talents are needed—"

"Let's hope they aren't," Myron interrupted.

Win shrugged again. Then he said, "Funny, isn't it?"

"What?"

"We haven't even mentioned Esperanza in all this. Why do you think that is?"

"I don't know."

"Perhaps," Win said, "we have some doubt about her innocence."

"No."

Win arched the eyebrow but said nothing.

"I'm not just being emotional," Myron said. "I've been thinking about it."

"And?"

"And it makes no sense. First off, why would Esperanza kill Clu? What's her motive?"

"The DA seems to think she killed him for the money."

"Right. And I think it's fair to say we both know better."

Win paused, nodded. "Esperanza would not kill for money, no."

"So we have no motive."

Win frowned. "I'd say that conclusion is at best premature."

"Okay, but now let's look at the evidence. The gun, for example."

"Go on," Win said.

"Think this through for a second. Esperanza has a major altercation with Clu in front of witnesses, right?"

"Yes."

Myron held up a finger. "One, would Esperanza be dumb enough to kill Clu so soon after a public fight?"

"Fair point," Win conceded. "But perhaps the battle in the garage just raised the stakes. Perhaps after that Esperanza realized that Clu was out of control."

"Fine, let's say that Esperanza was still dumb enough to kill him after the fight. She'd have to know she'd be a suspect, right? I mean, there were witnesses."

Win nodded slowly. "I'll go with that."

"So why was the murder weapon in the office? Esperanza isn't that stupid. She's worked with us before. She knows the ins and out. Hell, anybody with a television set would have known you're supposed to dump the gun."

Win hesitated. "I see what you're saying."

"So the gun had to be planted. And if the gun was planted, then it follows that the blood and the fibers were planted too."

"Logical." Win doing his best Mr. Spock. The Batphone rang again. Win picked up the receiver and dispatched the matter in seconds. They went back to thinking.

"On the other hand," Win said, "I have never encountered a perfectly logical murder."

"What do you mean?"

"Reality is messy and full of contradictions. Take the O.J. case."

"The what?"

"The O.J. case," Win repeated. "If all that blood was spilled and the Juice was drenched in it, why was so little found?"

"He changed clothes."

"So? Even if he did, you'd expect to find more than a few dashboard splatters, wouldn't you? If the Juice drove home and showered, why was no blood found on the tiles or in the pipes or what have you?"

"So you think O.J. was innocent?"

Win frowned again. "You are missing my point."

"Which is?"

"Murder investigations never make complete sense. There are always rips in the fabric of logic. Unexplainable flaws. Perhaps Esperanza made a mistake. Perhaps she did not believe the police would suspect her. Perhaps she thought the weapon would be safer in the office than, say, her house."

"She didn't kill him, Win."

Win spread his hands. "Who amongst us is incapable —given the right circumstances—of murder?"

Heavy silence.

Myron swallowed hard. "For the sake of argument, let's assume the weapon was planted."

Win nodded slowly, keeping his eyes on Myron's.

"The question is, who set her up?"

"And why," Win added.

"So we need to make a list of her enemies," Myron said.

"And ours."

"What?"

"This murder charge is seriously wounding both of

us," Win said. "We thus have to look at several possibilities."

"For example?"

"First," Win said, "we may be reading too much into the frame-up."

"How so?"

"This may not be a personal vendetta at all. Perhaps the murderer heard about the garage altercation and concluded that Esperanza would make a convenient patsy."

"So then this is all just a way of deflecting attention from the real killer? Nothing personal?"

"It's a possibility," Win said. "No more or less."

"Okay," Myron agreed, "what else?"

"The murderer wants to do Esperanza great harm."

"The obvious choice."

"For whatever that's worth, yes," Win said. "And possibility number three: The murderer wants to do one of us great harm."

"Or," Myron said, "our businesses."

"Yes."

Something like a giant cartoon anvil landed on Myron's head. "Someone like FJ."

Win merely smiled.

"And," Myron went on, "if Clu was doing something illicit, something that needed large amounts of cash—"

"Then FJ and his family would be a prime possible recipient," Win finished for him. "And of course, if we forget the money for a moment, FJ would relish any opportunity to crush you. What better way than decimating your business and incarcerating your best friend?"

"Two birds, one stone."

"Precisely."

Myron sat back, suddenly exhausted. "I don't relish the idea of tangling with the Aches."

"Neither do I," Win said.

"You? Before, you wanted to kill FJ."

"That's just my point. I can't anymore. If young FJ is behind this, we have to keep him alive in order to prove it. Trapping vermin is chancy. Simple extermination is the preferred course of action."

"So we've now eliminated your favorite option."

Win nodded. "Sad, no?"

"Tragic."

"But it gets worse, old friend."

"How's that?"

"Innocent or guilty," Win said, "Esperanza is concealing something from us."

Silence.

"We have no choice," Win said. "We need to investigate her too. Delve into her personal life a bit."

"I don't relish the idea of tangling with the Aches," Myron said, "but I really don't relish the idea of invading Esperanza's privacy."

"Be afraid," Win agreed. "Be very afraid."

CHAPTER 11

The first potential clue did two things to Myron: It scared the hell out of him, and it reminded him of *The Sound of Music.*

Myron liked the old Julie Andrews musical well enough—who didn't?—but he always found one song particularly dumb. One of the classics actually. ''My Favorite Things.'' The song made no sense. Ask a zillion people to list their absolute favorite things, and how many of them are going to list doorbells, for crying out loud? You know what, Millie? I love doorbells! To hell with strolling on a quiet beach or reading a great book or making love or seeing a Broadway musical. Doorbells, Millie. Doorbells punch my ticket. Sometimes I just run up to people's houses and press their doorbells and well, I think I'm man enough to admit I shudder.

Another puzzling ''favorite'' was brown paper packages tied up with string, mostly because it sounded like something sent by a mail-order pornographer (er, not that Myron would know that from personal experience). But that was what Myron found in the large stack of mail. Plain brown packaging. Typed address label with the word

Personal across the bottom. No return address. Post-marked New York City.

Myron slit open the brown paper package, shook it, and watched a floppy disk drop to his desktop.

Hello.

Myron picked it up, turned it over, turned it back. No label on it. No writing. Just a plain black square with the metal across the top. Myron studied it for a moment, shrugged, popped it into his computer, hit some keys. He was about to hit Windows Explorer and see what kind of file it was when something started to happen. Myron sat back and frowned. He hoped that the diskette didn't contain a computer virus of some sort. He should, after all, know better than to just stick a strange diskette into his computer. He didn't know where it had been, what sleazy computer drive it had been inserted into before, if it wore a condom or had a blood test. Nothing. His poor computer. Just "Wham, bam, thank you, RAM."

Groan.

The screen went black.

Myron tugged his ear. His finger stretched forward to strike the escape button—the escape button being the last refuge of a desperate computerphobe—when an image appeared on the screen. Myron froze.

It was a girl.

She had long, semistringy hair with two flips in front and an awkward smile. He guessed her age at around sixteen, braces fresh off, the eyes looking to the side, the backdrop a fading swirl of school-portrait rainbow. Yep, the picture belonged in a frame on Mommy and Daddy's mantel or a suburban high school yearbook circa 1985, the kind of thing with a life-summing write-up underneath it, a life-defining quote from James Taylor or Bruce Springsteen followed by So-So enjoyed being secretary/treasurer of the Key Club, her fondest memories including hanging out with Jenny and Sharon T at the Big W, popcorn in Mrs. Kennilworth's class, band practice behind the parking lot, that kind of apple-pie stuff. Typical. Kind of an obituary to adolescence.

Myron knew the girl.

Or at least he'd seen her before. He couldn't put his finger on where or when or if he'd seen her in person or in a photograph or what. But there was no doubt. He stared hard, hoping to conjure up a name or even a fleeting memory. Nothing. He kept staring. And that was when it happened.

The girl began to melt.

It was the only way to describe it. The girl's hair flips fell and blended into her flesh, her forehead sloped down, her nose dissolved, her eyes rolled back and then closed. Blood began to run down from the eye sockets, coating the face in crimson.

Myron bolted his chair back, nearly screaming.

The blood blanketed the image now, and for a moment Myron wondered if it would actually start coming out of the screen. A laughing noise came from the computer speakers. Not a psycho laugh or cruel laugh but the healthy, happy laugh of a teenage girl, a normal sound that raised the hairs on the back of Myron's neck as no howl ever could.

Without warning, the screen went mercifully black. The laughter stopped. And then the Windows 98 main menu reappeared.

Myron gulped down a few breaths. His hands gripped the edge of the desk to the point of white knuckles.

What the hell?

His heart beat against his rib cage as though it wanted to break free. He reached back and grabbed the brown paper wrappings. The postmark was almost three weeks old. Three weeks. This awful diskette had been sitting in his pile of mail since he'd run away. Why? Who had sent this to him? And who was the girl?

Myron's hand was still shaking when he picked up the phone. He dialed. Even though Myron had call block on his phone, a man answered by saying, "What's up, Myron?"

"I need your help, PT."

"Jesus, you sound like hell. This about Esperanza?"

"No."

"So what have you got?"

"A computer diskette. Three-and-half-inch floppy. I need it analyzed."

"Go to John Jay. Ask for Dr. Czerski. But if you're looking for a trace, it's pretty unlikely. What's this about?"

"I got this diskette in the mail. It contains a graphic of a teenage girl. In an AVI file of some sort."

"Who's the girl?"

"I don't know."

"I'll call Czerski. You head over."

Dr. Kirstin Czerski sported a white lab coat and a frown as yielding as a former East German swimmer's. Myron tried Smile Patent 17—moist Alan Alda, post-*M*A*S*H*.

"Hi," Myron said. "My name is—"

"The diskette." She held out her hand. He handed it to her. She looked at it for a second and headed for a door. "Wait here."

The door opened. Myron got a brief view of a room that looked like the bridge on *Battlestar Galactica*. Lots of metal and wires and lights and monitors and reel-to-reel tapes. The door closed. Myron stood in a sparsely decorated waiting room. Linoleum floor, three molded plastic chairs, brochures on a wall.

Myron's cellular phone rang again. He stared at it for a second. Six weeks ago he had turned the phone off. Now that it was back on, the contraption seemed to be making up for lost time. He pressed a button and brought it to his ear.

"Hello?"

"Hi, Myron."

Pow. The voice walloped him like a palm blast to the sternum. A rushing noise filled his ears, as though the phone were a seashell clamped against him. Myron slid into a yellow plastic chair.

"Hello, Jessica," he managed.

"I saw you on the news," she said, her voice a tad too controlled. "So I figured you'd turn your phone back on."

"Right."

More silence.

"I'm in Los Angeles," Jessica continued.

"Uh-huh."

"But I needed to tell you a few things."

"Oh?" Myron's Smooth-Lines Fountain—he just couldn't turn it off.

"First off, I'll be gone for at least another month. I didn't change the locks or anything so you can stay at the loft—"

"I'm, uh, bunking at Win's."

"Yeah, I figured. But if you need anything or if you want to clear your stuff out—"

"Right."

"Don't forget the TV too. That's yours."

"You can keep it," he said.

"Fine."

More silence.

Jessica said, "We're being so adult about this, aren't we?"

"Jess—"

"Don't. I called for a reason."

Myron kept quiet.

"Clu called you several times. At the loft, I mean."

Myron had guessed that.

"He sounded pretty desperate. I told him I didn't know where you were. He said that he had to find you. That he was worried about you."

"About me?"

"Yes. He came by once, looking like absolute shit. He grilled me for twenty minutes."

"About what?"

"About where you were. He said that he had to reach you—for your sake more than his. When I insisted that I didn't know where you were, he started scaring me."

"Scaring you how?"

"He asked how I knew you weren't dead."

"Clu said those words? About my being dead?"

"Yes. I actually called Win when he left."

"What did Win say?"

"That you were safe and that I shouldn't worry."

"What else?"

"I'm talking about Win here, Myron. He said—and I quote—'he's safe, don't worry.' Then he hung up. I let it drop. I figured that Clu was engaging in a little hyperbole to get my attention."

"That was probably it," Myron said.

"Yeah."

More silence.

"How are you?" she asked.

"I'm good. And you?"

"I'm trying to get over you," she said.

He could barely breathe. "Jess, we should talk—"

"Don't," she said again. "I don't want to talk, okay? Let me put it simply: If you change your mind, call me. You know the number. If not, have a nice life."

Click.

Myron put down the phone. He took several deep breaths. He looked at the phone. So simple. He did indeed know the number. How easy it would be to dial it.

"Worthless."

He looked up at Dr. Czerski. "Pardon?"

She held up the diskette. "You said there was graphic on it?"

Myron quickly explained what he had seen.

"It's not there now," she said. "It must have deleted itself."

"How?"

"You say the program ran automatically?"

"Yes."

"It probably self-extracted, self-ran, and then self-deleted. Simple."

"Aren't there special programs so you can undelete a file?"

"Yes. But this file did more than that. It reformatted the whole diskette. Probably the final command in the chain."

"Meaning?"

"Whatever you saw is gone forever."

"Is there anything else on the diskette?"

"No."

"Nothing we can trace? No unique characteristics or anything?"

She shook her head. "Typical diskette. Sold in every software store in the country. Standard formatting."

"How about fingerprints?"

"That's not my department."

And, Myron knew, it would be a waste of time. If someone had gone to the trouble of destroying any computer evidence, chances were pretty good that all fingerprints had been wiped off too.

"I'm busy." Dr. Czerski handed him back the diskette and left without so much as a back glance. Myron stared at it and shook his head.

What the hell was going on here?

The cell phone rang again. Myron picked it up.

"Mr. Bolitar?" It was Big Cyndi.

"Yes."

"I am going through Mr. Clu Haid's phone records, as you requested."

"And?"

"Are you coming back to the office, Mr. Bolitar?"

"I'm on the way there now."

"There is something here you might find bizarre."

CHAPTER 12

When the elevator opened, Big Cyndi was waiting for him. She'd finally scrubbed her face clean. All the makeup was gone. Must have used a sand blaster. Or a jackhammer.

She greeted him by saying, "Very bizarre, Mr. Bolitar."

"What's that?"

"Per your instructions, I was checking through Clu Haid's phone records," she said. Then she shook her head. "Very bizarre."

"What's bizarre?"

She handed him a sheet of paper. "I highlighted the number in yellow."

Myron looked at it while walking into this office. Big Cyndi followed, closing the door behind her. The number was in the 212 area code. That meant Manhattan. Other than that, it was totally unfamiliar. "What about it?"

"It's for a nightclub."

"Which one?"

"Take A Guess."

"Pardon?"

"That's the name of the place," Big Cyndi said. "Take A Guess. It's two blocks down from Leather-N-Lust." Leather-N-Lust was the S&M bar that employed Big Cyndi as a bouncer. Motto: Hurt The Ones You Love.

"You know this place?" he asked.

"A little."

"What kind of club is it?"

"Cross-dressers and transvestites, mostly. But they have a varied crowd."

Myron rubbed his temples. "When you say varied . . ."

"It's sort of an interesting concept really, Mr. Bolitar."

"I'm sure."

"When you go to Take A Guess, you never know for sure what you're getting. You know what I mean?"

Myron didn't have a clue. "Pardon my sexual naiveté, but could you explain?"

Big Cyndi scrunched her face in thought. It was not a pretty sight. "In part, it's what you might expect: men dress like women, women dress like men. But then sometimes a woman is just a woman and a man is just a man. Follow?"

Myron nodded. "Not even a little."

"That's why it's called Take A Guess. You never know for sure. For instance, you might see a beautiful woman who is unusually tall with a platinum wig. So you figure it's a he-she. But—and this is what makes Take A Guess special—maybe it's not."

"Not what?"

"A he-she. A transvestite or transsexual. Maybe it is indeed a beautiful woman who put on extra-high heels and a wig to confuse you."

"And the reason for this is?"

"That's the fun of the place. The doubt. There's a sign inside. TAKE A GUESS: IT'S ABOUT AMBIGUITY, NOT ANDROGYNY."

"Catchy."

"But that's the idea. It's a place of mystery. You bring someone home. You think it's a beautiful woman or a handsome man. But until the pants are all the way down, you're never sure. People come dressed to fool. You just never know until—well, you saw *The Crying Game*."

Myron made a face. "And this is a desirable thing?"

"If you're into that, sure."

"Into what?"

She smiled. "Exactly."

Myron rubbed the temples again. "So the patrons don't have a problem with"—he searched for the right word, but there wasn't one—"so a gay guy, for example, doesn't get pissed off when he finds out he brought home a woman?"

"It's why you go. The thrill. The uncertainty. The mystery."

"Sort of the sexual equivalent of a grab bag."

"Right."

"Except in this case, you can really be surprised by what you grab."

Big Cyndi considered that. "If you really think about it, Mr. Bolitar, there can be only one of two things."

He was no longer so sure.

"But I like your grab bag analogy," Big Cyndi continued. "You know what you're bringing to the party, but you have no idea what you're going to take home. One time a guy left with what he thought was an overweight woman. It turned out that it was a guy with a midget hiding under the dress."

"Please tell me you're joking."

Big Cyndi just looked at him.

"So," Myron continued, "you, uh, frequent this place?"

"I've been a couple of times. But not recently."

"Why not?"

"Two reasons. First, they compete with Leather-N-Lust. It's a different crowd, but we still draw from similar markets."

Myron nodded. "The pervert pool."

"They're not hurting anybody."

"At least nobody who doesn't want to be hurt."

She pouted, not a great look on a three-hundred-pound wrestler, especially without her mortarlike makeup. "Esperanza is right."

"About?"

"You can be very closed-minded."

"Yeah, I'm a regular Jerry Falwell. So what's the second reason?"

She hesitated. "I'm obviously for sexual freedom. I don't care what you're doing as long as it's consensual. And I've done some wild things myself, Mr. Bolitar." She looked straight at him. "*Very* wild."

Myron cringed, fearing she might share details.

"But Take A Guess started drawing the wrong kind of crowd," she said.

"Gee, that's surprising," Myron said. "You'd think a place like that would be a natural for vacationing families."

She shook her head. "You are so repressed, Mr. Bolitar."

"Because I like to know my partner's gender before getting naked?"

"Because of your attitude. People like you cause sexual hang-ups. Society becomes sexually repressed—so repressed, in fact, that they cross the line between sex and violence, between playacting and real danger. They reach a stage where they get off by hurting people who do not want to be hurt.''

''And Take A Guess attracts that kind of crowd?''

''More than most.''

Myron sat back and rubbed his face with both hands. He started hearing brain clicks. ''This might explain a few things,'' he said.

''Like what?''

''Why Bonnie finally threw Clu out for good. It's one thing to have a string of girlfriends. But if Clu was frequenting a place like this, if he started leaning toward''—again, what would be the word?—''toward whatever. And if Bonnie found out, well, it would explain the legal separation.'' He nodded to himself as he heard more internal clicks. ''And it would explain her odd behavior today.''

''How so?''

''She made a point of asking me not to dig too deeply. She just wanted me to clear Esperanza and then drop the investigation.''

Big Cyndi nodded. ''She was afraid this would get out.''

''Right. If something like this went public, what would it do to her kids?''

Another thought floating through Myron's brain got snagged on some jagged rock. He looked at Big Cyndi. ''I assume that Take A Guess appeals mostly to bisexuals. I mean, if you're not sure what you're getting, who better than someone who wouldn't care?''

''More like ambisexuals,'' Big Cyndi said. ''Or people who want some mystery. Who want something new.''

''But bisexuals too.''

''Yes, of course.''

''How about Esperanza?''

Big Cyndi bristled. "What about her?"

"Did she frequent this place?"

"I wouldn't know, Mr. Bolitar. And I don't see the relevance."

"I'm not asking because it gives me jollies. You want me to help her, right? That means digging where we don't want to dig."

"I understand that, Mr. Bolitar. But you know her better than I do."

"Not this side of her," Myron said.

"Esperanza is a private person. I really don't know. She usually has a steady, but I don't know if she's gone there or not."

Myron nodded. Didn't matter much. If Clu had been hanging out in such a place, it would give Hester Crimstein more reasonable doubt. A rough trade place complete with a reputation for violence—it was a natural recipe for disaster. Clu could have brought home the wrong package. Or been the wrong package. And there was the cash to consider. Blackmail money? Did a customer recognize him? Threaten him? Videotape him?

Yep, lots of murky reasonable doubt.

And a good place to search for the elusive girlfriend. Or boyfriend. Or in-between friend. He shook his head. It was not a question of the ethics or moral dilemma for Myron; deviancy simply confused him. Repugnancy aside, he didn't get it. Lack of imagination, he supposed.

"I'll have to pay the Take A Guess a visit," he said.

"Not alone," Big Cyndi said. "I'll go with you."

Subtle surveillance was out. "Fine."

"And not now. Take A Guess doesn't open until eleven."

"Okay. We'll go tonight then."

"I have just the outfit," she said. "What are you going to go as?"

"A repressed heterosexual man," he said. "All I'll have to do is slip on my Rockports." He looked at the phone record again. "You have another number highlighted in blue."

She nodded. "You mentioned an old friend named Billy Lee Palms."

"This his number?"

"No. Mr. Palms doesn't exist anywhere. No phone listing. And he hasn't paid taxes in four years."

"So whose number is this?"

"Mr. Palms's parents. Mr. Haid called them twice in the past month."

Myron checked the address. Westchester. He vaguely remembered meeting Billy Lee's parents during a Family Day at Duke. He looked at his watch. It would take an hour to get there. He grabbed his coat and headed for the elevator.

CHAPTER 13

Myron's car, the business's Ford Taurus, had been confiscated by the police, so he rented a maroon Mercury Cougar. He hoped the women would be able to resist. When he started the car, the radio was tuned to Lite FM 106.7. Patti LaBelle and Michael McDonald were crooning a sad lite staple entitled "On My Own." This once blissfully happy couple were breaking up. Tragic. So tragic that, as Michael McDonald put it, "Now we're up to talking divorce . . . and we weren't even married."

Myron shook his head. For this Michael McDonald left the Doobie Brothers?

In college Billy Lee Palms had been the quintessential party boy. He had sneaky good looks, jet black hair, and a magnetic, albeit oily, combination of charisma and machismo, the kind of thing that played well with young coeds away from home for the first time. At Duke the frat brothers had dubbed him Otter, the pseudosuave character in the movie *Animal House*. It fitted. Billy Lee was also a great baseball player, a catcher who managed to reach the major leagues for a half season, riding the bench for the Baltimore Orioles the year they won the World Series.

But that was years ago.

Myron knocked on the door. Seconds later the door swung open fast and wide. No warning, nothing. Strange. In this day and age people looked through peepholes or cracks in chain-held doors or at the very least asked who it was.

A woman he vaguely recognized as Mrs. Palms said, "Yes?" She was small with a squirrel mouth and eyes that bulged like something behind them was pushing to get out. Her hair was tied back, but several strands escaped and drooped in front of her face. She pushed them back with splayed fingers.

"Are you Mrs. Palms?" he asked.

"Yes."

"My name is Myron Bolitar. I went to Duke with Billy Lee."

Her voice dropped an octave or two. "Do you know where he is?"

"No, ma'am. Is he missing?"

She frowned and stepped back. "Come in, please."

Myron moved into the foyer. Mrs. Palms was already heading down a corridor. She pointed to her right without turning around or breaking stride. "Just go into Sarah's wedding room. I'll be there in a second."

"Yes, ma'am."

Sarah's wedding room?

He followed where she had pointed. When he turned the corner, he heard himself give a little gasp. Sarah's wedding room. The decor was run-of-the-mill living room, something out of a furniture store circular. An off-white couch and matching love seat formed a broken L, probably the monthly special, $695 for both, the couch might fold out into a Serta sleeper, something like that. The coffee table was a semi oak square, a short stack of attractive, unread magazines on one end, silk flowers in the middle, a couple of coffee books on the other end. The wall-to-wall carpeting was light beige, and there were two torchère lamps à la the Pottery Barn.

But the walls were anything but ordinary.

Myron had seen plenty of houses with photographs on the walls. They were hardly uncommon. He had even been in a house or two where the photographs dominated rather than complemented the surroundings. That too would hardly give him reason to pause. But this was beyond surreal. Sarah's Wedding Room—heck, it should be capitalized—was a re-creation of that event. Literally. Color wedding photographs had been blown up to life size and pasted on as a wallpaper substitute. The bride and groom smiled at him invitingly from the right. On the left, Billy Lee in a tux, probably the best man or maybe just an usher, smiled at him. Mrs. Palms, dressed in a summer gown, danced with her husband. In front of him were the wedding tables, lots of them. Guests looked up and smiled at him—all life size. It was as though a panoramic wedding photo had been blown up to the size of Rembrandt's *Night Watch*. People slow-danced. A band played. There was a minister of sorts and floral arrangements and a wedding cake and fine china and white linen—again, all life size.

"Please sit down."

Myron turned to Mrs. Palms. Was it the real Mrs. Palms or one of the reproductions? No, she was casually dressed. The real McCoy. He almost reached out and touched her to make sure. "Thank you," he said.

"This is our daughter Sarah's wedding. She was married four years ago."

"I see."

"It was a very special day for us."

"I'm sure."

"We had it at the Manor in West Orange. You know it?"

"I was bar mitzvahed there," Myron said.

"Really? Your parents must have very fond memories of the day."

"Yes." But now he wondered. I mean, Mom and Dad kept most of the photos in an album.

Mrs. Palms smiled at him. "It's odd, I know, but . . . oh, I've explained this a thousand times. What's one more?" She sighed, signaled to a couch. Myron sat. She did likewise.

Mrs. Palms folded her hands and looked at him with the blank stare of a woman who sat too close to life's big screen. "People take pictures of their most special times," she began too earnestly. "They want to capture the important moments. They want to enjoy them and savor them and relive them. But that's not what they do. They take the picture, they look at it once, and then they stick it in a box and forget about it. Not me. I remember the good times. I wallow in them—re-create them, if I can. After all, we live for those moments, don't we, Myron?"

He nodded.

"So when I sit in this room, it warms me. I'm surrounded by one of the happiest moments in my life. I've created the most positive aura imaginable."

He nodded again.

"I'm not a big art fan," she continued. "I don't relish the idea of hanging impersonal lithographs on the walls. What's the point of looking at images of people and places I don't know? I don't care that much about interior design. And I don't like antiques or phony-baloney Martha Stewart stuff. But do you know what I do find beautiful?" She stopped and looked at him expectantly.

Myron picked up his cue. "What?"

"My family," she replied. "My family is beautiful to me. My family is art. Does that make sense to you, Myron?"

"Yes." Oddly enough, it did.

"So I call this Sarah's Wedding Room. I know that's silly. Naming rooms. Blowing up old photographs and using them as wallpaper. But all the rooms are like this. Billy Lee's bedroom upstairs I call the Catcher's Mitt. It's where he still stays when he's here. I think it comforts him." She raised her eyebrows. "Would you like to see it?"

"Sure."

She practically leaped off the couch. The stairwell was plastered with giant, seemingly old black and whites. A stern-faced couple in wedding gear. A soldier in full uniform. "This is the Generational Wall. That's my great-grandparents over there. And Hank's. My husband. He died three years ago."

"I'm sorry."

She shrugged. "This stairwell goes back three generations. I think it's a nice way of remembering our ancestors."

Myron didn't argue. He looked at the photograph of the young couple, just starting out their life together, probably a little scared. Now they were dead.

Deep Thoughts by Myron Bolitar.

"I know what you're thinking," she said. "But is it any stranger than hanging oils of dead relatives? Just more lifelike."

Hard to argue.

The walls in the upstairs corridor featured some sort of costume party from the seventies. Lots of leisure suits and bell-bottoms. Myron didn't ask, and Mrs. Palms didn't explain. Just as well. She turned left and Myron trailed her into the Catcher's Mitt. It lived up to its billing. Billy Lee's baseball life was laid out like a Hall of Fame display room. It started with Billy Lee in Little League, squatting in his catcher's stance, his smile huge and strangely confident for so young a child. The years flashed by. Little League to Babe Ruth League to high school to Duke, ending with his one glorious year with the Orioles, Billy Lee proudly showing off his World Series ring. Myron studied the Duke photographs. One had been taken out in front of Psi U, their frat house. A uniformed Billy Lee had his arm around Clu, plenty of frat brothers in the background, including, he saw now, him and Win. Myron remembered when the picture had been taken. The baseball team had just beaten Florida State to win the national championship. The party had lasted three days.

"Mrs. Palms, where is Billy Lee?"

"I don't know."

"When you say you don't know—"

"He ran off," she interrupted. "Again."

"He's done this before?"

She stared at the wall. Her eyes were glassy now. "Maybe Billy Lee doesn't find this room comforting," she said softly. "Maybe it reminds him of what could have been." She turned to him. "When was the last time you saw Billy Lee?"

Myron tried to remember. "It's been a long time."

"How come?"

"We were never that close."

She pointed to the wall. "That's you? In the background?"

"That's right."

"Billy Lee spoke about you."

"Really?"

"He said you were a sports agent. Clu's agent, if I'm not mistaken."

"Yes."

"You stayed friendly with Clu then?"

"Yes."

She nodded as though this explained everything. "Why are you looking for my son, Myron?"

He was not sure how to explain. "You've heard about Clu's death?"

"Yes, of course. That poor boy. A lost soul. Like Billy Lee in many ways. I think that's why they were drawn to each other."

"Have you seen Clu lately?"

"Why do you want to know?"

In for a penny and all that. "I'm trying to find out who killed him."

Her body stiffened as though his words held a small electric shock. "And you think Billy Lee had something to do with it?"

"No, of course not." But even as he said it, he began to wonder. Clu is murdered; maybe his killer runs away. More reasonable doubt. "It's just that I know how close they were. I thought maybe Billy Lee could help me out."

Mrs. Palms was staring at the image of the two ballplayers in front of Psi U. She reached out as though to stroke her son's face. But she pulled back. "Billy Lee was handsome, wasn't he?"

"Yes."

"The girls," she said. "They all loved my Billy Lee."

"I'd never seen anybody better with them," he said.

That made her smile. She kept staring at the image of her son. It was kinda creepy. Myron remembered the old episode of *The Twilight Zone* where the aging movie queen escapes reality by stepping into one of her old movies. It looked like Mrs. Palms craved doing likewise.

She finally tore her eyes away. "Clu came by a few weeks ago."

"Can you be more specific?"

"Funny."

"What?"

"That's just what the police asked."

"The police were here?"

"Sure."

They must have gone through the phone records too, Myron thought. Or found another link.

"I'll tell you the same thing I told them. I can't be more specific."

"Do you know what Clu wanted?"

"He came to see Billy Lee."

"Billy Lee was here?"

"Yes."

"He lives here then?"

"On and off. The past few years have not been very good to my son."

Silence.

"I don't mean to pry," Myron began, "but—"

"What happened to Billy Lee?" she finished. "Life caught up with him, Myron. The drinking, the drugs, the womanizing. He had stints in rehab. Are you familiar with Rockwell?"

"No, ma'am."

"It's a private clinic. He finished his fourth trip to Rockwell not two months ago. But he couldn't stay clean. When you're in college or even in your twenties, you can survive it. When you're a big star and people are looking out for you, you can get away with it. But Billy Lee wasn't good enough to reach that level. So he had no one to fall back upon. Except me. And I'm not that strong.''

Myron swallowed. ''Do you know why Clu came to see Billy Lee?''

''For old times' sake, I guess. They went out. Maybe they had a few beers and chased women. I really don't know.''

''Did Clu visit Billy Lee a lot?''

''Well, Clu's been out of town,'' she said, a little too defensively. ''He was only traded back to this area a few months ago. But of course, you know that.''

''So this was just a casual visit?''

''I thought so at the time.''

''And now?''

''Now my son is missing and Clu is dead.''

Myron thought about it. ''Where does he usually go when he runs off like this?''

''Wherever. Billy Lee is a bit of a nomad. He goes off, he does whatever horrible thing he does to himself, and when he hits rock bottom, he comes back here.''

''So you don't know where he is?''

''That's right.''

''Any idea at all?''

''No.''

''No favorite haunts?''

''No.''

''A girlfriend maybe?''

''No one I know about anyway.''

''Any close friends he might stay with?''

''No,'' she said slowly. ''He has no friends like that.''

Myron took out his card and handed it to her. ''If you hear from him, Mrs. Palms, could you please let me know?''

She studied the card as they moved out of the room and back down the stairs.

Before she opened the door, Mrs. Palms said, "You were the basketball player."

"Yes."

"The one who hurt his knee."

First preseason game as a pro. Myron had been the Boston Celtics' first-round draft pick. A terrible collision and his career was over. Just like that. Finished before it started. "Yes."

"You managed to put it behind you," she said. "You managed to get on with your life and be happy and productive." She cocked her head. "Why couldn't Billy Lee?"

Myron had no answer—in part because he was not sure her supposition was entirely accurate. He said his goodbyes and left her alone with her ghosts.

CHAPTER 14

Myron checked his watch. Dinnertime. Mom and Dad were expecting him. He'd hit the Garden State Parkway when the cell phone rang again.

"Are you in the car?" Win asked. Always with the pleasantries.

"Yes."

"Flip on 1010 WINS. I'll call back."

One of New York's all-news radio stations. Myron did as he was told. The guy in the helicopter was finishing up the traffic report. He handed it back to the woman at the news desk. She provided the teaser: "The latest bombshell in the murder of baseball superstar Clu Haid. In sixty seconds."

It was a long sixty seconds. Myron had to put up with a truly annoying Dunkin' Donuts commercial, and then some excited bozo had a way of turning five thousand dollars into twenty thousand dollars, though a softer, fast-speaking voice added that it didn't work all the time and in fact you could lose money too and probably would and you'd have to be a major moron to take investment advice from a radio ad. Finally the woman at the news desk came back on. She told the audience her name—like anyone cared—the name of her male counterpart, and the time. Then:

"ABC is reporting from an anonymous source in the Bergen County district attorney's office that hairs and quote other bodily materials unquote matching the murder suspect Esperanza Diaz have been found at the murder scene. According to the source, DNA tests are pending, but preliminary tests show a clear match with Ms. Diaz. The source also says that the hairs, some small, were found in various locations throughout the house."

Myron felt a flutter beneath his heart. Small hairs, he thought. Euphemism for pubic.

"No further details are available, but the district attorney's office clearly believes that Mr. Clu Haid and Ms. Esperanza Diaz were having a sexual relationship. Stay tuned to 1010 WINS for all the details."

The cell phone rang. Myron picked it up. "Jesus Christ."

"Not even close," Win said.

"I'll call you right back." Myron hung up. He called Hester Crimstein's office. The secretary said that Ms. Crimstein was unavailable. Myron stressed that this was urgent. Ms. Crimstein was still unavailable. But, Myron asked, doesn't Ms. Crimstein have a cell phone? The secretary disconnected the call. Myron hit the memory button. Win picked up.

"What's your take on this?" Myron asked.

"Esperanza was sleeping with him," Win said.

"Maybe not."

"Yes, of course," Win said. "Perhaps someone planted Esperanza's pubic hairs at the murder scene."

"It could be a false leak."

"Could be."

"Or maybe she visited his apartment. To talk business."

"And left stray pubic hairs behind?"

"Maybe she used the bathroom. Maybe she—"

"Myron?"

"What?"

"Please don't go into further detail, thank you. There is something else to consider."

"What?"

"The E-Z Pass records."

"Right," Myron said. "She crossed the Washington Bridge an hour after the murder. We know that. But maybe that fits now. Esperanza and Clu have a big argument at the parking garage. Esperanza wants to clear the air. So she drives out to his apartment."

"And when she gets there?"

"I don't know. Maybe she saw the body and panicked."

"Yes, of course," Win said. "So she ripped out a few pubic hairs and ran."

"I didn't say it was her first visit out there."

"Indeed not."

"What do you mean?"

"The E-Z Pass records for the Ford Taurus. According to the bill that arrived last week, the car crossed the bridge eighteen times in the past month."

Myron frowned. "You're kidding."

"Yes, I am a mirthful fellow. I also took the liberty of checking the month before. Sixteen crosses of the Washington Bridge."

"Maybe she had another reason for going out to North Jersey."

"Yes, of course. The malls in Paramus are quite an attraction."

"Okay," Myron said. "Let's assume they were having an affair."

"That would seem most prudent, especially since it offers a reasonable explanation for much that has happened."

"How's that?"

"It would explain Esperanza's silence."

"How?"

"Lovers always make wonderful suspects," Win said. "If, for example, Esperanza and Clu were dancing the sheet mambo, then we can assume that the altercation in the parking garage was something of a lovers' tiff. All in all, this development looks bad for her. She would want to hide it."

"But from us?" Myron countered.

"Yes."

"Why? She trusts us."

"Several reasons come to mind. Her attorney probably ordered her not to say anything."

"That wouldn't stop her."

"It might. But more important, Esperanza was probably embarrassed. You have recently promoted her to partner. She was in charge of the entire operation. I know that you believe Esperanza is too tough to care about such things, but I do not think she would relish your disapproval."

Myron mulled that one over. It made some sense, but he wasn't sure he bought it entirely. "I still think we're missing something."

"That's because we're ignoring the strongest motive for her keeping silent."

"That being?"

"She killed him."

Win hung up on that cheery note. Myron took Northfield Avenue toward Livingston. The familiar landmarks of his hometown popped into view. He thought about the news report and what Win had said. Could Esperanza be the mystery woman, the reason for Clu and Bonnie's breakup? If so, why wouldn't Bonnie say that? Maybe she didn't know. Or maybe—

Hold the phone.

Maybe Clu and Esperanza met up at Take A Guess. Did they go there together or just bump into each other? Is that how the affair started? Did they go there and participate in —in whatever? Maybe it was an accident. Maybe they both arrived there in disguise and didn't realize who they were until, well, it was too late to stop? Did that make sense?

He made the right at Nero's Restaurant and onto Hobart Gap Road. Not far now. He was in the land of his childhood—check that, his entire life. He had lived here with his parents until a year or so ago, when he finally severed the apron strings and moved in with Jessica. Psychologists and psychiatrists and the like, he knew, would have a field day with the fact that he had lived with his parents into his thirties, theorizing all kinds of unnatural preoccupations that kept him so close to Mom and Dad. Maybe they'd be right. But for Myron, the answer had been far simpler. He liked them. Yes, they could be pests—what parents weren't?—and they liked to pry. But most of the pestering and prying were over the incidentals. They had given him privacy yet made him feel cared for and wanted. Was that unhealthy? Maybe. But it seemed a damn sight better than his friends who thrived on blaming their parents for any unhappiness in their lives.

He turned onto his street. The old neighborhood was wholly unspectacular. There were thousands like it in New Jersey, hundreds of thousands throughout the US of A.

This was suburbia, the backbone of this country, the battleground of the fabled American Dream. Corny to say, but Myron loved it here. Sure, there was unhappiness and dissatisfaction and fights and all that, but he still thought that this was the "realest" place he had ever been. He loved the basketball court in the driveway and the training wheels on the new two-wheelers and the routine and the walking to school and the caring too much about the color of the grass. This was living. This was what it was all about.

In the end Myron guessed that he and Jessica had broken up for all the classic reasons, albeit with a gender twist. He wanted to settle down, buy a house in the 'burbs, raise a family; Jessica, fearing commitment, did not. He pulled into the driveway now, shaking his head. Too simple an explanation. Too pat. The commitment stuff had been an ongoing source of tension, no question, but there was more to it. There was the recent tragedy, for one thing.

There was Brenda.

Mom rushed out the door, sprinting toward him with her arms spread wide. She always greeted him like he was a recently released POW, but today was something extra special. She threw her arms around him, nearly knocking him over. Dad trailed behind, equally excited but playing it cool. Dad had always been about balance, the total love without the smothering, the caring without pushing. An amazing man, his father. When Dad reached him, there was no handshake. The two men hugged fiercely and without any hint of embarrassment. Myron kissed his father's cheek. The familiar feel of Dad's rough skin made him understand a bit what Mrs. Palms was trying to accomplish with the wallpapered images.

"Are you hungry?" Mom asked. Always her opening gambit.

"A little."

"You want me to fix something?"

Everyone froze. Dad made a face. "You're going to cook?"

"What's the big deal?"

"Let me make sure I have the number of poison control."

"Oh, Al, that's so funny. Ha-ha, I can't stop laughing. What a funny man your father is, Myron."

"Actually, Ellen, go ahead and cook something. I need to drop a few pounds."

"Wow, what a knee slapper, Al. You're killing me here."

"Better than a fat farm."

"Ho-ho."

"Just the thought is better than an appetite suppressor."

"It's like being married to Shecky Greene." But she was smiling.

They were in the house now. Dad took Mom's hand. "Let me show you something, Ellen," Dad said. "See that big metal box over there? That's called an oven. O-v-e-n. Oven. See that knob, the one with all the numbers on it? That's how you turn it on."

"You're funnier than a sober Foster Brooks, Al."

But they were all smiling now. Dad was speaking the truth. Mom didn't cook. Almost never did. Her culinary skills could cause a prison riot. When he was a kid, Myron's favorite home-cooked dinner was Dad's scrambled eggs. Mom was an early career woman. The kitchen was a place to read magazines.

"What do you want to eat, Myron?" Mom asked. "Chinese maybe. From Fong's?"

"Sure."

"Al, call Fong's. Order something."

"Okay."

"Make sure you get shrimp with lobster sauce."

"I know."

"Myron loves Fong's shrimp with lobster sauce."

"I know, Ellen. I raised him too, remember?"

"You might forget."

"We've been ordering from Fong's for twenty-three years. We always order shrimp with lobster sauce."

"You might forget, Al. You're getting old. Didn't you forget to pick up my blouse at the laundry two days ago."

"It was closed."

"So you never picked up my blouse, am I right?"

"Of course not."

"I rest my case." She looked at her son. "Myron, sit. We need to talk. Al, call Fong's."

The men obeyed her orders. As always. Myron and Mom sat at the kitchen table.

"Listen to me closely," Mom said. "I know Esperanza is your friend. But Hester Crimstein is a fine lawyer. If she told Esperanza not to talk to you, it's the right thing."

"How do you know—"

"I've known Hester for years." Mom was a defense attorney, one of the best in the state. "We've worked cases together before. She called me. She said you're interfering."

"I'm not interfering."

"Actually she said you're bothering her and to butt out."

"She talked to you about this?"

"Of course. She wants you to leave her client alone."

"I can't."

"Why can't you?"

Myron squirmed a bit. "I have some information that might be important."

"Such as?"

"According to Clu's wife, he was having an affair."

"And you think Hester doesn't know that? The DA thinks he was having an affair with Esperanza."

"Wait a second." It was Dad. "I thought Esperanza was a lesbian."

"She's a bisexual, Al."

"A what?"

"Bisexual. It means she likes both boys and girls."

Dad thought about that. "I guess that's a good thing to be."

"What?"

"I mean, it gives you the double the options of everyone else."

"Great, Al, thanks for the insight." She rolled her eyes and turned back to Myron. "So Hester already knows that. What else?"

"Clu was desperate to find me before he was killed," Myron said.

"Most logically, *bubbe,* to say something incriminating about Esperanza."

"Not necessarily. Clu came to the loft. He told Jessica that I was in danger."

"And you think he meant it?"

"No, he was probably exaggerating. But shouldn't Hester Crimstein judge the significance?"

"She already has."

"What?"

"Clu came here too, darling." Her voice was suddenly

soft. "He told your father and me the same thing he told Jessica."

Myron didn't push it. If Clu had told his parents the same thing he told Jessica, if he had used all that death talk when Mom and Dad didn't know where Myron was . . .

As though reading his mind, Dad said, "I called Win. He said you were safe."

"Did he tell you where I was?"

Mom took that one. "We didn't ask."

Silence.

She reached over and put a hand on his arm. "You've been through a lot, Myron. Your father and I know that."

They both looked at him with the deep-caring eyes. They knew part of what happened. About his breakup with Jessica. About Brenda. But they would never know it all.

"Hester Crimstein knows what's she doing," Mom went on. "You have to let her do her job."

More silence.

"Al?"

"What?"

"Hang up the phone," she said. "Maybe we should go out to eat."

Myron checked his watch. "It'll have to be quick. I have to get back to the city."

"Oh?" Mom raised an eyebrow. "You have a date already?"

He thought about Big Cyndi's description of Take A Guess.

"Not likely," he said. "But you never know."

CHAPTER 15

From the outside Take A Guess looked pretty much like your standard Manhattan cantina-as-pickup-joint. The building was brick, the windows darkened to highlight the neon beer signs. Above the door, faded lettering spelled out *Take A Guess*. That was it. No "Bring Your Perversions." No "The Kinkier the Better." No "You Better Like Surprises." Nothing. A suit trudging home might happen by here, stop in, lay down his briefcase, spot something attractive, buy it a drink, make a few quasi-smooth moves warmed over from college mixers, take it home. Surprise, surprise.

Big Cyndi met him at the front door dressed like Earth, Wind, and Fire—not so much any one member as the entire group. "Ready?"

Myron hesitated, nodded.

When Big Cyndi pushed open the door, Myron held his breath and ducked in behind her. The interior too was not what he'd visualized. He had expected something . . . blatantly wacko, he guessed. Like the bar scene in *Star Wars* maybe. Instead Take A Guess just had the same neodesperate feel and stench of a zillion other singles' joints on a Friday night. A few patrons were colorfully dressed, but most wore khakis and business suits. There were also a handful of outrageously clad cross-dressers and leather devotees and one babe-a-rama packed into a vinyl catsuit, but nowadays you'd be hard pressed to find a Manhattan nightspot that didn't have any of that. Sure, some folks were in disguise, but when it came right down to it, who didn't wear a facade at a singles' bar?

Whoa, that was deep.

Heads and eyes swerved in their direction. For a moment Myron wondered why. But only for a moment. He was, after all, standing next to Big Cyndi, a six-six three-hundred-pound multihued mass blanketed with more sparkles than a Siegfried and Roy costume party. She drew the eye.

Big Cyndi seemed flattered by the attention. She lowered her eyes, playing demure, which was like Ed Asner playing coquettish. "I know the head bartender," she said. "His name is Pat."

"Male or female?"

She smiled, punched him on the arm. "Now you're getting the hang of it."

A jukebox played the Police's "Every Little Thing She Does Is Magic." Myron tried to count how many times Sting repeated the words *every little*. He lost count at a million.

They found two stools at the bar. Big Cyndi looked for Pat. Myron cased the joint, very detectivelike. He turned his back to the bar, eased his elbows against it, bobbed his head slightly to the music. Señor Slick. The babe-a-rama in the black catsuit caught his eye. She slithered to the seat next to him and curled into it. Myron flashed back to Julie Newmar as Cat Woman circa 1967, something he did far too often. This woman was dirty blond but otherwise frighteningly comparable.

Catsuit gave him a look that made him believe in telekinesis. "Hi," she said.

"Hi back." The Lady Slayer awakens.

She slowly reached for her neck and started toying with the catsuit's zipper. Myron managed to keep his tongue in the general vicinity of his mouth. He took a quick peek at Big Cyndi.

"Don't be too sure," Big Cyndi warned.

Myron frowned. There was cleavage here, for crying out loud. He stole another look—for the sake of science. Yep, cleavage. And plenty of it. He looked back at Big Cyndi and whispered, "Bosoms. Two of them."

Big Cyndi shrugged.

"My name is Thrill," Catsuit said.

"I'm Myron."

"Myron," she repeated, her tongue circling as though testing the word for taste. "I like that name. It's very manly."

"Er, thanks, I guess."

"You don't like your name?"

"Actually, I've always sort of hated it," he said. Then he gave her the big-guy look, cocking the eyebrow like Fabio going for deep thought. "But if you like it, maybe I'll reconsider."

Big Cyndi made a noise like a moose coughing up a turtle shell.

Thrill gave him another smoldering glance and picked up her drink. She did something that could roughly be called "taking a sip," but Myron doubted the Motion Picture Association would give it less than an R rating. "Tell me about yourself, Myron."

They started chatting. Pat, the bartender, was on break,

so Myron and Thrill kept at it for a good fifteen minutes. He didn't want to admit it, but he was sort of having fun. Thrill turned toward him, full body. She slid a little closer. Myron again looked for telltale gender signs. He checked for the two Five O'clocks: Shadow and Charlie. Nothing. He checked the cleavage again. Still there. Damn if he wasn't a trained detective.

Thrill put her hand on his thigh. It felt hot through his jeans. Myron stared at the hand for a moment. Was the size odd? He tried to figure out if it was big for a woman or maybe small for a man. His head started spinning.

"I don't mean to be rude," Myron finally said, "but you're a woman, right?"

Thrill threw her head back and laughed. Myron looked for an Adam's apple. She had a black ribbon tied around the neck. Made it hard to tell. The laugh was a touch hoarse, but oh, come on now. This couldn't be a guy. Not with that cleavage. Not when the catsuit was so tight about the, er, nether region, if you catch the drift.

"What's the difference?" Thrill asked.

"Pardon?"

"You find me attractive, don't you?"

"What I see."

"So?"

Myron raised his hands. "So—and let me just state this plainly—if, during a moment of passion, there is a second penis in the room . . . well, it definitely kills the mood for me."

She laughed. "No other penises, eh?"

"That's right. Just mine. I'm funny that way."

"Are you familiar with Woody Allen?" she asked.

"Of course."

"Then let me quote him." Myron stayed still. Thrill was about to quote the Woodman. If she was a she, Myron was close to proposing. " 'Sex is a beautiful thing between two people. Between five it's fantastic.' "

"Nice quote," Myron said.

"Do you know what it's from?"

"His old nightclub act. When Woody did stand-up comedy in the sixties."

Thrill nodded, pleased that the pupil had passed the test.

"But we're not talking group sex here," Myron said.

"Have you ever had group sex?" she asked.

"Well, uh, no."

"But if you did—if there were, say, five people—would it be a problem if one of them had a penis?"

"We're talking hypothetically here, right?"

"Unless you want me to call some friends."

"No, that's okay, really, thanks." Myron took a deep breath. "Yeah, okay, hypothetically, I guess it wouldn't be a huge problem, as long as the man kept his distance."

Thrill nodded. "But if I had a penis—"

"A major mood killer."

"I see." Thrill made small circles on Myron's thigh. "Admit you're curious."

"I am."

"So?"

"So I'm also curious about what goes through a person's mind when he jumps out of a skyscraper. Before he goes splat on the sidewalk."

She arched an eyebrow. "It's probably a hell of a rush."

"Yeah, but then there's that splat at the end."

"And in this case . . ."

"The splat would be a penis, yes."

"Interesting," Thrill said. "Suppose I'm a transsexual."

"Pardon?"

"Suppose I *had* a penis, but now it's gone. You'd be safe, right?"

"Wrong."

"Why?"

"Phantom penis," Myron said.

"Pardon?"

"Like in a war when a guy loses his limb and still thinks it's there. Phantom penis."

"But it's not your penis that would be missing."

"Still. Phantom penis."

"But that doesn't make any sense."

"Exactly."

Thrill showed him nice, even white teeth. Myron looked at them. Can't tell much about gender from teeth. Better to check the cleavage again. "You realize that you're massively insecure about your sexuality," she said.

"Because I like to know if a potential partner has a penis?"

"A real man wouldn't worry about being thought of as a fag."

"It's not what people think that bothers me."

"It's just the penis issue," she finished for him.

"Bingo."

"I still say you're sexually insecure."

Myron shrugged, palms raised. "Who isn't?"

"True." She shifted her rear. Vinyl on vinyl. Grrrr sound. "So why don't you ask me out on a date?"

"I think we just went over this."

"You find me attractive, right? What you see, I mean."

"Yes."

"And we're having a nice talk?"

"Yes."

"You find me interesting? Fun to be with?"

"Yes and yes."

"And you're single and unattached?"

He swallowed. "Two more yesses."

"So?"

"So—and again, don't take this personally—"

"But it's that penis thing again."

"Bingo."

Thrill leaned back, fiddled with the neckline zipper, pulled it up a bit. "Hey, it's a first date. We don't have to end up naked."

Myron thought about that. "Oh."

"You sound surprised."

"No . . . I mean—"

"Maybe I'm not that easy."

"My mistake for presuming . . . I mean, you're hanging out in this bar."

"So?"

"So I didn't think most of the patrons in here played hard to get. To quote Woody Allen, 'How did I misread those signs?' "

Thrill didn't hesitate. *"Play It Again, Sam."*

"If you are a woman," Myron said, "I may be falling in love."

"Thank you. And if we're reading signs from being in this bar, what are you doing here? You with your penis issue."

"Good point."

"So?"

"So what?"

"So why don't you ask me out?" Again with the smolder. "We could hold hands. Maybe kiss. You might even sneak a hand under my shirt, go for a little second base. The way you've been ogling, it's almost like you're there anyway."

"I'm not ogling," Myron said.

"No?"

"If I've been looking—and note I said *if*—it would be purely for the sake of gender clarification, I assure you."

"Thanks for straightening that out. But my point is, we can just go and have dinner. Or go to a movie. We don't have to have any genital contact."

Myron shook his head. "I'd still be wondering."

"Ah, but don't you like a little mystery?"

"I like mystery in lots of arenas. But when it comes to trouser content, well, I'm a pretty traditional guy."

Thrill shrugged. "I still don't understand why you're here."

"I'm looking for someone." He took out a photograph of Clu Haid and showed it to her. "Do you know him?"

Thrill looked at the photograph and frowned. "I thought you said you're a sports agent."

"I am. He was a client."

"Was?"

"He was murdered."

"He's the baseball player?"

Myron nodded. "Have you seen him here?"

Thrill grabbed a piece of paper and wrote something down. "Here's my phone number, Myron. Call me sometime."

"What about the guy in the photograph?"

Thrill handed him the scrap of paper, jumped off the stool, and undulated away. Myron watched her movements closely, looking for, umm, a concealed weapon. Big Cyndi elbowed him. He almost fell off the stool.

"This is Pat," Big Cyndi said.

Pat the bartender looked like someone Archie Bunker might have hired to work his place. He was mid-fifties, short, gray-haired, slouch-shouldered, world-weary. Even his mustache—one of those gray-turning-to-yellow models—drooped as though it'd seen it all. Pat's sleeves were rolled up, revealing Popeye-size forearms covered with hair. Myron hoped like hell Pat was a guy. This place was giving him a headache.

Behind Pat was a giant mirror. Next to that, a wall with the words *Customer Hall of Fame* painted in pink. The wall was covered with framed head shots of big-time right-wingers. Pat Buchanan. Jerry Falwell. Pat Robertson. Newt Gingrich. Jesse Helms.

Pat saw him looking at the photographs. "Ever notice that."

"Notice what?"

"How all the big antifags have sexually ambiguous first names? Pat, Chris, Jesse, Jerry. Could be a guy, could be a girl. See what I'm saying?"

Myron said, "Uh-huh."

"And what kind of name is Newt?" Pat added. "I mean, how the hell do you grow up with a healthy sexual attitude with a name like Newt?"

"I don't know."

"My theory?" Pat shrugged, wiped the bar with a dishrag. "These narrow assholes were all teased a lot as children. Makes them hostile on the whole gender issue."

"Interesting theory," Myron said. "But isn't your name Pat?"

"Yeah, well, I hate fags too," Pat said. "But they tip well."

Pat winked at Big Cyndi. Big Cyndi winked back. The jukebox changed songs. Lou Rawls crooned "Love Is in the Air." Timing.

The right-wing head shots were all "autographed." Jesse Helms's read: "I'm sore all over, Love and kisses, Jesse." Blunt. Several Xs and Os followed. There was also a big lipstick kiss impression as though Jesse himself had puckered up and laid down a wet one. Eeeuw.

Pat started cleaning out a beer mug with the dishrag. Casually. Myron half expected him to spit in it like in an old western. "So what can I get you?"

"Are you a sports fan?" Myron asked.

"You taking a poll?"

That line. It was always such a riot. Myron tried again. "Does the name Clu Haid mean anything to you?"

Myron watched for a reaction but didn't get one. Meant nothing. The guy looked like a lifetime bartender. They show about as much range as a *Baywatch* regular. Hmm. Now why was that show on his mind?

"I asked you—"

"Name means nothing to me."

Big Cyndi said, "Please, Pat."

He shot her a look. "You heard me, Big C. I don't know him."

Myron pressed it. "Never heard of Clu Haid?"

"That's right."

"How about the New York Yankees?"

"I haven't followed them since the Mick retired."

Myron put the photograph of Clu Haid on the bar. "Ever seen him in here?"

Someone called out for a draft. Pat drew it. When he came back, he spoke to Big Cyndi. "This guy a cop?"

"No," Big Cyndi said.

"Then the answer is no."

"And if I was a cop?" Myron asked.

"Then the answer would be no . . . sir." Myron noticed that Pat had never so much as glanced at the photograph. "I might also add a little song and dance about how I'm too busy to notice faces in here. And how most people, especially celebrities, don't show their real faces in here anyway."

"I see," Myron said. He reached into his wallet, took out a fifty. "And if I showed you a photograph of Ulysses S. Grant?"

The jukebox changed songs. The Flying Machine started crooning for Rosemarie to "smile a little smile for me, Rosemarie." The Flying Machine. Myron had remembered the group's name. What did that say about a man?

"Keep your money," Pat said. "Keep your picture. Keep your questions. I don't like trouble."

"And this guy means trouble?"

"I haven't even looked at the picture, pal. And I don't plan to. Take a hike."

Big Cyndi stepped in. "Pat," she said, "please can't you help"—she batted her eyelashes; picture two crabs on their backs in the blazing sun—"for me?"

"Hey, Big C, I love you, you know that. But suppose I came into Leather-N-Lust with pictures? You gonna be anxious to help?"

Big Cyndi thought about that. "I guess not."

"There you go. I got customers."

"Fine," Myron said. He picked up the photograph. "Then maybe I'll stick around. Pass the picture around the room. Ask some questions. Maybe I'll stake this place out. Indiscreetly. Take photos of people entering and leaving this fine establishment."

Pat shook his head, smiled a bit. "You're one dumb son of a bitch, you know that."

"I'll do it," Myron said. "I don't want to, but I'll camp out on your doorstep with a camera."

Pat gave Myron a long look. Hard to read. Part hostile

maybe. Mostly bored. "Big C, head out of here for a few minutes."

"No."

"Then I don't talk."

Myron turned to her, nodded. Big Cyndi shook her head. Myron pulled her aside. "What's the problem?"

"You shouldn't make threats in here, Mr. Bolitar."

"I know what I'm doing."

"I warned you about this place. I can't leave you alone."

"You'll be right outside. I can take care of myself."

When Big Cyndi frowned, her face resembled a freshly painted totem pole. "I don't like it."

"We have no choice."

She sighed. Picture Mount Vesuvius bubbling up a bit of lava. "Be careful."

"I will."

She lumbered toward the exit. The place was packed and Big Cyndi took up a wide berth. Still, people parted with a speed that would have made Moses jot notes. When she was all the way out the door, Myron turned back to Pat. "Well?"

"Well, you're a dumb asshole."

It happened without warning. Two hands snaked under Myron's arms, the fingers locking behind his neck. A classic full nelson. The hold was tightened, pushing back his arms like chicken wings. Myron felt something hot rip across his shoulder blades.

A voice near his ear whispered, "Care to dance, dreamboat?"

When it came to hand-to-hand combat, Myron was no Win, but he was no slouch either. He thus knew that if the perpetrator was good, there was no way to break a full nelson. That was why they were illegal in real wrestling matches. If you were standing, you could try to stomp on the person's instep. But only a moron fell for that, and a moron would not have had the speed or the strength to get this far. And Myron was not standing.

Myron's elbows were high up in the air, marionette fashion, his face helplessly exposed. The powerful arms locking him were covered in cardigan. Soft yellow cardigan, as a matter of fact. As in a soft yellow cardigan sweater. Jesus. Myron struggled. Nothing doing. The cardigan-clad arms pulled Myron's head back and then snapped it toward the bar, face first. Myron could do nothing but close his eyes. He tucked his chin just enough to keep his nose from taking the brunt of the blow. But his head bounced off the varnished teak in a way it was never intended to, jarring his skull. Something on his forehead split open. His head swam. He saw stars.

Another set of hands scooped up Myron's feet. He was in the air now and moving and very dizzy. Hands emptied his pockets. A door opened. Myron was carried through it into a dark room. The grip was released, and Myron fell like a potato sack onto his tailbone. The whole process, from the onset of the full nelson to the moment he was dumped on the floor, took all of eight seconds.

A light was snapped on. Myron touched his forehead and felt something sticky. Blood. He looked up at his attackers.

Two women.

No, cross-dressers. Both with blond wigs. One had gone with early-eighties Mall Girl hair—lots of height and teased more than a bed-wetter. The other one—the one with the soft yellow cardigan sweater (monogrammed, for those who cared)—had hair like Veronica Lake on a particularly nasty bender.

Myron started to get to his feet. Veronica Lake let out a

squeal and threw a side kick. The kick was fast and landed hard on his chest. Myron heard himself make a noise like "pluuu" and landed back on his rear. His hand automatically reached for his cellular. He'd hit the memory button and call Win. Then stall.

The phone was gone.

He looked up. Mall Girl had it. Damn. He took in his surroundings. There was a great view of the bar and Pat the bartender's back. He remembered the mirror. Of course. One-way glass. The patrons saw a mirror. The people back here saw, well, everything. Hard to steal from the till when you never knew who was watching.

The walls were corked and thus soundproof. The floor was cheap linoleum. Easier to clean, he guessed. Despite that, there were specks of blood on it. Not his. These specks were old and dried. But they were there. No mistaking them for something else. And Myron knew why. In a word: intimidation.

This was a classic pounding room. Lots of places have them. Especially sports arenas. Not so much now as in the old days. There was a time when an unruly·fan was more than just escorted out of the stadium. The security guards took him into a back room and pounded on him a bit. It was fairly safe. What could the unruly fan claim after the fact? He was drunk off his rocker, had probably gotten into a fight in the stands, whatever. So the security boys added a few extra bruises for good measure. Who's to say where the bruises came from? And if the unruly fan threatened to press charges or make noise, stadium officials could whack him back with charges of public drunkenness and assault and whatever else they could dream up. They could also produce a dozen security guards to back their story and none to back the unruly fan's.

So the fan let it drop. And the pounding rooms remained. Probably still do in some places.

Veronica Lake giggled. It was not a pretty sound. "Care to dance, dreamboat?" he-she asked again.

"Let's wait for a slow song," Myron said.

A third cross-dresser stepped into the room. A redhead. He-she looked a lot like Bonnie Franklin, the plucky mother on the old sitcom *One Day at a Time*. The resemblance was, in fact, rather uncanny—the perfect mix of determination and cutes. Spunky. Scrappy.

"Where's Schneider?" Myron asked.

No reply.

Veronica Lake said, "Stand up, dreamboat."

"The blood on the floor," Myron said.

"What?"

"It's a nice touch, but it's overkill, don't you think?"

Veronica Lake lifted her right foot and pulled on her heel. It came off. Sort of. The heel was a covering actually. A sheath. For a steel blade. Veronica showed it to Myron with an impressive display of martial art high kicks, the blade gleaming in the light.

Bonnie Franklin and Mall Girl started giggling.

Myron kept the fear at bay and looked steadily at Veronica Lake. "Are you new at cross-dressing?" he asked.

Veronica stopped kicking. "What?"

"I mean, aren't you taking the whole *stiletto* heel thing too far?"

Not his best joke, but anything to stall. Veronica looked at Mall Girl. Mall Girl looked at Bonnie Franklin. Then Veronica suddenly threw a sweep kick, leading with the blade heel. Myron saw the glint of steel shoot toward him. He rolled back, but the blade still sliced through his shirt and into his skin. He let out a little cry and looked down wide-eyed. The cut wasn't deep, but he was bleeding.

The three spread out, making fists. Bonnie Franklin had something in her hand. A black club maybe. Myron did not like this. He tried to spring to his feet, but again Veronica threw a kick. He leaped high, but the blade still hit his lower leg. He actually felt the blade get caught on the shin bone before scraping itself off.

Myron's heart was pounding now. More blood. Jesus Christ. Something about seeing your own blood. His breathing was too fast. *Keep cool,* he reminded himself. *Think.*

He faked left to the spot where Bonnie Franklin stood with the baton. Then he coiled right, his fist at the ready. Without hesitating, he threw a punch at the advancing Mall Girl. His knuckles landed flush below the eye and Mall Girl went down.

That was when Myron felt his heart stop.

There was a zapping sound and the back of his knee exploded. Myron spun in pure agony. His body jolted. Searing pain burst out of the nerve bundle behind the knee and traveled everywhere in an electric surge. He looked behind him. Bonnie Franklin had merely touched him with the baton. His legs seized up, lost power. He collapsed back to the floor and writhed fish-on-boat-deck fashion. His stomach clenched. Nausea consumed him.

"That was the lowest setting," Bonnie Franklin said, voice high-pitched little girl. "Just gets the cow's attention."

Myron looked up, trying to stop his body from quaking. Veronica lifted his leg and placed the heel blade near his face. One quick stomp and he was done. Bonnie showed him the cattle prod again. Myron felt a fresh shiver go through him. He looked through the one-way glass. No sign of Big Cyndi or any cavalry.

Now what?

Bonnie Franklin did the talking. "Why are you here?"

He focused on the cattle prod and how to avoid experiencing its wrath again. "I was asking about someone," he said.

Mall Girl had recovered. She-he stood up over him holding her-his face. "He hit me!" Her tone was a little deeper now, the shock and hurt dropping the feminine facade a bit.

Myron stayed still.

"You bitch!"

Mall Girl grimaced and threw a kick as though Myron's rib cage were a football. Myron saw the kick coming, saw the heel blade, saw the cattle prod, closed his eyes, and let it land.

He fell back.

Bonnie Franklin continued with the questions. "Who were you asking about?"

No secret. "Clu Haid."

"Why?"

"Because I wanted to know if he'd been here."

"Why?"

Telling them he was looking for his killer might not be the wisest course of action, especially if said killer was in the room. "He was a client of mine."

"So?"

"Bitch!" It was Mall Girl again. Another kick. It again landed on the bottom tip of the rib cage and hurt like hell. Myron swallowed away some bile that had worked its way up. He looked through the one-way glass again. Still no Big Cyndi. Blood flowed from the knife wounds to his chest and leg. His insides still trembled from the electric shock. He looked into the eyes of Veronica Lake. The calm eyes. Win had them too. The great ones always do.

"Who do you work for?" Bonnie asked.

"No one."

"Then why would you care if he came here?"

"I'm just trying to put some things together," he said.

"What things?"

"Just general stuff."

Bonnie Franklin looked at Veronica Lake. Both nodded. Then Bonnie Franklin made a show of turning up the cattle prod. " 'General stuff' is an unacceptable response."

Panic squeezed Myron's gut. "Wait—"

"No, I think not." Bonnie reached toward him with the cattle prod.

Myron's eyes widened. No choice really. He had to try it now. If the prod hit him again, he'd have nothing left. He just had to hope Veronica would not kill him.

He had been planning the move for the past ten seconds. Now he rolled all the way back over his neck and head. He landed on his feet and without warning shot himself forward as though from a cannon. The three crossdressers backed off, prepared for the attack. But an attack would be suicide. Myron knew that. There were three of them, two armed, at least one very good. Myron could never beat them. He needed to surprise them. So he did. By *not* going for them.

He went instead for the one-way glass.

His legs had pushed off full throttle, propelling him rocket-ship fashion toward the glass. By the time his three captors realized what he was doing, it was too late. Myron squeezed his eyes shut, made two fists, and hit the glass with his full weight, Superman style. He held nothing back. If the glass did not give, he was a dead man.

The glass shattered on impact.

The sound was enormous, all-consuming. Myron flew through it, glass clattering to the floor around him. When he landed, he tucked himself into a tight ball. He hit the floor and rolled. Tiny shards of mirror bit into his skin. He ignored the pain, kept rolling, crashing hard into the bar. Bottles fell.

Big Cyndi had talked about the place's reputation. Myron was counting on that. And the Take A Guess clientele did not disappoint.

A pure New York melee ensued.

Tables were thrown. People screamed. Someone flew over the bar and landed on top of Myron. More glass shattered. Myron tried to get to his feet, but it wasn't happening. From his right, he saw a door open. Mall Girl emerged.

"Bitch!"

Mall Girl started toward him, carrying Bonnie's cattle prod. Myron tried to scramble away, but he couldn't get his bearings. Mall Girl kept coming, drawing closer.

And then Mall Girl disappeared.

It was like a scene from a cartoon, where the big dog punches Sylvester the Cat, and Sylvester flies across the room and the oversize fist stays there for a few seconds.

In this case the oversize fist belonged to Big Cyndi.

Bodies flew. Glasses flew. Chairs flew. Big Cyndi ignored it all. She scooped Myron up and threw him over her shoulder like a firefighter. They rushed outside as police sirens clawed through the milky night air.

CHAPTER 16

Back at the Dakota, Win tsk-tsked and said, "You let a couple of girls beat you up?"

"They weren't girls."

Win took a sip of cognac. Myron gulped some Yoo-Hoo. "Tomorrow night," Win said, "we'll go back to this bar. Together."

It was not something Myron wanted to think about right now. Win called a doctor. It was after two in the morning, but the doctor, a gray-haired man straight from central casting, arrived in fifteen minutes. Nothing broken, he declared with a professional chuckle. Most of the medical treatment consisted of cleaning out the cuts from the heel blade and window bits. The two heel slices—the one on his stomach was shaped like a Z—required stitches. All in all, painful but relatively harmless.

The doctor tossed Myron some Tylenol with codeine, closed up his medical bag, tipped his hat, departed. Myron finished his Yoo-Hoo and stood slowly. He wanted to take a shower, but the doctor had told him to wait until the morning. He swallowed a couple of tablets and hit the sheets. When he fell asleep, he dreamed about Brenda.

In the morning he called Hester Crimstein at her apartment. The machine picked up. Myron said it was urgent. Midway through his message Hester took the call.

"I need to see Esperanza," he told the attorney. "Now."

Surprisingly, the attorney hesitated for only a moment before saying, "Okay."

"I killed someone," Myron said.

Esperanza sat across from him.

"I don't mean I actually fired a gun. But I might as well have. In many ways what I did was worse."

Esperanza kept her eyes on him. "This happened right before you ran away?"

"Within a couple of weeks, yes."

"But that's not why you left."

His mouth felt dry. "I guess not."

"You ran away because of Brenda."

Myron did not answer.

Esperanza crossed her arms. "So why are you sharing this little tidbit with me?"

"I'm not sure."

"I am," she said.

"Oh?"

"It's something of a ploy. You hoped that your big confession would help me open up."

"No," Myron said.

"Then?"

"You're the one I talk to about things like this."

She almost smiled. "Even now?"

"I don't understand why you're shutting me out," he said. "And okay, maybe I do hold out some hope that talking about this will help us return to—I don't know—some kind of sense of normalcy. Or maybe I just need to talk about this. Win wouldn't understand. The person I killed was evil incarnate. It would have presented him with a moral dilemma no more complex than choosing a tie.''

''And this moral dilemma haunts you?''

''The problem is,'' Myron said, ''it doesn't.''

Esperanza nodded. ''Ah.''

''The person deserved it,'' he went on. ''The courts had no evidence.''

''So you played vigilante.''

''In a sense.''

''And that bothers you? No, wait, it doesn't bother you.''

''Right.''

''So you're losing sleep over the fact that you're not losing sleep.''

He smiled, spread his hands. ''See why I come to you?''

Esperanza crossed her legs and looked up in the air. ''When I first met you and Win, I wondered about your friendship. About what first attracted you to each other. I thought maybe Win was a latent homosexual.''

''Why does everyone say that? Can't two men just—''

''I was wrong,'' she interrupted. ''And don't get all defensive, it'll make people wonder. You guys aren't gay. I realized that early on. Like I said, it was just a thought. Then I wondered if it was simply the old adage 'Opposites attract.' Maybe that's part of it.'' She stopped.

''And?'' Myron prompted.

''And maybe you two are more alike than either one of you wants to believe. I don't want to get too deep here, but Win sees you as his humanity. If you like him, he reasons, how bad can he be? You, on the other hand, see him as a cold dose of reality. Win's logic is scary, but it's oddly appealing. There is a little part in all of us that likes what he does, the same side of us that thinks the Iranians might be on to something when they cut off a thief's hand. You grew up with all that suburban liberal crap about the disadvantaged. But now real-life experience is teaching you that some people are just plain evil. It shifts you a little closer to Win."

"So you're saying I'm becoming like Win? Gee, that's comforting."

"I'm saying your reaction is human. I don't like it. I don't think it's right. You may indeed be sinking into a quagmire. Bending the rules is getting easier and easier for you. Maybe the person you killed deserved it, but if you want to hear that, if you want absolution, go to Win."

Silence.

Esperanza's fingers fluttered near her mouth, debating between biting the nails and plucking her lower lip. "You've always been the finest person I know," she said. "Don't let anybody change that, okay?"

He swallowed, nodded.

"You're not bending the rules anymore," she continued. "You're decimating them. Just yesterday you told me you'd lie under oath to protect me."

"That's different."

Esperanza looked straight at him. "Are you sure about that?"

"Yes. I'll do whatever I have to to protect you."

"Including breaking laws? That's my point, Myron."

He shifted in his chair.

"And one other thing," she said. "You're using this whole moral dilemma thing to distract yourself from two truths you don't want to face."

"What truths?"

"One, Brenda."

"And two?"

Esperanza smiled. "Skipped over one pretty fast."

"And two?" he repeated.

Her smile was gentle, understanding. "Two, it gets your mind off why you're really here."

"And why's that?"

"You're starting to do more than wonder if I killed Clu. And you're trying to find a way to rationalize it away if I did. You killed once, ergo it may be justifiable if I killed too. You just want to hear a reason."

"He hit you," Myron said. "In the parking garage."

She said nothing.

"The radio said they found pubic hairs in his apartment—"

"Don't go there," she said.

"I have to."

"Just stay out."

"I can't."

"I don't need your help."

"There's more to it than that. I'm involved in this."

"Only because you want to be."

"Did Clu tell you I was in danger?"

She said nothing.

"He told my parents that. And Jessica. I thought at first it was hyperbole. But maybe it's not. I got this weird diskette in the mail. There was an image of a young girl."

"You're ranting," she said. "You think you're ready for this, but you're not. Learn something from your past mistakes. Keep away from this."

"But it won't keep away from me," Myron said. "Why did Clu say I was in danger? Why did he hit you? What happened at the Take A Guess bar?"

She shook her head. "Guard."

The guard opened the door. Esperanza kept her eyes

down. She turned and left the room without looking back at Myron. Myron sat alone for a few seconds, gathered his thoughts. He checked his watch. Nine forty-five. Plenty of time to get to Yankee Stadium for his eleven o'clock meeting with Sophie and Jared Mayor. He had barely left the room when a man approached him.

"Mr. Bolitar?"

"Yes."

"This is for you."

The man handed him an envelope and disappeared. Myron opened it. A subpoena from the Bergen County district attorney's office. Case heading: "People of Bergen County v. Esperanza Diaz." Well, well. Esperanza and Hester had been right not to tell him anything.

He stuffed it into his pocket. At least now he wouldn't have to lie.

CHAPTER 17

Myron did what every good boy should do when he gets into legal trouble: He called his mommy.

"Your aunt Clara will handle the subpoena," Mom said.

Aunt Clara wasn't really his aunt, just an old friend from the neighborhood. On the High Holy Days she still pinched Myron's cheek and cried out, "What a *punim*!" Myron sort of hoped she wouldn't do that in front of the judge: "Your Honor, I ask you to look at this face: Is that a *punim* or is that a *punim*?"

"Okay," Myron said.

"I'll call her, she'll call the DA. In the meantime you say nothing, understand?"

"Yes."

"See now, Mr. Smarty Pants? See what I was telling you now? About Hester Crimstein being right?"

"Yeah, Mom, whatever."

"Don't whatever me. They've subpoenaed you. But because Esperanza wouldn't tell you anything, you can't hurt her case."

"I see that, Mom."

"Good. Now let me go call Aunt Clara."

She hung up. And Mr. Smarty Pants did likewise.

Bluntly put, Yankee Stadium was located in a cesspool section of the ever-eroding Bronx. It didn't much matter. Whenever you first caught sight of the famed sports edifice, you still fell into an immediate church hush. Couldn't help it. Memories swarmed in and burrowed down. Images flashed in and out. His youth. A small child crammed standing on the 4 train, holding Dad's seemingly giant hand, looking up into his gentle face, the pregame anticipation tingling through every part of him. Dad had caught a fly ball when Myron was five years old. He could still see it sometimes—the arc of white rawhide, the crowd standing, his dad's arm stretching to an impossible height, the ball landing on the palm with a happy smack, the warm beam coming off Dad's face when he handed the prized possession to his son. Myron still had that ball, browning in the basement of his parents' house.

Basketball was Myron's sport of choice, and football was probably his favorite to watch on TV. Tennis was the game of princes, golf the game of kings. But baseball was magic. Early childhood memories are faint, but almost every boy can recall his first major-league baseball game. He can remember the score, who hit a home run, who pitched. But mostly he remembers his father. The smell of his after-shave is wrapped up in the smells of baseball— the freshly cut grass, the summer air, the hot dogs, the stale popcorn, the spilled beer, the overoiled glove complete with baseball breaking in the pocket. He remembers the visiting team, the way Yaz tossed grounders to warm up Petrocelli at short, the way the hecklers made gentle fun of Frank Howard's TV commercials for Nestlé's Quik, the way the game's greats rounded second and slid head-first into third. You remember your sibling keeping stats, studying the lineups the way rabbinical scholars study the Talmud, baseball cards gripped in your hand, the ease and pace of a slow summer afternoon, Mom spending more time sunning herself than watching the action. You remember Dad buying you a pennant of the visiting team and later hanging it on your wall in a ceremony equal to the Celtics raising a banner in the old Boston Garden. You remember the way the players in the bullpen looked so relaxed, big wads of chew distorting their cheeks. You remember your healthy, respectful hate for the visiting team's superstars, the pure joy of going on Bat Day and treasuring that piece of wood as though it'd come straight from Honus Wagner's locker.

Show me a boy who didn't dream of being a big leaguer before age seven, before Training League or whatever slowly began to thin the herd in one of life's earliest lessons that the world can and will disappoint you. Show me a boy who doesn't remember wearing his Little League cap to school when the teachers would allow it, keeping it pitched high with a favorite baseball card tucked inside, wearing it to the dinner table, sleeping with it on the night table next to his bed. Show me a boy who doesn't remember playing catch with his father on the weekends or, better, on those precious summer nights when Dad would rush home from his job, shake off his work clothes, put on a T-shirt that was always a little too small, grab a mitt, and head into the backyard before the final rays faded away. Show me a boy who didn't stare in awe at how far his father could hit or throw a baseball—no matter how bad an athlete his father was, no matter how spastic or what have you—and for that shining moment Dad was transformed into a man of unimaginable ability and strength.

Only baseball had that magic.

The new majority owner of the New York Yankees was Sophie Mayor. She and her husband, Gary, had shocked the baseball world by buying the team from the longtime unpopular owner Vincent Riverton less than a year ago. Most fans had applauded. Vincent Riverton, a publishing mogul, had a love-hate relationship with the public (mostly hate) and the Mayors, a techno-nouveau-riche pair who had found their fortune through computer software, promised a more hands-off approach. Gary Mayor had grown up in the Bronx and promised a return to the days of the Mick and DiMaggio. The fans were thrilled.

But tragedy struck pretty fast. Two weeks before the deal to buy was finalized, Gary Mayor died of a sudden heart attack. Sophie Mayor, who had always been an equal, if not dominating, partner in the software business, insisted on going ahead with the transaction. She had public support and sympathy, but Gary and his roots had been the rope tethering her to the public. Sophie was a midwesterner, and with her love of hunting mixed with her background as a math genius, she hit the prenatally suspicious New Yorkers as being something of a kook.

Soon after taking over the helm, Sophie made her son Jared, a man with virtually no baseball experience, co-general manager. The public frowned. She made a quick trade, gutting the Yankee farm system on the chance that Clu Haid still had a good year or two left. The public cried. She had stood firm. She wanted a World Series in the Bronx immediately. Trading for Clu Haid was the way to get it. The public was skeptical.

But Clu pitched amazingly well during his first month with the team. His fastball was back over ninety, and his curves were breaking as if they were accepting signals from a remote control. He got better with each outing, and the Yankees grabbed first place. The public was appeased. For a little while anyway, Myron guessed. He had stopped paying attention, but he could imagine the backlash against the Mayor family when Clu tested positive for drugs.

Myron was led immediately into Sophie Mayor's office. She and Jared both stood to greet him. Sophie Mayor was probably mid-fifties, what was commonly called a handsome woman, her hair gray and neat, her back straight, her handshake firm, her arms tawny, her eyes twinkling with hints of mischief and cunning. Jared was twenty-fiveish. He wore his hair parted on the right with no hint of style, wire-rimmed glasses, a blue blazer, and a polka dot bow tie. Youths for George Will.

The office was sparsely decorated, or maybe it just appeared that way because the scene was dominated by a moose head hanging on a wall. A dead moose actually. A live moose is so hard to hang. Quite the decorating touch. Myron tried not to make a face. He almost said, "You must have hated this moose," à la Dudley Moore in *Arthur* but refrained. With age comes maturity.

Myron shook Jared's hand, then turned toward Sophie Mayor.

Sophie pounced. "Where the hell have you been, Myron?"

"Excuse me?"

She pointed to a chair. "Sit."

Like he was a dog. But he obeyed. Jared too. Sophie stayed on her feet and glowered down at him.

"In court yesterday they said something about your being in the Caribbean," she continued.

Myron made a noncommittal "uh-huh" sound.

"Where were you?"

"I was away."

"Away?"

"Yes."

She looked over at her son, then back at Myron. "For how long?"

"Three weeks."

"But Miss Diaz told me you were in town."

Myron said nothing.

Sophie Mayor made two fists and leaned toward him. "Why would she tell me that, Myron?"

"Because she didn't know where I was."

"In other words, she lied to me."

Myron did not bother replying.

"So where were you?" she pressed.

"Out of the country."

"The Caribbean?"

"Yes."

"And you never told anyone?"

Myron shifted in his chair, trying to find an opening or gain some sort of footing here. "I don't mean to sound rude," he said, "but I don't see how my whereabouts are any of your business."

"You don't?" A sharp chortle passed her lips. She looked at her son as if to say, *Do you believe this guy?*, then redirected her laser grays back toward Myron. "I relied on you," she said.

Myron said nothing.

"I bought this team and I decided to be hands-off. I know software. I know computers. I know business. I really don't know much about baseball. But I made one decision. I wanted Clu Haid. I had a feeling about him. I thought he still had something left. So I traded for him. People thought I was nuts—three good prospects for one has-been. I understood that concern. So I went to you, Myron, remember?"

"Yes."

"And you assured me he was going to stay clean."

"Wrong," Myron said. "I said he *wanted* to stay clean."

"Wanted, was going to . . . What is this, a lesson in semantics?"

"He was my client," Myron said. "It's my job to worry about his interests."

"And damn mine?"

"That's not what I said."

"Damn integrity and ethics too? Is that the way you work, Myron?"

"That's not it at all. Sure, we wanted this trade to happen—"

"You wanted it badly," she corrected him.

"Fine, we wanted it badly. But I never promised you he'd stay clean because it's not something I or anyone else can guarantee. I assured you we would try our hardest. I made it part of the deal. I gave you the right to randomly test him at any time."

"You *gave* me the right? I demanded it! And you fought me on it every step of the way."

"We shared the risk," Myron said. "I made his salary contingent on his staying clean. I let you put in a strict morals clause."

She smiled, crossed her arms. "You know who you sound like? Those hypocritical car commercials where General Motors or Ford tout all the pollution-saving devices they've put on their cars. As though they did it on their own. As though they woke up one day more concerned with the environment than the bottom line. They leave out the fact that the government forced them to put on those devices, that they fought the government tooth and nail the whole way."

"He was my client," Myron said again.

"And you think that's an all-purpose excuse?"

"It's my job to get him the best deal."

"Keep telling yourself that, Myron."

"I can't stop a man from returning to an addiction. You knew that."

"But you said you'd watch him. You said you'd work on keeping him straight."

Myron swallowed and shifted in his chair again. "Yes."

"But you didn't watch him, Myron, did you?"

Silence.

"You took a vacation and didn't tell anyone. You left Clu alone. You acted irresponsibly, and so I blame you in part for his falling off the wagon."

Myron opened his mouth, closed it. She was right, of course, but he didn't have the luxury of wallowing in that right now. Later. He'd think about his role in this later. The pain from last night's beating was angrily stirring from its snooze. He reached into his pocket and shook out a couple of extra-strength Tylenols.

Satisfied—or maybe satiated—Sophie Mayor sat down. Seeing the pills, she asked, "Would you like some water?"

"Please."

She nodded at Jared. Jared poured Myron a glass of water and handed it to him. Myron thanked him and swallowed the tablets. The placebo effect jumped in, and he immediately felt better.

Before Sophie Mayor could strike again, Myron tried to shift gears. "Tell me about Clu's failed drug test," he said.

Sophie Mayor looked puzzled. "What's to tell?"

"Clu claimed he was clean."

"And you believe that?"

"I want to look into it."

"Why?"

"Because when Clu was caught in the past, he begged forgiveness and promised to get help. He never pretended a test result was wrong."

She crossed her arms. "And that's evidence of what exactly?"

"Nothing. I'd just like to ask a few questions."

"Ask away then."

"How often did you test him?"

Sophie looked over at her son. His cue. Jared spoke for the first time since greeting Myron at the door. "At least once a week," he said.

"Urine tests?" Myron asked.

"Yes," Jared said.

"And he passed them all? I mean, except for the last one."

"Yes."

Myron shook his head. "Every week? And no other positives? Just that one?"

"That's right."

He looked back at Sophie. "Didn't you find that odd?"

"Why?" she countered. "He'd been trying to stay clean, and he fell off the wagon. It happens every day, doesn't it?"

It did, Myron guessed, and still something about it didn't sit right with him. "But Clu knew you were testing him?"

"I assume so, yes. We'd been testing him at least once a week."

"And how were the tests conducted?"

Sophie again looked over at Jared. Jared asked, "What do you mean?"

"Step by step," Myron said. "What did he do?"

Sophie took that one. "He peed in the cup, Myron. It's pretty simple."

It was never pretty simple. "Did someone watch him urinate?"

"What?"

"Did someone actually witness Clu peeing or did he step into a stall?" Myron said. "Was he naked when he did it or did he have on shorts—"

"What difference does any of that make?"

"Plenty. Clu had spent his lifetime beating these tests. If he knew they were coming, he'd be prepared."

"Prepared how?" Sophie asked.

"Lots of ways, depending on the sophistication of the test," Myron said. "If the testing was more primitive, you can put motor oil on your fingers and let the urine hit them while urinating. The phosphates throw the results out of whack. Some testers know this, so they check for phosphates. If the tester lets the guy urinate in a stall, he can strap clean urine onto his inner thigh and use that. Or the testee keeps the clean urine hidden in a condom or small balloon. He stores it in the lining of his boxer shorts maybe. Or between his toes. Under his armpit. In his mouth even."

"Are you serious?"

"It gets worse. If the testee gets tipped off a strict test is coming up—one where the administrators are watching every move he makes—he'll drain his bladder and use a catheter to pump in clean urine."

Sophie Mayor looked horror-stricken. "He pumps someone else's urine into his bladder?"

"Yes," Myron said.

"Jesus." Then she pinned him down with her eyes. "You seem to know quite a bit about this, Myron."

"So did Clu."

"What are you saying?"

"It raises some questions, that's all."

"He probably got caught by surprise."

"Maybe," Myron said. "But if you were testing him every week, how surprised could he have been?"

"He might have just messed up," Sophie went on. "Drug addicts have a way of doing that."

"Could be. But I'd like to speak with the person who administered the test."

"Dr. Stilwell," Jared said. "He's the team doctor. He handled it. Sawyer Wells assisted him."

"Sawyer Wells, as in the self-help guru?"

"He's a psychologist specializing in human behavior and an excellent motivational therapist," Jared corrected.

Motivational therapist. Uh-huh. "Are either of them around now?"

"No, I don't think so. But they'll be here later. We have a home game tonight."

"Who on the team was especially friendly with Clu? A coach, a player?"

"I really wouldn't know," Jared said.

"Who did he room with on the road?"

Sophie almost smiled. "You really were out of touch, weren't you?"

"Cabral," Jared said. "Enos Cabral. He's a Cuban pitcher."

Myron knew him. He nodded, glancing about, and that was when he saw it. His heart lurched, and it took all his willpower not to scream.

He had just been sweeping the room with his eyes,

taking the room in but not really seeing anything, just the normal thing everyone does, when an object snagged his gaze as though on a rusted hook. Myron froze. On the credenza. On the right side of the credenza, mixed in with the other framed photos and the trophies and those latex cubes that encased civic awards and the first issue of Mayor Software stock and the like. Right there. A framed photograph.

A framed photograph of the girl on the computer diskette.

Myron tried to maintain a calm facade. Deep breath in, deep breath out. But he could feel his pulse quicken. His mind fought through the haze, searching for a temporary clearing. He scanned his internal memory banks. *Okay, slow down. Breathe. Keep breathing.*

No wonder the girl had looked familiar to him.

But what was her deal? More memory bank scanning. She was Sophie Mayor's daughter, of course. Jared Mayor's sister. What was her name again? His recollections were vague. What had happened to her? A runaway, right? Ten, fifteen years ago. There had been an estrangement or something. Foul play was not suspected. Or was it? He didn't remember.

"Myron?"

He needed to think. Calmly. He needed space, time. He couldn't just blurt out, "Oh, I got this weird diskette with an image of your daughter melting in blood on it." He had to get out of here. Do some research. Think it through. He stood, clumsily looking at his watch.

"I have to go," he said.

"What?"

"I'd like to speak with Dr. Stilwell as soon as possible," he said.

Sophie's eyes stayed on him. "I don't see the relevance."

"I just explained—"

"What difference would it make? Clu is dead now. The drug test isn't relevant."

"There might be a connection."

"Between his death and a drug test?"

"Yes."

"I'm not sure I agree."

"I'd still like to check it out. I have that right."

"What right?"

"If the drug test was inconclusive, it changes things."

"Changes what—" Then Sophie stopped, smiled a bit, and nodded to herself. "I think I see now."

Myron said nothing.

"You mean in terms of his contract, don't you?"

"I have to go," he repeated.

She leaned back and recrossed her arms. "Well, Myron, I have to hand it to you. You are definitely an agent. Trying to squeeze one more commission out of a corpse, eh?"

Myron let the insult roll off. "If Clu was clean, his contract would still be valid. You'd owe the family at least three million dollars."

"So this is a shakedown? You're here for money?"

He glanced at the picture of the young girl again. He remembered the diskette, the laugh, the blood. "Right now," he said, "I'd just like to talk with the team doctor."

Sophie Mayor looked at him like he was a turd on the carpet. "Get out of my office, Myron."

"Will you let me speak to the doctor?"

"You don't have any legal standing here."

"I think I do."

"You don't, believe me. The blood money has run dry here. Get out, Myron. Now."

He took one more look at the photograph. Now was not the time to argue the point. He hurried out the door.

CHAPTER 18

Myron was starting to hurt. The Tylenol alone wasn't doing the trick. He had Tylenol with codeine in his back pocket, but he did not dare. He needed to stay sharp, and that stuff put him to sleep faster than, er, sex. He quickly cataloged the sore spots. His sliced-up shin hurt most, followed closely by his bruised ribs. The rest of the aches were an almost welcome distraction. But the pain made him conscious of every movement.

When he got back to his office, Big Cyndi handed him a huge pile of message slips.

"How many reporters have called?" he asked.

"I stopped counting, Mr. Bolitar."

"Any messages from Bruce Taylor?"

"Yes."

Bruce covered the Mets, not the Yankees. But every reporter wanted in on this story. Bruce was also something of a friend. He would know about Sophie Mayor's daughter. The question was, of course, how to raise the subject without getting him overly curious.

Myron closed his office door, sat down, dialed a number. A voice answered on the first ring.

"Taylor."

"Hey, Brucie."

"Myron? Jesus Christ. Hey, I appreciate you calling me back."

"Sure, Bruce. I love to cooperate with my favorite reporter."

Pause. Then: "Uh-oh."

"What?" Myron said.

"This is too easy."

"Pardon."

"Okay, Myron, let's skip the part where you break down my defenses with your supernatural charisma. Cut to it."

"I want to make a deal."

"I'm listening."

"I'm not willing to make a statement yet. But when I do, you get first crack. An exclusive."

"An exclusive? Sheesh, Myron, you really do know your media lingo, don't you?"

"I could have said scoop. It's one of my favorite words."

"Okay, Myron, great. So in return for your *not* telling me anything, you get what?"

"Just some information. But you don't read into anything that I ask and you don't report on it. You're just my source."

"More like your bitch," Bruce said.

"If that's what you're into."

"Not today, dear, I have a headache. So let me get this straight. You tell me nothing. I report nothing. In return I get to tell you everything. Sorry, big guy, no deal."

"Bye-bye, Brucie."

"Whoa, whoa, Myron, hold up. Christ, I'm not a general manager. Don't pull that negotiating crap on me.

Look, let's stop tugging each other's chains here. This is what we do: You give me something. A statement, anything. It can be as innocuous as you want to make it. But I want to be the first with a statement from Myron Bolitar. Then I tell you what you want, I keep quiet, you give me the exclusive scoop or whatever before everyone else. Deal?''

"Deal," Myron said. "Here's your statement: Esperanza Diaz did not kill Clu Haid. I stand behind her one hundred percent."

"Was she having an affair with Clu?"

"That's my statement, Bruce. Period."

"Okay, fine, but what's this about your being out of the country at the time of the murder?"

"A statement, Bruce. As in, 'no further comment.' As in, 'I'll be answering no questions today.' "

"Hey, it's already public knowledge. I just want a confirmation. You were in the Caribbean, right?"

"Right."

"Where in the Caribbean?"

"No comment."

"Why not? Were you really in the Cayman Islands?"

"No, I was not in the Caymans."

"Then where?"

See how reporters work? "No comment."

"I called you immediately following Clu's positive drug test. Esperanza said you were in town but would not comment."

"And I still won't," Myron said. "Now it's your turn, Bruce."

"Come on, Myron, you're giving me nothing here."

"We had a deal."

"Yeah, all right, sure, I want to be fair," he said in a

tone that made it clear he would start up again later. "Ask away."

Casual, casual. He couldn't just ask about Sophie Mayor's daughter. Subtlety. That was the key. Myron's office door opened, and Win swept into the room. Myron signaled with one finger. Win nodded and opened a closet door. There was a full-length mirror on the inside back. Win stared at his reflection and smiled. A nice way of passing the time.

"What were the rumors about Clu?" Myron asked.

"You mean before the positive test results?"

"Yes."

"Time bomb," Bruce said.

"Explain."

"He was pitching great, no question. And he looked good. Thinned down, seemed focused. But then a week or so before the drug test, he started looking like hell. Christ, you must have seen it, right? Or were you out of the country then too?"

"Just go on, Bruce."

"What else can I tell you? With Clu you've seen it a hundred times before. The guy breaks your heart. His arm was touched by God. The rest of him was, well, just touched, if you follow my meaning."

"So there were signs before the positive test?"

"Yeah, I guess. In hindsight, sure there were lots of signs. I hear his wife threw him out. He was unshaven, red-eyed, that kind of thing."

"It didn't have to be drugs," Myron said.

"True. It could have been booze."

"Or maybe it was just the strain of marital discord."

"Look, Myron, maybe some guys like Orel Hershiser get the benefit of the doubt. But when it comes to Clu Haid or Steve Howe or some other perennial screwup, you figure it's substance abuse, and eleven times out of ten you're right.''

Myron looked over at Win. Win had finished patting the blond locks and was now using the mirror to practice his different smiles. Right now he was working on roguish.

Subtle, Myron reminded himself, subtle. . . . "Bruce?"

"Yeah?"

"What can you tell me about Sophie Mayor?"

"What about her?"

"Nothing specific."

"Just curious, huh?"

"Right, curious."

"Sure you are," Bruce said.

"How much damage did Clu's drug test do to her?"

"Tremendous damage. But you know this. Sophie Mayor stuck her neck out, and for a while she was a genius. Then Clu fails the drug test, and presto, she's an idiotic bimbo who should let the men run things."

"So tell me about her background."

"Background?"

"Yes. I want to get a feel for her."

"Why?" Bruce asked. Then: "Ah, what the hell. She's from Kansas, I think, or Iowa or Indiana or Montana. Someplace like that. An aged Ivory Girl type. Loves fishing, hunting, all that nature stuff. She was also something of a math prodigy. Came East to go to MIT. That's where she met Gary Mayor. They got married and lived most of their lives as science professors. He taught at Brandeis; she taught at Tufts. They developed a software program for personal finance in the early eighties and suddenly went from middle-class professors to millionaires. They took the company public in '94 and changed the *m* to a *b*."

"The *m* to a *b*?"

"Millionaire to billionaire."

"Oh."

"So the Mayors did what lots of superwealthy people do: They bought a sports franchise. In this case, the Yankees. Gary Mayor grew up loving them. It was going to be a nice toy for him, but of course he never got to enjoy it."

Myron cleared his throat. "And they, uh, have children?" Señor Subtle-o.

"They had two. You know Jared. He's actually a pretty good kid, smart, went to your alma mater, Duke. But everyone hates him because he got the job through nepotism. His main responsibility is to keep an eye on Mommy's investment. My understanding is that he's actually pretty good at that and that he leaves the baseball to the baseball guys."

"Uh-huh."

"They also have a daughter. Or had a daughter."

With great effort, Win sighed, closed the closet door. So difficult to pull himself away from a mirror. He sat across from Myron looking, as always, completely at ease. Myron cleared his throat and said into the phone, "What do you mean, *had* a daughter?"

"The daughter's very estranged. Don't you remember the story?"

"Vaguely. She ran away, right?"

"Right. Her name was Lucy. She took off with a boyfriend, some grunge musician, a few weeks before her eighteenth birthday. This was, I don't know, ten, fifteen years ago. Before the Mayors had any money."

"So where does she live now?"

"Well, that's the thing. No one knows."

"I don't understand."

"She ran away, that much is known for sure. She left

them a note, I think. She was going to hit the road with her boyfriend and seek her fortune, the usual teenage stuff. Sophie and Gary Mayor were typical East Coast college professors who read too much Dr. Spock, so they gave their daughter 'space,' figuring of course that she'd come back.''

"But she didn't.''

"Duh.''

"And they never heard from her?''

"Duh again.''

"But I remember reading about this a few years ago. Didn't they start a search for her or something?''

"Yeah. First off, the boyfriend came back after a few months. They'd broken up and gone their separate ways. Big shock, right? Anyway, he didn't know where she went. So the Mayors called the police, but they treated it like no big deal. Lucy was eighteen by this time, and she had clearly run away on her own. There was no evidence of foul play or anything and remember that this was before the Mayors had beaucoup bucks.''

"And after they became rich?''

"Sophie and Gary tried to find her again. They made it like a search for the missing heiress. The tabloids loved it for a while. There were some wild reports but nothing concrete. Some say Lucy moved overseas. Some say she's living in a commune somewhere. Some say she's dead. Whatever. They never found her, and there was still no sign of foul play, so the story eventually petered out.''

Silence. Win looked at Myron and arched an eyebrow. Myron shook his head.

"So why the interest?'' Bruce asked.

"I just want to get a feel for the Mayors.''

"Uh-huh.''

"No big deal.''

"Okay, I buy that. Not."

"It's the truth," Myron lied. "And how about using a more up-to-date reference? No one says *not* anymore."

"They don't?" Pause: "Guess I gotta watch more MTV. But Vanilla Ice is still hip, right?"

"Ice, ice, baby."

"Fine, okay, we'll play it your way for now, Myron. But I don't know anything else about Lucy Mayor. You can try a search on Lexis. The papers might have more detail."

"Good idea, thanks. Listen, Bruce, I got another call coming in."

"What? You're just going to cut me loose?"

"That was our deal."

"So why all the questions about the Mayors?"

"Like I said, I want to get a feel for them."

"Does the phrase *what a crock* mean anything to you?"

"Good-bye, Bruce."

"Wait." Pause. Then Bruce said, "Something serious is going down here, right?"

"Clu Haid has been murdered. Esperanza's been arrested for the crime. I'd say that's pretty serious."

"There's more to it. Tell me that much. I won't print it, I promise."

"Truth, Bruce? I don't know yet."

"And when you do?"

"You'll be the first to know."

"You really think Esperanza's innocent? Even with all that evidence?"

"Yes."

"Call me, Myron. If you need anything else. I like Esperanza. I want to help if I can."

Myron hung up. He looked over at Win. Win seemed in

deep thought. He was tapping his chin with his index finger. They sat in silence for several seconds.

Win stopped tapping and asked, "Whatever happened to the King Family?"

"You mean the ones with the Christmas specials?"

Win nodded. "Every year you were supposed to watch the King Family Christmas Special. There must have been a hundred of the buggers—big Kings with beards, little Kings in knickers, Mommy Kings, Daddy Kings, Uncle and Aunt and Cousin Kings. Then one year—poof—they're gone. All of them. What happened?"

"I don't know."

"Strange, isn't it?"

"I guess."

"And what did the King clan do the rest of the year?"

"Prepared for the next Christmas special?"

"What a life, no?" Win said. "Christmas passes, and you start thinking about next Christmas. You live in a snow globe of Christmas."

"I guess."

"I wonder where they are now, all those suddenly unemployed Kings. Do they sell cars? Insurance? Are they drug dealers? Do they get sad every Christmas?"

"Yeah, poignant point, Win. By the way, did you come down here for a reason?"

"Discussing the King Family isn't reason enough? Weren't you the one who came up to my office because you didn't understand the meaning of a Sheena Easton song?"

"You're comparing the King Family to Sheena Easton?"

"Yes, well, in truth, I came up here to inform you that I quashed the subpoenas against Lock-Horne."

Myron shouldn't have been surprised. "The power of

payoffs," he said with a shake of his head. "It never fails to amaze me."

"*Payoff* is such an offensive term," Win said. "I prefer the more politically correct *assisting the contribution-challenged.*" He sat back, crossed his legs in that way of his, folded his hands on his lap. He gestured at the phone and said, "Explain."

So Myron did. He filled him in on everything, especially on the Lucy Mayor incident. When Myron was finished, Win said, "Puzzling."

"Agreed."

"But I am not sure I see a connection."

"Someone mails me a diskette with Lucy Mayor's image on it and a little while later Clu is murdered. You think that's just a coincidence?"

Win mulled that over. "Too early to tell," he concluded. "Let's do a little recap, shall we?"

"Go ahead."

"Let's start with a straight time line: Clu gets traded to New York, he pitches well, he gets thrown out by Bonnie, he starts collapsing, he fails a drug test, he desperately searches for you, he comes to me and withdraws two hundred thousand dollars, he strikes Esperanza, he gets murdered." Win stopped. "That sound fair?"

"Yes."

"Now let's explore some possible tangents from this line."

"Let's."

"One, our old fraternity chum Billy Lee Palms appears to be missing. Clu purportedly contacted him shortly before the murder. Aside from that, is there any reason to tie Billy Lee into all this?"

"Not really. And according to his mother, Billy Lee isn't the most dependable tool in the shed."

"So maybe his disappearance has nothing to do with this."

"Maybe.

"But that would be yet another bizarre coincidence," Win said.

"It would at that."

"Fine, let's move on for the moment. Tangent two, this Take A Guess nightspot."

"All we know is that Clu called them."

Win shook his head. "We know a great deal more."

"For example?"

"They overreacted to your visit. Tossing you out would have been one thing. Roughing you up a bit would have been one thing. But this sort of interrogation complete with knife slashes and electrocution—that's overkill."

"Meaning?"

"Meaning that you struck a nerve, poked the hive, stirred the nest, choose your favorite cliché."

"So they're connected into all this."

"Logical," Win said, again doing his best Spock.

"How?"

"Heavens, I haven't a clue."

Myron chewed it over a bit. "I had thought maybe Clu and Esperanza hooked up there."

"And now?"

"Let's say they did hook up there. What would be the big deal about that? Why the overkill?"

"So it's something else."

Myron nodded. "Any more tangents?"

"The big one," Win said. "The disappearance of Lucy Mayor."

"Which happened more than ten years ago."

"And we must confess that her connection is tenuous at best."

"So confessed," Myron said.

Win steepled his fingers and raised the pointers. "But the diskette was addressed to you."

"Yes."

"Ergo we cannot be sure that Lucy Mayor is connected to Clu Haid at all—"

"Right."

"—but we can be sure that Lucy Mayor is somehow connected to you."

"Me?" Myron made a face. "I can't imagine how."

"Think hard. Perhaps you met her once."

Myron shook his head. "Never."

"You might not have known. The woman has been living in some sort of clandestine state for a very long time. Perhaps she was someone you met in a bar, a one-night stand."

"I don't one-night stand."

"That's right," Win said. Then with flat eyes: "God, I wish I were you."

Myron waved him off. "But suppose you're right. Suppose I did meet her but didn't know it. So what? She decides to repay me by sending me a diskette of her face melting into a puddle of blood?"

Win nodded. "Puzzling."

"So where does that leave us?"

"Puzzled."

The speaker buzzed. Myron said, "Yes?"

Big Cyndi said, "Your father is on line one, Mr. Bolitar."

"Thank you." Myron picked up the receiver. "Hi, Dad."

"Hey, Myron. How are you?"

"Good."

"You readjusting to being home?"

"Yeah, I am."

"Happy to be back?"

Dad was stalling. "Yeah, Dad, I'm great."

"All this stuff with Esperanza. It must be keeping you hopping, huh?"

"I guess so, yeah."

"Soooo," Dad said, stretching out the word, "think you have time for lunch with your old man?"

There was a strain in the voice.

"Sure, Dad."

"How about tomorrow? At the club?"

Myron bit back a groan. Not the club. "Sure. Noon, okay?"

"Good, son, that'll be fine."

Dad didn't call him son very often. More like never. Myron switched hands. "Anything wrong, Dad?"

"No, no," he said too quickly. "Everything's fine. I just want to talk to you about something."

"About what?"

"It'll keep, no biggie. See you tomorrow."

Click.

Myron looked at Win. "That was my father."

"Yes, I picked up on that when Big Cyndi said your father was on the line. It was further reemphasized when you said 'Dad' four times during the conversation. I'm gifted that way."

"He wants to have lunch tomorrow."

Win nodded. "And I care because—?"

"Just telling you."

"I'll write about it in my diary tonight," Win said. "In the meantime, I had another thought, vis-à-vis Lucy Mayor."

"I'm listening."

"If you recall, we were trying to figure out who was being injured in all this."

"I recall."

"Clu obviously. Esperanza. You. I."

"Yes."

"Well, we must add a new person: Sophie Mayor."

Myron thought about it. Then he started nodding. "That could very well be the connection. If you wanted to destroy Sophie Mayor, what would you do? First, you'd do something to undermine any support she had with the Yankee fans and management."

"Clu Haid," Win said.

"Right. Then you might hit her in what has to be a vulnerable spot—her missing daughter. I mean, if someone sent her a similar diskette, can you imagine the horror?"

"Which raises an interesting question," Win said.

"What?"

"Are you going to tell her?"

"About the diskette?"

"No, about recent troop movements in Bosnia. Yes, the diskette."

Myron thought about it but not for very long. "I don't see where I have any choice. I have to tell her."

"Perhaps that too is part of the theoretical plan to wear her down," Win said. "Perhaps someone sent you the diskette knowing it would get back to her."

"Maybe. But she still has the right to know. It's not my place to decide what Sophie Mayor is strong enough to handle."

"Too true." Win rose. "I have some contacts trying to locate the official reports on Clu's murder—autopsy, crime scene, witness statements, labs, what have you. But everyone is tight-lipped."

"I got a possible source," Myron said.

"Oh?"

"The Bergen County medical examiner is Sally Li. I know her."

"Through Jessica's father?"

"Yes."

"Go for it," Win said.

Myron watched him head for the door. "Win?"

"Yes?"

"You have any thoughts on how I should break the news to Sophie Mayor?"

"None whatsoever."

Win left then. Myron stared at the phone. He picked it up and dialed Sophie Mayor's phone number. It took some time, but a secretary finally patched him through to her. Sophie sounded less than thrilled to hear his voice.

She opened sharply. "What?"

"We need to talk," Myron said. There was distortion on the line. A cell or car phone probably.

"We already talked."

"This is different."

Silence. Then: "I'm in the car right now, about a mile from my house out on the Island. How important is this?"

Myron picked up a pen. "Give me your address," he said. "I'll be right over."

CHAPTER 19

On the street the man was still reading a newspaper.

Myron's elevator trip down to the lobby featured mucho stops. Not atypical. No one spoke, of course, everyone busying themselves by staring up at the descending flashing numbers as though awaiting a UFO landing. In the lobby he joined the stream of suits and flowed out onto Park Avenue, salmons fighting upstream against the tide until, well, they died. Many of the suits walked with heads high, their expressions kick-ass-runway-model; others walked with backs bent, flesh versions of the statue on Fifth Avenue of Atlas carrying the world on his shoulders, but for them the world was simply too heavy.

Whoa, again with the deep.

Perfectly situated on the corner of Forty-sixth and Park, standing reading a newspaper but positioned in such way as to watch all entering or leaving the Lock-Horne building, was the same man Myron had noticed standing there when he entered.

Hmm.

Myron took out his cell phone and hit the programmed button.

"Articulate," Win said.

"I think I got a tail."

"Hold please." Maybe ten seconds passed. Then: "The newspaper on the corner."

Win keeps a variety of telescopes and binoculars in his office. Don't ask.

"Yep."

"Good Lord," Win said. "Could he be any more obvious?"

"Doubt it."

"Where's the pride in his work? Where's the professionalism?"

"Sad."

"That, my friend, is the whole problem with this country."

"Bad tails?"

"It's an example. Look at him. Does anybody really stand on a street corner and read a newspaper like that? He might as well cut out two eyeholes."

"Uh-huh," Myron said. "You got some free time?"

"But of course. How would you like to play it?"

"Back me up," Myron said.

"Give me five."

Myron waited five minutes. He stood there and studiously avoided looking at the tail. He checked his watch and huffed a bit as though he expected someone and was getting impatient. When the five minutes passed, Myron walked straight over to the tail.

The tail spotted his approach and ducked into the newspaper.

Myron kept walking until he stood directly next to the tail. The tail kept his face in the newspaper. Myron gave him Smile 8. Big and toothy. A televangelist being handed a hefty check. Early Wink Martindale. The tail kept his eyes on the newspaper. Myron kept smiling, his eyes wide as a clown's. The tail ignored him. Myron inched closer, leaned his *über*-wattage smile within inches of the tail's face, wriggled his eyebrows.

The tail snapped closed the newspaper and sighed. "Fine, hotshot, you made me. Congratulations."

Still with the Wink Martindale smile: "And thank you for playing our game! But don't worry, we won't let you go home empty-handed! You get the home version of Incompetent Tail and a year's subscription to *Modern Doofus*."

"Yeah, right, see you around."

"Wait! Final *Jeopardy!* round. Answer: He or she hired you to follow me."

"Bite me."

"Ooo, sorry, you needed to put that in the form of a question."

The tail started walking away. When he looked back, Myron gave him the smile and a big wave. "This has been a Mark Goodson-Bill Todman production. Good-bye, everybody!" More waving.

The tail shook his head and continued down the street, joining another stream of people. Lots of people in this stream; Win happened to be one of them. The tail would probably find a clearing and then call his boss. Win would listen in and learn all. What a plan.

Myron headed to his rented car. He circled the block once. No more tails. At least none as obvious as the last. No matter. He was driving out to the Mayor estate on Long Island. It didn't much matter if anyone knew.

He spent his time in the car working on the cell phone. He had two arena football players—indoor football on a smaller field, for those who don't know—both of whom were hoping to scratch a bench spot on an NFL roster before the waiver wire closed down. Myron called teams, but nobody was interested. Lots of people asked him about the murder. He brushed them off. He knew his efforts were fairly futile, but he stuck to it. Big of him. He tried concentrating on his work, tried to lose himself in the numb bliss of what he did for a living. But the world kept creeping in. He thought about Esperanza in jail. He thought about Jessica in California. He thought about Bonnie Haid and her fatherless boys at home. He thought about Clu in formaldehyde. He thought about his father's phone call. And strangely, he kept thinking about Terese alone on that island.

He blocked out the rest.

When he reached Muttontown, a section of Long Island that had somehow escaped him in the past, he turned right onto a heavily wooded road. He drove about two miles, passing maybe three driveways. He finally reached a simple iron gate with a small sign that read THE MAYORS. There were several security cameras and an intercom. He pressed the button. A woman's voice came on and said, "May I help you?"

"Myron Bolitar to see Sophie Mayor."

"Please drive up. Park in front of the house."

The gate opened. Myron drove up a rather steep hill. Tall hedges lined both sides of the driveway, giving the aura of being a rat in a maze. He spotted a few more security cameras. No sign of the house yet. When he reached the top of the hill, he hit upon a clearing. There was a slightly overgrown grass tennis court and croquet field. Very Norma Desmond. He made another turn. The house was dead straight ahead. It was a mansion, of course, though not as huge as some Myron had seen. Vines clung to pale yellow stucco. The windows looked leaded. The whole scene screamed Roaring Twenties. Myron half expected Scott and Zelda to pull up behind him in a slick roadster.

This part of the driveway was made up of small loose pebbles rather than pavement. His tires crunched them as it drew closer. There was a fountain in the middle of the circular drive, about fifteen feet in front of the door. Neptune stood naked with a triton in his hand. The fountain, Myron realized, was a smaller version of the one in the Piazza della Signoria in Florence. Water spouted up but not very high or with much enthusiasm, as if someone had set the water pressure on "light urination."

Myron parked the car. There was a perfectly square swimming pool on his right, complete with lily pads floating on the top. A poor man's Giverny. There were statues in the gardens, again something from old Italy or Greece or the like. Venus de Milo–like except with all the limbs.

He got out of the car and stopped. He thought about what he was about to unearth, and for a brief moment he considered turning back. *How,* he wondered again, *do I tell this woman about her missing daughter melting on a computer diskette?*

No answer came to him.

The door opened. A woman in casual clothes led him through a corridor and into a large room with high tin ceilings and lots of windows and a semidisappointing view of more white statues and woods. The interior was art deco, but it didn't try too hard. Nice. Except, of course, for the hunting trophies. Taxidermy birds of some sort sat on the shelves. The birds looked upset. Probably were. Who could blame them?

Myron turned and stared at a mounted deer. He waited for Sophie Mayor. The deer waited too. The deer seemed very patient.

"Go ahead," a voice said.

Myron turned around. It was Sophie Mayor. She was wearing dirt-smeared jeans and a plaid shirt, the very essence of the weekend botanist.

Never short of a witty opening gambit, Myron countered, "Go ahead and what?"

"Make the snide remark about hunting."

"I didn't say anything."

"Come, come, Myron. Don't you think hunting is barbaric?"

Myron shrugged. "I never really thought about it." Not true, but what the hey.

"But you don't approve, do you?"

"Not my place to approve."

"How tolerant." She smiled. "But you of course would never do it, am I right?"

"Hunt? No, it's not for me."

"You think it's inhumane." She gestured with her chin to the mounted deer. "Killing Bambi's mother and all."

"It's just not for me."

"I see. Are you a vegetarian?"

"I don't eat much red meat," Myron said.

"I'm not talking about your health. Do you ever eat any dead animals?"

"Yes."

"So do you think it's more humane to kill, say, a chicken or a cow than it is to kill a deer?"

"No."

"Do you know what kind of awful torture that cow goes through before it's slaughtered?"

"For food," Myron said.

"Pardon?"

"Slaughtered for food."

"I eat what I kill, Myron. Your friend up there"—she

nodded to the patient deer—"she was gutted and eaten. Feel better?"

Myron thought about that. "Uh, we're not having lunch, are we?"

That got a small chuckle. "I won't go into the whole food chain argument," Sophie Mayor said. "But God created a world where the only way to survive is to kill. Period. We all kill. Even the strict vegetarians have to plow fields. You don't think plowing kills small animals and insects?"

"I never really thought about it."

"Hunting is just more hands-on, more honest. When you sit down and eat an animal, you have no appreciation for the process, for the sacrifice made so that you could survive. You let someone else do the killing. You're above even thinking about it. When I eat an animal, I have a fuller understanding. I don't do it casually. I don't depersonalize it."

"Okay," Myron said, "while we're on the subject, what about those hunters who don't kill for food?"

"Most do eat what they kill."

"But what about those who kill for sport? I mean, isn't that part of it?"

"Yes."

"So what about that? What about killing merely for sport?"

"As opposed to what, Myron? Killing for a pair of shoes? Or a nice coat? Is spending a full day outdoors, coming to understand how nature works and appreciating her bountiful glory, is that worth any less than a leather pocketbook? If it's worth killing an animal because you prefer your belt made of animal skin instead of something man-made, is it not worth killing one because you simply enjoy the thrill of it?"

He said nothing.

"I'm sorry to ride you about this. But the hypocrisy of it all drives me somewhat batty. Everyone wants to save the whale, but what about the thousands of fish and shrimp a whale eats each day? Are their lives worthless because they aren't as cute? Ever notice how no one ever wants to save ugly animals? And the same people who think hunting is barbaric put up special fences so the deer can't eat their precious gardens. So the deers overpopulate and die of starvation. Is that better? And don't even get me started on those so-called ecofeminists. Men hunt, they say, but women are too genteel. Of all the sexist nonsense. They want to be environmentalists? They want to stay as close to a state of nature as possible? Then understand the one universal truth about nature: You either kill or you die."

They both turned and stared at the deer for a moment. Proof positive.

"You didn't come here for a lecture," she said.

Myron had welcomed this delay. But the time had come. "No, ma'am."

"Ma'am?" Sophie Mayor chuckled without a hint of humor. "That sounds grim, Myron."

Myron turned and looked at her. She met his gaze and held it.

"Call me Sophie," she said.

He nodded. "Can I ask you a very personal, maybe hurtful question, Sophie?"

"You can try."

"Have you heard anything from your daughter since she ran away?"

"No."

The answer came fast. Her gaze remained steady, her voice strong. But her face was losing color.

"Then you have no idea where she is?"

"No idea."

"Or even if she's . . ."

"Alive or dead," she finished for him. "None."

Her voice was so monotone it seemed on the verge of a scream. There was a quaking near her mouth now, a fault line starting to give way. Sophie Mayor stood and waited for his explanation, afraid perhaps to say any more.

"I got a diskette in the mail," he began.

She frowned. "What?"

"A computer diskette. It came in the mail. I put it in my A drive, and it just started up. I didn't have to hit any keys."

"Self-starting program," she said, suddenly the computer expert. "That's not complicated technology."

Myron cleared his throat. "A graphic came on. It started out as a photograph of your daughter."

Sophie Mayor took a step back.

"It was the same photograph that's in your office. On the right side of the credenza."

"That was Lucy's junior year of high school," she said. "The school portrait."

Myron nodded, though he didn't know why. "After a few seconds her image started melting on the screen."

"Melting?"

"Yes. It sort of dissolved into a puddle of, uh, blood. Then a sound came on. A teenage girl laughing, I think."

Sophie Mayor's eyes were glistening now. "I don't understand."

"Neither do I."

"This came in the mail?"

"Yes."

"On a floppy disk?"

"Yes," Myron said. Then he added for no reason: "A three-and-a-half-inch floppy."

"When?"

"It arrived in my office about two weeks ago."

"Why did you wait so long to tell me?" She put a hand up. "Oh, wait. You were out of the country."

"Yes."

"So when did you first see it?"

"Yesterday."

"But you saw me this morning. Why didn't you tell me then?"

"I didn't know who the girl was. Not at first anyway. Then when I was in your office, I saw the photograph on the credenza. I got confused. I wasn't sure what to say."

She nodded slowly. "So that explains your abrupt departure."

"Yes. I'm sorry."

"Do you have the diskette? My people will analyze it."

He reached into his pocket and withdrew it. "I don't think it'll be any help."

"Why not?"

"I took it to a police lab. They said it automatically reformatted itself."

"So the diskette is blank?"

"Yes."

It was as though her muscles had suddenly decided to flee the district. Sophie Mayor's legs gave way. She dropped to a chair. Her head lolled into her hands. Myron waited. There were no sounds. She just sat there, head in hands. When she looked up again, the gray eyes were tinged with red.

"You said something about a police lab."

He nodded.

"You used to work in law enforcement."

"Not really."

"I remember Clip Arnstein saying something about it."

Myron said nothing. Clip Arnstein was the man who had drafted Myron in the first round for the Boston Celtics. He also had a big mouth.

"You helped Clip when Greg Downing vanished," she continued.

"Yes."

"I've been hiring private investigators to search for Lucy for years. Supposedly the best in the world. Sometimes we seem to get close but . . ." Her voice drifted off, her eyes far away. She looked at the diskette in her hand as if it had suddenly materialized there. "Why would someone send this to you?"

"I don't know."

"Did you know my daughter?"

"No."

Sophie took a couple of careful breaths. "I want to show you something. Wait here a minute." It took maybe half that time. Myron had just begun to stare into the eyes of some dead bird, noting with some dismay how closely they resembled the eyes of some human beings he knew, and Sophie was back. She handed him a sheet of paper.

Myron looked at it. It was an artist's rendering of a woman nearing thirty years of age.

"It's from MIT," she explained. "My alma mater. A scientist there has developed a software package that helps with age progression. For missing people. So you can see what they might look like today. He made this up for me a few months ago."

Myron looked at the image of what the teenage Lucy might look like as a woman heading toward thirty. The effect was nothing short of startling. Oh, it looked like her, he guessed, but talk about ghosts, talk about life being a series of what-ifs, talk about the years slipping away and then smacking you in the face. Myron stared at the image, at the more conservative haircut, the small frown lines. How painful must it be for Sophie Mayor to look at this?

"Does she look familiar at all?" Sophie asked.

Myron shook his head. "No, I'm sorry."

"You're sure?"

"As sure as you can be in these situations."

"Will you help me find her?"

He wasn't sure how to answer. "I can't see how I can help."

"Clip said you're good at these things."

"I'm not. But even if I were, I can't see what I can do. You've hired experts already. You have the cops—"

"The police have been useless. They view Lucy as a runaway, period."

Myron said nothing.

"Do you think it's hopeless?" she asked.

"I don't know enough about it."

"She was a good girl, you know." Sophie Mayor smiled at him, her eyes misty with time travel. "Headstrong, sure. Too adventurous for her own good. But then again I raised Lucy to be independent. The police. They think she was simply a troubled kid. She wasn't. Just confused. Who isn't at that age? And it wasn't as if she ran off in the middle of the night without telling anyone."

Against his better judgment Myron asked, "Then what happened?"

"Lucy was a teenager, Myron. She was sullen and unhappy, and she didn't fit in. Her parents were college math professors and computer geeks. Her younger brother was considered a genius. She hated school. She wanted to see the world and live on the road. She had the whole rock 'n' roll fantasy. One day she told us she was going off with Owen."

"Owen was her boyfriend?"

She nodded. "An average musician who fronted a garage band, certain that his immense talent was being held back by them." She made a lemon-sucking face. "They wanted to run off and get a record deal and become famous. So Gary and I said okay. Lucy was like a wild bird trapped in a small cage. She wouldn't stop flapping her wings no matter what we did. Gary and I felt we had no choice in the matter. We even thought it might be good for her. Lots of her classmates were backpacking through Europe. What was the difference?"

She stopped and looked up at him. Myron waited. When she didn't say anything, he said, "And?"

"And we never heard from her again."

Silence.

She turned back to the mounted deer. The deer looked back at her with something akin, it seemed, to pity.

Myron said, "But Owen came back, right?"

"Yes." She was still staring at the deer. "He's a car salesman in New Jersey. He plays in a wedding band on weekends. Can you imagine? He dresses up in a cheap tuxedo and belts out 'Tie a Yellow Ribbon' and 'Celebration' and introduces the bridal party." She shook her head at the irony. "When Owen came back, the police questioned him, but he didn't know anything. Their story was so typical: They went out to Los Angeles, failed miserably, started fighting, and broke up after six months. Owen stayed out there another three months, certain this time it had been Lucy who was holding back his immense talent. When he failed again, he came back home with his tail between his legs. He said he hadn't seen Lucy since their breakup."

"The police checked it out?"

"So they said. But it was a dead end."

"Do you suspect Owen?"

"No," she said bitterly. "He's too big a nothing."

"Have there been any solid leads at all?"

"Solid?" She thought about it. "Not really. Several of the investigators we've hired think she joined a cult."

Myron made a face. "A cult?"

"Her personality fit the profile, they said. Despite my attempts to make her independent, they claim she was just the opposite—someone needing guidance, alone, suggestible, alienated from friends and family."

"I don't agree," Myron said.

She looked at him. "You said you never met Lucy."

"The psychological profile may be right, but I doubt she's with a cult."

"What makes you say that?"

"Cults like money. Lucy Mayor is the daughter of an extraordinarily wealthy family. Maybe you didn't have money when she first would have joined, but believe me, they'd know about you by now. And they would have been in touch, if for no other reason than to extort vast sums."

She started blinking again. Her eyes closed, and she turned her back to him. Myron took a step forward and then stopped, not sure what to do. He chose discretion, kept his distance, waited.

"The not knowing," Sophie Mayor said after some time had passed. "It gnaws at you. All day, all night, for twelve years. It never stops. It never goes away. When my husband's heart gave out, everyone was so shocked. Such a healthy man, they said. So young. Even now I don't know how I'll get through the day without him. But we rarely spoke about Lucy after she disappeared. We just lay in bed at night and pretended that the other one was asleep and stared at the ceiling and imagined all the horrors only parents with missing children can conjure up.''

More silence.

Myron had no idea what to say. But the silence was growing so thick he could barely breathe. "I'm sorry,'' he said.

She didn't look up.

"I'll go to the police,'' he said. "Tell them about the diskette.''

"What good will that do?''

"They'll investigate.''

"They already have. I told you. They think she's a runaway.''

"But now we have this new evidence. They'll take the case more seriously. I can even go to the media. It'll jump-start their coverage.''

She shook her head. Myron waited. She stood and wiped her palms on the thighs of her jeans. "The diskette,'' she said, "was sent to you.''

"Yes.''

"Addressed to you.''

"Yes.''

"So,'' she said, "someone is reaching out to you.''

Win had said something similar. "You don't know that,'' Myron said. "I don't want to douse your hopes, but it could be nothing more than a prank.''

"It's not a prank.''

"You can't be sure.''

"If it was a prank, it would have been sent to me. Or Jared. Or someone who knew her. It wasn't. It was sent to you. Someone is reaching out to you specifically. It might even be Lucy.''

He took a deep breath. "Again I don't want to douse your—"

"Don't patronize me, Myron. Just say what you want to say."

"Okay . . . if it were Lucy, why would she send an image of herself melting into a puddle of blood?"

Sophie Mayor did not wince, but she came close. "I don't know. Maybe you're right. Maybe it's not her. Maybe it's her killer. Either way, they're seeking *you* out. It's the first solid lead in years. And if we make it loud and public, I fear that whoever sent this will go back into hiding. I can't risk that."

"I don't know what I can do," Myron said.

"I'll pay you whatever you want. Name a price. A hundred thousand? A million?"

"It's not the money. I just don't see where I can help."

"You can investigate."

He shook his head. "My best friend and business partner is in jail for murder. My client was shot in his own home. I have other clients who rely on me for their job security."

"I see," she said. "So you don't have time, is that it?"

"It's not a question of time. I really have nothing to go on. No clue, no connection, no source. There's nothing to start with here."

Her eyes pinned him down. "You can start with you. You're my clue, my connection, my source." She reached out and took his hand. Her flesh was cold and hard. "All I'm asking is that you look closer."

"At what?"

"Maybe," she said, "at yourself."

Silence. They stood there, she holding his hand.

"That sounds good, Sophie, but I'm not sure what it means."

"You don't have children, do you?"

"No," Myron said. "But that doesn't mean I don't sympathize."

"So let me ask you, Myron: What would you do if you were me? What would you do if the first real clue in ten years just walked in your door?"

"The same thing you're doing."

So under the mounted deer, he told her he would keep his eyes open. He told her he would think about it. He told her he would try to figure out the connection.

CHAPTER 20

Back at the office Myron strapped on the Ultra Slim phone headset and started making phone calls. Very Jerry Maguire. Not just in appearance but in the fact that clients were abandoning him left and right. And he hadn't even written a mission statement.

Win called. "Newspaper Tail's name is Wayne Tunis. He lives in Staten Island and works in construction. He placed one call to a John McClain, telling him that he had been spotted. That's it. They're pretty careful."

"So we don't yet know who hired him?"

"That would be correct."

"When in doubt," Myron said, "we should go with the obvious choice."

"Young FJ?"

"Who else? He's been following me for months."

"Course of action?"

"I'd like to get him off my back."

"May I recommend a well-placed bullet through the back of the skull?"

"We've got enough problems without adding one more."

"Fine. Course of action?"

"We confront him."

"He usually hangs out at a Starbucks on Forty-ninth Street," Win said.

"Starbucks?"

"The old mob espresso bars have gone the way of leisure suits and disco music."

"Both of them are coming back."

"No," Win said, "bizarre mutations of them are coming back."

"Like coffee bars in place of espresso bars?"

"Then you understand."

"So let's pay FJ a visit."

"Give me twenty minutes," Win said before hanging up.

As soon as Myron hit the disconnect, Big Cyndi buzzed his line.

"Mr. Bolitar?"

"Yes?"

"A Miss or Mr. Thrill is on the phone," Big Cyndi said.

Myron closed his eyes. "You mean from last night?"

"Unless you know someone else named Thrill, Mr. Bolitar."

"Take a message."

"Both her words and tone suggest urgency, Mr. Bolitar."

Suggest urgency? "Fine. Patch her—or him—through."

"Yes, Mr. Bolitar."

There was a click.

"Myron?"

"Uh, yeah, hi, Thrill."

"That was some exit you made last night, big fella," Thrill said. "You really know how to impress a girl."

"Yeah, I usually don't jump through a plate glass window until the second date."

"So how come you haven't called me?"

"I've been really busy."

"I'm downstairs," Thrill said. "Tell the guard to let me up."

"It's not a good time. Like I said before—"

"Men rarely say no to Thrill. I must be losing my touch."

"It's not that," he said. "It's just that the timing is all wrong."

"Myron, my name isn't really Thrill."

"I hate to burst your bubble, but I kinda suspected it read something else on your birth certificate."

"No, that's not what I mean. Look, let me up. We need to talk about last night. About something that happened after you left."

So he shrugged and called down to the guard at the front desk and told him to let up anyone identifying themselves as Thrill. The guard was puzzled but said okay. The headset was still strapped on so Myron speed-dialed a sports apparel company. Before dashing to the Caribbean, Myron had been on the verge of landing a sneaker deal for a track and field client with said company. But now he was being put on hold. An assistant to an assistant finally came on the line. Myron asked him about the deal. It had fallen through, he was told. Why? he asked.

"Ask your client," the assistant said. "Oh, and ask his new agent too."

Click.

Myron closed his eyes and pulled off his headset. Damn.

There was a knock on his office door. The alien sound caused a ripple of pain. Esperanza had never knocked. Never. She prided herself on interrupting him. She would sooner give up a limb than knock.

"Come in."

The door opened. Someone stepped inside and said, "Surprise."

Myron tried not to stare. He took off the headset. "You're . . . ?"

"Thrill, yup."

Nothing was the same. Gone was the Cat Woman costume, the blond wig, the high heels, the, uh, prodigious bosom. Thrill was still female, thank heavens. Still quite attractive in her conservative navy suit with matching blouse, her hair done in a pixie style, her eyes less luminous behind round tortoiseshell glasses, her makeup now applied with a far lighter hand. Her figure was thinner, more toned, less, uh, shapely. Nothing to complain about, mind you. Just different.

"To answer your first question," she said, "when I dress like Thrill, I wear the aptly named Raquel Wonder Breast Enhancements."

Myron nodded. "That the stuff that looks like flattened Silly Putty?"

"The very. You jam them in your bra. Guess you've seen the infomercial on TV."

"Seen it? I bought the video."

Thrill laughed. Last night her laugh—not to mention her walk, her movements, her tone of voice, her choice of words—had been a double entendre. In the light of day the sound was melodic and almost childlike.

"I also strap on the aptly named Miracle Bra," she continued. "To lift it all up high."

"Any higher," Myron said, "and they could have doubled as earrings."

"Too true," she said. "The legs and ass, however, are mine. And for the record, I do not have a penis."

"So noted."

"Can I sit down?"

Myron looked at his watch. "I hate to be a pest—"

"You'll want to hear this, believe me." She sat in the chair in front of his desk. Myron folded his arms and leaned his butt on the desk's lip. "My real name is Nancy Sinclair. I don't dress like Thrill for kicks. I'm a journalist, and I'm doing a story on Take A Guess. An insider's look at what goes on, what kind of people go there, what makes them tick. In order to get people to open up, I go undercover as Thrill."

"So you do all this for a story?"

"I do all what?"

"Dress up and, uh . . . ." His gestures were unintelligible.

"Not that I see where it's even vaguely any of your concern, but the answer is no. I dress a part. I strike up conversations. I flirt. Period. I like to watch people's reaction to me."

"Oh." Then Myron cleared his throat and said, "Just, uh, out of curiosity, I'm not going to be in your story, am I? I mean, I've really never been there before and I was—"

"Relax. I recognized you as soon as you came in the door."

"You did?"

"I follow basketball. I got season tickets to the Dragons."

"I see." The Dragons were New Jersey's pro basketball team. Myron had tried a comeback with them not long ago.

"That's why I approached you."

"To see if I was into, uh, gender ambiguity?"

"Everyone else there is. Why not you?"

"But I explained to you that I was there to ask about someone."

"Clu Haid, right. Still, your reaction to me was interesting."

"I found you to be a witty conversationalist," Myron said.

"Uh-huh."

"And I also have a Julie-Newmar-as-Cat-Woman fetish."

"You'd be surprised how many people have that same fetish."

"No, I don't think I would be," Myron said. "So why are you here, Nancy?"

"Pat saw us talking last night."

"The bartender?"

"He's also one of the owners. He has shares in a couple of places in the city."

"And?"

"And after the smoke cleared from your exit, Pat pulled me aside."

"Because he saw us talking?"

"Because he saw me giving you my phone number."

"So?"

"So I'd never done that before."

"I'm flattered."

"Don't be. I'm just making a point. I come on to a ton of girls and guys and whatever in there. But I never give out a phone number."

"So why did you give it to me?"

"Because I was curious to see if you'd call. You rebuffed Thrill, so you clearly weren't there for sex. I wondered what you were up to."

Myron frowned. "That was the only reason?"

"Yes."

"Nothing about my rugged good looks and brawny body?"

"Oh, yeah. I almost forgot."

"So what did Pat want?"

"He wants me to bring you to another club tonight."

"Tonight?"

"Yes."

"How did he know I'd call?"

Again the smile. "Nancy Sinclair might not guarantee an immediate phone call . . ."

"But Thrill does?"

"Bosoms are empowerment. And if you didn't, he told me I could look up your business number in the phone book."

"Which is what you did."

"Yes. He also promised me you wouldn't be hurt."

"How comforting. And your interest in all this?"

"Isn't it obvious? A story. The Clu Haid murder is huge news. Now you're tying this week's murder-of-the-century to a kinky New York nightclub."

"I don't think I can help you."

"Cow dooky."

"Cow dooky?"

She shrugged.

"What else did Pat say to you?" Myron asked.

"Nothing much. He just said that he wanted to talk."

"If he wanted to talk, he could have looked up my phone number too."

"Thrill, not the brightest bulb on the tree, didn't pick up on that."

"But Nancy Sinclair did."

She smiled again. It was a damn nice smile. "Pat was also huddled up with Zorra."

"Who?"

"That's their psycho bouncer. A cross-dresser with a blond wig."

"Like Veronica Lake?"

She nodded. "He's absolutely nuts. Lift up your shirt."

"Pardon?"

"He can do anything with that razor heel. His favorite is a Z slash on the right side. You were in the back room with him."

Made sense. Myron hadn't made him miss. Zorra—Zorra?—just wanted to brand him. "I have one."

"He's seriously whacked out. Did some sort of stuff in the Persian Gulf War. Undercover. Worked for the Israelis too. There are all kinds of rumors about him, but if five percent of the stories I've heard are true, he's killed dozens."

Just what he needed—Cross-Dressing Mossad. "Did they talk about Clu at all?"

"No. But Pat said something about your trying to kill somebody."

"Me?"

"Yes."

"They think I killed Clu?"

"I don't think so. It sounded more like they thought you were at the club to find someone and kill him."

"Who?"

"No idea. They just said you were out to kill him."

"They didn't say who?"

"If they did, I didn't hear them." She smiled. "So do we have a date?"

"Guess so."

"You're not scared?"

"I'll have backup."

"Someone good?"

Myron nodded. "Oh, yeah."

"Then I better go home and strap up my breasts."

"Need any help?"

"My hero. But no, Myron, I think I can handle it myself."

"And if you can't?"

"I have your phone number," she said. "See you tonight."

CHAPTER 21

Win frowned. "Nonsurgical breast enhancements?"

"Yes. They're an accessory of some sort."

"An accessory? Like a matching pocketbook?"

"In a way." Then thinking about it, Myron added, "But they're probably more noticeable."

Win showed him the flat eyes. Myron shrugged.

"False advertising," Win said.

"Pardon?"

"Breast enhancements. It's false advertising. There should be a law."

"Right, Win. But the politicians in Washington— where are they when it comes to the real issues?"

"Then you understand."

"I understand that you're a snorting pig."

"A thousand pardons, O Enlightened One." Win put a hand to his ear and tilted his head to the side. "Tell me again, Myron: What first attracted you to this Thrill?"

"The catsuit," Myron said.

"I see. So if, say, Big Cyndi came into the office in the catsuit—"

"Hey, c'mon, I just ate a muffin."

"Exactly."

"Fine, I'm a pig too. Happy?"

"Yes, ecstatic. And perhaps you misread me. Perhaps I wish to outlaw such accessories because of what they do to a woman's self-esteem. Perhaps I tire of a society that forces unobtainable beauty on a woman—size four dresses with D cups."

"The key word here being *perhaps*."

Win smiled. "Love me for all my faults."

"What else is there?"

Win adjusted his tie. "FJ and the two oversized hormonal glands that guard him are at Starbucks. Shall we?"

"Let's. Then I want to head over to Yankee Stadium. I need to question a couple of folks."

"Sounds almost like a plan," Win said.

They strolled up Park Avenue. The light changed, and they waited at the corner. Myron stood next to a man in a business suit talking on a cell phone. Nothing unusual about that, except the man was having phone sex. He was actually rubbing his, uh, nether parts and saying into the phone, "Yeah, baby, like that," and other stuff not worth repeating. The light changed. The man crossed, still rubbing and talking. Talk about I Love New York.

"About tonight," Win said.

"Yes."

"You trust this Thrill?"

"She checks out."

"There is of course a chance that they'll just shoot you when you show up."

"I doubt it. This Pat is part owner. He wouldn't want the trouble in his own place."

"So you think they're extending this invitation to buy you a drink?"

"Could be," Myron said. "With my preference-crossing animal magnetism, I'm considered something of a tasty morsel to the swinger set.''

Win chose not to argue.

They headed east on Forty-ninth Street. The Starbucks was four blocks up on the right. When they arrived, Win signaled for Myron to wait. He leaned in and took a quick peek through the glass before backing away. ''Young FJ is at a table with someone,'' Win reported. ''Hans and Franz are two tables over. Only one other table is occupied.''

Myron nodded. ''Shall we?''

''You first,'' Win said. ''Let me trail.''

Myron had stopped questioning Win's methods a long time ago. He immediately stepped inside and headed toward FJ's table. Hans and Franz, the Mr. Universe Bookends, were still wearing the tank tops and the semipajama pants smeared with a pattern that resembled melted paisley. They bolted upright when Myron entered, fingers tightened into fists, necks in midcrack.

FJ was decked out in a light herringbone sports coat, collared shirt buttoned all the way to the top, cuffed pants, and Cole-Haan tasseled loafers. Too natty for words. He spotted Myron and raised his hand in the bruisers' direction. Hans and Franz froze.

''Hi, FJ,'' Myron said.

FJ was sipping something foamy; it kinda looked like shaving cream. ''Ah, Myron,'' he said with what he must have been sure was *savoir faire*. He gestured at his table companion. His companion got up without a word and scooted toward the exit like a scared gerbil. ''Please, Myron, join me. This is such a strange coincidence.''

''Oh?''

''You saved me a trip. I was just going to pay you a visit.'' FJ tossed Myron the snake smile. Myron let it land on the floor and watched it slither away. "I guess it's kismet, huh, Myron? Your coming here. Pure kismet."

FJ cracked up at that. Hans and Franz laughed too.

"Kismet," Myron repeated. "Good one."

FJ waved a modest hand as if to say, *I got a million like that*. "Please sit, Myron."

Myron pulled out a chair.

"Care for a drink?"

"An iced latte would be fine. Grande, skim, with a dash of vanilla."

FJ motioned to the guy working behind the coffee bar. "He's new," FJ confided.

"Who?"

"The guy working the espresso machine. The last guy who worked here made a wonderful latte. But he quit for moral reasons."

"Moral reasons?"

"They started selling Kenny G CDs," FJ said. "Suddenly he couldn't sleep at night. It was tearing him apart. Suppose an impressionable kid bought one? How could he live with himself? Pushing caffeine was okay. But Kenny G . . . the man had scruples."

Myron said, "Commendable."

Win chose that moment to enter. FJ spotted him and looked over at Hans and Franz. Win did not hesitate. He beelined straight toward FJ's table. Hans and Franz went to work. They stepped in Win's path and expanded their chests to dimensions large enough to apply for a parking permit. Win kept walking. Both men wore turtlenecks so high and loose they looked like something awaiting circumcision.

Hans managed a smirk. "You Win?"

"Yes," Win said, "me Win."

"You don't look so tough." Hans looked at Franz. "He look tough to you, Keith?"

Keith said, "Not so tough."

Win did not break stride. Almost casually and without the slightest warning, he struck Hans with the knife-edge of his hand behind the ear. Hans's whole body stiffened and then collapsed as though someone had ripped the skeleton out of him. Franz gaped at the sight. But not for long. In the same motion Win pirouetted and struck Franz in the oft vulnerable throat. An awful gurgling noise shot out of Franz's lips, as though he were choking on a slew of small bones. Win reached for the carotid artery, found it, and squeezed with his pointer and thumb. Franz's eyes closed, and he too slid into Nighty-Night Land.

The couple at the other table exited quickly. Win smiled down at the unconscious bruisers. Then he glanced at Myron. Myron shook his head. Win shrugged and turned to the guy manning the coffee bar.

"Barista," Win said. "One caffe mocha."

"What size?"

"Grande, please."

"Skim or whole milk?"

"Skim. I'm watching my figure."

"Right away."

Win joined Myron and FJ. He sat and crossed his legs. "Nice sports coat, FJ."

"Glad you like it, Win."

"It really brings out the demonic red in your eyes."

"Thank you."

"So where were we?"

Myron played along. "I was just about to tell FJ that I'm getting a little tired of the tail."

"And I was just about to tell Myron that I'm getting tired of him meddling in my affairs," FJ said.

Myron looked at Win. "Meddling? Does anybody really use that word anymore?"

Win thought about it. "The old man at the end of every *Scooby Doo*."

"Right. You meddling kids, stuff like that."

"You will never guess who does the voice for Shaggy," Win said.

"Who?"

"Casey Kasem."

"Get out," Myron said. "The top-forty radio guy?"

"The very same."

"Live and learn."

On the floor Hans and Franz started to stir. Win showed FJ the gun he had semihidden in his one hand. "For the safety of all concerned," Win said, "please ask your employees to refrain from moving."

FJ told them. He was not scared. His father was Frank Ache. That was protection enough. The muscles here were for show.

"You've been following me for weeks now," Myron said. "I want it to end."

"Then I suggest that you stop interfering with my company."

Myron sighed. "Fine, FJ, I'll bite. How am I interfering with your company?"

"Did you or did you not visit Sophie and Jared Mayor this morning?" FJ asked.

"You know I did."

"For what purpose?"

"It had nothing to do with you, FJ."

"Wrong answer."

"Wrong answer?"

"You visited the owner of the New York Yankees even

though you currently represent no one who plays for the team.''

"So?"

"So why were you there?"

Myron looked at Win. Win shrugged. "Not that I need to explain myself to you, FJ, but just to assuage your paranoid delusions, I was there about Clu Haid."

"What about him?"

"I was asking about his drug tests."

FJ's eyes narrowed. "That's interesting."

"Glad you think so, FJ."

"You see, I'm just a new guy trying to learn this confusing business."

"Uh-huh."

"I'm young and inexperienced."

Win said, "Ah, how often I've heard that line."

Myron just shook his head.

FJ leaned forward, his scaly features coming closer. Myron feared his tongue would dart out and sniff him. "I want to learn, Myron. So please tell me: What possible significance could Clu's drug test results have now?"

Myron quickly debated answering and decided, What's the harm? "If I can show the drug test was faulty, his contract would still be active."

FJ nodded, seeing the thought trail now. "You'd be able to get his contract paid out."

"Right."

"Do you have reason to believe that the test was faulty?"

"I'm afraid that's confidential, FJ. Agent-client privilege or whatever you want to call it. I'm sure you understand."

"I do," FJ said.

"Good."

"But you, Myron, are not his agent."

"I am still responsible for his estate's financial well-being. Clu's death doesn't alter my obligation."

"Wrong answer."

Myron looked at Win. "Again with the wrong answer?"

"You are not responsible." FJ reached to the floor and pulled a briefcase into view. He snapped it open with as much flair as possible. His finger danced through a stack of papers before withdrawing the one he sought. He handed it to Myron and smiled. Myron looked into FJ's eyes, and again he was reminded of the eyes of that mounted deer.

Myron skimmed it over. He read the first line, felt a thump, checked the signature. "What the hell is this?"

FJ's smile was like a dripping candle now. "Exactly what it looks like. Clu Haid changed representation. He fired MB SportsReps and hired TruPro."

He remembered what Sophie Mayor had said in her office, about his having no legal standing. "He never told us."

"Never told *us,* Myron, or never told *you*?"

"What the hell does that mean?"

"You weren't around. Perhaps he tried to tell you. Perhaps he told your associate."

"So he just happened by you, FJ?"

"How I recruit is none of your business. If you kept your clients happy, the best recruitment efforts wouldn't work."

Myron checked the date. "This is quite a coincidence, FJ."

"What's that?"

"He dies two days after he signs with you."

"Yes, Myron, I agree. I don't think it was a coincidence. Fortunately for me, it means that I had no motive to kill him. Unfortunately for the sizzling Esperanza, the opposite is true.''

Myron glanced over at Win. Win was staring down at Hans and Franz. They were both awake now, face to the floor, hands behind their heads. Customers occasionally came into the coffee bar. Some saw the two men on the floor and exited right away. Others were unfazed, walking past as though Hans and Franz were just two more Manhattan panhandlers.

''Very convenient,'' Myron said.

''What's that?''

''Clu signing with you so close to his death. On the surface it eliminates you as a serious suspect.''

''On the surface?''

''It draws attention away from you, makes it look like his death hurts your interests.''

''It does hurt my interests.''

Myron shook his head. ''He had failed a drug test. His contract was null and void. He's thirty-five years old with several suspensions. As a monetary commodity Clu was fairly worthless.''

''Clu had overcome adversity before,'' FJ said.

''Not like this. He was through.''

''If he stayed with MB, yes, that's probably true. But TruPro has influence. We would have found a way to relaunch his career.''

Doubtful. But all this raised some interesting questions. The signature looked real, the contract legit. So maybe Clu had left him. Why? Well, lots of reasons. His life was being flushed down the toilet while Myron lollygagged in the sands of the Caribbean. Okay, but why TruPro? Clu knew their reputation. He knew what the Aches were all about. Why would he choose them?

Unless he had to.

Unless Clu was in debt to them. Myron remembered the missing two hundred thousand dollars. Could Clu have been in debt to FJ? Had he gotten in too deep—so deep he had to sign with TruPro? But if that was the case, why not take out more money? He still had more in the account.

No, maybe this was far simpler. Maybe Clu got himself in big trouble. He looked to Myron for help. Myron wasn't there. Clu felt abandoned. He had no one. In desperation he turned to his old friend Billy Lee Palms. But Billy Lee was too messed up to help anyone. He looked again for Myron. But Myron was still gone, possibly avoiding him. Clu was weak and alone, and FJ was there with promises and power.

So maybe Clu didn't have an affair with Esperanza after all. Maybe Clu told her he was leaving the agency and she got upset and then he got upset. Maybe Clu gave her a good-bye smack in that garage.

Hmm.

But there were problems with that scenario too. If there was no affair, how do you explain Esperanza's hairs at the crime scene? How do you explain the blood in the car, the gun in the office, and Esperanza's continued silence?

FJ was still smiling.

"Let's cut to it," Myron said. "How do I get you off my back?"

"Stay away from my clients."

"The same way you stayed away from mine?"

"Tell you what, Myron." FJ sipped more shaving cream. "If I desert my clients for six weeks, I give you carte blanche to pursue them with as much gusto as you can muster."

Myron looked at Win. No solace. Scary as it might sound, FJ had a point.

"Esperanza has been indicted for Clu's murder," Myron said. "I'm involved until she's cleared. Outside of that, I'll stay out of your business. And you stay out of mine."

"Suppose she's not cleared," FJ said.

"What?"

"Have you considered the possibility that Esperanza did indeed kill him?"

"You know something I don't, FJ?"

FJ put his hand to his chest. "Me?" The most innocent lamb ever to lie next to a lion. "What would I know?" He finished his coffee whatever and stood. He looked down at his goons, then at Win. Win nodded. FJ told Hans and Franz to get up. They did. FJ ordered them out the door. They went out, heads high, chests out, eyes up, but still looking like a pair of whipped dogs.

"If you find anything that might help me get Clu's contract reinstated, you'll let me know?"

"Yeah," Myron said. "I'll let you know."

"Great. Then let's stay in touch, Myron."

"Oh," Myron said. "Let's."

CHAPTER 22

They took the subway to Yankee Stadium. The 4 train was fairly empty this time of the day. After they found seats, Myron asked, "Why did you beat up those two muscleheads?"

"You know why," Win said.

"Because they challenged you?"

"I hardly call what they mustered a challenge."

"So why did you beat them up?"

"Because it was simple."

"What?"

Win hated repeating himself.

"You overreacted," Myron said. "As usual."

"No, Myron, I reacted perfectly."

"Meaning?"

"I have a reputation, do I not?"

"As a violent psycho, yes."

"Exactly—a reputation that I've culled and created through what you call overreacting. You trade off that reputation sometimes, do you not?"

"I guess I do."

"It helps us?"

"I guess so."

"Guess nothing," Win said. "Friends and foes believe I snap too easily—overreact, as you put it. That I'm unstable, out of control. But that's nonsense, of course. I'm never out of control. Just the opposite. Every attack has been well thought out. The pros and cons have been weighed."

"And in this case, the pros won?"

"Yes."

"So you knew you were going to beat up those two before we entered?"

"I considered it. Once I realized that they were unarmed and that taking them out would be easy, I made the final decision."

"Just to enhance your reputation?"

"In a word, yes. My reputation keeps us safe. Why do you think FJ was ordered by his father not to kill you?"

"Because I'm a ray of sunshine? Because I make the world a better place for all?"

Win smiled. "Then you understand."

"Does it bother you at all, Win?"

"Does what?"

"Attacking someone like that."

"They're goons, Myron, not nuns."

"Still. You just walloped them without provocation."

"Oh, I see. You don't like the fact that I suckerpunched them. You would have preferred a fairer fight?"

"I guess not. But suppose you miscalculated?"

"Highly unlikely."

"Suppose one of them was better than you thought and didn't go down so easily. Suppose you had to maim or kill one."

"They're goons, Myron, not nuns."

"So you would have done it?"

"You know the answer to that."

"I guess I do."

"Who would have mourned their passing?" Win asked. "Two scums in the night who freely chose a profession that bullies and maims."

Myron did not answer. The train stopped. Passengers exited. Myron and Win stayed in their seats.

"But you enjoy it," Myron said.

Win said nothing.

"You have other reasons, sure, but you enjoy violence."

"And you don't, Myron?"

"Not like you."

"No, not like me. But you feel the rush."

"And I usually feel sick after it's all over."

"Well, Myron, that's probably because you're such a fine humanitarian."

They exited the subway at 161st Street and walked in silence to Yankee Stadium. Four hours to game time, but there were already several hundred fans lining up to watch the warm-ups. A giant Louisville Slugger bat cast a long shadow. Cops aplenty stood near clusters of unfazed ticket scalpers. Classic détente. There were hot dog carts, some with—gasp!—Yoo-Hoo umbrellas. Yum. At the press entrance Myron flashed his business card, the guard made a call, they were let in.

They traveled down the stairs on the right, reached the stadium tunnel, and emerged into bright sunshine and green grass. Myron and Win had just been discussing the nature of violence, and now Myron thought again about his dad's phone call. Myron had seen his father, the most gentle man he had ever known, grow violent only once. And it was here at Yankee Stadium.

When Myron was ten years old, his father had taken

him and his younger brother, Brad, to a game. Brad was five at the time. Dad had secured four seats in the upper tier, but at the last minute a business associate had given him two more seats three rows behind the Red Sox bench. Brad was a huge fan of the Red Sox. So Dad suggested that Brad and Myron sit by the dugout for a few innings. Dad would stay in the upper tier. Myron held Brad's hand, and they walked down to the box seats. The seats were, in a word, awesome.

Brad started cheering his five-year-old lungs out. Cheering like mad. He spotted Carl Yastrzemski in the batter's box and started calling out, "Yaz! Yaz!" The guy sitting in front of them turned around. He was maybe twenty-five and bearded and looked a bit like a church image of Jesus. "That's enough," the bearded guy snapped at Brad. "Quiet down."

Brad looked hurt.

"Don't listen to him," Myron said. "You're allowed to yell."

The bearded man's hands moved fast. He grabbed the ten-year-old Myron by his shirt, bunching the Yankee emblem in his seemingly giant fist, and pulled Myron closer to him. There was beer on his breath. "He's giving my girlfriend a headache. He shuts up now."

Fear engulfed Myron. Tears filled his eyes, but he wouldn't let them escape. He remembered being shocked, scared, and mostly, for some unknown reason, ashamed. The bearded man glared at Myron another few seconds and then pushed him back. Myron grabbed Brad's hand and rushed back to the upper tier. He tried to pretend everything was all right, but ten-year-olds are not great actors, and Dad could read his son as if he lived inside his skull.

"What's wrong?" Dad asked.

Myron hesitated. Dad asked again. Myron finally told him what happened. And something happened to Myron's father, something Myron had never seen before or since. There was an explosion in his eyes. His face turned red; his eyes went black.

"I'll be right back," he said.

Myron watched the rest through binoculars. Dad moved down to the seat behind the Red Sox dugout. His father's face was still red. Myron saw Dad cup his hands around his mouth, lean forward, and start screaming for all he was worth. The red in his face turned to crimson. Dad kept screaming. The bearded man tried to ignore him. Dad leaned into his ear à la Mike Tyson and screamed some more. When the bearded man finally turned around, Dad did something that shocked Myron to the core. He pushed the man. He pushed the man twice and then gestured toward the exit, the international sign inviting another man to step outside. The guy with the beard refused. Dad pushed him again.

Two security guards raced down the steps and broke it up. No one was tossed. Dad came back to the upper tier. "Go back down," Dad said. "He won't bother you again."

But Myron and Brad shook their heads. They liked the seats up here better.

Win said, "Time traveling again, are we?"

Myron nodded.

"You realize, of course, that you are far too young for so many reflective spells."

"Yeah, I know."

A group of Yankee players were sitting on the outfield grass, legs sprawled, hands back, still kids under the collars waiting for their Little League game to start. A man in a too-nicely-fitted suit was talking to them. The man gestured wildly, smiling and enthusiastic and as enraptured with life as the new born-again on the block. Myron recognized him. Sawyer Wells, the motivational speaker né con man of the moment. Two years ago Wells was an unknown charlatan, spouting the standard reworded dogma about finding yourself, unlocking your potential, doing something for yourself—as though people weren't self-centered enough. His big break came when the Mayors hired him to do talks for their workforce. The speeches were, if not original, successful, and Sawyer Wells caught on. He got a book deal—cleverly monikered *The Wells Guide to Wellness*—along with an infomercial, audiotapes, video, a planner, the full self-help schematic. Fortune 500 companies started hiring him. When the Mayors took over the Yankees, they brought him on board as a consulting motivational psychologist or some such drivel.

When Sawyer Wells spotted Win, he almost started panting.

"He smells a new client," Myron said.

"Or perhaps he's never seen anyone quite this handsome before."

"Oh, yeah," Myron said. "That's probably it."

Wells turned back to the players, shouted out a bit more enthusiasm, spasmed with gestures, clapped once, and then bade them good-bye. He looked back over at Win. He waved. He waved hard. Then he started bounding over like a puppy chasing a new squeaky toy or a politician chasing a potential contributor.

Win frowned. "In a word, decaf."

Myron nodded.

"You want me to befriend him?" Win asked.

"He was supposedly present for the drug tests. And he's also the team psychologist. He probably hears a lot of rumors."

"Fine," Win said. "You take the roommate. I'll take Sawyer."

Enos Cabral was a good-looking wiry Cuban with a flame-throwing fastball and breaking pitches that still needed work. He was twenty-four, but he had the kind of looks that probably got him carded at any liquor store. He stood watching batting practice, his body slack except for his mouth. Like most relief pitchers, he chewed gum or tobacco with the ferocity of a lion gnawing on a recently downed gazelle.

Myron introduced himself.

Enos shook his hand and said, "I know who you are."

"Oh?"

"Clu talked about you a lot. He thought I should sign with you."

A pang. "Clu said that?"

"I wanted a change," Enos continued. "My agent. He treats me well, no? And he made me a rich man."

"I don't mean to knock the importance of good representation, Enos, but you made you a rich man. An agent facilitates. He doesn't create."

Enos nodded. "You know my story?"

The thumbnail sketch. The boat trip had been rough. Very rough. For a week everyone had assumed they had been lost at sea. When they finally did pop up, only two of the eight Cubans were still alive. One of the dead was Enos's brother Hector, considered the best player to come out of Cuba in the past decade. Enos, considered the lesser talent, was nearly dead of dehydration.

"Just what I've read in the papers," Myron said.

"My agent. He was there when I arrived. I had family in Miami. When he heard about the Cabral brothers, he loaned them money. He paid for my hospital stay. He gave me money and jewelry and a car. He promised me more money. And I have it.''

''So what's the problem?''

''He has no soul.''

''You want an agent with a soul?''

Enos shrugged. ''I'm Catholic,'' he said. ''We believe in miracles.''

They both laughed.

Enos seemed to be studying Myron. ''Clu was always suspicious of people. Even me. He had something of a hard shell.''

''I know,'' Myron said.

''But he believed in you. He said you were a good man. He said that he had trusted you with his life and would gladly do so again.''

Another pang. ''Clu was also a lousy judge of character.''

''I don't think so.''

''Enos, I wanted to talk to you about Clu's last few weeks.''

He raised an eyebrow. ''I thought you came here to recruit me.''

''No,'' Myron said. Then: ''But have you heard the expression *killing two birds with one stone*?''

Enos laughed. ''What do you want to know?''

''Were you surprised when Clu failed the drug test?''

He picked up a bat. He gripped and regripped it in his hands. Finding the right groove. Funny. He was an American League pitcher. He would probably never have the opportunity to bat. ''I have trouble understanding addictions,'' he said. ''Where I come from, yes, a man may try to drink away his world, if he can afford it. You live in such stink, why not leave, no? But here, when you have as much as Clu had . . .''

He didn't finish the thought. No point in stating the obvious.

"One time Clu tried to explain it to me," Enos continued. " 'Sometimes,' he said, 'you don't want to escape the world; sometimes you want to escape yourself.' " He cocked his head. "Do you believe that?"

"Not really," Myron said. "Like a lot of cute phrases, it sounds good. But it also sounds like a load of self-rationalization."

Enos smiled. "You're mad at him."

"I guess I am."

"Don't be. He was a very unhappy man, Myron. A man who needs so much excess . . . there is something broken inside him, no?"

Myron said nothing.

"Clu tried. He fought hard, you have no idea. He wouldn't go out at night. If our room had a minibar, he'd make them take it out. He didn't hang out with old friends because he was afraid of what he might do. He was scared all the time. He fought long and hard."

"And he lost," Myron added.

"I never saw him take drugs. I never saw him drink."

"But you noticed changes."

Enos nodded. "His life began to fall apart. So many bad things happened."

"What bad things?"

The organ music revved immediately into high gear, the legendary Eddie Layton opening up with his rendition of that ballpark classic "The Girl from Ipanema." Enos lifted the bat to his shoulder, then lowered it again. "I feel uncomfortable talking about this."

"I'm not prying for the fun of it. I'm trying to find out who killed him."

"The papers said your secretary did it."

"They're wrong."

Enos stared at the bat as though there were a message hidden beneath the word *Louisville*. Myron tried to prompt him.

"Clu withdrew two hundred thousand dollars not long before he died," Myron said. "Was he having financial problems?"

"If he did, I didn't see it."

"Did he gamble?"

"I didn't see him him gamble, no."

"Do you know that he changed agents?"

Enos looked surprised. "He fired you?"

"Apparently he was going to."

"I didn't know," he said. "I know he was looking for you. But no, I didn't know that."

"So what was it then, Enos? What made him cave?"

He lifted his eyes and blinked into the sun. The perfect weather for a night game. Soon fans would arrive, and memories would be made. Happened every night in stadiums around the world. It was always some kid's first game.

"His marriage," Enos said. "That was the big thing, I think. You know Bonnie?"

"Yes."

"Clu loved her very much."

"He had an odd way of showing it."

Enos smiled. "Sleeping with all those women. I think he did it more to hurt himself than anyone else."

"That sounds like another one of those big, fat rationalizations, Enos. Clu may have made self-destruction an art form. But that's not an excuse for what he put her through."

"I think he'd agree with that. But Clu hurt himself most of all."

"Don't kid yourself. He hurt Bonnie too."

"Yes, you're right, of course. But he still loved her. When she threw him out, it hurt him so much. You have no idea."

"What can you tell me about their breakup?"

Another hesitation. "Not much to tell. Clu felt betrayed, angry."

"You know that Clu had fooled around before."

"Yes."

"So what made it different this time? Bonnie was used to his straying. What made her finally snap? Who was his girlfriend?"

Enos looked puzzled. "You think Bonnie threw him out over a girl?"

"She didn't?"

Enos shook his head.

"You're sure."

"It was never about girls with Clu. They were just part of the drugs and alcohol. They were easy for him to give up."

Myron was confused. "So he wasn't having an affair?"

"No," Enos said. "*She* was."

That was when it clicked. Myron felt a cold wave roll through him, squeezing the pit of his stomach. He barely said good-bye before he hurried away.

He knew Bonnie would be home.

The car had barely come to a full stop when he shot out the driver's door. There were perhaps a dozen other vehicles parked on the street. Mourners. The front door was opened. Myron headed inside without knocking. He wanted to find Bonnie and confront her and end this. But she wasn't in the living room. Just mourners. Some approached him, slowing him down. He offered his condolences to Clu's mother, her face ravaged with grief. He shook other hands, trying to swim through the thick sea of grief-stricken and glad-handers and find Bonnie. He finally spotted her outside in the backyard. She sat alone on the deck, her knees tucked under her chin, watching her children play. He steeled himself and pushed open the sliding glass doors.

The porch was cedarwood and overlooked a large swing set. Clu's boys were on it, both dressed in red ties and untucked short-sleeve shirts. They ran and laughed. Miniature versions of their dead father, their smiles so like his, their features eternal echoes of Clu's. Bonnie watched them. Her back was to Myron, a cigarette in her hand. She did not turn around as he approached.

"Clu didn't have the affair," Myron said. "You did."

Bonnie inhaled deeply and let it out. "Great timing, Myron."

"That can't be helped."

"Can't we talk about this later?"

Myron waited a beat. Then: "I know who you were sleeping with."

She stiffened. Myron looked down at her. She finally turned and met his gaze.

"Let's take a walk," Bonnie said.

She reached out a hand, and Myron helped her to her feet.

They walked down the backyard to a wooded area. The din of traffic filtered through a sound barrier up the hill. The house was spanking new, large and innately nouveau-riche. Airy, lots of windows, cathedral ceilings, small living room, huge kitchen flowing into huge California room, huge master bedroom, closets large enough to double as Gap outlets. Probably went for about eight hundred thou. Beautiful and sterile and soulless. Needing to be lived in a bit. Properly aged like a fine Merlot.

"I didn't know you smoked," he said.

"You don't know a lot of things about me, Myron."

Touché. He looked at her profile, and again he saw that young coed heading into the fraternity basement. He flashed back to that very moment, to the sound of Clu's sharp intake of air when he first laid eyes on her. Suppose she'd come down a little later, after Clu had passed out or hooked up with another woman. Suppose she had gone to another frat party that night. Dumb thoughts—life's arbitrary forks in the road, the series of what ifs—but there you go.

"So what makes you think I was the one having an affair?" she said.

"Clu told Enos."

"Clu lied."

"No," Myron said.

They kept walking. Bonnie took a last drag and tossed the cigarette on the ground. "My property," she said. "I'm allowed."

Myron said nothing.

"Did Clu tell Enos who he thought I was sleeping with?"

"No."

"But you think you know who this mystery lover is."

"Yes," Myron said. "It's Esperanza."

Silence.

"Would you believe me if I insisted you were wrong?" she said.

"You'd have a lot of explaining to do."

"How's that?"

"Let's start with you coming to my office after Esperanza was arrested."

"Okay."

"You wanted to know what they had on her—that was the real reason. I wondered why you warned me away from finding the truth. You told me to clear my friend but not dig too hard."

She nodded. "And you think I said that because I didn't want you to know about this affair?"

"Yes. But there's more. Like Esperanza's silence, for one thing. Win and I theorized that she didn't want us to know about her affair with Clu. It would look bad on several levels to be having an affair with a client. But to be having an affair with a client's wife? What could be dumber than that?"

"That's hardly evidence, Myron."

"I'm not finished. You see, all the evidence that points to an affair between Esperanza and Clu actually points to an affair between you two. The physical evidence, for example. The pubic hairs and DNA found at the Fort Lee apartment. I started thinking about that. You and Clu lived there for a short time. Then you moved into this house. But you still had the lease on the apartment. So before you threw him out, it was empty, right?"

"Right."

"What better place to meet for a tryst? It wasn't Clu and Esperanza meeting there. It was you two."

Bonnie said nothing.

"The E-Z Pass records—most of the bridge crossings were on days when the Yankees were out of town. So Esperanza wasn't coming out to see Clu. She was coming out to see you. I checked the office phone records. She never called the apartment after you threw Clu out—only this house. Why? Clu wasn't living here. You were."

She took out another cigarette and struck a match.

"And lastly, the fight in the garage when Clu struck Esperanza. That bothered the hell out of me. Why would he hit her? Because she broke off an affair? That didn't make sense. Because he wanted to find me or was crazed from taking drugs? Again, no. I couldn't figure it out. But now the answer is obvious. Esperanza was having an affair with his wife. He blamed her for breaking up the marriage. Enos said the breakup shook him to the core. What could be worse for a psyche as fragile as Clu's than his wife having an affair with a woman?"

Her voice was sharp. "Are you blaming me for his death?"

"Depends. Did you kill him?"

"Would it help if I said no?"

"It would be a start."

She smiled, but there was no joy in it. Like the house, it was beautiful and sterile and almost soulless. "Do you want to hear something funny?" she said. "Clu's beating the drugs and the drinking didn't help our marriage—it ended it. For so long Clu was . . . I don't know . . . a work in progress. I blamed his shortcomings on the drugs and drinking and all that. But once he finally exorcised his demons, what was left was just"—she lifted her palms and shrugged—"just him. I saw Clu clearly for the first time, Myron, and you know what I realized? I didn't love him."

Myron said nothing.

"And don't blame Esperanza. It wasn't her fault. I held on purely for the sake of my kids, and when Esperanza came along—" Bonnie stopped, and this time her smile seemed more genuine. "You want to hear something else funny? I'm not a lesbian. I'm not even a bisexual. It's just . . . she treated me tenderly. We had sex, sure, but it was never about sex. I know that sounds weird, but her gender was irrelevant. Esperanza is just a beautiful person, and I fell in love with that. Does that make sense?"

"You know how this looks," Myron said.

"Of course I know how it looks. Two dykes got together and offed the husband. Why do you think we're trying so hard to keep it secret? The weakness in their case right now is motive. But if they find out we were lovers—"

"Did you kill him?"

"What do you expect me to say to that, Myron?"

"I'd like to hear it."

"No, we didn't kill him. I was leaving him. Why would I throw him out and start filing papers if I planned on killing him?"

"To prevent a scandal that would surely hurt your kids."

She made a face. "Come on, Myron."

"So how do you explain the gun in the office and the blood in the car?"

"I can't."

Myron thought about it. His head hurt—from the physical altercation or this latest revelation, he couldn't say. He tried to concentrate through the haze. "Who else knows about the affair?"

"Just Esperanza's lawyer, Hester Crimstein."

"No one else?"

"No one. We were very discreet."

"You're sure?"

"Yes. Why?"

"Because," Myron said, "if I were going to murder Clu and I wanted to frame someone for it, his wife's lover would be my first choice."

Bonnie saw where he was heading. "So you think the killer knew about us?"

"It might explain a lot."

"I didn't tell anyone. And Esperanza said she didn't either."

Pow. Right between the eyes. "You couldn't have been too careful," Myron said.

"What makes you say that?"

"Clu found out, didn't he?"

She thought about it, nodded.

"Did you tell him?" he asked.

"No."

"What did you say when you threw him out?"

She shrugged. "That there was no one else. That was true in a sense. It wasn't about Esperanza."

"So how did he find out?"

"I don't know. I assumed he became obsessed. That he followed me."

"And he found out the truth?"

"Yes."

"And then he went after Esperanza and attacked her?"

"Yes."

"And before he has a chance to tell anyone else about this, before it has a chance of getting out and hurting either of you, he ends up dead. And the murder weapon ends up with Esperanza. And Clu's blood ends up in the car she's been driving. And the E-Z Pass records show Esperanza came back to New York an hour after the murder."

"Again, yes."

Myron shook his head. "It doesn't look good, Bonnie."

"That's what I've been trying to tell you," she said. "If even you won't believe us, how do you think a jury is going to react?"

There was no need to answer. They headed back to the house then. The two young boys were still at play, oblivious of what was going on around them. Myron watched for a moment. *Fatherless,* he thought, shuddering at the word. With one last look he turned and walked away.

CHAPTER 24

Thrill, not Nancy Sinclair, met him outside a bar called the Biker Wannabee. Honesty in advertising. Nice to see.

"Howdy," Myron said. Tex Bolitar.

Her smile was full of pornographic promise. Totally into Thrill mode now. "Howdy yourself, pardner," she cooed. With some women, every syllable is cooed. "How do I look?"

"Mighty tasty, ma'am. But I think I prefer you as Nancy."

"Liar."

Myron shrugged, not sure if he was telling the truth or not. This whole thing reminded him of when Barbara Eden would play her evil sister on *I Dream of Jeannie*. He was often torn back then too, not sure if Larry Hagman should stay with Jeannie or run off with the enticingly evil sister. But hey, talk about your great dilemmas.

"I thought you were bringing backup," Thrill said.

"I am."

"Where is he?"

"If things go well, you won't see him."

"How mysterious."

"Isn't it?"

They headed inside and grabbed a corner booth in the back. Yep, biker wanna-be. Lots of guys aiming for that hairy, Vietnam vet–cum–hit-the-road look. The jukebox played "God Only Knows (What I'd Be Without You)" —the Beach Boys, but unlike anything else the Beach Boys did. The song was a plaintive wail, and despite its pop misgivings, it always struck Myron to the bone, the trepidation of what the future might hold so naked in Brian's voice, the words so hauntingly simple. Especially now.

Thrill was studying his face. "You okay?" she asked.

"Fine. So what happens next?"

"We order a drink, I guess."

Five minutes passed. "Lonely Boy" came on the jukebox. Andrew Gold. Serious seventies AM bubble gum. Chorus: "Oh, oh, oh . . . oh what a lonely boy . . . oh what a lonely boy . . . oh what a lonely boy." By the time the chorus was repeated for the eighth time, Myron had it down pat so he sang along. Megamemory. Maybe he should do an infomercial.

Men at nearby tables checked out Thrill, some surreptitiously, most not. Thrill's smile was practically a leer now, sinking deeper into the role.

"You get into this," Myron said.

"It's a part, Myron. We're all actors on a stage and all that."

"But you enjoy the attention."

"So?"

"So I was just saying."

She shrugged. "I find it fascinating."

"What's that?"

"What a large bosom does to a man. They get so obsessed."

"You just reached the conclusion that men are mammary-obsessed? I hate to break this to you, Nancy, but the research has been done."

"But it's weird when you think about it."

"I try not to."

"Bosoms do weird things to men, no doubt," she said, "but I don't like what they do to women either."

"How's that?"

Thrill put her palms on the table. "Okay, everyone knows that we women put too much of our self-worth into our bodies. Old news, right?"

"Right."

"I know it, you know it, everyone knows it. And unlike my more feminist sisters, I don't blame men for this."

"You don't?"

"*Mademoiselle, Vogue, Bazaar, Glamour*—those are run by women and have a totally female clientele. They want to change the image, start there. Why ask the men to change a perception that women themselves won't change?"

"Refreshing viewpoint," Myron noted.

"But bosoms do funny things to people. Men, okay, that's obvious. They become brain-dead. It's as if the nipples shoot out like two grapefruit spoons, dig into their frontal lobe, and scrape away all cognitive thought."

Myron looked up, the imagery giving him pause.

"But for women, well, it starts when you're young. A girl develops early. Adolescent boys start lusting after her. How do her girlfriends react? They take it out on her. They're jealous of the attention or feeling inadequate or whatever. But they take it out on the young girl who can't help what her body is going through. With me?"

"Yes."

"Even now. Look at the glances the women in here

give me. Pure hatred. You get a group of women together and a chesty counterpart walks by and they all sigh, 'Oh, please.' Professional women, for example, feel the urge to dress down—not just because of leering men but because of women. Because of how women treat them. A businesswoman sees a big-chested businesswoman with a better title—well, she got the job because of her tits. Plain and simple. Might be true, might not be. Is this animosity spawned again from dormant jealousy or a misplaced feeling of inadequacy or because they unfairly equate bosoms with stupidity? Any way you look at it, it's an ugly thing.''

''I never really thought about it,'' Myron said.

''And finally I don't like what it does to me.''

''Your reaction to seeing a big chest or having one?''

''The latter.''

''Why?''

''Because the big-breasted woman gets used to it. She takes it for granted. She uses them to her advantage.''

''So?''

''What do you mean, so?''

''All attractive people do that,'' Myron said. ''It's not just bosoms. If a woman is beautiful, she knows it and uses it. Nothing wrong with that. Men use it too, if they can. Sometimes—I'm ashamed to admit this—even I shake my little tush to get my way.''

''Shocking.''

''Well, not really. Because it never works.''

''I think you're being modest. But either way, don't you see anything wrong with that?''

''With what?''

''With using a physical attribute to get your way.''

''I didn't say there was nothing wrong with it. I'm simply noting that what you're talking about is not merely a mammarial phenomenon.''

She made a face. "Mammarial phenomenon?"

Myron shrugged, and mercifully the waitress came over. Myron made a point of not looking anywhere near her chest, which was tantamount to telling yourself not to scratch that irksome itch. The waitress had a pen behind her ear. Her overtreated hair aimed for on-the-farm strawberry blond but landed far closer to fell-at-the-4H-fair cotton candy.

"Get you?" she said. Skipping the preliminaries like "Hello" and "What can I . . . ?"

"Rob Roy," Thrill said.

The pen came out of the ear holster, jotted it down, back in the holster. Wyatt Earp. "You?" she said to Myron.

Myron doubted that they had any Yoo-Hoo. "A diet soda, please."

She looked at him as if he'd ordered a bedpan.

"Maybe a beer," Myron said.

She clacked her gum. "Bud, Michelob, or some pansy brew?"

"Pansy would be fine, thank you," Myron said. "And do you have any of those little cocktail umbrellas?"

The waitress rolled her eyes and walked away.

They chatted for a while. Myron had just started relaxing and yes, even enjoying himself when Thrill said, "Behind you. By the door."

He was not much in the mood for clandestine games. They wanted him here for a reason. No sense beating around the bush. He turned without an iota of subtlety and spotted Pat the bartender and Veronica Lake aka Zorra dressed again in a cashmere sweater—peach-toned, for those keeping score—long skirt, and a strand of pearls. Zorra, the Steroid Debutante. Myron shook his head. Bonnie Franklin and Mall Girl were nowhere to be seen.

Myron gave a big wave. "Over here, fellas!"

Pat scowled, feigning surprise. He looked toward Zorra, She-Man of the Saber Heel. Zorra showed nothing. The great ones never do. Myron always wondered if their blaséness was an act or if, in truth, nothing really surprised them. Probably a bit of both.

Pat strode toward their table, acting as though he were shocked—shocked!—that Myron was in his bar. Zorra followed, more gliding than walking, the eyes soaking in everything. Like Win, Zorra moved economically—albeit in stylish red pumps—no motion wasted. Pat was still scowling when he reached the table.

"What the hell are you doing here, Bolitar?" Pat asked.

Myron nodded. "Not bad, but it could use work. Do me a favor. Try it again. But add a little gasp first. Gasp, what the hell are you doing here, Bolitar? Like that. Better yet, why not give a wry shake of your head and say something like 'All the gin joints in all the world, you have to walk into mine—two nights in a row.' "

Zorra was smiling now.

"You're crazy," Pat said.

"Pat." It was Zorra. He looked at Pat and shook his head just once. The shake said, Stop with the games.

Pat turned to Thrill. "Do me a favor, hon."

Thrill offered up breathless. "Sure, Pat."

"Go powder your nose or something, okay?"

Myron made a face. "Go powder your nose?" He looked pleadingly at Zorra. Zorra's small shrug was semiapologetic. "What next, Pat? You going to threaten to make me sleep with the fishes? Make me an offer I can't refuse. I mean, go powder your nose?"

Pat was fuming. He looked over at Thrill. "Please, hon."

"No problem, Pat." She slid out of the booth. Pat and Zorra immediately took her place. Myron frowned at the change in scenery.

"We need some information," Pat said.

"Yeah, I picked up on that last night," Myron said.

"That got out of control. I'm sorry."

"I bet."

"Hey, we let you go, right?"

"As soon as I was electrocuted with a cattle prod, slashed twice with a heel blade, kicked in the ribs, and then jumped through a glass mirror. Yeah, you let me go."

Pat smiled. "If Zorra here didn't want you to escape, you wouldn't have escaped. Get my meaning?"

Myron looked at Zorra. Zorra looked at Myron. Myron said, "A peach sweater with red pumps?"

Zorra smiled, shrugged.

"Zorra here could have killed you easy as pie," Pat continued.

"Right, fine, Zorra is a tough guy, you're super-generous to me. Get to it."

"Why were you asking about Clu Haid?"

"Sorry to disappoint you, but I was telling you the truth last night. I'm trying to find his killer."

"So what does my club have to do with that?"

"Before I got dragged into the back room, I would have said, 'Nothing.' But now, well, that's what I'd like to know."

Pat looked at Zorra. Zorra did not move. Pat said, "We want to take you for a ride."

"Damn."

"What?"

"You'd gone nearly three minutes without a mob cliché. Then you come up with the take a ride bit. It's sad really. Can I powder my nose first?"

"You want to crack wise or you want to come with us?"

"I can do both," Myron said. "I'm rather multi-talented."

Pat shook his head. "Let's go." Myron started to slide out the booth.

"No," Zorra said.

Everyone stopped. "What's wrong?" Pat said.

Zorra looked at Myron. "We are not interested in hurting you," Zorra said.

More reassurances.

"But we can't let you know where you're going, dreamboat. You'll have to be blindfolded."

"You're kidding, right?"

"No."

"Fine, blindfold me. Let's go."

"No," Zorra said again.

"What now?"

"Your friend Win. Zorra assumes he's close by."

"Who?"

Zorra smiled. He-she wasn't pretty. Lots of transvestites are. Lots of times you can't even tell. But Zorra had a five o'clock shadow (a look Myron found to be less than alluring in a woman), big hands with hairy knuckles (ditto), a skewered wig (call him picky), a rather masculine, whispery voice (*comme ci, comme ça*) and despite the outer trappings, Zorra looked like, well, à guy wearing a dress. "Don't insult Zorra's intelligence, dreamboat."

"You see him?"

"If Zorra could," Zorra said, "then someone has grossly overexaggerated his reputation."

"So what makes you so sure Win's here?"

"You're doing it again," Zorra said.

"Doing what?"

"Insulting Zorra's intelligence."

Nothing like a psycho who refers to himself in the third person.

"Please ask him to come forward," Zorra said. "We have no interest in hurting anyone. But Zorra knows that your colleague will follow wherever you go. Then Zorra will have to follow him. It will lead to conflict. None of us wants that."

Win's voice came from Myron's cell phone. Must have taken off the mute. "What guarantee do we have that Myron will return?"

Myron lifted the cell phone into view.

"You and Zorra will sit and enjoy a drink, dreamboat," Zorra said into the phone. "Myron will travel with Pat."

"Travel where?" Myron asked.

"We can't tell you."

Myron frowned. "Is this cloak-and-dagger stuff really necessary?"

Pat leaned back now, letting Zorra handle it. "You have questions, we have questions," Zorra said. "This meeting is the only way to satisfy both."

"So why can't we talk here?"

"Impossible."

"Why?"

"You have to go with Pat."

"Where?"

"Zorra cannot tell you."

"Who are you taking me to see?"

"Zorra cannot tell you that either."

Myron said, "Does the fate of the free world rest in Zorra's maintaining silence?"

Zorra adjusted his lips, forming what he probably read someplace was known as a smile. "You mock Zorra. But Zorra has kept silent before. Zorra has seen horrors you cannot imagine. Zorra has been tortured. For weeks on end. Zorra has felt pain that makes what you felt with that cattle prod seem like a lover's kiss.''

Myron nodded solemnly. "Wow," he said.

Zorra spread his hands. Hairy knuckles and pink nail polish. Hold me back. "We can always choose to part ways, dreamboat."

From the cell phone Win said, "Good idea."

Myron lifted the receiver. "What?"

"If we agree to their terms," Win said, "I cannot guarantee they won't kill you."

"Zorra guarantees it," Zorra said. "With her life."

Myron said, "Excuse me?"

"Zorra stays here with Win," Zorra went on, the glint in the overmascaraed eye sparkling anew. Something was there, and it was not lucidity. "Zorra will be unarmed. If you don't return in perfect health, Win kills Zorra."

"Heck of a guarantee," Myron said. "Ever thought about becoming a car mechanic?"

Win entered the bar now. He walked straight toward the table, sat down, hands under it. "If you'd be so kind," Win said to Zorra and Pat, "please put all hands on the table."

They did.

"And, Ms. Zorra, if you wouldn't mind kicking off your heels?"

"Sure, dreamboat." Win kept his eyes on Zorra. Zorra kept his on Win. There would be no blinking here. Win said, "I still cannot guarantee his safety. Yes, I have the option of killing you if he does not return. But for all I know, Pat the Bunny here doesn't give a rodent's buttocks about you."

"Hey," Pat said, "you have my word."

Win just looked at him for a moment. Then he turned

back to Zorra. "Myron goes armed. Pat drives. Myron keeps the gun on him."

Zorra shook his head. "Impossible."

"Then we have no deal."

Zorra shrugged. "Then Zorra and Pat must bid you adieu."

They rose to leave. Myron knew that Win wouldn't call them back. He whispered to Win, "I need to know what's going on here."

Win shrugged. "It's a mistake," he said, "but it's your call."

Myron looked up. "We agree," he said.

Zorra sat back down. Under the table Win kept the gun on him.

"Myron keeps his cell phone on," Win said. "I listen to every word."

Zorra nodded. "Fair enough."

Pat and Myron started to leave.

"Oh, Pat?" Win said.

Pat stopped.

Win's voice was how's-the-weather casual. "If Myron isn't returned, I may or may not kill Zorra. I will decide at the appropriate time. Either way, I will use all my considerable influence and money and time and effort to find you. I will offer rewards. I will search. I will not sleep. I will find you. And when I do, I *won't* kill you. Do you understand?"

Pat swallowed, nodded.

"Go," Win said.

CHAPTER 25

When they reached the car, Pat frisked him. Nothing. Then he handed Myron a black hood. "Put this on."

Myron made a face. "Tell me you're joking."

"Put it on. Then lie down in the backseat. Don't look up."

Myron rolled his eyes, but he did as he was asked. His six-four frame wasn't all that comfortable, but he made do. Big of him. Pat got in the front seat and started the car.

"Quick suggestion," Myron said.

"What did you say?"

"Next time you do this, try vacuuming out the car first. It's disgusting back here."

Pat drove. Myron tried to concentrate, listening for sounds that would give him a clue where they were going. That always worked on TV. The guy would hear, say, a boat horn and know he'd gone to Pier 12 or something, and they'd all rush in and find him. But all Myron heard were, not surprisingly, traffic noises: the occasional horn, cars passing or being passed, loud radios, that kind of thing. He tried to keep track of turns and distances but quickly realized the futility. What did he think he was, a human compass?

The drive lasted maybe ten minutes. Not enough time to leave the city. Clue: He was still in Manhattan. Gee, that was helpful. Pat turned off the engine.

"You can sit up," he said. "But keep the hood on."

"You sure the hood goes with this ensemble? I want to look my best for Mr. Big."

"Someone once tell you were funny, Bolitar?"

"You're right. Black goes with everything."

Pat sighed. When nervous, some people run. Some hide. Some grow silent. Some get chatty. And some make dumb jokes.

Pat helped Myron out of the car and led him by the elbow. Myron again tried to pick up sounds. The cooing of a seagull maybe. That too always seemed to happen on TV. But in New York seagulls didn't coo as much as phlegm cough. And if you heard a seagull in New York, it was more likely you were near a trash canister than a pier. Myron tried to think of the last time he had seen a seagull in New York. There was a picture of one on a sign for his favorite bagel store. Caption: "If a bird flying over the sea is a seagull, what do you call a bird flying over the bay?" Clever when you think about it.

The two men walked—where to, Myron had no idea. He stumbled on uneven pavement, but Pat kept him upright. Another clue. Find the spot in Manhattan with uneven pavement. Christ, he practically had the guy cornered.

They walked up what felt like a stoop and entered a room with heat and humidity slightly more stifling than a Burmese forest fire. Myron was still blindfolded, but light from what might be a bare bulb filtered through the cloth. The room reeked of mildew and steam and dried sweat—

like the most popular sauna at Jack La Lanne's gone to seed. It was hard to breathe through the hood. Pat put a hand on Myron's shoulder.

"Sit," Pat said before pushing down slightly.

Myron sat. He heard Pat's footsteps, then low voices. Whispers actually. Mostly from Pat. An argument of some sort. Footsteps again. Coming closer to Myron. A body suddenly cut off the bare lightbulb, bathing Myron in total darkness. One more step. Someone stopped directly over him.

"Hello, Myron," the voice said.

There was a tremor there, an almost manic twang in the tone. But there was no doubt. Myron was not great with names and faces, but voices were imprints. Memories flooded in. After all these years his recall was instantaneous.

"Hello, Billy Lee."

The missing Billy Lee Palms, to be exact. Former frat brother and Duke baseball star. Former best bud of Clu Haid. Son of Mrs. My-Life-Is-but-a-Wallpaper-Tapestry.

"Mind if I take the hood off now?" Myron asked.

"Not at all."

Myron reached up and grabbed the top of the hood. He pulled it off. Billy Lee was standing over him. Or at least he assumed it was Billy Lee. It was as if the former pretty boy had been kidnapped and replaced with this fleshier counterpart. Billy Lee's formerly prominent cheekbones looked malleable, tallow skin in mid-shed clung to sagging features, his eyes sunken deeper than any pirate treasure, his complexion the gray of a city street after a rainfall. His hair was greasy and jutting all over the place, as unwashed as any MTV video jockey's.

Billy Lee was also holding what looked liked a sawed-off shotgun about six inches from Myron's face.

"He's holding what looks like a sawed-off shotgun about six inches from my face," Myron said for the benefit of the cell phone.

Billy Lee giggled. That sound too was familiar.

"Bonnie Franklin," Myron said.

"What?"

"Last night. You were the one who hit me with the cattle prod."

Billy Lee spread his hands impossibly wide. "Bingo, baby!"

Myron shook his head. "You definitely look better with the makeup, Billy Lee."

Billy Lee giggled again and retrained the shotgun on Myron. Then he held out his free hand. "Give me the phone."

Myron hesitated but not for long. The sunken eyes, once Myron could see them, were wet and unfocused and tinged with a dull red. Billy Lee's body was one tremor. Myron checked out the short sleeves and saw the needle tracks. Billy Lee looked like the wildest and most unpredictable of animals: a cornered junkie. Myron handed him the phone. Billy Lee put it to his ear.

"Win?"

Win's voice was clear. "Yes, Billy Lee."

"Go to hell."

Billy Lee giggled again. Then he clicked off the phone, untethering them from the outside world, and Myron felt the dread rise in his chest.

Billy Lee stuck the phone in Myron's pocket and looked over at Pat. "Tie him to the chair."

Pat said, "What?"

"Tie him to the chair. There's rope right behind it."

"Tie him how? I look like a goddamn Boy Scout?"

"Just wrap it around him and tie a knot. I want to slow him down in case he gets dumb before I kill him."

Pat moved toward Myron. Billy Lee kept an eye on Myron.

Myron said, "It's not really a good idea to upset Win."

"Win doesn't scare me."

Myron shook his head.

"What?"

"I knew you were strung out," Myron said. "But I didn't realize how badly."

Pat started winding the rope around Myron's chest. "Maybe you should call him back," Pat said. If the San Andreas quaked like his voice, they'd be calling for an evacuation. "We don't need him searching for us too, you know what I'm saying?"

"Don't worry about it," Billy Lee said.

"And Zorra's still there—"

"Don't worry about it!" Screaming this time. A shrill, awful scream. The shotgun bounced closer to Myron's face. Myron tensed his body, preparing to make a move before the rope was knotted. But Billy Lee jumped back suddenly, as if realizing for the first time that Myron was in the room.

Nobody spoke. Pat tightened the rope and tied it in a knot. Not well done, but it'd serve its stated purpose—i.e., slow him down so that Billy Lee would have plenty of time to blow Myron's head off.

"You trying to kill me, Myron?"

Strange question. "No," Myron said.

Billy Lee's fist slammed into the lower part of Myron's belly. Myron doubled over, the air gone, his lungs spasming in the pure, naked need for oxygen. He felt tears push into his eyes.

"Don't lie to me, asshole."

Myron fought for breath.

Billy Lee sniffed, wiped his face with his sleeve. "Why are you trying to kill me?"

Myron tried to respond, but it took too long. Billy Lee hit him hard with the butt of the shotgun, exactly on the Z spot Zorra had sliced into him the night before. The stitches split apart, and blood mushroomed onto Myron's shirt. His head began to swim. Billy Lee giggled some more. Then he raised the butt of the shotgun over his head and started it in an arc toward Myron's head.

"Billy Lee!" Pat shouted.

Myron saw it coming, but there was no escape. He managed to tilt the chair with his toes and roll back. The blow glanced the top of his head, scraping his scalp. The chair teetered over, and Myron's head banged against the wooden floor. His skull tingled.

Oh Christ . . .

He looked up. Billy Lee was raising the butt of the shotgun again. A straight blow would crush his skull. Myron tried to roll, but he was hopelessly tangled up. Billy Lee smiled down at him. He held the shotgun high above his head, letting the moment drag out, watching Myron struggle the way some people watch an injured ant before stomping it with their foot.

Billy Lee suddenly frowned. He lowered the weapon, studying it for a moment. "Hmm," he said. "Might break my gun that way."

Myron felt Billy Lee grab his shoulders and lift him and the chair back up. The shotgun was at eye level now.

"Fuck it," Billy Lee said. "Might as well just shoot your sorry ass, am I right?"

Myron barely heard the giggling now. When a gun is pointed so directly in your face, it has a tendency to block out everything else. The double barrel's opening grows, moves closer, surrounds you until everything you are and see and hear is consumed in its black mouth.

Pat tried again. "Billy Lee . . ."

Myron felt the sweat under his arms begin to gush. Calm. Keep the tone calm. Don't excite him. "Tell me what's going on, Billy Lee. I want to help."

Billy Lee snickered, the shotgun still shaking in his hand. "You want to help me?"

"Yes."

That made him laugh. "Bullshit, Myron. Total bullshit."

Myron kept still.

"We were never even friends, were we, Myron? I mean, we were frat brothers, and we hung out and stuff. But we were never really friends."

Myron tried to keep his eyes on Billy Lee's. "This is a heck of a time to go tiptoeing through the past, Billy Lee."

"I'm trying to make a point here, asshole. You're peddling this crap about wanting to help me. Like we're friends. But that's a load of bullshit. We're not friends. You never really liked me."

Never really liked me. Like they were third graders during recess. "I still helped pull your ass out of a few fires, Billy Lee."

The smile. "Not my ass, Myron. Clu's. It was always about Clu, wasn't it? The drunk driving thing when we were living in Massachusetts. You didn't drive up to save my ass. You drove up because of Clu. And that brawl at that bar in the city. That was also because of Clu."

Billy Lee suddenly tilted his head like a dog hearing a new sound. "Why weren't we friends, Myron?"

"Because you didn't invite me to your birthday party at the roller rink?"

"Don't fuck with me, asshole."

"I liked you just fine, Billy Lee. You were a fun guy."

"But it got tired after a while, didn't it? My whole act, I mean. While I was a college star, it was pretty cool, right? But when I failed in the pros, I wasn't so cute and funny anymore. I was suddenly pathetic. That sound about right, Myron?"

"You say so."

"So what about Clu?"

"What about him?"

"You were friends with him."

"Yes."

"Why? Clu partied the same way. Maybe even harder. He was always getting his ass in trouble. Why were you his friend?"

"This is stupid, Billy Lee."

"Is it?"

"Put the gun down already."

Billy Lee's smile was wide and knowing and somewhere just south of sane. "I'll tell you why you stayed friendly with Clu. Because he was a better baseball player than me. He was going to the bigs. And you knew that. That's the only difference between Clu Haid and Billy Lee Palms. He got drunk and took drugs and screwed tons of women, but it was all so funny because he was a pro."

"So what are you trying to say, Billy Lee?" Myron countered. "That pro athletes are treated differently from the rest of us? Hell of a revelation."

But the revelation sat uneasily on Myron. Probably because Billy Lee's words, while wholly irrelevant, were at least in part true. Clu was charming and quirky simply because he was a pro athlete. But if the velocity of his fastball had dropped a few miles per hour, if the rotation of his arm had been just a little askew or if his finger position had not allowed for good ball movement on his pitches, Clu would have ended up like Billy Lee. Alternate worlds—totally different lives and fates—are right there, separated by a curtain no thicker than membrane. But with athletes, you can see your alternate life a little too clearly. You have the ability to throw the ball just a little faster than the next guy, you end up a god rather than the most pitiful of mortals. You get the girls, the fame, the big house, the money instead of the rats, the dull anonymity, the crummy apartment, the menial job. You get to go on TV and offer life insights. People want to be near you and hear you speak and touch the hem of your cloak. Just because you can hurl the rawhide with great velocity or put an orange ball in a metallic circle or swing a stick with a slightly more pure arc. You are special.

Nuts when you think about it.

"Did you kill him, Billy Lee?" Myron said.

Billy Lee looked like he'd been slapped. "What?"

"You were jealous of Clu. He had everything. He left you behind."

"He was my best friend!"

"A long time ago, Billy Lee."

Myron again debated making a move. He could try to slip the ropes—they were not on very tightly—but it would take time and he was still too far away. He wondered how Win was reacting to being cut off from all this and shuddered. Not worth dwelling upon.

A funny, tranquil flat line crossed Billy Lee's face. He stopped shaking, looked straight at Myron without jerking or twitching. His voice was suddenly soft.

"Enough," he said.

Silence.

"I have to kill you, Myron. It's self-defense."

"What are you talking about?"

"You killed Clu. And now you want to kill me."

"That's crazy."

"Maybe you had your secretary do it. And she got caught. Or maybe Win did it. That guy's always been your lapdog. Or maybe you did it yourself, Myron. The gun was found in your office, right? The blood in your car?"

"Why would I kill Clu?"

"You use people, Myron. You used him to start up your business. But after he failed his last drug test, Clu was finished. So you figured, why not cut your losses?"

"That makes no sense," Myron said. "And even if it did, why would I want to kill you?"

"Because I can talk too."

"Talk about what?"

"About how helpful you are."

Tears started rolling down Billy Lee's face. His voice tailed off. And Myron knew he was in huge trouble.

The moment of calm was over. The barrel of the gun was shaking. Myron tested the ropes. Nope. Despite the heat, something icy flooded his veins. He was trapped. No chance of making a move.

Billy Lee tried to giggle again, but something inside him was too weary now. "Bye."

Panic squeezed Myron's insides. Billy Lee was only seconds away from killing him. Period. There was no chance of talking him out of it. The combo of drugs and paranoia had scooped out all his ability to reason. Myron accessed his options and liked none of them.

"Win," Myron said.

"I already told you. I ain't afraid of him."

"I'm not talking to you." Myron glanced over at Pat. The bartender was breathing hard, and his shoulders were drooping as though someone had packed them with wet sand. "Once he pulls that trigger," Myron said to him, "I'm better off than you are."

Pat started toward Billy Lee. "Let's just calm down a second, Billy Lee. Think this through, okay?"

"I'm going to kill him."

"Billy Lee, this Win guy. I've heard stories—"

"You don't understand, Pat. You just don't get it."

"Then tell me, man. I'm here to help."

"After I kill him."

Billy Lee stepped toward Myron. He put the barrel of the gun against Myron's temple. Myron went rigid.

"Don't!"

Pat was close enough now. Or at least that was what he thought. He made his move, diving for Billy Lee's legs. But beneath the diminished drug addict lurked some of the athlete's old reflexes. Enough of them anyway. Billy Lee spun and fired. The bullet hit Pat's chest. For the briefest moment Pat looked surprised. Then he went down.

Billy Lee screamed, "Pat!" He dropped onto his knees and crawled toward the still body.

Myron's heart was flapping like a caged condor. He did not wait. He struggled with the ropes. No go. He slid down in a frenzied slither. The rope was tighter than he thought, but he made some headway.

"Pat!" Billy Lee screamed again.

Myron's knees were on the floor now, his body contorted, his spine bow-bending in a way it was never supposed to. Billy Lee was wailing over a too-silent Pat. The rope got caught under Myron's chin, pushing his head back and temporarily strangling him. How long did he have? How long before Billy Lee regained his senses? Impossible to say. Myron tilted his chin even higher, and the rope began to pass over him. He was almost out.

Billy Lee startled and turned around.

Myron was still caught in the rope. The two men locked eyes. It was over. Billy Lee lifted the shotgun. Maybe eight feet separated them. Myron saw the barrel, saw Billy Lee's eyes, saw the distance.

No chance. Too late.

The gun fired.

The first bullet hit Billy Lee's hand. He screamed in pain and dropped the shotgun. The second bullet hit Billy Lee's knee. Another scream. Blood spurted. The third bullet came so fast Billy Lee didn't have time to hit the floor. His head flew back from the impact, his legs splaying in midair. Billy Lee dropped out of sight like something at a shooting gallery.

The room was still.

Myron pulled the rope the rest of the way off and rolled into a corner.

"Win?" he shouted.

No answer.

"Win?"

Nothing.

Pat and Billy Lee did not so much as twitch. Myron stood, the only sound his own breath. Blood. Everywhere blood. They had to be dead. Myron pressed back into the corner. Someone was watching him. He knew that now. He crossed the room and looked out a window. He looked left. Nothing. He looked right.

Someone stood in the shadows. A silhouette. Fear engulfed Myron. The silhouette seemed to hover and then vanished into the darkness. Myron spun around and found the doorknob. He threw the door open and began to run.

CHAPTER 26

He vomited three blocks away. He pulled up, leaned against a building, and puked his guts out. Several homeless men stopped and applauded. Myron gave a wave, acknowledging his fans. Welcome to New York.

Myron tried his cell phone, but it'd been crushed in the melee. He found a street sign and saw that he was only ten blocks south of the Biker Wannabee bar, in the meatpacking district near the West Side Highway. He jogged, holding his side, trying to stop the blood flow. He located a working pay phone, a feat that in this section of Manhattan normally involved a burning bush, and dialed Win's cellular.

Win picked up on the first ring. "Articulate."

"They're dead," Myron said. "Both of them."

"Explain."

Myron did.

When he finished, Win said, "I'll be there in three minutes."

"I have to call the cops."

"Unwise."

"Why?"

"They will not believe your tale of woe," Win said, "especially the part about a mystery savior."

"Meaning they'll think you killed them?"

"Precisely."

Win had a point.

"But we'd be able to clear it up," Myron said.

"Yes perhaps, eventually. But it would take serious time."

"Time we don't have."

"Then you understand."

Myron thought about it. "But witnesses saw me leave the bar with Pat."

"So?"

"So the police will question people. They'll learn about that. They'll be able to place me at the scene."

"No more."

"What?"

"On the phone. No more discussion. I'll be there in three minutes."

"What about Zorra? What did you do to him?"

But Win was already off the line. Myron hung up the phone. A new set of homeless guys eyed him like he was a dropped sandwich. Myron met their gaze and did not look away until they did. He was not in the mood to be afraid anymore tonight.

A car pulled up in the promised three minutes. A Chevy Nova. Win had a collection of them—all old, all very used, all untraceable. Disposable cars, he called them. Win liked to use them for certain night activities. Don't ask.

The front passenger door opened. Myron glanced inside and saw Win behind the wheel. Myron slid in next to him.

"The die is cast," Win said.

"What?"

"The police are already at the scene. It was on the scanner."

Bad news. "I can still come forward."

"Yes, of course. And why, Mr. Bolitar, did you not call the police? Why, in fact, did you call your friend before the proper authorities? Are you or are you not suspected of aiding Ms. Esperanza Diaz in the murder of Billy Lee Palms's oldest friend? What exactly were you doing in that bar in the first place? Why would Mr. Palms want to kill you?"

"It can all be explained."

Win shrugged. "Your call."

"Just as it was my call to go alone with Pat."

"Yes."

"Which I called wrong."

"Yes. You were too vulnerable going in like that. There were other ways."

"What other ways?"

"We could have grabbed Pat at another time and made him tell us."

"Made him?"

"Yes."

"You mean, rough him up? Or torture him?"

"Yes."

"I don't do that."

"Grow up," Win said. "It is a simple cost-benefit analysis: By causing temporary discomfort to a malfeasant, you greatly lower the risk of being killed. It's a no-brainer." Win glanced at him. "By the way, you look like hell."

"You should see the other guy," he said. Then: "Did you kill Zorra?"

Win smiled. "You know me better than that."

"No, Win, I don't. Did you kill him?"

Win pulled up to the Biker Wannabee bar. He put the car in park. "Take a look inside."

"Why are we back here?"

"Two reasons. One, you never left."

"I didn't?"

"That's what I'll swear to. You were here all night. You just walked Pat out for a moment. Thrill will back me on it." He smiled. "So will Zorra."

"You didn't kill him?"

"Her. Zorra prefers to be called a her."

"Her. You didn't kill her?"

"Of course not."

They got out of the car.

"I'm surprised," Myron said.

"Why?"

"Usually when you threaten—"

"I never threatened Zorra. I threatened Pat. I said I *may* kill Zorra. But what would have been the point? Should Zorra suffer because a drugged-out psychotic like Billy Lee Palms hangs up a phone? Methinks not."

Myron shook his head. "You're a constant surprise."

Win stopped. "And lately you're a constant screwup. You got lucky. Zorra said she'd be willing to use her life to guarantee your safety. I recognized that she couldn't do it. It's why I told you not to go."

"I didn't think I had a choice."

"Now you know better."

"Maybe."

Win put a stilling hand on Myron's arm. "You're not over her yet. Esperanza has a point when she tells you that."

Myron nodded. Win dropped his arm.

"Take this," Win said, handing him a small bottle. "Please."

Trial-size mouthwash. Count on Win. They made their way inside the Biker Wannabee. Myron stopped in the bathroom, rinsed out his mouth, splashed water on his face, checked the wound. It hurt. He looked in the mirror. His face was still tan from his three weeks with Terese, but Win was right: He looked like hell.

He met up with Win outside the bathroom door. "You said two reasons before, that there were two reasons you wanted me to come back here."

"Reason two," Win said. "Nancy—or Thrill, if you prefer. She was worried about you. I thought it best if you saw her."

When they reached the corner booth, Zorra and Thrill were busy chatting like, well, two single women at a bar.

Zorra smiled at Myron. "Zorra is sorry, dreamboat."

"Not your fault," Myron said.

"Zorra means that they're dead," Zorra said. "Zorra would have liked a few hours alone with them first."

"Yeah," Myron said. "Pity."

"Zorra already told Win all Zorra knows, which is very little. Zorra is just a beautiful hired gun. She likes to know as little as possible."

"But you worked for Pat?"

He-she nodded, but the wig did not. "Zorra was a bouncer and bodyguard. Do you believe that? Zorra Avrahaim having to settle for work as a common bouncer?"

"Yeah, times are tough. So what was Pat into?"

"A little of everything. Mostly drugs."

"And how were Billy Lee and Pat connected?"

"Billy Lee claimed to be his uncle." Zorra shrugged. "But that could have been a lie."

"Did you ever meet Clu Haid?"

"No."

"Do you know why Billy Lee was hiding?"

"He was terrified. He thought someone was trying to kill him."

"That someone being me?"

"So it seemed."

Myron couldn't figure that one out. He asked a few more questions, but there was nothing else to learn. Win offered his hand. Zorra took it and stepped out of the booth. She handled the high heels well. Not everyone does.

Zorra kissed Win on the cheek. "Thanks for not killing Zorra, dreamboat."

Win bowed slightly. "A pleasure, madame." Win the charmer. "I'll walk you out."

Myron slid into the booth next to Thrill. Without saying a word, she grabbed his face with both hands and kissed him hard. He kissed her back. Win and his mouthwash. What a guy.

When they came up for air, Thrill said, "You do know how to show a girl a good time."

"Ditto."

"You also scared the hell out of me."

"I didn't mean to."

She searched his face. "Are you okay?"

"I will be."

"Part of me wants to invite you back to my place."

He said nothing, lowering his eyes. She kept her eyes on his face.

"This is it, isn't it?" she said. "You won't call, will you?"

Myron said, "You're beautiful, intelligent, fun—"

"And about to get the big kiss-off."

"It's not you."

"Oh, that's original. Don't tell me. It's you, right?"

He tried a smile. "You know me so well."

"I'd like to."

"I'm damaged goods, Nancy."

"Who isn't?"

"I'm just over a long-term relationship—"

"Who said anything about a relationship? We could just go out, right?"

"No."

"What?"

"I don't work that way," he said. "I can't help it. I go out with someone, I start picturing kids and a backyard barbecue and a rusted hoop in the driveway. I try to size up all that stuff right away."

She looked at him. "Christ, you're strange."

Hard to argue.

She started fiddling with a mixing straw. "And you can't imagine me in any of those domestic settings?"

"Just the opposite," Myron said. "That's the problem."

"I see. At least I think I see." She shifted in her seat. "I better go."

"I'll take you home."

"No, I'll get a taxi."

"That's not necessary."

"I think it is. Good night, Myron."

She walked away. Myron stood. Win moved up next to him. They watched her disappear out the door.

"You'll make sure she gets home safely?" Myron asked.

Win nodded. "I already called a car service for her."

"Thanks."

Silence. Then Win put his hand on Myron's shoulder.

"May I make one observation at this juncture?" Win asked.

"Shoot."

"You're a total moron."

They stopped at the doctor's apartment on the Upper West Side. He restitched the wound, making a tsk-tsk noise as he sewed. When they reached Win's apartment at the Dakota building, the two friends settled into the Louis the Someteenth decor with their favorite beverages. Myron chugged on a Yoo-Hoo; Win sipped an amber liquor.

Win flipped channels with a remote control. He stopped on CNN. Myron looked at the screen and thought of Terese on that island by herself. He checked the time. This was normally Terese's anchor slot. A bad dye job filled in. Myron wondered when or if Terese would be back on the air. And he wondered why he kept thinking about her.

Win turned the TV off. "Need a refill?"

Myron shook his head. "So what did Sawyer Wells tell you?"

"Not very much, I'm afraid. Clu was a drug addict. He tried to help him. Blah, blah, blah. Sawyer is leaving the Yankees, you know."

"I didn't."

"He credits them with raising him out of obscurity. But alas, now it's time for dear Sawyer to take hold of his reins and motivate more minions. He's going to start touring soon."

"Like a rock star?"

Win nodded. "Complete with overpriced T-shirts."

"Are they black?"

"I don't know. But at the end of each performance he encores after frenzied fans flick their Bics and shout, 'Freebird!' "

"That's so 1977."

"Isn't it? But I did a little checking. Guess who's sponsoring the tour."

"Budweiser, the undisputed King of Beer?"

"Close," Win said. "His new publisher. Riverton Press."

"As in Vincent Riverton, former owner of the New York Yankees?"

"The very."

Myron whistled, processed it, came up with nothing. "With all the buyouts in publishing, Riverton owns half the books in town. Probably means nothing."

"Probably," Win agreed. "If you have more questions, Sawyer is giving a seminar tomorrow at the Cagemore Auditorium at Reston University. He invited me to attend. I'm allowed to bring a date."

"I don't put out on the first date."

"And you're proud of that?"

Myron took a deep chug. Maybe he was getting older, but Yoo-Hoo didn't have the same kick anymore. He craved a venti-size skim iced latte with a splash of vanilla, though he hated ordering it in front of other men. "I'm going to try to find out about Clu's autopsy tomorrow."

"Through this Sally Li?"

Myron nodded. "She's been in court, but she's supposed to be back at the morgue tomorrow morning."

"Think she'll tell you anything?"

"I don't know."

"You may have to turn on the charm again," Win said. "Is this Sally Li of the heterosexual persuasion?"

"She is now," Myron said. "But once I turn on the charm—"

"All bets are off, yes."

"Charm so potent," Myron said, "he can turn a woman against men."

"You should print that on your business card." Win did that snifter circle, palm up and under the glass. "Before our old chum Billy Lee perished, did he reveal anything of import?"

"Not really," Myron said. "Just that he thought I was the one who killed Clu and now wanted to kill him."

"Hmm."

"Hmm what?"

"Once again, your name rears its ugly head."

"He was a strung-out addict."

"I see," Win said. "So he was just ranting?"

Silence.

"Somehow," Myron said, "I keep ending up in the middle of this."

"So it seems."

"But I can't imagine why."

"Life's little mysteries."

"I also can't figure out how Billy Lee fits into any of this: into Clu's murder, into Esperanza's affair with Bonnie, into Clu getting thrown off the team, into Clu signing with FJ, into any of it."

Win put down his snifter and stood. "I suggest we sleep on it."

Good advice. Myron crawled under the covers and plunged immediately into slumber land. It was several hours later—after the REM and alpha sleep cycles, when he started rising to consciousness and his brain activity started going haywire—that it came to him. He thought again about FJ and about his having tailed Myron. He thought about what FJ had said, about how he had even seen Myron at the cemetery before Myron disappeared with Terese in the Caribbean.

And a big click sounded in his head.

CHAPTER 27

He called FJ at nine in the morning. FJ's secretary said that Mr. Ache could not be disturbed. Myron told her it was urgent. Sorry, Mr. Ache was out of the office. But, Myron reminded her, you just said he could not be disturbed. He cannot be disturbed, the secretary countered, because he is not in the office. Ah.

"Tell him I want to meet with him," Myron said. "And it has to be today."

"I can't promise you—"

"Just tell him."

He looked at his watch. He was meeting Dad at "the Club" at noon. It gave him time to try to rendezvous with Sally Li, chief medical examiner for Bergen County. He called her office and told her he wanted to talk.

"Not here," Sally said. "You know the Fashion Center?"

"It's one of the malls on Route Seventeen, right?"

"On the Ridgewood Avenue intersection, yeah. There's a sub shop outside the Bed, Bath and Beyond. Meet me there in an hour."

"Bed, Bath and Beyond is part of the Fashion Center?"

"Must have something to do with the Beyond part."

She hung up. He got in the rental car and started out to Paramus, New Jersey. Motto: There's No Such Thing as Too Much Commerce. The town of Paramus was like a muggy, jam-packed elevator with some jerk holding the door-open button and shouting, "Come on, we can squeeze in one more strip mall."

Nothing about the Fashion Center was particularly fashionable; the mall was in fact so unhip that teenagers didn't even hang out there. Sally Li sat on a bench, an unlit cigarette dangling from her lips. She wore green hospital scrubs and rubber sports sandals with no socks— footwear sported by many a coroner because it made cleaning off blood and guts and other human debris easy with a simple garden hose.

Okay, a little background here: For the past decade or so, Myron had been involved in an on-again, off-again romance with Jessica Culver. More recently they'd been in love. They'd moved in together. And now it was over. Or so he thought. He was not sure what exactly had happened. Objective observers might point to Brenda. She came along and changed a lot of things. But Myron was not sure.

So what's that have to do with Sally Li?

Jessica's father, Adam Culver, had been the Bergen County chief medical examiner until he was murdered several years ago. Sally Li, his assistant and close friend, had taken his place. That was how Myron knew her.

He approached. "Another no-smoking mall?"

"No one uses the word *no* anymore," Sally said. "They say *free* instead. This isn't a no-smoking mall; it's a smoke-free zone. Next they'll call underwater an air-free zone. Or the Senate a brain-free zone."

"So why did you want to meet here?"

Sally sighed, sat up. "Because you want to know about Clu Haid's autopsy, right?"

Myron hesitated, nodded.

"Well, my superiors—and I use that term knowing I don't even have equals—would frown upon seeing us together. In fact, they'd probably try to fire my ass."

"So why take the risk?" he asked.

"First off, I'm going to change jobs. I'm going back West, probably UCLA. Second, I'm cute, female, and what they now call Asian-American. It makes it harder to fire me. I might make a stink and the politically ambitious hate to look like they're beating up a minority. Third, you're a good guy. You figured out the truth when Adam was killed. I figure I owe you." She took the cigarette out of her mouth, put it back in the package, took out another one, put it in her mouth. "So what do you want to know?"

"Just like that?"

"Just like that."

Myron said, "I thought I'd have to turn on my charm."

"Only if you want to get me naked." She waved a hand. "Ah, who am I kidding? Go ahead, Myron, fire away."

"Injuries?" Myron asked.

"Four bullet wounds."

"I thought there were three."

"So did we at first. Two to the head, both at close range, either one of which would have been fatal. The cops thought there was only one. There was another in the right calf, and another in the back between the shoulder blades."

"Longer range?"

"Yeah, I'd say at least five feet. Looked liked thirty-eights, but I don't do ballistics."

"You were at the scene, right?"

"Yup."

"Could you tell if there was forced entry?"

"The cops said no."

Myron sat back and nodded to himself. "Let me see if I got the DA's theory right. Correct me if I'm wrong."

"I look forward to it."

"They figure Clu knew the killer. He let him or her in voluntarily, they talked or whatever, and something went wrong. The killer draws a gun, Clu runs, the killer fires two shots. One hits his calf, the other his back. Could you tell which came first?"

"Which what?"

"The calf shot or the back shot."

"No," Sally said.

"Okay, so Clu goes down. He's hurt but not dead. The killer puts the gun to Clu's head. Bang, bang."

Sally arched an eyebrow. "I'm impressed."

"Thanks."

"As far as it goes."

"Pardon?"

She sighed and shifted on the bench. "There are problems."

"Such as?"

"The body was moved."

Myron felt his pulse pick up. "Clu was killed someplace else?"

"No. But his body was moved. After he was killed."

"I don't understand."

"The lividity wasn't affected, so the blood didn't have time to settle. But he was dragged around on the floor, probably immediately after death, though it could be up to an hour later. And the room was tossed."

"The killer was searching for something," Myron said. "Probably the two hundred thousand dollars."

"Don't know about that. But there were blood smears all over the place."

"What do you mean, smears?"

"Look, I'm an ME. I don't interpret crime scenes. But the place was a mess. Overturned furniture and book-shelves, drawers emptied out, and blood everywhere. On the walls. And on the floor. Like he'd been dragged like a rag doll."

"Maybe he was dragging himself around. After he was shot in the leg and back."

"Could be, I guess. Of course it's hard to drag yourself across walls unless you're Spider-Man."

Myron's blood chilled a few degrees. He tried to sort and sift and process. How did all this fit? The killer was on a rampage to find the cash. Okay, that makes sense. But why drag around the body? Why smear the walls with blood?

"We're not finished," Sally said.

Myron blinked as though coming out of a trance.

"I also ran a full tox screen on the deceased. Know what I found?"

"Heroin?"

She shook her head. "El Zippo."

"What?"

"*Nada*, nothing, the big zero."

"Clu was clean?"

"Not even a Tums."

Myron made a face. "But that could have been tempo-rary, right? I mean, the drugs might have just been out of his system."

"Nope."

"What do you mean, nope?"

"Let's keep the science simple here, shall we? If a guy abuses drugs or alcohol, it shows up somewhere. Enlarged heart, liver damage, lung modules, whatever. And it did. There was no question that Clu Haid had liked some pretty potent chemicals. *Had,* Myron. Had. There are other tests —hair tests, for example—that give you a more recent snapshot. And those were clean. Which means he'd been off the stuff for a while.''

"But he failed a drug test two weeks ago."

She shrugged.

"Are you telling me that test was fixed?"

Sally held up both hands. "Not me. I'm telling you that my data disputes that data. I never said anything about a fix. It could have been an innocent error. There are such things as false positives."

Myron's head swam. Clu had been clean. His body had been dragged around after being shot four times. Why? None of this made any sense.

They chatted a few more minutes, mostly about the past, and headed for the exit ten minutes later. Myron started back to his car. Time to see Dad. He tried the new cellular—count on Win to have "extras" lying about his apartment—and called Win.

"Articulate," Win answered.

"Clu was right. The drug test was fixed."

Win said, "My, my."

"Sawyer Wells witnessed the drug test."

"More my, my."

"What time is he doing the motivational talk at Reston?"

"Two o'clock," Win said.

"In the mood to get motivated?"

"You have no idea."

The Club.

Brooklake Country Club, to be more exact, though there was no brook, no lake, and they were not in the country. It was, however, most definitely a club. As Myron's car made its way up the steep drive, the clubhouse's white Greco-Roman pillars rising through the clouds, childhood memories popped up in fluorescent flashes. It was how he always saw the place. In flashes. Not always pleasant ones.

The Club was the epitome of nouveau-riche, Myron's wealthy brethren proving that they could be just as tacky and exclusive as their goyish counterparts. Older women with perpetual tans on large, freckled chests sat by the pool, their hair shellacked into place by fake French hairdressers to the point where the strands resembled frozen fiber optics, never allowing it, God forbid, to touch the water, sleeping, he imagined, without putting their heads down lest they shatter the dos like so much Venetian glass; there were nose jobs and liposuction and face-lifts so extreme that the ears almost touched in the back, the overall effect bizarrely sexy in the same way you might find

Yvonne De Carlo on *The Munsters* sexy; women fighting off old age and on the surface winning, but Myron wondered if they doth protest too much, their fear just a little too bare in the scar-revealing, harsh overhead lights of the dining room.

Men and women were separated at the Club, the women animatedly playing mah-jongg, the men silently chewing on cigars over a hand of cards; women still had special tee times so as not to interfere with the breadwinners'—i.e., their husbands'—precious leisure moments; there was tennis too, but that was more for fashion than exercise, giving everyone an excuse to wear sweatsuits that rarely encountered sweat, couples sometimes sporting matching ones; a men's grill, a women's lounge, the oak boards memorializing golf champions in gold leaf, the same man winning seven years in a row, now dead, the large locker rooms with masseur's tables, the bathrooms with combs sitting in blue alcohol, the pickle-and-coleslaw bar, cleat marks on the rug, the Founders Board with his grandparents' names still on it, immigrant dining room help, all referred to by their first names, always smiling too hard and at the ready.

What shocked Myron now was that people *his* age were members. The same young girls who had sneered at their mothers' idleness now abandoned their own foundering careers to "raise" the kids—read: hire nannies—came here to lunch and bore each other silly with a continuous game of one-upmanship. The men Myron's age had manicures and long hair and were well fed and too well dressed, kicking back with their cellular phones and casually swearing to a colleague. Their kids were there too, dark-eyed youngsters walking through the clubhouse with hand-held video games and Walkmans and too regal a bearing.

All conversations were inane and depressed the hell out of Myron. The grandpas in Myron's day had the good sense not to talk much to one another, just discarding and picking up what was dealt, occasionally grumbling about a local sports team; the grandmothers interrogated one another, measuring their own children and grandchildren against the competition, seeking an opponent's weakness and any conversational opening to jab forward with tales of offspring heroics, no one really listening, just preparing for the next frontal assault, familial pride getting confused with self-worth and desperation.

The main clubhouse dining room was as expected: waaaay too overstated. The green carpeting, the curtains that resembled corduroy leisure suits, the gold tablecloths on huge round mahogany, the floral centerpieces piled too high and with no sense of proportion, not unlike the plates traipsing down the buffet line. Myron remembered attending a sports-themed bar mitzvah here as a child: jukeboxes, posters, pennants, a Wiffle ball batting cage, a basket for foul shots, an artist wanna-be stuck sketching sports-related caricatures of thirteen-year-old boys—thirteen-year-old boys being God's most obnoxious creation short of television lawyers—and a wedding band complete with an overweight lead singer who handed the kids silver dollars shrouded in leather pouches that were emblazoned with the band's phone number.

But this view—these flashes—were too quick and thus simplistic. Myron knew that. His remembrances were all screwed up about this place—the derision blending with the nostalgia—but he also remembered coming here as a child for family dinners, his clip-on tie slightly askew, sent by Mom into the inner sanctum of the men's card room to find his grandfather, the undisputed family patriarch, the room reeking of cigar smoke, his pop-pop greeting him with a ferocious embrace, his gruff compatriots who wore golf shirts that were too loud and too tight, barely acknowledging the interloper because their own grandkids would do the same soon, the card game trickling down, participant by participant.

These same people he so easily picked apart were the first generation fully out of Russia or Poland or Ukraine or some other shtetl-laced combat zone. They'd hit the New World running—running away from the past, the poverty, the fear—and they just ran a bit too far. But under the hair and the jewelry and the gold lamé, no mother bear would ever be so quick to kill for her cubs, the women's hard eyes still seeking out the pogrom in the distance, suspicious, always expecting the worst, bracing themselves to take the blow for their children.

Myron's dad sat in a yellow, pseudo-leather swivel chair in the brunch room, fitting in with this crowd about as well as a camel-riding mufti. Dad did not belong here. Never had. He didn't play golf or tennis or cards. He didn't swim and he didn't brag and he didn't brunch and he didn't talk stock tips. He wore his work clothes of all things: charcoal gray slacks, loafers, and a white dress shirt over a sleeveless white undershirt. His eyes were dark, his skin pale olive, his nose jutting forward like a hand waiting to be shook.

Interestingly enough, Dad was not a member of Brooklake. Dad's parents, on the other hand, had been founding members, or in the case of Pop-pop, a ninety-two-year-old quasi vegetable whose rich life had been dissolved into useless fragments by Alzheimer's, still was. Dad hated the place, but he kept up the membership for the sake of his father. That meant showing up every once in a while. Dad looked at it as a small price to pay.

When Dad spotted Myron, he rose, more slowly than

usual, and suddenly the obvious hit Myron: The cycle was beginning anew. Dad was the age Pop-pop had been back then, the age of the people they'd made fun of, his ink-black hair wispy, static gray now. The thought was far from comforting.

"Over here!" Dad called, though Myron had seen him. Myron threaded his way through the brunchers, mostly overkept women who constantly pendulumed between chewing and chatting, bits of coleslaw caught in the corners of their glossy mouths, water glasses stained with pink lipstick. They eyed Myron as he walked by for three reasons: under forty, male, no marriage band. Measuring his son-in-law potential. Always on the lookout, though not necessarily for their own daughters, the yenta from the shtetl never too far away.

Myron hugged his father and as always kissed his cheek. The cheek still felt wonderfully rough, but the skin was loosening. The scent of Old Spice wafted gently in the air, as comforting as any hot chocolate on the coldest of days. Dad hugged him back, released, then hugged him again. No one noticed the display of affection. Such acts were not uncommon here.

The two men sat. The paper place mats had an overhead diagram of the golf course's eighteen holes and an ornate letter *B* in the middle. The club's logo. Dad picked up a stubby green pencil, a golf pencil, to scribble down their order. That was how it worked. The menu had not changed in thirty years. As a kid Myron always ordered either the Monte Cristo or Reuben sandwich. Today he asked for a bagel with lox and cream cheese. Dad wrote it down.

"So," Dad began. "Getting acclimated to being back?"

"Yeah, I think so."

"Hell of a thing with Esperanza."

"She didn't do it."

Dad nodded. "Your mother tells me that you've been subpoenaed."

"Yep. But I don't know anything."

"You listen to your aunt Clara. She's a smart lady. Always has been. Even in school, Clara was the smartest girl in the class."

"I will."

The waitress came by. Dad handed her the order. He turned back to Myron and shrugged. "It's getting near the end of the month," Dad said. "I have to use your pop-pop's minimum before the thirtieth. I didn't want the money to go to waste."

"This place is fine."

Dad made a face signaling disagreement. He grabbed some bread, buttered it, then pushed it away. He shifted in his chair. Myron watched him. Dad was working up to something.

"So you and Jessica broke up?"

In all the years Myron had been dating Jessica, Dad had never inquired about their relationship past the polite questions. It just wasn't his way. He'd ask how Jessica was, what she was up to, when her next book was coming out. He was polite and friendly and greeted her warmly, but he'd never given a true indication of how he really felt about her. Mom had made her own feelings on the subject crystal clear: Jessica was not good enough for her son, but then again, who was? Dad was like a great newscaster, the kind of guy who asks questions without giving the viewer any hint of how he was really leaning on the issue.

"I think it's over," Myron said.

"Because"—Dad stopped, looked away, looked back —"of Brenda?"

"I'm not sure."

"I'm not big on giving advice. You know that. Maybe I should have been. I read those life instruction books fathers write for their children. You ever see those?"

"Yes."

"All kinds of wisdom in there. Like: Watch a sunrise once a year. Why? Suppose you want to sleep in? Another one: Overtip a breakfast waitress. But suppose she's grumpy? Suppose she's really bad? Maybe that's why I never dealt with it. I always see the other side."

Myron smiled.

"So I was never big on advice. But I have learned one thing for sure. One thing. So listen to me because this is important."

"Okay."

"The most important decision you'll ever make is who you marry," Dad said. "You can take every other decision you'll ever make, add them together, and it still won't be as important as that one. Suppose you choose the wrong job, for example. With the right wife, that's not a problem. She'll encourage you to make a change, cheer you on no matter what. You understand?"

"Yes."

"Remember that, okay?"

"Okay."

"You have to love her more than anything in the world. But she has to love you just as much. Your priority should be her happiness, and her priority should be yours. That's a funny thing—caring about someone more than yourself. It's not easy. So don't look at her as just a sexual object or as just a friend to talk to. Picture every day with the person. Picture paying bills with that person, raising children with that person, being stuck in a hot room with no air-conditioning and a screaming baby with that person. Am I making sense?''

''Yes.'' Myron smiled and folded his hands on the table. ''Is that how it is with you and Mom? Is she all those things to you?''

''All those things,'' Dad agreed, ''plus a pain in the *tuchus*.''

Myron laughed.

''If you promise not to tell your mother, I'll let you in on a little secret.''

''What?''

He leaned in and whispered conspiratorially. ''When your mother walks in the room—even now, even after all these years, if she were to, say, stroll by us right now—my heart still does a little two-step. You understand what I'm saying?''

''I think so, yeah. That used to happen with Jess.''

Dad spread his hands. ''Enough then.''

''Are you saying Jessica is that person?''

''Not my place to say one way or the other.''

''Do you think I'm making a mistake?''

Dad shrugged. ''You'll figure that out, Myron. I have tremendous confidence in you. Maybe that's why I never gave you much advice. Maybe I always thought you were smart enough without me.''

''Bull.''

''Or maybe it was easier parenting, I don't know.''

''Or maybe you led by example,'' Myron said. ''Maybe you led gently. Maybe you showed rather than told.''

''Yeah, well, whatever.''

They fell into silence. The women around them chatted up their white noise.

Dad said, ''I turn sixty-eight this year.''

"I know."

"Not a young man anymore."

Myron shook his head. "Not old either."

"True enough."

More silence.

"I'm selling the business," Dad said.

Myron froze. He saw the warehouse in Newark, the place Dad had worked for as long as Myron could remember. The *schmata* business—in Dad's case, undergarments. He could picture Dad with his ink-black hair in his glass-walled warehouse office, barking out orders, sleeves rolled up, Eloise, his long-time secretary, fetching him whatever he needed before he knew he needed it.

"I'm too old for it now," Dad went on. "So I'm getting out. I spoke to Artie Bernstein. You remember Artie?"

Myron managed a nod.

"The man's a rat bastard, but he's been dying to buy me out for years. Right now his offer is garbage, but I still might take it."

Myron blinked. "You're selling?"

"Yes. And your mother is going to cut back at the law firm."

"I don't understand."

Dad put a hand on Myron's arm. "We're tired, Myron."

Myron felt two giant hands press down on his chest.

"We're also buying a place in Florida."

"Florida?"

"Yes."

"You're moving to Florida?" Myron's Theory on East Coast Jewish Life: You grow up, you get married, you have kids, you go to Florida, you die.

"No, maybe part of the year, I don't know. Your

mother and I are going to start traveling a little more.''
Dad paused. "So we'll probably sell the house.''

They'd owned that house Myron's entire life. Myron looked down at the table. He grabbed a wrapped Saltine cracker from the bread basket and tore open the cellophane.

"Are you okay?'' Dad asked.

"I'm fine,'' he said. But he wasn't fine. And he couldn't articulate why, even to himself.

The waitress served them. Dad was having a salad with cottage cheese. Dad hated cottage cheese. They ate in silence. Myron kept feeling tears sting his eyes. Silly.

"There's one other thing,'' Dad said.

Myron looked up. "What?''

"It's not a big deal really. I didn't even want to tell you, but your mother thought I should. And you know how it is with your mother. When she has something in her mind, God himself—''

"What is it, Dad?''

Dad fixed his eyes on Myron's. "I want you to know this has nothing to do with you or your going to the Caribbean.''

"Dad, what?''

"While you were gone''—Dad shrugged and started blinking; he put down his fork, and there was the faintest quiver in his lower lip—"I had some chest pains.''

Myron felt his own heart sputter. He saw Dad with the ink-black hair at Yankee Stadium. He saw Dad's face turning red when he told him about the bearded man. He saw Dad rise and storm off to avenge his sons.

When Myron spoke, his voice sounded tinny and far away. "Chest pains?''

"Don't make a thing of it.''

"You had a heart attack?''

"Let's not blow it out of proportion. The doctors weren't sure what it was. It was just some chest pains, that's all. I was out of the hospital in two days."

"The hospital?" More images: Dad waking up with the pains, Mom starting to cry, calling an ambulance, rushing to the hospital, the oxygen mask on his face, Mom holding his hand, both their faces devoid of any color. . . .

And then something broke open. Myron couldn't stop himself. He got up and half sprinted to the bathroom. Someone said hello to him, called out his name, but he kept moving. He pushed open the bathroom door, opened a stall, locked himself in, and nearly collapsed.

Myron started to cry.

Deep, bone-crushing cries, full-body sobs. Just when he thought he couldn't cry anymore. Something inside him had finally given way, and now he sobbed without pause or letup.

Myron heard the bathroom door open. Someone leaned against the stall door. Dad's voice, when he finally spoke, was barely a whisper. "I'm fine, Myron."

But Myron again saw Dad at Yankee Stadium. The ink-black hair was gone, replaced with the gray, fly-away wisps. Myron saw Dad challenge the bearded man. He saw the bearded man rise, and then he saw Dad clutch his chest and fall to the ground.

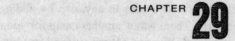

CHAPTER **29**

Myron tried to shake it off. No choice really. But he couldn't stop thinking about it. And he couldn't stop worrying. Worrying had never been his style in the past, even when a crisis loomed. All of a sudden he had the worryqueasies in his stomach. It was true what they said: The older you become, the more you are like your parents. Soon he'd be telling a kid not to stick his elbow out the car window or he'd lose it.

Win met him in front of the auditorium. He was in classic Win pose, eyes level, arms crossed, totally relaxed. He wore designer sunglasses and looked ultrasleek. *GQ* casual.

"Problem?" Win said.

"No."

Win shrugged.

"I thought we were going to meet inside," Myron said.

"That would mean I'd have to listen to more of Sawyer Wells."

"That bad?"

"Imagine, if you will, a Mariah Carey–Michael Bolton duet," Win said.

"Eeuw."

Win checked his watch. "He should be finishing up now. We must be brave."

They headed inside. The Cagemore Center was a sprawling facility that featured oodles of concert and lecture halls that could be cut to any size by sliding walls back and forth. There was a summer camp for young children in one room. Win and Myron stopped and listened to the children sing "Farmer in the Dell." The sound made Myron smile.

". . . the farmer in the dell, the farmer in the dell, hi-ho-the-dairy-o, the farmer in the dell . . ."

Win turned to Myron. "What's a dell?" Win asked.

"No idea."

Win shrugged and moved on to the main auditorium. There was a table out front selling Sawyer Wells paraphernalia. Cassettes, videos, books, magazines, posters, pennants (though what one does with a Sawyer Wells pennant went beyond Myron's capacity to imagine) and yep, T-shirts. Groovy titles too: *The Wells Guide to Wellness, The Wells Rules for Wellness, Key to Wellness: It's All About You.* Myron shook his head.

The auditorium was packed, the crowd so silent they'd put the Vatican to shame. Up on the stage, jittering to and fro like Robin Williams in his stand-up comic days, was the self-help guru himself. Sawyer Wells was resplendent in a business suit with the jacket off, shirt cuffs turned once, fancy suspenders cutting into his shoulders. A good look for a self-help guru: The expensive suit makes you reek of success while the jacket off and rolled-up sleeves give you the air of a regular guy. A perfectly balanced ensemble.

"It's all about you," Sawyer Wells told the enraptured audience. "If you remember nothing else today, remember that. It's all about you. Make everything about you. Every decision is about you. Everything you see, everything you touch is a reflection of you. No . . . more than that—it *is* you. You are everything. And everything is you."

Win leaned toward Myron. "Isn't that a song?"

"The Stylistics, I think. Circa early seventies."

"I want you to remember that," Sawyer continued. "Visualize. Visualize everything as you. Your family is you. Your job is you. When you're walking down the street, that beautiful tree is you. That blooming rose is you."

Win said, "That dirty commode at the bus terminal."

Myron nodded. "You."

"You see the boss, the leader, the breadwinner, the successful, fulfilled person. That person is you. No one can lead you because the leader is you. You stand in front of your opponent, and you know you can win because you are your opponent. And you know how to beat you. Remember you are your opponent. Your opponent is you."

Win frowned. "But don't you know how to beat you too?"

"It's a paradox," Myron agreed.

"You fear the unknown," Sawyer Wells ranted. "You fear success. You fear taking chances. But now you know that the unknown is you. Success is you. Taking chances is you. You don't fear you, do you?"

Win frowned.

"Listen to Mozart. Take long walks. Ask yourself what you did today. Do that every night. Before you go to sleep, ask yourself if the world is better because of you. After all, it's your world. You are the world."

Win said, "If he breaks into a rendition of 'We Are the World,' I'm using my gun."

"But you are your gun," Myron countered.

"And he is my gun too."

"Right."

Win considered that. "So if he is my gun and my gun kills him, it's a suicide."

"Take responsibility for your actions," Wells said. "That's one of the Wells Rules for Wellness. Take responsibility. Cher once said, 'Excuses won't lift your butt, 'kay?' Listen to that. Believe that with all your heart."

The man was quoting Cher. The crowd was nodding. There is no God.

"Confess something about yourself to a friend—something awful, something you'd never want anyone to know. You'll feel better. You'll still see that you're worthy of love. And since your friend is you, you are really just telling yourself. Have an interest in everything. Thirst for knowledge. That's another rule. Remember that it's all about you. When you learn about other things, you are actually learning about yourself. Get to know you better."

Win looked at Myron, his face pained.

"Let's wait outside," Myron said.

But luck was with them. Two sentences later Sawyer Wells was done. The crowd went ballistic. They stood, they applauded, they hooted like an old Arsenio Hall audience.

Win shook his head. "Four hundred dollars a pop."

"That what this thing costs?"

"He is your money."

People approached the stage, stretching their hands toward the heavens in the vain hope that Sawyer Wells might reach out and touch them. Myron and Win watched. The table with the Wells paraphernalia was swarmed now like rotting fruit with buzzing flies.

"The citified version of a tent revival," Win noted.

Myron nodded.

Eventually Sawyer Wells waved and ran offstage. The crowd continued to cheer and purchase. Myron half expected a voice-over to announce that Elvis had left the building. Win and Myron swam through the crowd.

"Come," Win said. "I have backstage passes."

"Please tell me you're joking."

He wasn't. They actually said "Backstage Pass" on them. A plainclothes security guard scowled at them and scrutinized the passes as if they were the Zapruder film. Satisfied, he let them past the velvet rope. Yep, velvet rope. Sawyer Wells spotted Win and bounced toward them.

"So glad you could come, Win!" He turned to Myron and stuck out his hand. "Hi, I'm Sawyer Wells."

Myron shook it. "Myron Bolitar."

Sawyer's smile flickered but stayed on. "Nice to meet you, Myron."

Myron decided to try a frontal assault. "Why did you fix Clu Haid's drug test so it would appear he was taking heroin?"

The smile was still there, but it wasn't sitting right. "Pardon?"

"Clu Haid. The name ring a bell?"

"Of course. As I told Win yesterday, I worked very hard with him."

"Worked how?"

"To keep him off drugs. I have an extensive background as a drug counselor. That's how I was trained. To help addicts."

"Not so different from what you're doing now," Myron said.

"Pardon?"

"People with addictive personalities need an addiction. If it's not booze or drugs, maybe it's religion or self-help mumbo jumbo. They're simply swapping addictions; we hope to one less damaging.''

Sawyer Wells overnodded. "That's a really interesting viewpoint, Myron."

"Gee, thanks, Sawyer."

"I learned much about human frailty, about our lack of self-esteem, from addicts like Clu Haid. As I said, I worked very hard with him. His failure hurt me greatly."

Win said, "Because it was your failure."

"Pardon?"

"You are everything, and everything is you," Win said. "You are Clu Haid. He failed, ergo you failed."

Sawyer Wells maintained the smile. But it was different when he looked at Win. His gestures were tighter too, more controlled. He was one of those guys who tried to imitate the person with whom he was conversing. Myron hated that. "I see you came in at the end of my seminar, Win."

"Did I misunderstand your message?"

"No, it's not that. But a man creates his own world. That's my point. You are what you create, what you perceive. Take responsibility. That's the most important component of the Wells Guide to Wellness. You take responsibility for your own actions. And you admit fault. You know what the two most beautiful sentences in the world are?"

Win opened his mouth, stopped, looked at Myron, shook his head. "Too easy," he said.

" 'I am responsible,' " Sawyer continued. " 'It's my fault.' " He turned toward Myron. "Say it, Myron."

"What?"

"Come on. It's exhilarating. Say, 'I am responsible. It's my fault.' Stop passing the buck in your life. Say it. Come on, I'll say it with you. Win, you too."

Myron and Sawyer said, "I am responsible. It's my fault." Win remained silent.

"Feel better?" Sawyer said.

"It was almost like sex," Myron said.

"It can be powerful, yes."

"Yeah, uh-huh. Look, Sawyer, I'm not here to critique your seminar. I want to know about Clu's drug test. It was fixed. We have evidence that proves that fact. You helped administer that test. I want to know why you made it look like Clu was on drugs."

"I don't know what you're talking about."

"The autopsy shows conclusively that Clu hadn't taken drugs for at least two months before his death. Yet you tested him positive two weeks ago."

"Maybe the test was faulty," Sawyer said.

Win tsk-tsked. "Say, 'I am responsible. It's my fault.'"

"Stop passing the buck in your life," Myron added.

"Come on, Sawyer. It's exhilarating."

"That's not funny," Sawyer said.

"Wait," Win said. "You are everything, thus you are the drug test."

"And you are a positive guy," Myron added.

"Ergo the test result was positive."

Sawyer said, "I think I've had just about enough."

"You're finished, Wells," Myron said. "I'll blab to the papers."

"I don't know what you're talking about. I don't know anything about a fixed test."

"Want to hear my theory?" Myron said.

"No."

"You're leaving the Yankees and going to work for Vincent Riverton, right?"

"I'm not working exclusively for anyone. His conglomerate publishes my book."

"He's also Sophie Mayor's archenemy."

"You don't know that," Sawyer said.

"He lived for owning the team. When she took over, he was pissed. She ends up being everything New York wants in an owner because she minds her own business. She makes only one move, acquiring Clu Haid, and it's a beauty. Clu pitches better than anyone dared hope. The Yankees start heading for greatness. Then you step in. Clu fails a drug test. Sophie Mayor looks incompetent. The Yankees tumble."

Sawyer seemed to recoup a bit. Something in what Myron had just said had given him a new lease. Odd. "That makes no sense whatsoever."

"What part?"

"All of it," Sawyer said, chest back out. "Sophie Mayor has been good to me. I was working as a drug counselor at the Sloan State and Rockwell rehab centers when she gave me my chance to move up. Why would I want to hurt her?"

"You tell me."

"I have no idea. I firmly believed that Clu was on drugs. If he wasn't, then the test was faulty."

"You know the results are double-tested. There was no mistake. Someone had to fix it."

"It wasn't me. Maybe you should speak to Dr. Stilwell."

"But you were there? You admit that?"

"Yes, I was there. And I will no longer dignify your questions with answers." With that Sawyer Wells abruptly spun and stormed off.

"I don't think he liked us," Myron said.

"But if it's all about you, then we are he."

"So he doesn't like himself?"

"Sad, isn't it?"

"Not to mention confusing," Myron said.

They headed for the exit.

"So where to, O Motivated One?" Win asked.

"Starbucks."

"Latte time?"

Myron shook his head. "Confront FJ time."

CHAPTER 30

FJ was not there. Myron called his office again. The same secretary told him that FJ was still unavailable. Myron repeated that it was imperative that he speak to Francis Ache Junior as soon as humanly possible. The secretary remained unimpressed.

Myron returned to his office.

Big Cyndi wore a bright green spandex bodysuit with a slogan across the chest—this on a woman who could barely squeeze into a caftan. The fabric screamed in pain, the letters in the slogan so elongated that Myron couldn't read them, kinda like what happens to Silly Putty after you press it against a newspaper headline and stretch it out.

"Lots of clients have been calling, Mr. Bolitar," Big Cyndi said. "They are not pleased by your absence."

"I'll take care of it," he said.

She gave him the messages. "Oh, and Jared Mayor called," she said. "He seemed very anxious to talk to you."

"Okay, thanks."

He called Jared Mayor first. He was in his mother's

office at Yankee Stadium. Sophie switched on the speakerphone.

"You called?" Myron said.

"I was hoping you could give us an update," Jared said.

"I think someone is setting up your mother."

Sophie said, "Setting me up how?"

"Clu's drug test was a fix. He was clean."

"I know you want to believe that—"

"I have proof," Myron said.

Silence.

"What kind of proof?" Jared asked.

"There's no time for that now. But trust me on this. Clu was clean."

"Who would have fixed the test?" Sophie asked.

"That's what I want to know. The logical suspects are Dr. Stilwell and Sawyer Wells."

"But why would they want to hurt Clu?"

"Not Clu, Sophie. You. It fits in with everything else we have. Raising the specter of your missing daughter, taking your big baseball trade and turning it against you— I think someone's out to hurt you."

"You're jumping to conclusions," Sophie said.

"Could be."

"Who would want to hurt me?"

"I'm sure you've made your share of enemies. How about Vincent Riverton, for one?"

"Riverton? No. Our whole takeover was far more amicable than the press portrayed it."

"Still, I wouldn't rule him out."

"Listen, Myron, I don't really care about any of this. I just want you to find my daughter."

"They're probably connected."

"How?"

Myron changed ears. "You want me to be blunt, right?"

"Absolutely."

"Then I have to remind you what the odds are that your daughter is still alive."

"Slim," she said.

"Very slim."

"No, I'll stay with slim. In fact, I think it's better than slim."

"Do you really believe Lucy is alive someplace?"

"Yes."

"She's out there somewhere, waiting to be found?"

"Yes."

"Then the big question," Myron said, "is why."

"What do you mean?"

"Why isn't she home?" he asked. "Do you think someone's been holding her hostage all these years?"

"I don't know."

"Well, what other choices are there? If Lucy is still alive, why hasn't she come home? Or phoned home? What is she hiding from?"

Silence.

Sophie broke it. "You think someone has resurrected my daughter's memory as part of some vendetta against me?"

Myron was not sure how to answer. "I think it's a possibility we have to consider."

"I appreciate your bluntness, Myron. I want you to remain honest with me. Don't hold back. But I'll also keep my hope. When your child disappears into thin air, it creates a huge void. I need something to fill that void, Myron. So until I find out otherwise, I'll fill it with hope."

Myron said, "I understand."

"Then you'll keep looking."

There was a knock on the door. Myron put his hand over the phone and said to come in. Big Cyndi opened the door. Myron gestured to a chair. She took it. In the bright green she looked a bit like a planet.

"I'm not sure what I can do, Sophie."

"Jared will investigate Clu's drug test," she said. "If there was anything amiss, he'll find out about it. You keep your eyes open for my daughter. You may be right about Lucy's fate. Then again you may be wrong. Don't give up."

Before he could reply, the line was disconnected. Myron put the phone back in the cradle.

"Well?" Big Cyndi asked.

"She still has hope."

Big Cyndi scrunched up her face. "There's a fine line between hope and delusion, Mr. Bolitar," she said. "I think Ms. Mayor may have crossed it."

Myron nodded. He shifted in his chair. "Something I can do for you?" he asked.

She shook her head. Her head was a nearly perfect cube and reminded Myron of the old game of Rock'Em Sock'Em Robots. Not sure what else to do, Myron folded his hands and put them on his desk. He wondered how many times he had been alone with Big Cyndi like this. Less than a handful for sure. Wrong to say, but she made him uncomfortable.

After some time had passed, Big Cyndi said, "My mother was a big, ugly woman."

Myron had no comeback for that one.

"And like most big, ugly women, she was a shrinking violet. That's how it is with big, ugly women, Mr. Bolitar. They get used to standing alone in the corner. They hide. They become angry and defensive. They keep their heads down, and they let themselves be treated with disdain and disgust and—"

She stopped suddenly, waved a meaty paw. Myron sat still.

"I hated my mother," she said. "I swore that I would never be like that."

Myron risked a small nod.

"That's why you have to save Esperanza."

"I'm not sure I see the connection."

"She's the only one who sees past this."

"Past what?"

She thought about that one for a moment. "What's the first thing you think when you see me, Mr. Bolitar?"

"I don't know."

"People like to stare," she said.

"Hard to blame them, don't you think?" Myron said. "I mean, the way you dress and stuff."

She smiled. "I'd rather see shock on their faces than pity," she said. "And I'd rather they see brazen or outrageous than shrinking or scared or sad. Do you understand?"

"I think so."

"I'm not standing alone in the corner anymore. I've done enough of that."

Myron, unsure what to say, settled for a nod.

"When I was nineteen, I started wrestling professionally. And of course I was cast as a villain. I sneered. I made faces. I cheated. I hit opponents when they weren't looking. It was all an act, of course. But that was my job."

Myron sat back and listened.

"One night I was scheduled to fight Esperanza—Little Pocahontas, I should say. It was the first time we'd met. She was already the most beloved wrestler on the circuit. Cute and pretty and small and all the things . . . all the things that I'm not. Anyway, we were performing in some high school gym outside Scranton. The script was the usual. A back-and-forth match. Esperanza winning with her skill. Me cheating. Twice I was supposed to nearly have her pinned when the crowd would go wild and she'd start stamping her foot, like the cheers were giving her strength, and then everyone would start clapping in unison with her stomps. You know how it works, right?''

Myron nodded.

''She was supposed to pin me with a backflip at the fifteen-minute mark. We executed it perfectly. Then as she was raising her hands in victory, I was supposed to sneak up on her and whack her in the back with a metal chair. Again it went perfectly. She collapsed to the canvas. The crowd gasped. I, the Human Volcano—that's what I was called then—raised my hands in victory. They started booing and throwing things. I sneered. The announcers acted all concerned for poor Little Pocahontas. They brought out the stretcher. Again you've seen the same act a million times on cable.''

He nodded again.

''So there was another match or two, and then the crowd was ushered out. I decided not to change until I got back to the motel. I left for the bus a few minutes before the other girls. It was dark, of course. Nearly midnight. But some of the spectators were still out there. They confronted me. There must have been twenty of them. They started shouting at me. I decided to play back. I did my ring sneer and flexed''—her voice caught—''and that was when a rock hit me square in the mouth.''

Myron kept perfectly still.

''I started bleeding. Then another rock hit me in the shoulder. I couldn't believe what was happening. I tried to head back inside, but they circled around me. I didn't know what to do. They started moving in closer. I ducked down. Someone hit me over the head with a beer bottle. My knees hit the pavement. Then someone kicked me in the stomach and someone else pulled my hair.''

She stopped. Her eyes blinked a few times and she looked up and away. Myron thought about reaching out to her, but he didn't. Later he'd wonder why.

"And that's when Esperanza stepped in," Big Cyndi said after a few moments had passed. "She jumped over someone in the crowd and landed right on me. The morons thought she was there to help beat me up. But she just wanted to put herself between me and the blows. She told them to stop. But they wouldn't listen. One of them pulled her away so they could keep beating me. I felt another kick. Someone yanked my hair so hard my neck snapped back. I really thought they were going to kill me.''

Big Cyndi stopped again and took a deep breath. Myron stayed where he was and waited.

"You know what Esperanza did then?" she asked.

He shook his head.

"She announced that we were going to be tag team partners. Just like that. She shouted that after she'd been taken off on the stretcher, I'd visited her and we realized that we were actually long-lost sisters. The Human Volcano was now going to be called Big Chief Mama and we were going to be partners and friends. Some of the spectators backed off then. Others looked wary. 'It's a trap!' they warned her. 'The Human Volcano is setting you up!' But Esperanza insisted. She helped me to my feet and by then the police showed up and the moment was over. The crowd dispersed pretty easily.''

Big Cyndi threw up her thick arms and smiled. "The end.''

Myron smiled back. "So that's how you two became tag team partners?"

"That's how. When the president of FLOW heard about the incident, he decided to capitalize on it. The rest, as they say, is history."

They both sat back in silence, still smiling. After some time had passed, Myron said, "I had my heart broken six years ago."

Big Cyndi nodded. "By Jessica, right?"

"Right. I walked in on her with another man. A guy named Doug." He paused. He could not believe he was telling her this. And it still hurt. After all this time it still hurt. "Jessica left me then. Isn't that weird? I didn't throw her out. She just left. We didn't speak for four years—until she came back and we started up again. But you know about that."

Big Cyndi made a face. "Esperanza hates Jessica."

"Yeah, I know. She doesn't exactly go to pains to hide that fact."

"She calls her Queen Bitch."

"When she's in a good mood," Myron said. "But that's why. Up until we broke up that first time, she was more or less indifferent. But after that—"

"Esperanza doesn't forgive easily," Big Cyndi said. "Not when it comes to her friends."

"Right. Anyway, I was devastated. Win was no help. When it comes to matters of the heart, well, it's like explaining Mozart to a deaf man. So about a week after Jess left me, I moped into the office. Esperanza had two airplane tickets in her hand. 'We're going away,' she said. 'Where?' I asked. 'Don't worry about it,' she said. 'I already called your folks. I told them we'd be gone for a week.'" Myron smiled. "My parents love Esperanza."

"That should tell you something," Big Cyndi said.

"I told her I didn't have any clothes. She pointed to two suitcases on the floor. 'I bought you all you'll need.' I protested, but I didn't have much left, and you know Esperanza."

"Stubborn," Big Cyndi said.

"To put it mildly. You know where she took me?"

Big Cyndi smiled. "On a cruise. Esperanza told me about it."

"Right. One of those big new ships with four hundred meals a day. And she made me go to every dumb activity. I even made a wallet. We drank. We danced. We played friggin' bingo. We slept in the same bed and she held me and we never so much as kissed."

They sat for another long moment, both smiling again.

"We never asked her for help," Big Cyndi said. "Esperanza just knows and does the right thing."

"And now it's our turn," Myron said.

"Yes."

"She's still hiding something from me."

Big Cyndi nodded. "I know."

"Do you know what it is?"

"No," she said.

Myron leaned back. "We'll save her anyway," he said.

At eight o'clock Win called down to Myron's office. "Meet me at the apartment in an hour. I have a surprise for you."

"I'm not much in the mood for surprises, Win."

Click.

Great. He tried FJ's office again. No answer. He didn't much like waiting. FJ was a key in all this, he was sure of it now. But what choice did he have? It was getting late anyway. Better to go home and be surprised by whatever Win had in store and then get some rest.

The subway was still crowded at eight-thirty; the so-called Manhattan rush hour had grown to more like five or six. People worked too hard, Myron decided. He got off and walked to the Dakota. The same doorman was there. He had been given instructions to let Myron in at any time, that indeed Myron was now officially a resident of the Dakota, but the doorman still made a face like there was a bad odor whenever he passed.

Myron took the elevator up, fumbled for his key, and opened the door.

"Win?"

"He's not here."

Myron turned. Terese Collins gave him a small smile.

"Surprise," she said.

He gaped. "You left the island?"

Terese glanced in a nearby mirror, then back at him. "Apparently."

"But—"

"Not now."

She stepped toward him and they embraced. He kissed her. They fumbled with buttons and zippers and snaps. Neither one spoke. They made it into the bedroom, and then they made love.

When it was over, they clung to each other, the sheets tangled and binding them close together. Myron rested his cheek against her soft breast, hearing her heartbeat. Her chest was hitching a bit, and he knew that she was quietly crying.

"Tell me," he said.

"No." Terese's hand stroked his hair. "Why did you leave?"

"A friend is in trouble."

"That sounds so noble."

Again with that word. "I thought we agreed we wouldn't do this," he said.

"You complaining?"

"Hardly," he said. "Just curious why you changed your mind."

"Does it matter?"

"I don't think so."

She stroked his hair some more. He closed his eyes, not moving, wanting only to enjoy the wonderful suppleness of her skin against his cheek and ride the rise and fall of her chest.

"Your friend in trouble," she said. "It's Esperanza Diaz."

"Win told you?"

"I read it in the papers."

He kept his eyes closed.

"Tell me about it," she said.

"We were never great at talking on the island."

"Yeah, but that was then, this is now."

"Meaning?"

"Meaning you look a little worse for wear," she said. "I think you'll need the recovery time."

Myron smiled. "Oysters. The island had oysters."

"So tell me."

So he did. Everything. She stroked his hair. She interrupted a lot with follow-up questions, relaxing in the more familiar role of interviewer. It took him almost an hour.

"Some story," she said.

"Yes."

"Does it hurt? I mean, where you got beaten up?"

"Yes. But I'm a tough guy."

She kissed the top of his head. "No," she said. "You're not."

They sat in comfortable silence.

"I remember the Lucy Mayor disappearance," Terese said. "At least the second round."

"The second round?"

"When the Mayors had the money to run the big campaign to find her. Before that there really wasn't much of a story. An eighteen-year-old runaway. No big deal."

"You remember anything that might help me?"

"No. I hate covering stories like that. And not just for the obvious reason that lives are being shattered."

"Then what?"

"There's just too much denial," she said.

"Denial?"

"Yes."

"You mean with the family?"

"No, with the public. People block when it comes to their children. They deny because it's too painful to accept. They tell themselves it can't happen to them. God is not that fickle. There has to be a reason. Do you remember the Louise Woodward case a couple of years ago?"

"The nanny who killed the baby in Massachusetts?"

"Reduced to manslaughter by the judge, but yes. The public kept denying, even those who thought she was guilty. The mother shouldn't have been working, they said. Never mind the fact that the mother worked only part-time and came home at lunch every day to breast-feed the baby. It was her fault. And the father. He should have checked out the nanny's background better. The parents should have been more careful."

"I remember," Myron said.

"In the Mayors' case it was the same kind of thing. If Lucy Mayor had been raised right, she would have never run away in the first place. That's what I mean by denial. It's too painful to think about, so you block and convince yourself it can't happen to you."

"Do you think there's any merit to that argument in this case?"

"What do you mean?"

"Were Lucy Mayor's parents part of the problem?"

Terese's voice was soft. "It's not important."

"What makes you say that?"

She was silent, her breathing a little more hitched again.

"Terese?"

"Sometimes," she said, "a parent is to blame. But that doesn't change anything. Because either way—your fault or not—your child is gone and that's all that matters."

More silence.

Myron broke it. "You okay?" he asked.

"Fine."

"Sophie Mayor told me that the worst part was the not knowing."

"She's wrong," Terese said.

Myron wanted to ask her more, but she got out of bed then. When she came back, they made love again—languid and bittersweet, as the song says—both feeling loss, both searching for something in the moment or at least settling for the numb.

They were still snarled in the sheets when the phone woke Myron early in the morning. He reached over her head and picked up the receiver.

"Hello?"

"What's so important?"

It was FJ. Myron quickly sat up.

"We need to chat," Myron said.

"Again?"

"Yes."

"When?"

"Now."

"Starbucks," FJ said. "And Myron?"

"What?"

"Tell Win to stay outside."

CHAPTER 31

FJ sat alone at the same table. He had his legs crossed at the knee and sipped as if maybe there were something in the bottom of the cup he wanted no part of. A bit of foam clung to his upper lip. His face was clean and wax-treatment smooth. Myron checked for Hans and Franz or some new goons, but nobody was there. FJ smiled and as always, something cold scrambled down Myron's back.

"Where's Win?" FJ asked.

"Outside," Myron said.

"Good. Have a seat."

"I know why Clu signed with you, FJ."

"Care for an iced latte? You take it skim, correct?"

"It was bugging the hell out of me," Myron said. "Why would Clu sign with you? Don't get me wrong. He had every reason to leave MB. But he knew about TruPro's reputation. Why would he go there?"

"Because we offer a valuable service."

"At first I figured it was a gambling or drug debt. It's how your dad always worked. He gets his hooks into someone, and then he gnaws on the carcass. But Clu was clean. And he had plenty of cash. So that wasn't it."

FJ put his elbow on the table and leaned his chin against his palm. "This is so fascinating, Myron."

"It gets better. When I ran off to the Caribbean, you were keeping tabs on me. Because of the whole Brenda Slaughter situation. You even admitted it when I first got back, remember? You knew I'd been visiting the cemetery."

"A very poignant moment for us all," FJ agreed.

"When I vanished, you still wanted to keep tabs on me. If anything, my disappearance probably piqued your curiosity. You also saw an opening for TruPro, but that's not here or there. You wanted to know where I was. But I wasn't around. So you did the next best thing: You followed Esperanza, my partner and closest friend."

FJ made a clucking noise. "And here I thought Win was your closest friend."

"They both are. But that's not the point. Following Win would be too difficult. He'd spot the tail before you even had him in place. So you followed Esperanza instead."

"I still don't see what any of this has to do with Clu's decision to improve his representation."

"I was missing. You knew that. You took advantage. You called my clients, telling them that I'd abandoned them."

"Was I wrong?"

"I don't care about that now. You saw a weakness and you exploited it. You couldn't help yourself. It's how you were raised."

"Ouch."

"But the important thing here is that you were following Esperanza, hoping she'd lead you to me or at least give you a clue to how long I'd be gone. You followed her out to New Jersey. And you stumbled upon something you were never supposed to learn.''

His smile was positively wet. ''And what would that be?''

''Wipe that smile off your face, FJ. You're no better than a peeping Tom. Even your father wouldn't stoop that low.''

''Oh, you'd be surprised how low my father would stoop.''

''You're a pervert, and worse, you used what you learned as leverage against a client. Clu went nuts when Bonnie threw him out. He had no idea why. But now you knew. So you made a deal with him. He signs with TruPro, he learns the truth about his wife.''

FJ leaned back, recrossed the legs, folded his hands, and placed them on his lap. ''Quite a spin, Myron.''

''It's true, isn't it?''

FJ tilted his head in a maybe-yes, maybe-no fashion. ''Let me tell you how I see it,'' he began. ''Clu Haid's old agency, MB SportsReps, was clearly screwing him. In every way. His agent—that would be you, Myron—abandoned him when he needed him most. Your partner—that would be the lovely and rather lithe Esperanza—was engaging in a lick fest with his wife. True?''

Myron said nothing.

FJ unfolded the hands, took a sip of foam, refolded the hands. ''What I did,'' he continued, ''was take Clu Haid out of this awful situation. I brought him to an agency that would not abuse his trust. An agency that would look out for his interests. One of the ways we do that is through information. Valuable information. So the client understands what is happening to him. That's part of an agent's job, Myron. One of our agencies engaged in questionable ethics here. And it wasn't TruPro.''

It was a reverse spin, but it was also true. One day, when Myron had the time to dwell upon them, the words would undoubtedly wound. But not now.

"So you admit it?"

FJ shrugged.

"But if you were following Esperanza, you know she didn't do it."

Again the head tilt. "Do I?"

"Stop playing games with me, FJ."

"Please hold a moment." FJ took out his cell phone and dialed a number. He stood, walked toward the corner, chatted. He put the phone between his shoulder and ear, took out a pen and paper, jotted something down. He hung up and returned to the table.

"You were saying?"

"Did Esperanza do it?"

He smiled. "You want the truth?"

"Yes."

"I don't know. Honest. Yes, I followed her. But as I am sure you know, even lesbian scenes get repetitive. So after a while we'd stop watching her once she crossed the Washington Bridge. There was no point."

"So you really don't know who killed Clu?"

"Afraid not."

"Are you still following me, FJ?"

"No."

"Last night. You didn't have a man on me?"

"No. And truth be told, I didn't have a man on you when you came in here yesterday."

"The guy I spotted outside my office wasn't yours?"

"Sorry, no."

Myron was missing something here.

FJ leaned forward again. His smile was so creepy that

his teeth seemed to wiggle. "How far are you willing to go to save Esperanza?" he whispered.

"You know how far."

"The ends of the earth?"

"What are you getting at, FJ?"

"You're right, of course. I did learn about Esperanza and Bonnie. And I saw an opening. So I called Clu at the apartment in Fort Lee. But he wasn't there. I left a rather intriguing message on his machine. Something to the effect of 'I know who your wife is sleeping with.' He called me back on my private line within the hour."

"When was this?"

"What . . . three days before his death?"

"What did he say?"

"His reaction was the obvious. But the *what* is not nearly as important as the *where*."

"The where?"

"I have caller ID on my private line." FJ sat back. "Clu was out of town when he returned my call."

"Where?"

FJ took his time. He picked up the coffee, took a long sip, made an aaah noise as if he were filming a 7-Up commercial, put the cup back down. He looked at Myron. Then he shook his head. "Not so fast."

Myron waited.

"My specialty, as you've now seen, is gathering information. Information is power. It's currency. It's cash. I just don't give away cash."

"How much, FJ?"

"Not money, Myron. I don't want your money. I could buy you ten times over; we both know that."

"So what do you want?"

He took another long sip. Myron wanted so very much

to reach across the table and throttle him. "Sure you don't want anything to drink?"

"Cut the crap, FJ."

"Temper, temper."

Myron made two fists and hid them under the table. He willed himself to stay calm. "What do you want, FJ?"

"You are familiar, are you not, with Dean Pashaian and Larry Vitale."

"They're two of my clients."

"Correction. They are seriously considering leaving MB Sports-Reps and joining TruPro. They are on the fence as we speak. So here is my deal. You stop pursuing them. You don't call them and hand them crap about TruPro being run by gangsters. You promise to do that"— he showed Myron the piece of paper he'd been writing on in the corner—"I give you the number Clu called from."

"Your agency will destroy their careers. It always does."

FJ smiled again. "I can guarantee you, Myron, that no one on my staff will have a lesbian affair with their wives."

"No deal."

"Good-bye then." FJ stood.

"Wait."

"Your promise or I walk."

"Let's talk about this," Myron said. "We can come up with something."

"Good-bye."

FJ started for the door.

"Okay," Myron said.

FJ put a hand to his ear. "I missed that."

Selling out two clients. What would he stoop to next, running political campaigns? "You have a deal. I won't talk to them."

FJ spread his hands. "You really are a master negotiator, Myron. I'm in awe of your skills."

"Where did he call from, FJ?"

"Here's the phone number." He handed Myron the piece of paper. Myron read it and sprinted back to the car.

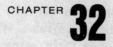

Myron was on the cell phone before he reached Win. He pressed in the number and heard three rings.

"Hamlet Motel," a man said.

"Where are you located?"

"In Wilston. On Route Nine off Ninety-one."

Myron thanked the man and hung up. Win looked at him. Myron dialed Bonnie's number. Bonnie's mother answered. Myron identified himself and asked to speak with Bonnie.

"She was very upset after you left yesterday," Bonnie's mother said.

"I'm sorry about that."

"Why do you want to talk to her?"

"Please. It's very important."

"She's in mourning. You realize that. Their marriage may have been in trouble—"

"I understand that, Mrs. Cohen. Please let me speak to her."

A deep sigh, but two minutes later Bonnie came on. "What is it, Myron?"

"What does the Hamlet Motel in Wilston, Massachusetts, mean to you?"

Myron thought he heard a short intake of air. "Nothing."

"You and Clu lived there, didn't you?"

"Not at the motel."

"I mean, in Wilston. When Clu was playing for the Bisons in the minor leagues."

"You know we did."

"And Billy Lee Palms. He lived there too. At the same time."

"Not Wilston. I think he was in Deerfield. It's the neighboring town."

"So what was Clu doing staying at the Hamlet Motel three days before he died?"

Silence.

"Bonnie?"

"I don't have the slightest idea."

"Think. Why would Clu need to go up there?"

"I don't know. Maybe he was visiting an old friend."

"What old friend?"

"Myron, you're not listening. I don't know. I haven't been up there in almost ten years. But we lived there for eight months. Maybe he made a friend. Maybe he went up there to fish or take a vacation or get away from it all. I don't know."

Myron gripped the phone. "You're lying to me, Bonnie."

Silence.

"Please," he said. "I'm just trying to help Esperanza."

"Let me ask you something, Myron."

"What?"

"You keep digging and digging, right? I asked you not

to. Esperanza asked you not to. Hester Crimstein asked you not to. But you keep digging.''

''Is there a question in there?''

''It's coming now: Has all your digging helped? Has all your digging made Esperanza look more guilty or less?''

Myron hesitated. But it didn't matter. Bonnie hung up before he had the chance to answer. Myron put the phone back in his lap. He looked at Win.

''I'll take Awful Songs for two hundred, Alex,'' Win said.

''What?''

''Answer: Barry Manilow and Eastern Standard.''

Myron almost smiled. ''What is 'Time in New England,' Alex?''

''Correct answer.'' Win shook his head. ''Sometimes when our minds are that in tune—''

''Yeah,'' Myron said. ''It's scary.''

''Shall we?''

Myron thought about it. ''I don't think we have a choice.''

''Call Terese first.''

Myron nodded, started dialing. ''You know how to get there?''

''Yes.''

''It'll probably take three hours.''

Win hit the accelerator. No easy trick in midtown Manhattan. ''Try two.''

CHAPTER **33**

Wilston is in western Massachusetts, about an hour shy of the New Hampshire and Vermont borders. You could still see remnants of the old days, the oft artistically rendered New England town with V-shaped brick walks, colonial clapboard homes, the historical society bronze signs welded onto the front of every other building, the white-steepled chapel in the center of the town—the whole scene screaming for the lush leaves of autumn or a major snowstorm. But like everywhere else in the US of A, the superstore boom was playing havoc with the historical. The roads between these postcard villages had widened over the years, as though guilty of gluttony, feeding off the warehouse-size stores that now lined them. The stores sucked out the character and the quaintness and left in their wake a universal blandness that plagued the byroads and highways of America. Maine to Minnesota, North Carolina to Nevada—there was little texture and individuality left. It was about Home Depot and Office Max and the price clubs.

On the other hand, whining about the changes progress imposes upon us and longing for the good ol' days make for easy pickings. Harder to answer the question of why, if these changes are so bad, do every place and everybody so quickly and warmly welcome them.

Wilston had the classic New England Christmas card–conservative facade, but it was a college town, the college in question being Wilston College, and was thus liberal—liberal in the way only a college town can be, liberal in the way only the young can be, liberal in the way only the isolated and protected and rose-tinted can be. But that was okay. In fact, that was how it should be.

But even Wilston was changing. Yes, the old signs of liberalism were there: the tofu sweet shop, the migrant-friendly coffeehouse, the lesbian bookstore, the shop with the black lightbulbs and the pot paraphernalia, the clothing store that sold only ponchos. But the franchises were sneaking in quietly, slowly eating away at the gray stone corners: Dunkin' Donuts, Angelo's Sub Shop, Baskin-Robbins, Seattle Coffee.

Myron started softly singing "Time in New England."

Win looked at him. "You realize, of course, that I'm well armed."

"Hey, you're the one who got the song stuck in my head."

They sped through town—with Win driving, you only sped—and arrived at the Hamlet Motel, a quasi-dump on Route 9 hovering on the town's edge. A sign advertised FREE HBO! and the ice machine was so large you could see it from your average space station. Myron checked his watch. Less than two hours to get here. Win parked the Jag.

"I don't get it," Myron said. "Why would Clu stay here?"

"Free HBO?"

"More likely because he could pay in cash. That's why

we didn't see anything about this on his credit cards. But why wouldn't he want anyone to know he was here?''

"Such good questions," Win said. "Perhaps you should go inside and see if you can find some of the answers."

They both stepped out of the car. Win noticed a restaurant next door. "I'll try there," he said. "You take the desk clerk."

Myron nodded. The desk clerk, definitely a college kid on break, sat behind the counter and stared straight ahead at nothing. He could have looked more bored, but only if a qualified physician induced a coma. Myron took a glance around and spotted the computer terminal. This was a good thing.

"Hello?"

The kid's eyes slid toward Myron. "Yeah?"

"This computer. It keeps track of outgoing calls, right? Even local ones."

The kid's eyes narrowed. "Who wants to know?"

"I need to see records for all outgoing guest calls from the tenth and eleventh of this month."

That got the kid to his feet. "You a cop? Let me see your badge."

"I'm not a cop."

"Then—"

"I'll pay you five hundred dollars for the information." No sense in playing around here, Myron thought. "No one will ever know."

The kid hesitated but not for long. "Hell, even if I get canned, that's more money than I clear in a month. What dates did you need?"

Myron told him. The kid punched a few buttons. The printer started cranking. It all fitted on one sheet. Myron handed the kid the money. The kid handed him the sheet. Myron quickly scanned the list.

Instant bingo.

He spotted the long-distance call to FJ's office. It had come from room 117. Myron looked for other calls made from the same room. Clu had called his answering machine at home twice. Okay, good, fine. Now how about something more local? No reason to come up here just to make long-distance calls.

Bingo again.

Room 117. The first call on the list. A local number. Myron's heart started pumping, his breath growing shallow. He was close now. So close. He walked outside. The driveway was gravel. He kicked it around a bit. He took out his phone and was about to dial the number. No. That might be a mistake. He should learn all he could first. If he called, he might tip someone off. Of course, he didn't know whom he'd tip off or how they'd be tipped off or what they'd be tipped off about. But he didn't want to screw up now. He had the phone number. Big Cyndi at the office would have a reverse directory. These were easy to come by now. Any software store sold CD-ROMs that had the entire country's phone books on them or you could visit www.infospace.com on the Web. You plug in a number, it tells you who the number belongs to and where they live. More progress.

He called Big Cyndi.

"I was just about to call you, Mr. Bolitar."

"Oh?"

"I have Hester Crimstein on the line. She says that she urgently needs to talk to you."

"Okay, put her through in a sec. Big Cyndi?"

"Yes."

"About what you said yesterday. About people staring. I'm sorry if—"

"No pity, Mr. Bolitar. Remember?"

"Yes."

"Please don't change a thing, okay?"

"Okay."

"I mean it."

"Put Hester Crimstein through," he said. "And while I'm on the line, do you know where Esperanza keeps the reverse phone directory CDs?"

"Yes."

"I want you to look up a number for me." He read it off to her. She repeated it. Then she put Hester Crimstein through.

"Where are you?" the attorney barked at him.

"Why do you care?"

Hester was not pleased. "God damn it, Myron, stop acting like a child. Where are you?"

"None of your business."

"You're not helping."

"What do you want, Hester?"

"You're on a cell phone, right?"

"Right."

"Then we don't know if the line is safe," she said. "We have to meet right away. I'll be in my office."

"No can do."

"Look, do you want to help Esperanza or not?"

"You know the answer to that."

"Then get your ass in here, pronto," Hester said. "We got a problem, and I think you can help."

"What kind of problem?"

"Not on the phone. I'll be waiting for you."

"It'll take me some time," Myron said.

Silence.

"Why will it take some time, Myron?"

"It just will."

"It's almost noon," she said. "When can I expect you?"

"Not until at least six."

"That's too late."

"Sorry."

She sighed. "Myron, get here now. Esperanza wants to see you."

Myron's heart did a little flip. "I thought she was in jail."

"I just got her released. It's hush-hush. Get your ass over here, Myron. Get over here now."

Myron and Win stood in the Hamlet Motel parking lot.

"What do you make of it?" Win asked.

"I don't like it," Myron said.

"How so?"

"Why is Hester Crimstein so desperate to see me all of a sudden? She's been trying to get rid of me from the moment I returned. Now I'm the answer to a problem?"

"It is bizarre," Win agreed.

"And not only that, I don't like this whole hush-hush release for Esperanza."

"It happens."

"Sure, it happens. But if it did, why hasn't Esperanza called me? Why is Hester making the call for her?"

"Why indeed?"

Myron thought about it. "Do you think she's involved in all this?"

"I cannot imagine how," Win said. Then: "Except that she may have spoken to Bonnie Haid."

"So?"

"So then she may have deduced that we are in Wilston."

"And now she urgently wants us to return," Myron said.

"Yes."

"So she's trying to get us out of Wilston."

"It is a possibility," Win said.

"So what is she afraid we'll find?"

Win shrugged. "She's Esperanza's advocate."

"So something detrimental to Esperanza."

"Logical," Win said.

A couple in their eighties stumbled out of one of the motel rooms. The old man had his arm around the woman's shoulder. They both looked postsex. At noon. Nice to see. Myron and Win watched them in silence.

"I pushed too hard last time," Myron said.

Win did not reply.

"You warned me. You told me I didn't keep my eye on the prize. But I didn't listen."

Win still said nothing.

"Am I doing the same now?"

"You are not good at letting things go," Win said.

"That's not an answer."

Win frowned. "I'm not some holy wise man on the mount," he said. "I don't have all the answers."

"I want to know what you think."

Win squinted, though the sun was pretty much gone by now. "Last time, you lost sight of your goal," he said. "Do you know what your goal is this time?"

Myron thought about it. "Freeing Esperanza," he said. "And finding the truth."

Win smiled. "And if those two are mutually contradictory?"

"Then I bury the truth."

Win nodded. "You seem to have a good handle on the goal."

"Should I let it go anyway?" Myron asked.

Win looked at him. "There's one other complication."

"What's that?"

"Lucy Mayor."

"I'm not actively looking for her. I'd love to find her, but I don't expect to."

"Still," Win said, "she is your personal connection into all this."

Myron shook his head.

"The diskette came to you, Myron. You can't run away from that. You're not built that way. Somehow you and this missing girl are linked."

Silence.

Myron checked the address and name Big Cyndi had given him. The phone was listed to a Barbara Cromwell at 12 Claremont Road. The name meant nothing to him. "There's a rental car place down the street," Myron said. "You go back. Talk to Hester Crimstein. See what you can learn."

"And you?"

"I'm going to check out Barbara Cromwell of Twelve Claremont Road."

"Sounds like a plan," Win said.

"A good one?"

"I didn't say that."

Massachusetts, like Myron's home state of New Jersey, can quickly turn from big city to full-fledged town to hicksville. That was the case here. Twelve Claremont Road—why the numbers reached twelve when the whole road had only three buildings on it Myron could not say— was an old farmhouse. At least it looked old. The color, probably once a deep red, had faded to a barely visible, watery pastel. The top of the structure curled forward as though suffering from osteoporosis. The front roof over-hang had split down the middle, the right lip dipping for-ward like the mouth of a stroke victim. There were loose boards and major cracks and the grass was tall enough to go on the adult rides at a Six Flags.

He stopped in front of Barbara Cromwell's house and debated his approach. He hit the redial button and Big Cyndi answered.

"Got anything yet?"

"Not very much, Mr. Bolitar. Barbara Cromwell is thirty-one years old. She was divorced four years ago from a Lawrence Cromwell."

"Children?"

"That's all I have right now, Mr. Bolitar. I'm terribly sorry."

He thanked her and said to keep trying. He looked back at the house. There was a dull, steady thudding in his chest. Thirty-one years old. He reached into his pocket and took out the computer rendering of the aged Lucy Mayor. He stared at it. How old would Lucy be if she were still alive? Twenty-nine, maybe thirty. Close in age, but who cares? He shook the thought away, but it didn't go easy.

Now what?

He turned off the engine. A curtain jumped in an upstairs window. Spotted. No choice now. He opened the door and walked up the drive. It had been paved at one time, but the grass now laid claim to all but a few patches of tar. The side yard had one of those plastic Fisher-Price tree houses with a slide and rope ladder; the loud yellow, blue, and red of the play set shone through the brown grass like gems against black velvet. He reached the door. No bell, so he knocked and waited.

He could hear house sounds, someone running, someone whispering. A child called out, "Mom!" Someone hushed him.

Myron heard footsteps, and then a woman said, "Yes?"

"Ms. Cromwell?"

"What do you want?"

"Ms. Cromwell, my name is Myron Bolitar. I'd like to talk to you a moment."

"I don't want to buy anything."

"No, ma'am, I'm not selling—"

"And I don't accept door-to-door solicitations. You want a donation, you ask by mail."

"I'm not here for any of that."

Brief silence.

"Then what do you want?" she said.

"Ms. Cromwell"—he'd clipped on his most reassuring voice now—"would you mind opening your door?"

"I'm calling the police."

"No, no, please, just wait a second."

"What do you want?"

"I want to ask you about Clu Haid."

There was a long pause. The little boy started talking again. The woman hushed him. "I don't know anybody by that name."

"Please open the door, Ms. Cromwell. We need to talk."

"Look, mister, I'm friendly with all the cops around here. I say the word, they'll lock you up for trespassing."

"I understand your concerns," Myron said. "How about if we talk by phone?"

"Just go away."

The little boy started crying.

"Go away," she repeated. "Or I'll call the police."

More crying.

"Okay," Myron said. "I'm leaving." Then, figuring what the hey, he shouted, "Does the name Lucy Mayor mean anything to you?"

The child's crying was the only reply.

Myron let loose a sigh and started back to the car. Now what? He hadn't even been able to see her. Maybe he could poke around the house, try to peek in a window. Oh, that was a great idea. Get arrested for peeping. Or worse, scare a little kid. And she'd call the cops for sure—

Hold the phone.

Barbara Cromwell said that she was friendly with the police in town. But so was Myron. In a way. Wilston was the town where Clu had been nabbed on that first drunk driving charge when he was in the minors. Myron had gotten him off with the help of two cops. He scanned the memory banks for names. It didn't take him long. The arresting officer was named Kobler. Myron didn't remember his first name. The sheriff was a guy named Ron Lemmon. Lemmon was in his fifties then. He might have retired. But odds were pretty good one of them would still be on the force. They might know something about the mysterious Barbara Cromwell.

Worth a shot anyway.

CHAPTER 35

One might expect the Wilston police station to be in a dinky little building. Not so. It was in the basement of a tall, fortresslike structure of dark, old brick. The steps down had one of those old bomb shelter signs, the black and yellow triangles still bright in the ominous circle. The image brought back memories of Burnet Hill Elementary School and the old bombing drills, a somewhat intense activity in which children were taught that crouching in a corridor was a suitable defense against a Soviet nuclear blitzkrieg.

Myron had never been to the station house before. After Clu's accident he'd met with the two cops in the back booth of a diner on Route 9. The whole episode took less than ten minutes. No one wanted to hurt the up-and-coming superstar. No one wanted to ruin Clu's promising young career. Dollars changed hands—some for the arresting officer, some for the sheriff in charge. Donations, they'd called it with a chuckle. Everyone smiled.

The desk sergeant looked up at Myron when he came in. He was around thirty and, like so many cops nowadays, built as if he spent more time in the weight room than the doughnut shop. His nametag read "Hobert." "May I help you?"

"Does Sheriff Lemmon still work here?"

"No, sorry to say. Ron died, oh, gotta be a year now. Retired about two years before that."

"I'm sorry to hear that."

"Yeah, cancer. Ate through him like a hungry rat." Hobert shrugged as if to say, What can you do?

"How about a guy named Kobler? I think he was a deputy about ten years ago."

Hobert's voice was suddenly tight. "Eddie's not on the force anymore."

"Does he still live in the area?"

"No. I think he lives in Wyoming. May I ask your name, sir?"

"Myron Bolitar."

"Your name sounds familiar."

"I used to play basketball."

"Nah, that's not it. I hate basketball." He thought a moment, then shook his head. "So why are you asking about two former cops?"

"They're sort of old friends."

Hobert looked doubtful.

"I wanted to ask them about someone a client of mine has become involved with."

"A client?"

Myron put on his helpless-puppy-dog smile. He usually used it on old ladies, but hey, waste not, want not. "I'm a sports agent. My job is to look after athletes and, well, make sure they're not being taken advantage of. So this client of mine has an interest in a lady who lives in town. I just wanted to make sure she's not a gold digger or anything."

Two words: *truly lame.*

Hobert said, "What's her name?"

"Barbara Cromwell."

The officer blinked. "This a joke?"

"No."

"One of your athletes is interested in dating Barbara Cromwell?"

Myron tried a little backpedal. "I might have gotten the name wrong," he said.

"I think maybe you have."

"Why's that?"

"You mentioned Ron Lemmon before. The old sheriff."

"Right."

"Barbara Cromwell is his daughter."

For a moment Myron just stood there. A fan whirred. A phone rang. Hobert said, "Excuse me a second," and picked it up. Myron heard none of it. Someone had frozen the moment. Someone had suspended him above a dark hole, giving Myron plenty of time to stare down at the nothingness, until suddenly the same someone let go. Myron plunged down into the black, his hands wheeling, his body turning, waiting, almost hoping, to smash against the bottom.

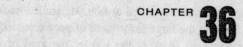

CHAPTER 36

Myron stumbled back outside. He walked the town square. He grabbed something to eat at a Mexican place, wolfing it down without even tasting the food. Win called.

"We were correct," Win said. "Hester Crimstein was trying to divert our attention."

"She admitted it?"

"No. She offers no explanation. She claims that she will speak with you and only you and only in person. She then pushed me for details on your whereabouts."

No surprise.

"Would you like me to"—Win paused—"interrogate her?"

"Please no," Myron said. "Ethics aside, I don't think there's much need anymore."

"Oh?"

"Sawyer Wells said he was a drug counselor at Rockwell."

"I remember."

"Billy Lee Palms was treated at Rockwell. His mother mentioned it when I visited her house."

"Hmm," Win said. "Wonderful coincidence."

"Not a coincidence," Myron said. "It explains everything."

When he finished talking to Win, he strolled the main street of Wilston seven or eight times over. The shopkeepers, light on business, smiled at him. He smiled back. He nodded hello to the large assortment of people passing by. The town was so stuck in the sixties, the kind of place where people still wore unkempt beards and black caps and looked like Seals and Crofts at an outdoor concert. He liked it here. He liked it a lot.

He thought about his mother and his father. He thought about them getting old and wondered why he could not accept it. He thought about how his father's "chest pains" were partially his fault, how the strain of his running away had at least tangentially contributed to what happened. He thought about what it would have been like for his parents if they had suffered the same fate as Sophie and Gary Mayor, if he had disappeared at seventeen without a trace and were never found. He thought about Jessica and how she claimed she would fight for him. He thought about Brenda and what he had done. He thought about Terese and last night and what, if anything, it meant. He thought about Win and Esperanza and the sacrifices that friends make.

For a long time he did not think about Clu's murder or Billy Lee's death. He did not think about Lucy Mayor and her disappearance and his connection to it. But that lasted only so long. Eventually he made a few phone calls, did some digging, confirmed what he already suspected.

The answers never come with cries of "Eureka!" You stumble toward them, often in total darkness. You stagger through an unlit room at night, tripping over the unseen, lumbering forward, bruising your shins, toppling over and righting yourself, feeling your way across the walls and hoping your hand happens upon the light switch. And then —to keep within this piss-poor but sadly accurate analogy —when you find the switch, when you flick it on and bathe the room in light, sometimes the room is just as you pictured it. And then sometimes, like now, you wonder if you'd have been better off staying forever stumbling in the dark.

Win of course would say that Myron was limiting the analogy. He would point out that there were other options. You could simply leave the room. You could let your eyes get accustomed to the dark, and while you would never see everything clearly, that was okay. You could even flick the switch back off once you turned it on. In the case of Horace and Brenda Slaughter, Win would be right. In the case of Clu Haid, Myron was not so sure.

He had found the light switch. He had flicked it on. But the analogy did not hold—and not just because it was a dumb one from the start. Everything in the room was still murky, as though he were looking through a shower curtain. He could see lights and shadows. He could make out shapes. But to know exactly what had happened, he would have to push aside the curtain.

He could still back off, let the curtain rest or even flick the light back off. But that was the problem with darkness and Win's options. In the dark you cannot see the rot fester. The rot is free to continue to eat away, undisturbed, until it consumes everything, even the man huddled in the corner, trying like hell to stay away from that damned light switch.

So Myron got in his car. He drove back out to the farmhouse on Claremont Road. He knocked on the door, and again Barbara Cromwell told him to go away. "I know why Clu Haid came here," he told her. He kept talking. And eventually she let him in.

When he left, Myron called Win again. They talked a long time. First about Clu Haid's murder. Then about Myron's dad. It helped. But not a lot. He called Terese and told her what he knew. She said that she'd tried to check some of the facts with her sources.

"So Win was right," Terese said. "You are personally connected."

"Yes."

"I blame myself every day," Terese said. "You get used to it."

Again he wanted to ask more. Again he knew that it wasn't time.

Myron made two more calls on the cell phone. The first was to the law office of Hester Crimstein.

"Where are you?" Hester snapped.

"I assume you're in contact with Bonnie Haid," he said.

Pause. Then: "Oh Christ, Myron, what did you do?"

"They aren't telling you everything, Hester. In fact, I bet Esperanza barely told you anything."

"Where are you, dammit?"

"I'll be in your office in three hours. Have Bonnie there."

His final call was to Sophie Mayor. When she answered, he said three words: "I found Lucy."

CHAPTER 37

Myron tried to drive like Win, but that was beyond his capabilities. He sped, but he still hit construction on Route 95. You always hit construction on Route 95. It was a Connecticut state law. He listened to the radio. He made phone calls. He felt frightened.

Hester Crimstein was a senior partner in a high-rise, higher-bill, mega New York law firm. The attractive receptionist had clearly been expecting him. She led him down a hallway lined with what looked like mahogany wallpaper and into a conference room. There was a rectangular table big enough to seat twenty, pens and legal pads in front of each chair, billable no doubt to some unsuspecting client at wildly inflated prices. Hester Crimstein sat next to Bonnie Haid, their backs to the window. They started to rise when he entered.

"Don't bother," he said.

Both women stopped.

"What's this all about?" Hester asked.

Myron ignored her and looked at Bonnie. "You almost told me, didn't you, Bonnie? When I first came back. You said you wondered if we did Clu a disservice by helping him. You wondered if our sheltering him and protecting him had eventually led to his death. I said you were wrong. The only person to blame is the person who shot him. But I didn't know everything, did I?''

"What the hell are you talking about?'' Hester said.

"I want to tell you a story,'' he said.

"What?''

"Just listen, Hester. You might find out what you've gotten yourself involved in.''

Hester closed her mouth. Bonnie kept silent.

"Twelve years ago,'' Myron said, "Clu Haid and Billy Lee Palms were minor-league players for a team called the New England Bisons. They were both young and reckless in the way athletes tend to be. The world was their oyster, they thought they were the cat's pajamas, you know the fairy tale. I won't insult you by going into details.''

Both women slid back into their seats. Myron sat across from them and continued.

"One day Clu Haid drove drunk—well, he probably drove drunk more than once, but on this occasion he wrapped his car around a tree. Bonnie''—he gestured to her with his chin—"was injured in the accident. She suffered a bad concussion and spent several days in the hospital. Clu was unhurt. Billy Lee broke a finger. When it happened, Clu panicked. A drunk driving charge could ruin a young athlete, even as little as twelve years ago. I had just signed him to several profitable endorsement deals. He was going to move up to the majors in a matter of months. So he did what a lot of athletes did. He found someone who'd get him out of trouble. His agent. Me. I drove up to the scene like a madman. I met with the arresting officer, a guy named Eddie Kobler, and the town sheriff, Ron Lemmon.''

Hester Crimstein said, "I don't understand any of this."

"Give me time, you will," Myron said. "The officers and I came to an understanding. It happens all the time with big-time athletes. Matters like this are swept under the rug. Clu was a good kid, we all agreed. No reason to destroy his life over this little incident. It was a somewhat victimless crime—the only person hurt was Clu's own wife. So money changed hands, and an agreement was reached. Clu wasn't drunk. He swerved to avoid another car. That's what caused the accident. Billy Lee Palms and Bonnie would swear to it. Incident over and forgotten."

Hester wore her annoyed-but-curious scowl. Bonnie's face was losing color fast.

"It's twelve years later now," Myron said. "And the incident is almost like one of those mummy curses. The drunk driver, Clu, is murdered. His best friend and passenger, Billy Lee Palms, is shot to death—I won't call that murder because the shooter saved my life. The sheriff I bought off—he died of prostate cancer. Nothing too strange about that or perhaps God got to him before the mummy. And as for Eddie Kobler, the other officer, he was caught last year taking bribes in a big drug string. He was arrested and plea-bargained down. His wife left him. His kids won't talk to him. He lives alone in a bottle in Wyoming."

"How do you know about this Kobler guy?" Hester Crimstein asked.

"A local cop named Hobert told me what happened. A reporter friend confirmed it."

"I still don't see the relevance," Hester said.

"That's because Esperanza kept you in the dark," Myron said. "I was wondering how much she told you. Apparently not much. Probably just insisted that I be kept totally out of this, right?''

Hester gave him the courtroom eyes. ''Are you saying Esperanza has something to do with all this?''

''No.''

''You're the one who committed a crime here, Myron. You bribed two police officers.''

''And there's the rub,'' Myron said.

''What are you talking about?''

''Even that night something struck me as odd about the whole incident. The three of them in the car together. Why? Bonnie didn't much care for Billy Lee Palms. Sure, she'd go out with Clu and Clu would go out with Billy Lee and maybe they'd even double-date or something. But why were the three of them in that car so late at night?''

Hester Crimstein stayed the lawyer. ''Are you saying one of them wasn't in the car?''

''No. I'm saying that there were four people in the car, not three.''

''What?''

They both looked at Bonnie. Bonnie lowered her head.

''Who were the four?'' Hester asked.

''Bonnie and Clu were one couple.'' Myron tried to meet Bonnie's eyes, but she wouldn't look up. ''Billy Lee Palms and Lucy Mayor were the other.''

Hester Crimstein looked as if she'd been hit with a two-by-four. ''Lucy Mayor?'' she repeated. ''As in the missing Mayor girl?''

''Yes.''

''Jesus Christ.''

Myron kept his eyes on Bonnie. Eventually she raised her head. ''It's true, isn't it?''

Hester Crimstein said, ''She's not talking.''

''Yes,'' Bonnie said. ''It's true.''

"But you never knew what happened to her, did you?"

Bonnie hesitated. "Not then, no."

"What did Clu tell you?"

"That you bought her off too," Bonnie said. "Like with the police. He said you paid her to keep silent."

Myron nodded. It made sense. "There's one thing I don't get. There was a ton of publicity about Lucy Mayor a few years back. You must have seen her picture in the paper."

"I did."

"Didn't it ring a bell?"

"No. You have to remember. I only saw her that one time. You know Billy Lee. A different girl every night. And Clu and I sat in the front. Her hair was a different color too. She was a blonde then. So I didn't know."

"And neither did Clu."

"That's right."

"But eventually you learned the truth."

"Eventually," she said.

"Whoa," Hester Crimstein said. "I'm not following any of this. What does an old traffic accident have to do with Clu's murder?"

"Everything," Myron said.

"You better explain, Myron. And while you're at it, why did Esperanza get framed for it?"

"That was a mistake."

"What?"

"Esperanza wasn't the one they intended to frame," Myron said. "I was."

CHAPTER 38

Yankee Stadium hunched over in the night, crouching shoulders low as though trying to escape the glow from its own lights. Myron parked in Lot 14, where the executives and players parked. There were only three other cars there. The night guard at the press entrance said he was expected, that the Mayors would meet him on the field. Myron moved down the lower tier and hopped the wall near the batter's box. The stadium lights were on, but nobody was there. He stood alone on the field and took a deep breath. Even in the Bronx nothing smelled like a baseball diamond. He turned toward the visitor's dugout, scanning the lower boxes and finding the exact seats he and his brother had sat in all those years ago. Funny what you remember. He walked toward the pitcher's mound, the grass making a gentle whooshing sound, and sat down on the rubber and waited. Clu's home. The one place he'd always felt at peace.

Should have buried him here, Myron thought. *Under a pitcher's mound.*

He stared up into the thousands of seats, empty like the shattered eyes of the dead, the vacant stadium merely a body now without a soul. The whites of the foul lines were muddied, nearly dirt-toned now. They'd be put down anew tomorrow before game time.

People say that baseball is a metaphor for life. Myron did not know about that, but staring down the foul line, he wondered. The line between good and evil is not so different from the foul line on a baseball field. It's often made of stuff as flimsy as lime. It tends to fade over time. It needs to be constantly redrawn. And if enough players trample on it, the line becomes smeared and blurred to the point where fair is foul and foul is fair, where good and evil become indistinguishable from each other.

Jared Mayor's voice broke the stillness. "You said you found my sister."

Myron squinted toward the dugout. "I lied," he said.

Jared stepped up the cement stairs. Sophie followed. Myron rose to his feet. Jared started to say something more, but his mother put her hand on his arm. They kept walking as though they were coaches coming out to talk to the relief pitcher.

"Your sister is dead," Myron said. "But you both know that."

They kept walking.

"She was killed in a drunk driving accident," he went on. "She died on impact."

"Maybe," Sophie said.

Myron looked confused. "Maybe?"

"Maybe she died on impact, maybe she didn't," Sophie continued. "Clu Haid and Billy Lee Palms weren't doctors. They were dumb, drunk jocks. Lucy might have just been injured. She may have been alive. A doctor might have been able to save her."

Myron nodded. "I guess that's possible."

"Go on," Sophie said. "I want to hear what you have to say."

"Whatever your daughter's condition actually was, Clu and Billy Lee believed that she was dead. Clu was terrified. Drunk driving charges would be serious enough, but this was vehicular homicide. You don't walk away from that, no matter how far your curveball breaks. He and Billy Lee panicked. I don't know the details here. Sawyer Wells can tell us. My guess is that they hid the body. It was a quiet road, but there still wouldn't be enough time to bury Lucy before the police and ambulance arrived. So they probably stashed her in the brush. And when it all calmed down, they came back and buried her. Like I said, I don't know the details. I don't think they're particularly relevant. What is relevant is that Clu and Billy Lee got rid of the body."

Jared stepped into Myron's face. "You can't prove any of this."

Myron ignored him, keeping his eyes on Jared's mother. "The years pass. Lucy is gone. But not in the minds of Clu Haid and Billy Lee Palms. Maybe I'm over-analyzing. Maybe I'm being too easy on them. But I think what they did that night defined the rest of their lives. Their self-destructive tendencies. The drugs—"

"You're being too easy," Sophie said.

Myron waited.

"Don't give them credit for having consciences," she continued. "They were worthless scum."

"Maybe you're right. I shouldn't analyze. And I guess it doesn't matter. Clu and Billy Lee may have created their own hell, but it wasn't close to the agony your family experienced. You told me about the awful torment of not knowing the truth, how it lives with you every day. With Lucy dead and buried like that, the torment just went on."

Sophie's head was still high. There was no flinch in her. "Do you know how we finally learned our daughter's fate?"

"From Sawyer Wells," Myron said. "The Wells Rules of Wellness, Rule Eight: 'Confess something about yourself to a friend—something awful, something you'd never want anyone to know. You'll feel better. You'll still see that you're worthy of love.' Sawyer was a drug counselor at Rockwell. Billy Lee was a patient there. My guess is that he caught him during a withdrawal episode. When he was delirious probably. He did what his therapist asked. Rule eight. He confessed the worst thing he could imagine, the one moment in his life that shaped all others. Sawyer suddenly saw his ticket out of Rockwell and into the spotlight. Through the wealthy Mayor family, owners of Mayor Software. So he went to you and your husband. And he told you what he'd heard."

Again Jared said, "You have no proof of any of this!"

And again Sophie silenced him with her hand. "Go on, Myron," she said. "What happened then?"

"With this new information, you found your daughter's body. I don't know if your private investigators did it or if you just used your money and influence to keep the authorities quiet. It wouldn't have been difficult for someone in your position."

"I see," Sophie said. "But if all that's true, why would I want to keep it quiet? Why not prosecute Clu and Billy Lee—and even you?"

"Because you couldn't," Myron said.

"Why not?"

"The corpse had been buried for twelve years. There was no evidence there. The car was long gone—no evidence there either. The police report listed a Breathalyzer test that showed Clu was not drunk. So what did you have:

the ranting of a drug addict going through withdrawal? Billy Lee's confession to Sawyer Wells would probably be suppressed, and even if it wasn't, so what? His testimony about the police payoffs was complete hearsay since he wasn't even there when it happened. You realized all that, didn't you?''

She said nothing.

''And that meant justice was up to you, Sophie. You and Gary would have to avenge your daughter.'' He stopped, looked at Jared, then back at Sophie. ''You told me about a void. You said that you preferred to fill that void with hope.''

Sophie nodded. ''I did.''

''And when the hope was gone—when the discovery of your daughter's body sucked it all away—you and your husband still needed to fill that void.''

''Yes.''

''So you filled it with revenge.''

She fixed her gaze on his. ''Do you blame us, Myron?''

He said nothing.

''The crooked sheriff was dying of cancer,'' Sophie said. ''There was nothing to be done about him. The other officer, well, as your friend Win could tell you, money is influence. The Federal Bureau of Investigation set him up at our behest. He took the bait. And yes, I shattered his life. Gladly.''

''But Clu was the one you wanted to hurt most,'' Myron said.

''Hurt nothing. I wanted to crush him.''

''But he too was fairly broken down,'' Myron said. ''In order to really crush him, you had to give him hope. Just like you and Gary had all these years. Give him hope, then snatch it away. Hope hurts like nothing else. You knew that. So you and your husband bought the Yankees. You overpaid, but so what? You had the money. You didn't care. Gary died soon after the transaction.''

''From heartache,'' Sophie interrupted. She raised her head, and for the first time he saw a tear. ''From years of heartache.''

''But you carried on without him.''

''Yes.''

''You concentrated on one thing and one thing only: getting Clu in your grasp. It was a silly trade—everyone thought so—and it was strange coming from an owner who kept out of every other baseball decision. But it was all about getting Clu on the team. That's the only reason you bought the Yankees. To give Clu a last chance. And even better, Clu cooperated. He started straightening out his life. He was clean and sober. He was pitching well. He was as happy as Clu Haid was ever going to get. You had him in the palm of your hand.''

''And then you closed your fist.''

Jared put his arm around her shoulders and pressed her close.

''I don't know the order,'' Myron went on. ''You sent Clu a computer diskette like you sent me. Bonnie told me that. She also told me that you blackmailed him. Anonymously. That explains the missing two hundred thousand dollars. You made him live in terror. And Bonnie even inadvertently helped you by filing for divorce. Now Clu was in the perfect position for your coup de grace: the drug test. You fixed it so he would fail. Sawyer helped. Who better, since he already knew what was going on? It worked beautifully. Not only did it destroy Clu, but it also diverted any attention from you. Who would ever suspect you, especially since the test seemingly hurt you too? But you didn't care about any of that. The Yankees meant nothing to you except as a vehicle to destroy Clu Haid.''

"So true," Sophie said.

"Don't," Jared said.

She shook her head and patted her son's arm. "It's okay."

"Clu had no idea the girl he buried in the woods was your daughter. But after you bombarded him with the calls and the diskette and especially after he failed the drug test, he put it together. But what could he do about it? He certainly couldn't say the drug test was fixed because he'd killed Lucy Mayor. He was trapped. He tried to figure out how you'd learned the truth. He thought maybe it was Barbara Cromwell."

"Who?"

"Barbara Cromwell. She's Sheriff Lemmon's daughter."

"How did she know?"

"Because as quiet as you tried to keep the investigation, Wilston is a small town. The sheriff was tipped off about the discovery. He was dying. He had no money. His family was poor. So he told his daughter about what had really happened that night. She could never get in trouble for it—it was his crime, not hers. And they could use the information to blackmail Clu Haid. Which they did. On several occasions. Clu figured Barbara had been the one who opened her mouth. When he called her to find out if she'd told anyone, Barbara played coy. She demanded more money. So Clu drove up to Wilston a few days later. He refused to pay her. He said it was over."

Sophie nodded. "So that's how you put it together."

"It was the final piece, yes," Myron said. "When I realized that Clu had visited Lemmon's daughter, it all fell into place. But I'm still surprised, Sophie."

"Surprised about what?"

"That you killed him. That you let Clu out of his misery."

Jared's arm dropped off his mother. "What are you talking about?" he said.

"Let him speak," Sophie said. "Go on, Myron."

"What more is there?"

"For starters," she said, "how about your part in all this?"

A lead block formed in his chest. He said nothing.

"You're not going to claim that you were blameless in all this, are you, Myron?"

His voice was soft. "No."

In the distance, out beyond center field, a janitor started cleaning off the memorials to the Yankees' greats. He sprayed and wiped, working, Myron knew from past stadium visits, on Lou Gehrig's stone. The Iron Horse. Such bravery in the face of so awful a death.

"You've done this too, haven't you?" Sophie said.

Myron kept his eyes on the janitor. "Done what?" But he knew.

"I've looked into your past," she said. "You and your business associate often take the law into your own hands, am I right? You play judge and jury."

Myron said nothing.

"That's all I did. For the sake of my daughter's memory."

The blurry line between fair and foul again. "So you decided to frame me for Clu's murder."

"Yes."

"The perfect way to wreak vengeance on me for bribing the officers."

"I thought so at the time."

"But you messed up, Sophie. You ended up framing the wrong person."

"That was an accident."

Myron shook his head. "I should have seen it," he said. "Even Billy Lee Palms said it, but I didn't pay attention. And Hester Crimstein said it to me the first time I met her."

"Said what?"

"They both pointed out that the blood was found in *my* car, the gun in *my* office. Maybe I killed Clu, they said. A logical deduction except for one thing. I was out of the country. You didn't know that, Sophie. You didn't know that Esperanza and Big Cyndi were playing a shell game with everybody, pretending I was still around. That's why you were so upset with me when you found out I'd been away. I messed up your plan. You also didn't know that Clu had an altercation with Esperanza. So all the evidence that was supposed to point to me—"

"Pointed instead to your associate, Miss Diaz," Sophie said.

"Exactly," Myron said. "But there's one other thing I want to clear up."

"More than one thing," Sophie corrected.

"What?"

"There's more than one thing you'll want to clear up," Sophie said. "But please go ahead. What would you like to know?"

"You were the one who had me followed," he said. "The guy I spotted outside the Lock-Horne building. He was yours."

"Yes. I knew Clu had tried to hook up with you. I hoped the same might happen with Billy Lee Palms."

"Which it did. Billy Lee thought that maybe I killed Clu to keep my part in the crime buried. He thought I wanted to kill him too."

"It makes sense," she agreed. "You had a lot to lose."

"So you were following me then? At the bar?"

"Yes."

"Personally?"

She smiled. "I grew up a hunter and a tracker, Myron. The city or the woods, it makes little difference."

"You saved my life," he said.

She did not reply.

"Why?"

"You know why. I didn't come there to kill Billy Lee Palms. But there are degrees of guilt. Simply put, he was more guilty than you. When it came down to a question of you or him, I chose to kill him. You deserve to be punished, Myron. But you didn't deserve to be killed by scum like Billy Lee Palms."

"Judge and jury again?"

"Luckily for you, Myron, yes."

He sat down hard on the pitcher's mound, his whole body suddenly drained. "I can't just let you get away with this," he said. "I may sympathize. But you killed Clu Haid in cold blood."

"No."

"What?"

"I didn't kill Clu Haid."

"I don't expect you to confess."

"Expect or don't expect. I didn't kill him."

Myron frowned. "You had to. It all adds up."

Her eyes remained placid pools. Myron's head started spinning. He turned and looked up at Jared.

"He didn't kill him either," Sophie said.

"One of you did," Myron said.

"No."

Myron looked at Jared. Jared said nothing. Myron opened his mouth, closed it, tried to come up with something.

"Think, Myron." Sophie crossed her arms and smiled at him. "I told you my philosophy when you were last here. I'm a hunter. I don't hate what I kill. Just the opposite. I respect what I kill. I honor my kill. I consider the animal brave and noble. Killing, in fact, can be merciful. That's why I kill with one shot. Not Billy Lee Palms, of course. I wanted him to have at least a few moments of agony and fear. And of course, I would never show Clu Haid mercy."

Myron tried to sort through it. "But—"

And then he heard yet another click. His conversation with Sally Li started uncoiling in his head.

The crime scene . . .

Christ, the crime scene. It was in such a state of disarray. Blood on the walls. Blood on the floor. Because blood splatters would show the truth. So splatter some more. Destroy the evidence. Fire more shots into the corpse. To the calf, to the back, even to the head. Take the gun with you. Mess things up. Cover up what really happened.

"Oh God . . ."

Sophie nodded at him.

Myron's mouth felt dry as a sandstorm. "Clu committed suicide?"

Sophie tried a smile, but she just couldn't quite make it.

Myron started to stand, his bad knee audibly creaking as he rose. "The end of his marriage, the failed drug test, but mostly the past coming back at him—it was all too much. He shot himself in the head. The other shots were just to throw the police off. The crime scene was messed up so no one would be able to analyze the blood splatters and see it was a suicide. It was all a diversion."

"A coward to the end," Sophie said.

"But how did you know he killed himself? Did you have his place bugged or under surveillance?"

"Nothing so technical, Myron. He wanted us to find him—me specifically."

Myron just stared at her.

"We were supposed to have our big confrontation that night. Yes, Clu had hit rock bottom, Myron. But I was not through with him. Not by a long shot. An animal deserved a quick kill. Not Clu Haid. But when Jared and I arrived, he'd already taken the gutless way out."

"And the money?"

"It was there. As you noted, the anonymous stranger who sent him the diskette and made all those phone calls was blackmailing him. But he knew it was us. I took the money that night and donated it to the Child Welfare Institute."

"You caused him to kill himself."

She shook her head, her posture still ramrod. "Nobody causes someone to kill himself. Clu Haid chose his fate. It was not what I intended but—"

"Intended? He's dead, Sophie."

"Yes, but it was not what I *intended*. Just as you, Myron, did not *intend* to cover up my daughter's murder."

Silence.

"You took advantage of his death," Myron said. "You planted the blood and gun in my car and office. Or you hired someone to do it."

"Yes."

He shook his head. "The truth has to come out," he said.

"No."

"I'm not letting Esperanza rot in jail—"

"It's done," Sophie Mayor said.

"What?"

"My attorney is meeting with the DA as we speak.

Anonymously, of course. They won't know whom he represents.''

"I don't understand."

"I kept evidence that night," she said. "I took pictures of the body. They'll test Clu's hand for powder residue. I even have a suicide note, if need be. The charges against Esperanza will be dropped. She'll be released in the morning. It's over."

"The DA isn't going to settle for that. He's going to want to know the whole story."

"Life is full of wants, Myron. But the DA won't get it in this case. He'll just have to live with that reality. And in the end it's just a suicide anyway. High profile or not, it won't be a priority." She reached into her pocket and took out a piece of paper. "Here," she said. "It's Clu's suicide note."

Myron hesitated. He took the note, immediately recognizing Clu's handwriting. He started reading:

Dear Mrs. Mayor,
The torment has gone on long enough. I know you won't accept my apology and I can't say that I blame you. But I also don't have the strength to face you. I've been running away from that night all my life. I hurt my family and my friends, but I hurt nobody so much as I hurt you. I hope my death gives you some measure of comfort.
I am the one to blame for what happened. Billy Lee Palms just did what I told him to. The same goes for Myron Bolitar. I paid off the police. Myron just delivered the money. He never knew the truth. My wife was knocked out in the accident. She also never knew the truth and she still doesn't.
The money is all here. Do with it what you will. Tell Bonnie that I'm sorry and that I understand everything.

And let my children know that their father always loved them. They were the only thing pure and good in my life. You, of all people, should understand that.

Clu Haid

Myron read the note again. He pictured Clu writing it, then putting it aside, then picking up the gun and pressing it against his head. Did he close his eyes then? Did he think of his children, the two boys with his smile, before he pulled the trigger? Did he hesitate at all?

His eyes stayed on the note. "You didn't believe him," he said.

"About the culpability of the others? No. I knew he was lying. You, for example. You were more than a delivery boy. You bribed those officers."

"Clu lied to protect us," Myron said. "In the end he sacrificed himself for those he loved."

Sophie frowned. "Don't make him out to be a martyr."

"I'm not. But you just can't walk away from what you did."

"I did nothing."

"You made a man—the father of two boys—kill himself."

"He made a choice, that's all."

"He didn't deserve that."

"And my daughter didn't deserve to be murdered and buried in an anonymous pit," she said.

Myron looked up into the stadium lights, letting them blind him a bit.

"Clu was off drugs," he said. "You'll pay the rest of his salary."

"No."

"You'll also let the world know—and his children—that in the end Clu wasn't on drugs."

"No," Sophie said again. "The world won't know that. And they also won't know Clu was a murderer. I'd say that's a pretty good bargain, wouldn't you?"

He read the note again, tears stinging his eyes.

"One heroic moment in the end doesn't redeem him," Sophie said.

"But it says something."

"Go home, Myron. And be glad it's over. If the truth were ever to come out, there is only one guilty party left to take the fall."

Myron nodded. "Me."

"Yes."

They stared at each other.

"I didn't know about your daughter," he said.

"I know that now."

"You thought I helped Clu cover it up."

"No, I *know* you helped Clu cover it up. What I wasn't sure about is if you knew what you were doing. It was why I asked you to look for Lucy—so I could see how deep your involvement was."

"The void," Myron said.

"What about it?"

"Did this help fill it?"

Sophie thought about it. "Strangely enough, the answer is yes, I think. It doesn't bring Lucy back. But I feel as though she's been properly buried now. I think we can begin to heal."

"So we all just go on?"

Sophie smiled. "What else can we do?"

She nodded to Jared. Jared took his mother's hand, and they started back for the dugout.

"I am very sorry," Myron said.

Sophie stopped. She dropped her son's hand and studied Myron for a moment, her eyes moving over his face.

"You committed a felony by bribing those police officers. You put my family and me through years of agony. You probably contributed to my husband's premature death. You had a hand in the deaths of Clu Haid and Billy Lee Palms. And in the end you made me commit horrible acts I always thought I was incapable of committing." She stepped back toward her son, her gaze more tired now than accusatory. "I won't hurt you any further. But if you don't mind, I'll let you keep your apology."

She gave Myron a moment for rebuttal. He didn't use it. They strode down the steps and disappeared, leaving Myron alone with the grass and the dirt and the bright stadium lights.

CHAPTER 39

In the lot Win frowned and holstered his .44. "No one even pulled a gun."

Myron said nothing. He got into his car. Win got into his. Myron's cellular phone rang before he had driven five minutes. It was Hester Crimstein.

"They're dropping the charges," she said to him. "Esperanza will be out tomorrow morning. They're offering up a full exoneration and apology if we promise not to sue."

"Will you accept that?"

"It's up to Esperanza. But I think she'll agree."

Myron drove to Bonnie's house. Her mother opened the door and looked angry. Myron pushed past her and found Bonnie alone. He showed her the note. She cried. He held her. He looked in on the two sleeping boys and stayed in the doorway until Bonnie's mother tapped him on the shoulder and asked him to leave. He did.

He headed back to Win's apartment. When he opened the door, Terese's suitcase was by the entrance. She stepped into the foyer.

"You're packed," Myron said.

She smiled. "I love a man who misses nothing."

He waited.

"I'm leaving in an hour for Atlanta," she said.

"Oh."

"I spoke to my boss at CNN. Ratings have been down. He wants me back on the air tomorrow."

"Oh," Myron said again.

Terese pulled at a ring on her finger. "You ever try a long-distance relationship?" she asked.

"No."

"Might be worth a try."

"Might be," he said.

"I hear the sex is great."

"That's never been our trouble, Terese."

"No," she said. "It hasn't."

He checked his watch. "Only an hour, you said?"

She smiled. "Actually, an hour and ten minutes."

"Whew," he said, moving closer.

At midnight Myron and Win were in the living room watching television.

"You'll miss her," Win said.

"I'm flying down to Atlanta this weekend."

Win nodded. "Best-case scenario."

"Meaning?"

"Meaning you are the pitiful, needy type who feels incomplete without a steady girlfriend. Who better than a career woman who lives a thousand miles away?"

More silence. They watched a repeat of *Frasier* on Channel 11. The show was starting to grow on them both.

"An agent represents his clients," Win said during a commercial. "You're his advocate. You can't worry about the repercussions."

"You really believe that?"

"Sure, why not?"

Myron shrugged. "Yeah, why not?" He watched another commercial. "Esperanza said I'm starting to get too comfortable with breaking the rules."

Win said nothing.

"Truth is," Myron said, "I've been doing it for a while. I paid off police officers to cover up a crime."

"You didn't know the severity."

"Does that matter?"

"Of course it does."

Myron shook his head. "We trample on that damned foul line until we can't see it anymore," he said softly.

"What are you talking about?"

"I'm talking about us. Sophie Mayor said that you and I do the same thing she did. We take the law into our own hands. We break the rules."

"So?"

"So it's not right."

Win frowned. "Oh, please."

"The innocent get hurt."

"The police hurt the innocent too."

"Not like this. Esperanza suffered when she had nothing to do with any of this. Clu deserved to be punished, but what happened to Lucy Mayor was still an accident."

Win drummed his chin with two fingers. "If we put aside an argument on the relative severity of drunk driving," he said, "in the end it was not merely an accident. Clu chose to bury the body. The fact that he couldn't live with it doesn't excuse it."

"We can't keep doing this, Win."

"Keep doing what?"

"Breaking the rules."

"Let me pose a question to you, Myron." Win continued his chin drumming. "Suppose you were Sophie

Mayor and Lucy Mayor were your daughter. What would you have done?"

"Maybe the same thing," Myron said. "Does that make it right?"

"Depends," Win said.

"On?"

"On the Clu Haid factor: Can you live with yourself?"

"That's it?"

"That's it. Can you live with yourself? I know that I could."

"And you're comfortable with that?"

"With what?"

"With a world where people take the law into their own hands," Myron said.

"Good lord, no. I'm not prescribing this remedy for others."

"Just you."

Win shrugged. "I trust my judgment. I'd trust yours too. But now you want to go back in time and take an alternate route. Life is not like that. You made a decision. It was a good one based on what you knew. A tough call, but aren't they all? It could have worked out the other way. Clu might have smartened up from the experience, become a better person. My point is, you can't concern yourself with distant, impossible-to-see consequences."

"Just worry about the here and now."

"Precisely."

"And what you can live with."

"Yes.

"So maybe next time," Myron said, "I should opt for doing the right thing."

Win shook his head. "You're confusing the right thing with the legal or seemingly moral thing. But that's not the real world. Sometimes the good guys break the rules because they know better.''

Myron smiled. "They cross the foul line. Just for a second. Just to do good. Then they scramble back into fair territory. But when you do that too often, you start smearing the line.''

"Perhaps the line is supposed to be smeared,'' Win said.

"Perhaps.''

"On balance, you and I do good.''

"That balance might be better if we didn't stray across the line so much—even if that meant letting a few more injustices remain injustices.''

Win shrugged. "Your call.''

Myron sat back. "You know what's bothering me the most about this conversation?''

"What's that?''

"That I don't think it'll change anything. That I think you're probably right.''

"But you're not sure,'' Win said.

"No, I'm not sure.''

"And you still don't like it.''

"I definitely don't like it,'' Myron said.

Win nodded. "That's all I wanted to hear.''

Big Cyndi was totally in orange. An orange sweatshirt. Orange parachute pants like something stolen from MC Hammer's 1989 closet. Dyed orange hair. Orange fingernail polish. Orange—don't ask how—skin. She looked like a mutant teenage carrot.

"Orange is Esperanza's favorite color," she told Myron.

"No, it's not."

"It's not?"

Myron shook his head. "Blue is." For a moment, he pictured a giant Smurf.

Big Cyndi mulled that one over. "Orange is her second favorite color?"

"Sure, I guess."

Satisfied, Big Cyndi smiled and strung up a sign across the reception area that read WELCOME BACK, ESPERANZA!

Myron moved into his inner office. He made some calls, managed to do a little work, kept listening for the elevator.

Finally, the elevator dinged at 10:00 A.M. The doors slid open. Myron stayed put. He heard Big Cyndi's squeal of delight; the floors below them almost evacuated at the sound. He felt the vibrations of Big Cyndi leaping to her feet. Myron stood now and still waited. He heard cries and sighs and reassurances.

Two minutes later Esperanza entered Myron's office. She didn't knock. As always.

Their hug was a little awkward. Myron backed off, shoved his hands in his pockets. "Welcome back."

Esperanza tried a smile. "Thanks."

Silence.

"You knew about my personal involvement the whole time, didn't you?"

Esperanza said nothing.

"That's the part I could never resolve," Myron said.

"Myron, don't—"

"You're my best friend," he continued. "You know I'd do anything for you. So I couldn't for the life of me figure out why you wouldn't talk to me. It made no sense. At first I thought you were angry at me for disappearing. But that isn't like you. Then I thought you had an affair with Clu and you didn't want me to know. But that was wrong. Then I thought it was because you had an affair with Bonnie—"

"Showing very poor judgment," Esperanza added.

"Yes. But I'm hardly in a position to lecture you. And you wouldn't be afraid to tell me about it. Especially with the stakes so high. So I kept wondering, What could be so bad that you wouldn't talk to me? Win thought that the only explanation was that you did indeed kill Clu."

"That Win," Esperanza said. "Always the sunny side."

"But even that wouldn't do it. I'd still stick by you. You knew that. There is only one reason you wouldn't tell me the truth—"

Esperanza sighed. "I need a shower."

"You were protecting me."

She looked at him. "Don't get all mushy on me, okay? I hate when you do that."

"Bonnie told you about the car accident. About my bribing the cops."

"Pillow talk," Esperanza said with a shrug.

"And once you were arrested, you made her swear to keep her mouth shut. Not for your sake or hers. But for mine. You knew that if the bribes ever became public, I'd be ruined. I'd committed a serious felony. I'd be disbarred or worse. And you knew that if I ever found out, you wouldn't be able to stop me from telling the DA because it would've been enough to get you off."

Esperanza put her hands on her hips. "Is there a point to this, Myron?"

"Thank you," he said.

"Nothing to thank me for. You were too weak coming off Brenda. I was afraid you'd do something stupid. You have that habit."

He hugged her again. She hugged him back. Nothing felt awkward this time. When they broke the embrace, he stepped back. "Thank you."

"Stop saying that."

"You are my best friend."

"And I did it for my sake too, Myron. For the business. My business."

"I know."

"So do we still have any clients left?" she asked.

"A few."

"Maybe we better get on the horn then."

"Maybe," he said. "I love you, Esperanza."

"Shut up before I puke my guts out."

"And you love me."

"If you start singing 'Barney,' I'll kill you. I've already done prison time. I'm not afraid to do more."

Big Cyndi stuck her head in. She was smiling. With the orange skin, she looked like the most frightening jack-o'-lantern imaginable. "Marty Towey on line two."

"I'll take it," Esperanza said.

"And I have Enos Cabral on line three."

"Mine," said Myron.

At the end of a wonderfully long workday Win came into the office. "I spoke to Esperanza," he said. "We're all doing pizza and old CBS Sunday at my place."

"I can't."

Win arched an eyebrow. *"All in the Family, M*A*S*H, Mary Tyler Moore, Bob Newhart, Carol Burnett?"*

"Sorry."

"The Sammy Davis episode of *All in the Family*?"

"Not tonight, Win."

Win looked concerned. "I know you want to punish yourself," he said, "but this is taking self-flagellation too far."

Myron smiled. "It's not that."

"Don't tell me you want to be alone. You never want to be alone."

"Sorry, I got other plans," Myron said.

Win arched the eyebrow, turned, left without another word.

Myron picked up the phone. He dialed the familiar number. "I'm on my way," he said.

"Good," Mom said. "I already called Fong's. I got two orders of shrimp with lobster sauce."

"Mom?"

"What?"

"I really don't like their shrimp in lobster sauce anymore."

"What? You've always loved it. It's your favorite."

"Not since I was fourteen."

"So how come you never told me?"

"I have. Several times."

"And what, you expect me to remember every little thing? So what are you trying to tell me, Myron, your taste buds are too mature for Fong's shrimp with lobster sauce now? Who do you think you are, the Galloping Gourmet or something?"

Myron heard his father yell in the background. "Stop bothering the boy."

"Who's bothering him? Myron, am I bothering you?"

"And tell him to hurry," Dad shouted. "The game's almost on."

"Big deal, Al. He doesn't care."

Myron said, "Tell Dad I'm on my way."

"Drive slowly, Myron. There's no rush. The game will wait."

"Okay, Mom."

"Wear a seat belt."

"Sure thing."

"And your father has a surprise for you."

"Ellen!" It was Dad again.

"What's the big deal, Al?"

"I wanted to tell him—"

"Oh stop being silly, Al. Myron?"

"Yeah, Mom?"

"Your father bought tickets to a Mets game. For Sunday. Just the two of you."

Myron swallowed, said nothing.

"They're playing the Tunas," Mom said.

"The Marlins!" Dad shouted.

"Tunas, marlins—what's the difference? You going to be a marine biologist now, Al? Is that what you're going to do with your leisure time, study fish?"

Myron smiled.

"Myron, you there?"

"I'm on my way, Mom."

He hung up. He slapped his thighs and stood. He said good night to Esperanza and Big Cyndi. He stepped into the elevator and managed a smile. Friends and lovers were great, he thought, but sometimes a boy just wanted his mom and dad.

HARLAN COBEN, winner of the Edgar Award, the Shamus Award, and the Anthony Award, is the author of eight other critically acclaimed novels: *Deal Breaker, Drop Shot, Fade Away, Back Spin, One False Move, Darkest Fear, Tell No One,* and *Gone for Good.* He lives in New Jersey with his wife and four children. Visit his website at www.harlancoben.com.